THE CONSEQUENCE OF CHOICE

NATALIE SAMMONS

BLOODHOUND
— BOOKS —

www.bloodhoundbooks.com

Print ISBN 978-1-914614-87-3

To my family.

The room, although full, was eerily silent. Serious faces pored over red leather-bound folders.

Patiently, Professor Alice Franklin waited. She had been sitting, at the edge of the stage, for almost an hour whilst the reality of the situation was absorbed.

Professor Franklin had known that this day was coming. In truth, she believed that everyone in this room knew it was coming, but now, being here, the weight of it was crushing.

Her research had been conclusive. Every variable considered, and still the same grave result was produced.

For years she was hushed, her research pushed aside as nonsense, identified as the worst-case scenario unlikely to ever occur. Now though, with the expiration of the last fossil fuels imminent, she had been summoned to the United Nations World Summit to present her work.

The UN were worried. *They should be.*

The last two days had been exhausting. Professor Franklin had presented her research, all of it, in its entirety. They needed to have all the facts in front of them, she'd realised, if she, no, if *they* were to make decisions that mattered, that saved lives. This was her one opportunity to stress the gravity of what faced them if drastic action wasn't taken.

She had been interrogated, laughed at and applauded.

With quiet resolve, she'd endured it, allowing her research to speak for itself.

This project had been her life's work, had been the reason she got out of bed each morning. When everything else in her life had been falling apart around her, this alone had kept her going, kept her focused. It had provided her with a purpose, a lifeline, and she believed in it wholeheartedly.

All she had to do was wait.

'There will be an uproar!' declared the French President, his accent nasal.

Professor Franklin approached the podium. As she did, she surreptitiously straightened her suit jacket and tucked a loose strand of her shoulder length, silvery-grey hair behind her ear.

After tapping at a keyboard, a screen high on the wall behind her illuminated a ten-digit number. The last digit multiplied, then dropped before increasing and increasing again.

'This is the Worldometer,' Professor Franklin announced poignantly into the microphone. 'As you can see, the numbers are duplicating at an expeditious rate, a reflection of our swelling population.'

Again, she paused, just momentarily, as the digits on the screen continued to escalate. 'I appreciate that there will be some initial opposition to the change, however, I can assure you that to protect our species as well as the planet, this is the only way forward,' she said, confident in her response.

'How long do you foresee this lasting?' a female translator interjected on behalf of the South African president.

Professor Franklin took a moment to consider how best to respond.

'From all my research, you can see the severity of the issue. The population is increasing by approximately eighty-three million people every year. This cannot and will not be rectified overnight. I have deduced that for the Worldometer to begin to show signs of slowing down, it will take at least two generations.' Professor Franklin swallowed hard against the indignation rising within the audience. She had to forge on, no matter how difficult it became. 'However, to restore the planet to a more sustainable equilibrium, I estimate four generations.'

Uproar exploded throughout the auditorium.

Many of the UN members were on their feet. The cacophony of voices, overwhelming, as every member debated and contested her solution. Her heart raced and her palms sweated. She had anticipated their reactions, long before they'd experienced them. She had been here, many times, had fought desperately to uncover an alternative. There wasn't one.

She knew she had to weather this storm.

Professor Franklin absorbed their consternation. Watched as disgust and fear filled their faces. Sympathised as they tried, in vain, to shout their way out of this otherwise-bleak situation.

'Surely, there has to be another way?' demanded a voice louder than the others.

Professor Franklin searched the sea of solemn faces staring back at her, silence once again descending. She would like to tell them that there was an easier way, that they could plant more trees, grow more food, eat vegan, in fact, she had looked at the impact of all of these avenues, none of it, however, would be enough, not if the population continued to surge. Her research had been conclusive.

'I can assure you, there isn't,' she returned with finality.

'How must we begin?' the English Prime Minister asked, his hair unusually dishevelled, a reflection of how Professor Franklin was feeling.

She knew that this was the moment when everything, for everyone, would change and she was going to be deemed responsible. 'You enforce a change in the law.'

1

ELSPETH

MARCH 7TH 2035

E yes wide in shock, Elspeth stood motionless. She blinked slowly, trying to absorb what it meant. Silently she was still praying that it would change.

It didn't.

A cold fear gripped her. Her stomach lurched.

'Shit,' she growled.

Raking her fingers through her hair, she caught sight of herself in the oval mirror above the sink. Hands resting on the sink's edge, she leaned forward, the tip of her nose brushed against it. She scrutinised her appearance.

Her once-hazel eyes appeared dull, her skin, previously fresh, now tired. She knew she looked different, she just hoped that no one else had noticed.

Peering down, it was still there. Unchanged.

She slammed her hands on the sink. 'Fuck!'

'You all right in there, Ellie?' Artie called from the other side of the door.

Her head whipped towards him. 'Yeah, I'm fine,' she croaked, desperately trying to remain calm against the hysteria bubbling inside her.

'Okay. I'm gonna put the kettle on, do you want a cuppa?'

'No,' she snapped, before adding more softly, 'thank you.' The words were thick and heavy on her tongue.

She listened as his slippered feet padded away from the door and down the stairs.

What had he heard? She panicked, heart pounding.

Nothing, there had been nothing voiced to betray her.

What would they think, if they found out? No, she didn't want to entertain those thoughts, wasn't ready to think beyond now.

She couldn't have asked for better flatmates really. Elspeth had moved to Brighton from Storrington, twenty miles north-west of the Sussex city, almost a year ago.

Having qualified as a nurse, she had taken a job in the local hospital on the special care baby unit. The commute home after a nightshift had soon become taxing. She decided that she needed to be nearer to the hospital, not to mention that, at twenty-three, she knew it was probably time to fly the nest.

This had been the first and only house that she'd looked at. Brooke and Artie had been so relaxed, rather than interviewing her, they'd chatted, about everything from films to politics. It was only when the Chinese takeaway arrived that Brooke voiced what they'd all been thinking, 'The room's yours, of course! It's like we've all been mates for years.'

The house was Brooke's, Elspeth later learned. She'd inherited it when her father had passed away. Elspeth suspected that Brooke had been lonely, rattling around in the four-bedroom, two-bathroom townhouse all by herself.

Elspeth loved living there.

'Now you've gone and fucked it all up,' she spat at her reflection. Pushing herself back from the sink, Elspeth grabbed hold of the white stick and slumped down on the toilet seat. She looked again.

Two blue lines beamed back at her.

Pregnant.

She was pregnant.

One small error in judgement, an accident really, was going to ruin her entire life. Drilled into her from a young age, she'd read the stories, seen the newspaper reports; babies removed the moment they're delivered, forced sterilisation and a minimum sentence of ten years. There were prisons, she'd heard, with cells reserved especially for unapproved women.

Women just like her.

2

ALICE

OCTOBER 2025

The phone rang again. It had been ringing incessantly since the previous day.

Professor Alice Franklin cursed her misdirected nostalgia. She knew no one else maintained a landline these days, and yet she had held on to it, not wanting to let go, though she wasn't sure how much more of the bloody ringing she could take.

Alice didn't doubt that every brief pause between calls only allowed another reporter to pick up where the last one had left off.

Maybe she should've expected to be hounded, but this wasn't her doing, didn't they see that? She was desperately trying to undo what everyone else had done.

Walking over to the window, Alice carefully edged the curtain aside, just a fraction.

Despondently, she peered at the ever-enlarging circus of reporters camped outside.

Haphazardly parked vans obscured the pavement. Alice frowned. Her neighbours would no doubt be complaining soon enough.

The reporters were chatting and laughing loudly, perhaps at

her expense, whilst cameras were being positioned around her home, making it impossible to leave.

A loud sigh escaped her lips. How could they be so blind? She was the scapegoat, the fall guy.

On the coffee table, her mobile vibrated furiously, joining in the discord of noise overwhelming her.

Letting go of the curtain which fell lazily back into place, Alice moved towards the table. She didn't, however, pick up the phone. Instead, she leant forward, slightly tilting her head to read its flashing display.

Unknown.

Her brow furrowed. They had that number now too. She groaned inwardly.

Then to add to the din, the doorbell rang. Once, twice, then a third time.

She was hemmed in, like a caged animal, in her own home. Her sanctuary had become her prison.

She was desperate to go outside, to tell them all to fuck off, to leave her alone. In fact, she wanted to scream it at them but she had been told not to talk to the press, not yet.

Furious with having become their target, she grabbed the phone and yanked it away from the wall, the cord ripping free.

'That's better!' she said with a defiant nod as silence momentarily filled the room.

'Professor Franklin? Alice? We just want to hear your side, to give you an opportunity to explain,' called a female voice through her letterbox.

My side! Alice's eyes widened with anger. She didn't have a side, she was neutral, and this was not her fault. Why were they treating her like a criminal? It felt like she had been found guilty. But guilty of what? Caring? Making a difference?

'That's it, I've done nothing wrong!' Alice declared to the empty lounge before striding towards the front door.

Unlocking the deadbolt and turning the key, she was fired up. Alice hadn't thought through what she wanted to say, what needed to be said, but she had to say something. She refused to be a sitting duck any longer.

Wrenching the door open wide, Alice found her colleague Mark there, his hand raised, poised ready to knock.

'Mark!' Alice's confusion unmistakable.

Behind Mark, cameras flashed and reporters hollered her name. Without looking back, Mark gently but swiftly guided Alice back into the hallway, slamming the door shut behind him.

'What were you thinking?'

Alice shook her head. 'I don't know. I just wanted to explain, to make them see that this was the only way.' She sagged then, deflated.

'Okay,' Mark responded slowly. 'Can I make a suggestion though?'

Alice wasn't sure she needed any more advice. In fact, the prospect of one more person telling her what to do, even her closest friend and colleague, made her want to scream like a banshee.

Mark, knowing Alice all too well, seemed to realise that he may have just put his size ten foot in it. With a reassuring hand placed on her shoulder he said, 'I was just going to suggest that next time you feel like heading out to confront the paparazzi, you may want to get dressed first.'

Slowly, Alice looked down. Curiously, she found her favourite blue silk pyjamas glaring back at her.

'Well, that's just fantastic!' she moaned. 'I can already see tomorrow's headline, Professor Franklin; mad as a box of frogs.'

Mark smiled sympathetically. He had been by Alice's side throughout this whole fiasco. He had participated in the research, supported the plan. And now, he was seeing Alice, only Alice, receiving the full brunt of the public's hatred. They had turned against her almost instantaneously. Vilified her for telling the truth, for insisting upon rational but radical action.

'Come on. I brought coffee and croissants.' Mark smiled, raising his left hand to indicate the pair of recyclable cups and paper bag of goodies.

'You're a lifesaver.' Alice smirked, taking the bag from him and heading back to the lounge. She hadn't felt able to leave her Brighton home since the reporters began arriving the previous morning and as Alice often worked long hours, she had developed a rather lax attitude to proper food shopping. A habit she had been cursing herself for all morning, as the contents of her fridge: half a courgette, an out-of-date yoghurt and some butter, left little to be desired.

Hungrily, Alice delved into the ham and cheese croissant, that was until Mark poignantly laid the daily tabloid on the table right under her nose.

'I don't want to read it.' She knew she was being childish.

Mark frowned. 'Fine.' He theatrically snatched up the paper and turned it round to face him. 'Then I'll just have to give you the edited highlights.'

For a few minutes they were silent, apart from the low hum of Alice's mobile, which she had shoved under a sofa cushion and continued to vibrate relentlessly, whilst Mark scanned through the many pages dedicated to Alice and her work.

'Okay, well there is a poll as to whether the British population agree with the new law, seventy per cent against, I'm afraid, but it was to be expected. Although glass half full, means that thirty per cent agreed.' He offered her a consoling smile before continuing. 'They have picked apart your qualifications and questioned the authenticity of your research, again that was to be expected. After that... it just blithers on about human rights and freedom of choice. Funny, isn't it, they can't see beyond their own small existence. Anyway...' He exhaled loudly, folded up the paper and ceremoniously chucked it across the floor.

He always did have an eccentric flair, maybe that's why they worked so well together. They complemented each other, perhaps. Alice knew she was prone to being singled-minded. She lived for her work and could often be found alone in the office on a Sunday. Perhaps the lack of a private life compounded this, or was this void in her life a result of it?

Mark on the other hand managed to enjoy a vibrant social life outside of work, often disappearing with John, his better half, to some party or other and would typically be the one to sigh dramatically before suggesting she didn't work too late, when Alice politely declined his invitation, as she so often did.

She was pleased to have his company though. She felt like she would have gone stir-crazy otherwise.

'Oh, also... I forgot to mention that a protest group has been set up, headed by some human rights lawyer and they're planning to have the law overturned,' he added nonchalantly.

'What?' Alice jumped to her feet, almost spilling her coffee.

'Alice, calm down! They're not going to get very far. This is an international collective plan to manage the world's population. We can't be seen to be doing anything differently, can we? The law is in place and it is going to be enforced, you heard the prime minister's speech. One child per family. End of.'

3

ELSPETH

DECEMBER 31ST 2034

'What are you drinking?' Dr Nick shouted into Elspeth's ear, his breath caressing her skin.

'What?'

'I said, what are you drinking?' he repeated a little louder.

'Oh! Pink gin and tonic, please.' She couldn't help smiling.

'Pink gin and tonic,' he parroted. 'Right. I'm off to the bar! I may be some time!'

Elspeth blushed at the closeness which hadn't gone unnoticed by some of their group. He was shamelessly flirting with her and why shouldn't she enjoy his attention? After all she was single, unattached, sadly available. No, he wasn't her typical type, he was perhaps a little too pretty for her liking, a little too well-groomed. Just then an image sprang into her mind, but she dispelled it quickly, not wanting to think about anyone else.

Besides, she thought, he's cute. She wouldn't go as far as saying that she had a crush on him, but she wasn't blind. He was very attractive, with his emerald-green eyes and smooth skin, if not a little arrogant.

In fact, Elspeth suspected that some of the other nurses on

the ward thought the same thing. And why wouldn't they? He was very charming, she knew, staring after him as he ordered their drinks at the bar, although no one had ever come out and said anything. Well, not to her anyway.

New Year's Eve in Brighton and the bar was heaving. Hundreds of people were squeezed, body to body, into the snug trendy bar. The live band was adding just the right sort of atmosphere; light-hearted and playful without being too imposing.

Elspeth stood with several of her work colleagues. In truth, she hadn't planned on going out, she always felt that New Year's Eve was a little false, like people were trying too hard to look like they were having a good time when really all they wanted to do was curl up on their sofas and go to bed before midnight.

Surprisingly, though, she was having fun, even if she was surrounded by lots of hot sweaty bodies and the queue to the bar was three deep.

'Pink gin and tonic.' Nick smiled, handing Elspeth the large gin glass.

'Thanks.' Sipping her gin, Elspeth pulled a face as the raspberry-coloured liquid slid down the back of her throat. 'Wow, that's strong!' She coughed against the burn.

'I got you a double.' He laughed easily.

'Oh, right. Thanks.'

Elspeth was a lousy drunk, although she very much appreciated the occasional drink. A glass of wine with dinner was manageable, a drink or two when out with friends she could tolerate but anything more became problematic. Uninhibited, that's how Brooke had described her after one too many drinks on their first night out together as housemates.

Elspeth couldn't recall the night itself, nor the events which Brooke took pleasure in recounting for her. The headache, lack of shoes and absent bra the following morning, however, were evidence enough that Elspeth needed to curb her enthusiasm when alcohol was involved.

Nick hadn't noticed her wariness, his attention focused towards their group. Jane, a forty-something ward sister with salt-and-pepper hair and large-framed glasses, was excitedly holding up a tray of shots filled with a clear liquid.

It was always the quiet ones. Elspeth sighed, a sense of unease creeping in as she knew that one of those small but inevitably lethal drinks would be for her.

Nick, clearly delighted by the challenge, took a small glass for himself and without a moment's hesitation, put it to his lips, tipped his head back and swallowed the shot, all to the cheers of the group around him.

'Your turn,' he announced suddenly, face looking flushed, as he snatched up another glass and thrust it at Elspeth.

'Oh! No, I don't think I should.' She shook her head for good measure.

'Come on.' Nick pressed the glass into her hand. 'Lighten up, it's only a drink, I mean what's the worst that can happen?'

'Come on. Down the hatch!' Jane encouraged, her tray empty.

'Down it!' Someone else laughed.

Compelled by the persistence of her colleagues and not wanting to be seen as a killjoy, Elspeth inhaled deeply, put the glass to her lips and quickly poured the syrup into her mouth, swallowing it in one go. Almost instantly she grimaced and coughed against the sweet-yet-sickly taste of liquorice.

Nick gently placed a hand against Elspeth's lower back and leant into her. 'Jane certainly is a wild card.'

Whether the double gin and liquorice shot had started to take effect or whether it was Nick's hand, which had continued to rest lightly against Elspeth's back, she was starting to feel rather flushed and definitely a little fuzzy around the edges.

Soon, Elspeth found herself swaying to the music, lightly at first and then more enthusiastically as her colleagues joined her.

She loved to dance, to feel the music pulsing through her body. It made her feel free. Her movements became more exaggerated, her arms and legs becoming extensions of her hips.

Repeatedly, she found her empty glass efficiently replaced with an overflowing one.

As the evening progressed, her cheeks flared from the alcohol and her eyes became glassy.

Nick's hand had somehow found its way into Elspeth's free hand, his thumb gently drawing circles across her skin.

Although their group had loosely remained in a circle, Elspeth was focused solely on Nick. She watched his eyes, which were fixated on her, drinking in every movement her body made as she danced. A shiver ran down her spine. She was relishing his attention, savouring his obvious desire.

Another shot found its way to her lips. This one slid down easier, the warmth of the alcohol almost pleasant.

'You are so beautiful!' Nick declared unexpectedly, his speech tainted by the alcohol.

'You're not too bad yourself.' She giggled. She was flirting, no, *they* were flirting and she liked it.

Nick leant forward and as if it were the most common of acts between them, he gently pressed his lips to Elspeth's. For a moment, she didn't respond. Then, as her brain caught up with her lips, she kissed him back.

At first the kiss was gentle, sweet even, before a raw hunger took over. His hands slid around her waist as hers encircled his neck.

No one else in the room mattered. They were enthralled by each other.

Eventually, they pulled apart, breathlessly.

With a subtle tilt of his head, Nick indicated towards the door. 'Shall we get out of here?'

A knowing look passed between them.

Elspeth nodded firmly.

4

SAM

FEBRUARY 2ND 2035

Detective Inspector Sam Wakley sat at her desk, a steaming mug of black sweetened coffee firmly grasped in her right hand. At seven in the morning she wasn't scheduled to start work for another hour but she hadn't been able to sleep, not after the previous day's debacle.

It should have been an easy bust.

The planning had been months in the making and meticulous down to the last detail. The intel had been foolproof, or so she had thought.

Now she was going to have to face the music. Getting hauled into Smithers' office was inevitable, her perfect record would be tarnished, and if that wasn't enough to bear, the entire office were laughing at her.

How could she have gotten it so wrong? She shook her head, attempting to dispel the negative thoughts. She just needed to write her report, to accept the unavoidable slap on the wrist and to move on. But that was easier said than done.

Turning on the computer, she waited silently whilst the machine sprang to life. As soon as the screen lit up an email notification flashed, as if it had been waiting, tapping its pixel foot for her arrival.

Slowly, Sam dragged the mouse across to the email before hesitating. She didn't want to open it, she already knew what it would say and that it would hurt like hell.

Stop procrastinating.

Sucking in a deep breath, she clicked on it. The email popped open.

`My office. 9am.`

'Damn!' Sam cursed reading the email. This was bad. Gone were the pleasantries; there was no cushioning the blow, it was straight to the point. She could practically hear Smithers' fury in those three words.

A bead of sweat materialised above Sam's top lip. She was nervous and that pissed her off. What happened hadn't been her fault.

Leaning back in her cool leather chair, she cradled her mug between both hands and closed her eyes. She needed to compose herself.

Sam had always been different to other girls, somewhat of an outcast. She'd demanded, forcefully at times, to be called Sam rather than Samantha, she'd preferred her black hair short, chose riding a bike over dancing, she thought crying was pointless, and she had always wanted to work for the police. Her appointment into the special branch division, The Enforcers, had been the pinnacle of her career, one she wore like a badge of honour. She had proven her worth to everyone who had ever doubted her strength and commitment, to all those kids that had picked on her in the playground, who had called her a freak and pathetic. She wasn't such a loser now.

Driven and determined, Sam had qualified top of her class.

She wasn't liked by many, she knew that, but she also knew she was admired for her work ethic, first to arrive, last to leave. She had a nose for the job, always sensing the truth amongst the lies. *So how...*

'No!' she growled at herself. 'Enough self-pitying. This was your case. You fucked up, now you've got to deal with it.'

Pep talk done, she sat forward again and pulled open the case file. She would go through it all with a fine toothcomb later, unpicking every single detail, cross referencing every statement, scrutinising every step she'd taken. Now, though, she had to compile some semblance of a report to satisfy the powers that be.

At five to nine, Sam stood stiffly outside Detective Chief Inspector Smithers' office door. *DCI Smithers*, she thought with a sneer, taking in the plaque hung outside his door. *That job should have been mine, but Smithers is one of the boys, rubbing shoulders with all the right people.* She should have known she'd never stood a chance. Of course, that wasn't what they told her... No. They went with more experience in the special branches field, a few more years under her belt, the usual shit that meant *we've chosen someone we like and that's not you.* She sighed loudly. Now was not the time, as this path never led anywhere productive.

Restlessly, she tugged the hem of her black fitted suit jacket before running her hand over her already-smooth bobbed hair. She wanted to look together, unfazed by the previous day's debacle, even though that wasn't how she was feeling internally.

She checked her watch. Nine o'clock. She disliked being made to wait but she would have to make an exception.

'Sam. Come in.' Smithers was unsmiling as he opened the door to her.

His office was obviously nicer than hers. A perk of his promotion, she thought, trying to keep a handle on her jealousy. She admired the large mahogany desk, the separate meeting desk and the full-length windows letting in the morning light.

Smithers indicated to a chair with a lazy wave of his hand. 'Take a seat,' he instructed as he marched around the desk taking his seat, a very comfortable looking red leather office chair.

'Well,' he began, leaning forward with clasped hands resting on the desk in front of him, 'that was an absolute fucking balls-up.' His voice had risen an octave and his cheeks flushed. 'What the hell happened yesterday? I've got the press crawling up my arse and let me tell you, it's very uncomfortable. So, what I want, no, what I need is an explanation and I want it now!'

Sam cleared her throat. 'The suspect produced papers—'

'Papers!' Smithers stuttered, interjecting. A fine spray of spit flew across the desk and landed in small wet globules on the well-polished desktop. Disgusted, Sam pushed further back in her seat. 'I didn't have you pegged as incompetent,' Smithers continued, 'but clearly I was wrong. How could you have over-looked something as basic as that?'

'I can assure you her documentation was one of the first things I checked—'

He was starting to turn a shade of puce, Sam noticed despondently. But seeing as how he wasn't actually prepared to hear her out, she reasoned there was little she could do.

'Then how is it she could produce paperwork?' he asked, standing up. He began pacing. 'I'm getting it in the neck from our superiors. You know we can't afford the bad press. We're still wading through protesters and lawsuits, and this shit doesn't help. They can't shut the department down but they can sure as hell reduce our funding and numbers!'

'I am certain that her papers were forged,' Sam finally added, her conviction evident.

Smithers' eyes widened and he paused his pacing to stare indignantly at her. 'I do not want you looking into this any further. Do you hear me? You've done enough. We'll be lucky if this one doesn't sue. No, you will submit your report, the case will be closed and you will spend the next month on desk duty.'

Sam struggled to keep her features neutral. She barely managed a civil nod to let him know she had heard him, under the barrage of emotions suddenly overwhelming her.

He couldn't be serious. She was their best field agent, and he knew it. The department would suffer because he wanted to demonstrate his authority, to prove he was the boss. This wasn't about the case, she decided, this was because he felt threatened by her and her impeccable record. He wanted to discredit her, to eliminate her as a possible opponent for his job.

Her dislike for him was starting to turn to hatred.

'Do you understand me, Sam?' Smithers demanded.

'Yes, sir,' she replied, her fury barely contained behind her placid facade.

5

ELSPETH

JANUARY 1ST 2035

The sun seeped in from around the curtains, illuminating the large bed in an otherwise stark room.

Elspeth, coming to, winced against the brightness filtering through her closed eyelids. Heavily, she turned over, not yet ready to face the day. Behind her left eye, a persistent, needling pain throbbed.

Screwing her eyes shut, she willed the headache to disappear. Unsurprisingly it didn't.

She knew she should get something, some water or paracetamol or maybe a new head, but the thought of getting out of her warm cosy bed stopped her.

Hushed voices drifted in from somewhere outside the room. More awake, Elspeth found herself trying to tune into the dull tones but she couldn't make out what was being said. After a while her intrigue piqued, she forced her eyes open.

'Oh,' she said, genuinely startled.

Instinctively, she sat up, her head protesting at the sudden movement.

The room around her was completely alien. The four walls

were an unimaginative cream. Apart from the bed, which Elspeth guessed to be super king size, a pair of cream bedside tables and a built-in wardrobe, the room was empty.

Cautiously, she looked around, a bubble of panic starting to rise. Where was she? There were no pictures, no ornaments, nothing with any sort of personality to help her recall how she'd got there and with who.

Tentatively she ran her hands over the cream silk duvet wrapped around her before she grabbed a handful of it and tugged it away from her.

'Shit!' she whispered at the sight of her naked body.

Leaning over the edge of the bed, Elspeth located her clothes in a crumpled pile on the cream carpeted floor.

'What have you gotten yourself into this time?' she scolded. Closing her eyes, Elspeth vigorously rubbed at the spot above her eyebrow where her head hurt the most, whilst trying to piece together the night before. 'What did you do?'

The memories suddenly surfaced with such clarity that a wave of nausea rolled over her. With a groan, she remembered the drinks, the double gins and shots, dancing with Nick, the way she'd practically draped herself on him. 'Argh,' she moaned, then there was the kissing, and in front of their colleagues no less. Her cheeks reddened in embarrassment.

She had left with him, she recalled with a sinking feeling, had gotten in a taxi with him. His hands had been all over her body, her mouth pressed hungrily against his. The rest of the journey was a blur, for which she was thankful. She wasn't ready to remember any of the more-sordid details yet, although there was a dull ache between her legs which told her all she needed to know.

She knew she had nothing to feel ashamed about, she wasn't attached, she hadn't done anything wrong, and yet, she did.

Brooke was right, Elspeth begrudgingly acknowledged, she really shouldn't drink.

She was cursing her reckless behaviour when the voices outside momentarily grew loudly. The thought of facing others, knowing what she'd done, filled her with cold dread. But she couldn't hide in the bedroom forever, could she?

No, you can't. She sighed. Instincts kicked in. She knew she needed to get dressed, to get out of there as fast as she could manage. The bed, which had only moments ago been like a sanctuary, was suddenly unwelcoming and strange. She desperately wanted to be at home, somewhere familiar.

Elspeth was feeling exceedingly uncomfortable, she wasn't someone who did this sort of thing. Even in the early stages of a relationship, Elspeth had always felt stupendously awkward with morning-after etiquette.

Sweeping up her clothes from the floor, a wave of relief at the previous night's wardrobe choice, fitted jeans and a lace vest top, settled over her. At least it would feel less like doing the walk of shame, as she wouldn't stand out compared to everyone else wrapped up against the winter cold.

Hastily, she dressed. Wanting to keep her remaining dignity intact, Elspeth looked for a mirror. She wanted to at least leave with some semblance of togetherness, even if her head was pounding so hard she was squinting against the pain and her cheeks were flushed with embarrassment.

There wasn't a mirror.

Seriously, who doesn't have a mirror in their bedroom?

Realistically, she knew there was bound to be smudged mascara blackening the underneath of her eyes and that her long brown hair would be tangled in clumps. Licking her thumb, she expertly ran it under each eye, wiping away what she could, before raking her fingers through her hair, freeing the tangled strands. That would have to do.

Feeling as put together as she was going to get, Elspeth sucked in a deep breath and in one swift movement, like ripping off a plaster, she yanked open the bedroom door.

Unexpectedly, Elspeth stepped straight into a large open-plan lounge and kitchen.

She had no recollection of this room. She eyed the space, disorientated. This room, like the bedroom, was also a bland vision in cream, the walls, the kitchen units and of course the large L-shaped couch.

Nick, perched on the edge of the couch, with his back to her, was staring intently at the television. *That explains the voices.* Relief flooded through Elspeth, grateful that she didn't have to face a room of strangers.

Still battling against her headache, Elspeth picked up a few snatches of the onscreen debate which Nick was clearly immersed in. That environmental activist woman, Greta some-thing or other, was arguing fervently with some big-wig from one of the last remaining oil companies. Elspeth struggled to absorb the argument, she needed coffee and paracetamol and in that order.

'Good morning,' she mumbled to Nick, her tongue feeling furry.

'Oh, hey,' he replied flatly, without so much as a glance in her direction. 'There's some coffee in the pot on the side.' He motioned with a distracted wave of his hand.

Taken back by his coolness, Elspeth remained unmoving. Unexpectedly, she found herself torn between her desire to run for the safety of home and trying to salvage some sort of equilib-rium from this intensely awkward situation. *Did I do some-thing?* she wondered, feeling perplexed by his off-handedness. *Why do you even care?* she thought, more forcefully, aware that she had just been planning to run out of there as if the place was on fire.

Eventually, the smell of caffeine drifting from the kitchen won.

Touching the coffee pot, Elspeth was relieved to find it still steaming. A brief hunt through some cupboards located the ceramic cups. Pouring herself half a cup, she stood silently in the immaculate kitchen whilst the coffee kicked in.

The flat, she observed, was verging on being clinical, it was like a show home but not in a good way. It was minimalist; all cream and with nothing personal of any description. Maybe he was renting, she considered, trying to justify its sparseness that was a complete contrast to her home, which was cluttered, colourful and warm.

Swallowing the dregs from her cup, Elspeth placed it in the sink and collected her strewn possessions. Her discarded strappy shoes, her black handbag and her fitted leather jacket. All the while Nick continued to pretend she wasn't there.

She hadn't expected him to profess his undying love for her, no, but some polite conversation, a conspiring smile, anything would have been a marked improvement on the cold shoulder she was getting.

True, he was arrogant at work, full of himself in an unashamed way, she just hadn't expected it from him now, after last night. Not that she really cared, she wouldn't be making the same mistake twice. No, if she hadn't been sure before, she was certain now, it had been a massive fucking error in judgement.

With her shoes firmly on her feet, Elspeth was about to duck out the front door when Nick called after her, 'Elle!' She turned back, anger flaring at the presumptuous way he'd short-ened her name. Was it meant to be charming? Endearing even? It wasn't. He was still facing the television. 'Last night was fun. We should do it again sometime!'

A look of disgust instantly distorted Elspeth's pretty features. *The nerve!* Yanking the door open, she walked through it, then as hard as she could, she slammed it behind her. Yes, it was childish, but it made her feel the tiniest bit better.

Stood in the empty corridor, Elspeth took several ragged breaths as irrational tears rolled down her cheeks.

'Arsehole!' she spat back to the door before she strode off, desperate for a shower and her own bed.

6

ALICE

NOVEMBER, 2025

S at safely in the rear of her chauffeur-driven car, Alice
breathed a sigh of relief. She couldn't wait to get home,
confident in the knowledge that most, if not all, of the paparazzi
would still be at the press conference. Having played her part,
she'd made a quick exit, leaving the floundering prime minister
in front of the cameras.

She would open a bottle of Prosecco and order in a Chinese
takeaway. *I've earned it*, she thought defiantly.

Making herself more comfortable, she undid the top button
of her crisp white blouse and slid her feet out of her highly-
polished black brogues.

The press conference had been orchestrated by the prime
minister's people. Alice had little choice in attending considering her role as the leading epidemiologist on this worldwide
collaboration. Considering how the press had been hounding
her, the chance to address them officially had also been appeal-
ing. Only, her speech had been stripped right back, the hard
truth that she'd wanted to present, just like she had to the UN,
had been reconfigured into a gentle cajoling message by some

public relations team. She hadn't been allowed to be honest, to push back, to tell them that this was not her doing alone.

It was some small consolation that she had at least been accompanied by the prime minister himself and the commissioner of police.

The attending press had been ruthless.

Naively, Alice had believed the public would demonstrate the same stoicism shown during the Covid pandemic. A sense of camaraderie against adversity, a uniting of the masses against a common enemy. After all, it was not as if this was an entirely new concept. China had previously utilised a one-child law for over thirty years to manage their overpopulation.

She was sorely mistaken.

This threat unfortunately didn't have the same punch. The devastating footprint that humanity was having on the world wasn't like a wolf outside their door, demanding their attention. They could ignore it and they were. All they saw was the law restricting their human rights.

Maybe I'm being too harsh, Alice considered. *It is a lot to absorb after all and I've had years to do it.*

Even at this stage, Alice found herself sympathising with the public, their stories, their heartbreak. The argument that one child was not enough pulled at her heartstrings, it really did. But then... she knew she would have been overjoyed with one child, a single perfect baby. Life, however, had not blessed her in that way.

Maybe she understood more than most.

A loud sigh escaped her lips.

Cautiously, her driver glanced back at her through his rear-view mirror. She offered a weak smile before turning her attention to the outside world dashing past her at high speed.

Arriving home, she was surprised and disheartened to find a handful of press still camped outside. Either they had broken every speed limit going to beat her back, or they weren't deemed important enough to have been granted press passes to the conference in the first place.

Thankful for the tinted windows, Alice swiftly slipped her brogues back on and rebuttoned her blouse, keen to present as professional after her previous pyjama incident.

On Alice's word, the driver exited the car. Efficiently, he bypassed the paparazzi, navigating his way to the rear car door.

Inhaling deeply, Alice rolled back her shoulders and grabbed hold of her Louis Vuitton handbag. She was as ready as she was going to be.

The moment the door was opened for her, she swiftly slid out of the back seat.

The driver, instantly switching roles, became Alice's body-guard. He shielded her from the stalking press with his larger-than-average body. With outstretched arms, he cleared a path for them, whilst keeping the vultures at bay.

A barrage of questions were thrown at Alice, her name, shouted repeatedly until it sounded strange and unfamiliar, all the while cameras flashed incessantly, like lightning striking, in her peripheral vision.

Reaching the safety of her front door, the driver waited patiently whilst her trembling hand struggled to get the key in the damned lock.

Calm down, she told herself gently. The worst was over.

'Thank you.' She smiled sincerely at the driver, the door finally swinging open.

Alice disappeared into the safety of her home, leaving the driver to fend for himself.

Half-empty silver containers laid open upon the coffee table with the remnants of now-cold Chinese food. A bottle of Prosecco sat upturned in the ice bucket, drained of its contents, the ice long since melted.

Quietly sitting in her favourite chair, Alice held a small envelope carefully in her hand. The food had satisfied her but the wine had sedated her. It had made her thoughtful.

Morose, Alice had found herself hunting through the back of her wardrobe. There, she'd uncovered the simple cream-coloured box.

With the sleeve of her chunky-knit cardigan, Alice had wiped away the thin layer of dust from the lid. She knew exactly what she was looking for in the box.

Hunting through its contents, she was careful not to linger too long on any one item, there were things that she didn't want to remember.

'Ah,' she breathed, finding what she wanted.

Leaving everything else discarded on the floor, Alice returned to the living room.

The conference had brought something to the surface, some long-buried past, and fuelled by alcohol Alice wanted to face it, to relive it, to remember the truth in it.

With such care, she opened the envelope and slid out the small embossed card. Delicately, she ran her hand over it, the memories flashing back violently.

Maybe I'm not ready, she panicked. But her hands continue to move subconsciously, unfolding the card.

'Oh!' She gasped, stricken by such instant and engulfing grief. Tears stung her eyes as her fingers caressed the image in the grainy photograph.

Her beautiful baby.

They had been ecstatic when she'd found out she was

expecting. Alice recalled how she had even taken two tests to be sure, unconvinced by the first.

They had been trying ever since their wedding night and after two long years Alice had practically given up on the idea. Resigned herself to the fact that it was not meant to be, that she had heart-breakingly missed some crucial fertility window. They should have known really, should have realised that being thirty-nine meant the odds had been stacked so heavily against them. Hoping became futile and only led to disappointment after disappointment.

At the time, she had been working tirelessly and if she was honest, her relationship with Gregory had become strained. The pressure and failure of falling pregnant had become like a cavernous space between them, a blackness which prevented them from reaching out to each other. Then there had been that night out in London.

It was the nausea that made her wonder, everything made her want to throw up, the smell of coffee was the worst. She hadn't told Gregory, not until the second test, two days later, had read positive.

She remembered sadly, how they had lived in a bubble of bliss for weeks, brought back together by their joy. They'd spent hours talking baby names, nursery themes and equipment.

Gregory had brought a birth-to-baby book to read and they'd delighted in watching online videos together.

Then at the twelve-week scan, their world had been shattered. Ripped apart by the news that their precious baby had no heartbeat.

Alice bitterly wiped away her tears. She had just wanted to remember that it was real, that for a few short months she had been a mother.

Sucking in ragged breaths, she carefully returned the scan picture back into its envelope.

How dare those reports claim that she couldn't, no, wasn't able to understand what it felt like to have their rights to motherhood restricted, not having children of her own.

They may know the ending of my story but they are clueless to its beginning. I was a mother once.

With drying eyes, Alice pushed her anger back down, hiding it away. With a renewed sense of conviction, she reminded herself that this was the right course of action, the only viable course of action.

And besides, they could still have a child, a perfect beautiful child each. They had absolutely no right to feel hard done by.

None whatsoever.

7

ARTIE

MARCH 3RD 2035

Dumping the shopping on the kitchen counter, Artie shrugged off his coat, slinging it carelessly over the back of a chair.

'Alexa,' he commanded, 'play Coldplay.'

'Playing songs by Coldplay,' Alexa responded, the kitchen filling with the pleasing tones of his favourite band. *Such a shame they're not together anymore*, he thought fleetingly.

Dancing around the island in the centre of the kitchen, Artie began unpacking his shopping. Lamb chops, two red peppers, a bag of spinach, tomatoes and a rather expensive bottle of red wine. It didn't escape him that he'd chosen Elspeth's favourite bottle, he hadn't meant to, he had just – picked it up.

Without lingering on the thought any longer, he leisurely grabbed a wine glass from the shelf and poured himself a very generous measure.

Taking a sip, he eyed all the ingredients spread out in front of him. A gentle wave of contentment washing over him, a smile transformed his face as he set to work on dinner.

Sunday night dinner had become something of a tradition.

Artie couldn't quite remember why or how it started, but he unabashedly loved it.

Any excuse to spend a couple of hours in the kitchen with his favourite tunes playing and some new creation cooking. *What better way was there to spend Sunday?*

Admittedly, not all his creations had been entirely edible; there had been some burnt dinners and some misjudged flavours, there had even been a very unfortunate seafood incident.

Not your finest hour, he thought with a light chuckle. They hadn't been laughing when they'd been fighting over who got to vomit in the toilet first.

Now, though, he could confidently say that he'd mastered the art of cooking a decent curry, with the girls favouring his lamb chop curry.

Soon, Artie had a selection of pots simmering on the cooker when Elspeth wandered in, slumping listlessly into a chair at the dining table.

'Hey,' Artie's tone cheerful. Without asking, he took down another wine glass, half-filled it and placed it down in front of Elspeth.

'Oh, thanks.'

He watched as her hands circled the glass, noticed as it remained firmly fixed on the table in front of her. 'Rough day?'

'You could say that.'

With a light frown, Artie turned from her momentarily. Adding a pinch of chilli powder to the sauce, he gave the pot a vigorous stir. Satisfied with its rich red consistency, he tapped the wooden spoon firmly on the pot's edge, then gently placed it on the chopping board. Taking his wine glass, he leant on the kitchen island, full attention turned to Elspeth. 'What happened?'

'Huh?' Elspeth mumbled, clearly distracted. 'Oh. It's a long story,' she added, trying a little too hard to sound nonchalant.

'I've got time.' Artie smiled kindly. He desperately wanted things to be better between them. He was trying to be normal, admittedly it was hard, but he was putting his feelings aside and carrying on, just like she wanted.

But there was still this strangeness that hadn't been there before, like they were both trying too hard, and he didn't know what to do to move past it.

Patiently, Artie waited, all the while studying her. Purple shadows underlined her eyes, her beautiful wavy hair hung lifeless around her face, casting a shadow over her features. *She looks washed out*, he realised, pained. She hadn't been herself for several weeks.

Yes, he'd noticed, it was hard not to. He'd wanted to ask her, to point it out, and yet he hadn't. He could never seem to find the right words, words that couldn't be misinterpreted, that wouldn't add to the layer of weirdness between them.

An image of the previous summer barrelled into his mind.

The warmth of the sun, the gentle fuzz from the cocktails, the closeness of her body, the curve of her lips.

Artie had been desperate to kiss Elspeth. From the moment she'd moved in, he knew he was in trouble.

She had been beautifully carefree that day, they had laughed and joked, and he couldn't stand it any longer. The desire to touch her, to hold her had been too much to bear. He'd leaned in, almost anticipating her rebuff. But she'd simply giggled, the most delightful sound that made his heart soar and she'd kissed him back. That night with her...

Stop! He had to get over it, to get over her. She had made her feelings extremely clear, it had been a mistake, one she had clearly regretted.

He didn't though. How could he?

Looking at her now, it was obvious that something was wrong. He was struggling to see that girl from the beach. She was staring ahead, a hollowness in her eyes which frightened him. It was as if she were lost in some other place. He wondered where she disappeared in those moments.

He couldn't ignore it any longer, couldn't keep pretending that she was all right, because evidently, she wasn't.

'Maybe another time,' she finally said. An air of sadness in her resolve.

'Ellie?'

She interrupted him, stopping him with a cold look, one which practically screamed at him to drop it.

Frustration bubbled just below the surface. How did she expect him to leave it? Artie fought the urge to snap at her, to take her by the shoulders and shake her. He wanted to shout at her, to tell her that whatever it was, he would help. Surely she knew that, didn't she? But before he could push the words out of his mouth, Brooke bustled in, cutting him off.

'Hey, guys! Oh, something smells good!' Brooke chirped, oblivious to the tense atmosphere.

Artie couldn't help it, he sighed loudly, loud enough to ensure that Elspeth heard him.

Noisily, Brooke dragged out a chair, sitting down. 'You not drinking that?' she casually asked Elspeth, indicating to the still-half-full glass of wine.

With a shake of her head, she removed her hands from the glass allowing Brooke to claim it.

Brooke drank deeply.

Artie, of course, didn't miss this. Partly because he was watching and partly because it was so unusual for Elspeth to give up a good red that easily.

His brow knitted tightly together. *It must be serious.*

He wasn't pretending to be super in tune to all her

emotions, but he knew enough to know she was worried, really worried about something. And he wanted to know what.

'Oh, that's the good stuff.' Brooke giggled, raising her glass in a toast towards Artie which drew him out of his brooding. 'What's for dinner?'

'Lamb chop curry, rice, garlic naan bread and some chutney.' A note of pride found its way into his voice. 'It'll only be ten more minutes.'

'Yum. My favourite.'

With Artie's attention returned to the dinner, Brooke filled the room with light-hearted chatter.

Occasionally Elspeth responded with a well-timed 'ah-ha' or a nod, but Artie could see she wasn't listening, not really. Her eyes were glazed over, as though she was lost in her own thoughts.

He'd never seen her like this, so absorbed by a problem and unable to confide in him. Now, though, wasn't the time to pursue this further he knew, not with Brooke there.

As much as he adored Brooke, she lacked empathy for others, often twisting a problem until it reflected something she had experienced herself, something much worse. Ultimately she ended up making you feel idiotic and insignificant for even giving your worry a second thought. It wasn't done maliciously. He suspected that she didn't even realise what she was doing, it was just what happened with Brooke. She was fairly self-absorbed.

The timer sounded loudly.

'Dinner is served.' Artie smiled tightly, his mood diminishing before he'd even placed the pots in the middle of the table.

'It's a feast.' Brooke smiled, wide-eyed. Without waiting, she dived in, helping herself.

Artie sat down, his plate piled high.

Discreetly, he watched Elspeth serve herself. She spooned a small handful of rice and the tiniest bit of curry sauce onto her plate. She then proceeded to push it around, absent-mindedly, the redness of the curry slowly bleeding into the white rice. All the while her gaze transfixed on a nothingness, Artie desperately wished he could see.

'Are you not very hungry?' Brooke piped up, having noticed Elspeth's lack of appetite.

'Not really. It's really good, though, Artie, probably one of your best,' she lied. 'I think I'm going to get an early night. Sorry,' she added without looking up.

Quietly, she shuffled out of the room, leaving her untouched dinner on the table and Artie in knots.

'That was weird,' Brooke said with fleeting concern, then just as quickly, she delved back into her dinner, Elspeth's behaviour already forgotten.

Yes, it was, Artie thought. *That was very peculiar.*

8

SAM

MARCH 9TH 2035

'It's that or nothing. I thought you would've been desperate to get back out in the field. Your choice. Take it or leave it,' Smithers said with a light shrug.

Sam knew he didn't give a shit whether she took this job or not, he would probably be happy if she never left her desk again. But she had obediently done her desk-duty time, so she likely felt compelled to offer her this case. Besides, she was still their best agent. If there was a case to build, she would be the one to do it.

Quietly, anticipation took root. The theft of a controlled item held a hefty penalty. This could be a case worthy of restoring her damaged reputation.

And yet, she couldn't help feeling like she was being set up, sent out on a fool's errand. Was there something he wasn't telling her? She wouldn't expect anything less from Smithers, he disliked her as much as she loathed him.

Sam was clenching her teeth so hard her jaw started to protest. She knew if she took the job, she'd get out of the office, get a chance to redeem herself. Her initial suspicion waned.

God, she wanted something to sink her teeth into, something other than paperwork. Not that she wanted Smithers to know that, her pride had taken enough of a battering already.

'Well?'

'I'll do it,' she grunted, feigning disinterest.

With a frown, he chucked a brown folder across the table towards her. 'Everything you'll need is in there.'

Seizing the folder, she turned to leave.

'Sam!' Smithers called after her. 'Don't balls this one up!'

Walking into the hospital, the smell of disinfectant and something else, something pungent, filled Sam's nostrils. With some difficulty she managed to keep her face neutral, managed not to screw it up in disgust.

Even in her nondescript black trouser suit Sam stood out in the otherwise clinical space. She looked ill at ease.

Her shiny black court shoes echoed in the muted silence of the waiting room as she strode towards the reception desk, not wanting to linger any longer than was absolutely necessary.

This was her version of Hell. Sick people made her very uncomfortable.

'Where's the maternity ward?' she demanded from the elderly man sat behind the desk.

'Thirteenth floor. Take the corridor, lifts on the right,' he instructed, unfazed by her abruptness.

Following his instruction, she quickly entered an exceptionally large lift. Hitting the button, Sam stepped back whilst the doors slid closed.

Putting all her effort into her breathing, Sam relaxed a fraction. Enough to recount the information she had on the case when the lift sharply ground to a halt on level eight.

Instinctively, Sam jabbed at the buttons on the wall. The doors, however, slid open.

Two men wearing scrubs expertly manoeuvred a large hospital bed into the lift right next to her. They were quickly followed by a young-looking nurse holding a clipboard.

The nurse gave a curt nod in Sam's direction without making eye contact before she leant forward, selecting floor ten.

You have to be kidding me. A wave of nausea mixed with repulsion washed over her. Sam was pinned between the wall and the bed, which was housing an exceedingly overweight woman.

Sam's eyes impulsively drifted over the woman. She was pallid, and although her eyes were closed the skin around them was sunken and dark. Her left arm, strategically positioned on top of the sheet, was covered in bruises, the fresh kind that were a rainbow of purples, blues and yellows.

Taped in the back of her hand was a small tube. Sam followed the course of the tubing which led to a bag of clear liquid hanging securely on a hook at the head of the bed. Gastric band, Sam decided, somewhat cynically, before turning her attention back to her breathing.

In and out, in and out.

'Thanks,' one of the porters said curtly, as the lift opened on level ten. Sam didn't respond as they wheeled the still-unconscious patient out, presumably taking her to a ward for recovery.

Sam exhaled loudly as the doors once again scraped shut.

By the time she arrived on level thirteen, she was feeling thoroughly irritated.

Make it brief, she told herself in an attempt to gain a modicum of control over her discomfort.

The large fire doors to the ward were firmly secured, Sam noted as she tried them. Standing in front of the intercom she waited impatiently to be buzzed in.

Finally, she heard the resounding click of the lock.

Walking in, she paused momentarily, assessing the ward.

The reception desk was positioned immediately in front of the entrance. There was what appeared to be a single U-shaped corridor running behind the desk, with no other exits immediately visible.

Unlikely to have been opportunistic, Sam decided.

Striding to the desk, several women in nursing tunics turned to look at her. Without hesitation, she returned their stares, aware that these women were probably feeling an inflated sense of importance, sat behind the desk.

Not for much longer. She sensed a challenge.

'Where's the ward sister?' Sam demanded.

'Can I help you?' a young woman asked, her voice a little uncertain.

Sam, feeling an arrogant sense of pleasure at the woman's obvious discomfort, smiled wickedly. 'Not unless you're the ward sister?'

'I'm Judith Chesterfield, the ward sister,' the eldest of the women interrupted. 'And you are?'

Shame, Sam thought fleetingly, she was rather enjoying belittling that girl.

Reaching into the inside pocket of her blazer, Sam pulled out a small black wallet. Opening it, Sam turned it towards the sister, displaying her badge. 'I'm Detective Inspector Sam Wakley from The Enforcers, here to investigate the report you submitted.'

The eyes of the two other staff members widened in what was unmistakably surprise, Sam noticed. *Interesting.* The theft had clearly not been made common knowledge, although she knew that her department's reputation did precede them, often making people instantly uncomfortable.

It was fair to say that her team had earnt itself quite the

reputation. Admittedly, in its infancy there were a lot of grey areas which needed scratching out. Sam had personally been involved in advising and strategising with the legal team as to how they could adequately police the law, ensuring that there were no discrepancies or loopholes. The law had therefore had to evolve somewhat. One child per family still applied, however, only on application and only if approved.

'Ah, yes. Thank you for coming so promptly. Would you like to follow me?' Judith said uneasily.

Sam nodded in reply.

Silently, they made their way towards the far end of the corridor. Each of the doors on the left revealed occupied maternity rooms, whilst on the right were cupboards, storage rooms and Judith's office.

'Please take a seat,' Judith said, closing the office door behind them.

Her office was nothing more than a glorified cupboard, Sam realised instantly. The cheap and tired-looking desk with two plastic chairs, one positioned on either side, occupied most of the space. A tall metal filing cabinet took up one free wall whilst a large wall-mounted calendar filled the other.

Sam perched on the edge of her chair; back straight and face serious. Judith practically shrank into her seat under the weight of Sam's stare. *Good*, Sam thought with a sense of satisfaction.

'You're busy?'

The ward sister blinked, absorbing the meaning in the detective's question. 'The unit?' She finally understood. 'Yes, well, since the number of deliveries has significantly reduced over the past few years, they closed all of our smaller sister sites. We are the only remaining maternity unit for the whole of the South East. So yes, we're always busy.'

'So, you submitted a report about a missing test kit?' Sam moved on, without acknowledging the sister's thinly veiled complaint. Sam extracted a small notebook and pen from a pocket in her blazer.

Judith nodded. 'Yes, that's correct.'

'When did you notice it was missing?' Sam enquired, getting straight to the point. She already knew this information, she just wanted to hear it, to unpick the details again. Sometimes people overlooked things, something they perceived as small and insignificant, which could in fact be very pertinent to the case. And it was Sam's job to determine what was of importance to this case.

'I'm sure you'll find everything you need in my initial report,' Judith bristled.

Despite Sam's smile, her face remained deadly serious. 'Why don't you indulge me? Tell me what happened, starting from the beginning.'

Judith raised her brow sceptically, her dislike for the officer evident. Sam didn't care though, she wanted to ensure that her position of authority was established from the get-go. She would be the one asking the questions, not answering them.

Sighing heavily, the ward sister relented. 'It was reported to me on March seventh.'

'Reported to you?' Sam repeated.

Judith cleared her throat nervously. 'Yes. It was noted to be missing during the night shift when the staff reviewed our controlled items. It was brought to my attention when I arrived on the morning of the seventh.'

'Could it have been used or misplaced?' Sam wanted to cover the most likely of scenarios early.

Judith pursed her lips together, perhaps offended by the insinuation that an error had been made, but Sam was unfazed, she had to be sure, she had to consider all the possibilities.

'As I said, pregnancy tests are a controlled item,' Judith stated firmly. 'We are required to keep a record of all our stock.

Each time one is used it has to be signed out by two staff members. We are not in the habit of misplacing restricted items,' she added for good measure.

Sam scribbled a few notes in her pad: *controlled item, two staff, located where?*

She moved on. 'Where are they kept?'

'In the treatment room, in a locked cupboard.'

'And who has access to the keys for that cupboard?' Sam twirled her pen absent-mindedly in her hand.

'They are the responsibility of the senior staff member on each shift, however...' Judith readjusted herself in her chair, a look of unease marring her expression. 'Often the keys are... stored, at the reception desk so that they are easily accessible in case of an emergency.'

Damn! Sam's jaw tightened at this admission.

What should have been an open and shut case just got complicated.

'So, let me make sure I've understood you correctly. The keys for your restricted and controlled items are left *unattended* at the reception desk where anyone on this ward could have accessed them?' Sam didn't attempt to hide her condescending tone.

Sam studied the sister as she sucked in a deep breath, which she then blew out her nose in one long stream. 'Only our midwives should be using them, after all we don't advertise where they are kept... but yes. That is a possibility,' she replied sullenly.

Sam thought for a moment. She jotted down a few more notes, then shut her pad firmly, tucking it into her pocket along with her pen. 'I'll need the contact details of every staff member who was working that shift and the shift before. Also, a list of all mothers who were on the unit at that time, along with the names of any visitors. I assume you keep a log of sorts?'

'Of course,' Judith replied clearly irritated. 'I'll need some time to–'

'Here's my card, you can email me all the details. Preferably within the next twenty-four hours,' Sam interrupted, sliding an inoffensive business card across the table to the appalled-looking ward sister. 'I'll show myself out,' Sam said flatly, already making her way out of the door.

9

ELSPETH

FEBRUARY 28TH 2035

Aggressively, she wiped away the vomit remnants from her mouth with the back of her hand. The taste of acid lingering unpleasantly on her tongue.

Crumpled in a heap on the floor by the toilet, Elspeth was spent.

Weakly, she raised her hand and flushed the toilet.

She had been sick every morning for the past week. At first she had been convinced that it was something she'd eaten, then as it didn't ease she began to suspect a bug. By the fourth morning, however, realisation twinned with fear started to settle in.

Perhaps there was a plausible explanation, she'd hoped. Another reason why food cooking made her nauseous and why she had to make a mad dash to the bathroom every morning to expel the tiniest amount of food she'd managed to stomach the evening before.

Her thoughts drifted back to that night with Nick. Had they been reckless? They had both been inebriated, she knew, but perhaps he had thought of it. She certainly hadn't.

Argh! She just couldn't remember. Elspeth prayed that he'd

thought of it, that he'd used precautions, but then – what was wrong with her?

Using the toilet seat for support, she hauled herself up. Shakily, she made her way across to the sink. Splashing cold water on her face first, Elspeth rinsed the taste of vomit from her mouth.

Feeling mildly better, she cautiously moved to the middle of the bathroom. Standing in front of the full-length mirror fixed to the back of the door, she turned to the side and lifted her jumper. She examined her reflection.

Do I look any different? she wondered. Her eyes traced her frame. She inspected the shape of her stomach. Was that a slight curve? Was her body changing? Tentatively, she ran her hand over her stomach. Would you even start to show at this point? A cold unease settled. She shook her head, not equipped to deal with the thoughts swirling around in her mind.

Frustrated, she dropped her hand and tugged her jumper back into place. 'You're just being dramatic,' she told the dishevelled woman staring back at her from within the mirror. A bead of hope, or was it denial, starting to take root.

Back in her room, tucked safely under her duvet, Elspeth scrolled through the calendar on her phone. She went back through the current month, then January, then back to December.

'There,' she whispered softly. December 18th was starred. Her last period was just over two months earlier.

Panic gripped hold of her like an iron fist.

Just think rationally. She attempted to soothe herself, to dispel her thoughts. *Your periods have always been erratic, this doesn't necessarily mean anything.*

But the vomiting?

Spontaneously, she typed 'How to know if you're pregnant' into her phone.

Thousands of websites quickly filled the screen. Aimlessly she started searching, unsure of what exactly she was looking for, perhaps something to disprove her wildest fears, an explanation other than *that*.

Random words jumped out at her as she chased reassurance. Morning sickness, swollen breasts, cravings, scans, midwife appointments, pregnancy tests. Elspeth wanted to stop looking but she'd not yet found anything to alleviate her worries.

At the bottom of the second page of websites, she spotted something which sent a cold chill shooting down her spine.

The Enforcers arrest unauthorised pregnant woman.

For a moment, her finger hovered over the link, she knew she shouldn't read it, knew nothing positive would come from knowing what it said, but her curiosity, morbid as it was, was too great. She clicked the link.

A newspaper article from two years earlier flashed up on the screen. Under the headline, a grainy picture of a heavily pregnant woman in handcuffs, flanked by two large men, stared back at her. *Police*, Elspeth knew, the hairs on the back of her neck rising.

Scanning the article, Elspeth soon discovered this woman's fate: unplanned, single, prosecution, sterilisation and adoption.

Petrified, she abruptly launched her phone across the room, desperate to be as far away from it as possible. It landed with a thud against the carpeted floor.

What if that's me? Alone and afraid, Elspeth silently sobbed into her pillow, tears cascading down her face.

Dread flooded through her. What had she done? An overwhelming sense of loneliness engulfed her, like a black cloud. She knew she couldn't risk telling anyone, and that included Artie and Brooke, and yet that was all she wanted to do. She wanted to tell someone, to have someone hold her, someone to tell her it was going to be okay, that they would help her figure out what to do.

The shame, the uncertainty was oppressive, it was pressing against her chest like a vice, trying to squeeze the life out of her.

Uncertainty. The word resonated.

That was what she needed, certainty.

She sat up.

I need a pregnancy test.

But that task in itself seemed insurmountable not to mention profoundly dangerous. If she were to be caught stealing a controlled item, even if it turned out to be negative, Elspeth suspected that she would be made an example of and sentenced to months, if not years, in prison.

She swallowed against the lump which had risen in her throat.

What other choice did she have? She needed to know, one way or the other.

10

ARTIE

MARCH 7TH 2035

A rtie sat in front of the two expensive-looking computer screens, dominating the small desk in his bedroom.

Casually he tapped away on the keyboard. Streams of indecipherable codes appeared on the left screen which in turn manipulated a graphic blueprint on the right.

A phone buzzed.

Artie yanked open a drawer under the right screen. Without glancing away from the computer, he grabbed hold of the phone and answered the call.

'Yep?'

Artie listened as a familiar voice asked when the information would be ready.

'A few more hours,' Artie instructed as he continued typing, the phone wedged between his ear and his shoulder.

'Will it be traceable?' the caller asked.

Artie rolled his eyes. 'Do you want it to be traceable?' A hint of sarcasm to his voice.

'No. No, definitely not,' the caller stuttered, frightened.

'Then it won't be traceable.'

'Okay, good.'

'I'll call you when it's done.' Artie ended the call before the caller had an opportunity to respond. Chucking the phone back in the drawer, he slammed it shut with more force than was necessary.

'Fucking amateurs.' He sighed.

Sometimes... make that all the time, Artie found himself wondering if he should do something different, just so that he didn't have to deal with all these rookie fuckwits.

But who was he kidding, he was great at what he did, in fact he would go so far as to say he was one of the best in the business.

Artie could hack into just about any computer system going.

By fifteen, he'd already hacked the school's computer system, and it was fair to say that his GCSE results were a surprise to everyone except himself.

By sixteen he had repeatedly hacked the Metropolitan Police's main database and was free to roam through their entire network. He could crack any firewall, break any code and gain access to all kinds of information.

Needless to say, with a talent like his, Artie soon found himself gainfully employed.

In his early career he had been desperate to prove himself, his skills. He'd wanted the recognition and accolades that came with being the best. So, without hesitation he'd accept the most ambitious jobs, the jobs that he soon realised others wouldn't touch, wouldn't risk. Yes, he'd been paid handsomely and yes, his reputation preceded him, but he soon found it impossible to remain under the radar that way.

At the age of twenty-two, Artie had been arrested under suspicion of hacking into classified government documents. Although there wasn't enough to charge him in the end, he'd spent an unacceptable amount of time confined within the miserable walls of a cell.

It had been a wake-up call.

He had gotten lazy. He hadn't covered his tracks well enough but more than that, he'd grown big-headed. It had been a steep learning curve, but Artie came to realise he didn't need to keep proving himself. Beyond that he knew that if he got caught again, especially as he was certain the police were still watching him, he would end up spending the rest of his life behind bars, and that was not an option.

Prison was not an option.

With an exceedingly healthy bank balance, not to mention the offshore accounts, and a reputation which was just about intact, Artie made the momentous decision to walk away, to leave everything he had known and everyone behind and start again. A clean slate.

So Artie left London, without a single word to anybody.

It had been surprisingly easy.

Thinking back, 'good riddance' sprang to his mind. He was sure there were a few pissed off low-lifes who had cursed him for leaving them high and dry. He didn't care though. There wasn't a single person from his old life that he missed, not one.

It was only after an unplanned night out in Brighton that Artie had happened upon Brooke, drinking alone in the quiet corner of a not-so-quiet bar. She had looked lost and at that time, Artie knew how she felt. He'd known that he wanted her company, and that she probably needed his.

Over a bottle of wine, she had divulged her life story. Having recently lost her dad to cancer she found that without him there, her house was not only empty but also lonely. She had suggested Artie move in, first as a sort of off-hand joke fuelled by too much alcohol and then with growing conviction, as though she had just stumbled upon the solution to all her problems, and wouldn't risk letting go. And that solution was Artie.

The rest, as they say, was history.

Under the guise of a freelance web designer, Artie had started over.

With absolute care, Artie only accepted simple cases, ones which wouldn't draw any unwanted attention in his direction. Clients who needed information disappearing from records or money moved around as inconspicuously as possible or official documents forged. All untraceable and all profitable.

Needless to say, these run-of-the-mill jobs often meant a nervous jittery sort of client, the type of person who typically kept their noses clean, who had slipped up and needed help.

But they were the worst type, Artie soon realised, whiny and needy.

Annoyance flaring, Artie pushed himself away from the computer.

'I need a break.' He headed out of his room in search of a distraction.

In the hallway, a furious shout from Elspeth in the bathroom, startled him. Cautiously, he took a step towards the door.

'You all right in there, Ellie?' he called out, not attempting to hide his concern.

There was a pause. It was long enough for his heart to beat a little faster. He raised his hand ready to knock when she finally responded. 'Yeah, I'm fine.'

Artie's brow creased. She definitely didn't sound all right but he knew there was no point in arguing, knew she wouldn't talk to him.

Even though every muscle in his arms were taut, his spiralling tattoos straining against the tension and he had balled his hands into fists, he forced himself to respond calmly. 'Okay,' he replied, hesitantly. 'I'm gonna put the kettle on, do you want a cuppa?'

He waited, ear turned to the door. What was he listening

for? He didn't know, perhaps for some small, insignificant reason to kick the door down, an excuse to give in to the impulses cursing through his veins.

'No. Thank you,' she called out meekly.

Artie released a slow steady breath through his nose and slowly he unfurled his clenched fists.

Disappointment emanated from every pore of his body.

Without another word, he padded downstairs.

In the silence of the kitchen, Artie's frustration became deafening. He knew something was wrong with Elspeth, she hadn't been herself for weeks. It was like she was keeping a secret, a secret which was eating away at her and he just didn't know what it was – if only she'd talk to him. But then he knew he was as guilty as she was when it came to that. They had polite, civilised conversations, avoiding anything that may rock the boat, that may stir up old emotions.

When Elspeth moved in, it was fair to say that Artie had been intrigued if not a little besotted by her. He had known his fair share of women in the past and Elspeth was unlike any of them.

She was beautiful in a very natural way, clever but not a know-it-all and she was funny, always knowing just what to say to make him smile. She wasn't afraid to be herself and that was what Artie loved the most.

Not that he had ever said those words to her, of course. Perhaps he would have, if things had turned out differently.

Maybe it's guy trouble? The thought appeared out of nowhere and with it a note of jealousy, stirring deep in the pit of his stomach before he brushed it off. *No, it isn't that.* He would have known if she was seeing someone, Brooke would have let it slip at the very least. But what then? A work issue, a family issue, a parking ticket?

Artie was grappling to find a concrete reason to hold on to.

An idea crawled into his mind then, like a snake slithering towards its prey.

He could check. To see if it was a problem that he could make disappear for her, but–

He sighed loudly.

Yes, he had previously run a background check on Elspeth and no, he wasn't proud of himself. He had just wanted to know a little more about who he was sharing his home with, he had told himself at the time.

He had learned little about her really. She had grown up in a small village, living all her life in one house. The only child of parents who were still together. She had completed a degree in paediatrics, achieving a first, no less. Some moderate savings in her bank account, the standard student loans but nothing else to her name. She'd never been arrested and up until recently she'd never even had a credit card.

He wondered whether he should revisit this, to see if something had changed, something which would have Elspeth so clearly out of sorts that she looked ill.

Would she hate me for prying?

It would be different now, he reasoned. This wasn't about protecting himself from an unknown threat, this would be snooping, although for all intents and purposes it would be for a very good reason. He would be helping. Wouldn't he?

Torn with indecision, Artie turned the kettle on. As it slowly boiled, he dropped a teabag into his favourite mug.

Eventually, the kettle's noisy bubbling drew him out of his pondering. Maybe it wouldn't hurt to check a couple of databases, the police, the nursing council, that sort of thing to make sure her name didn't pop up. *Just to rule out a few possibilities*, he told himself.

Having made a cuppa, Artie headed back upstairs feeling even more tightly wound than he had been ten minutes previously. Not only was he brooding over Elspeth, he knew there was a whiney arse-wipe waiting on him for some information and they would only get more annoying if he didn't deliver soon.

'I need a holiday!' he groaned, shutting the bedroom door behind him.

11

ALICE

FEBRUARY, 2026

'I don't think you've understood. The recommendation is one child *per* family,' Professor Alice Franklin repeated, placing a slight exaggeration on the 'per' in the hope of making herself clear.

The conference room within the Metropolitan Police headquarters was a vast yet drab room. The metal-framed chairs covered in rough blue fabric were tired and vandalised with a multitude of unidentifiable stains although best guess would be coffee, whilst the table was a large monstrosity of MDF.

'I appreciate the recommendation, however, we have to make this manageable to police,' the commissioner of police Gemima Curtis, replied curtly from the head of the table.

Alice had met her at several press conferences recently. They had been attempting to demonstrate a united front to the press and therefore to the population. It hadn't stopped the rioting, or the petitioning or the threats though. A note of anger seeped into Alice's otherwise-calm facade as she recalled the last and most terrifying of threats she'd received. A death threat, tied to a brick, which had smashed its way through her lounge window. Thankfully, she'd been in the kitchen at the time, or else she suspected it would have collided with the back of her head.

She pushed the memory away.

Every other seat around the table was occupied by unfamiliar faces. And they all seemed uninterested.

Alice was used to being questioned in public, explaining her research, defending it even, this felt different, however. Like a formality that they were begrudgingly suffering through.

'It seems to me as though you are taking what is a fair and simple law and twisting it up into knots.' Alice's frustration was obvious.

'May I interrupt?' a woman to the left of Curtis asked.

'By all means,' Curtis responded with a little wave of her hand.

The woman fixed Alice with a hard stare. 'Detective Inspector Sam Wakley,' she said briskly without any pleasantries. 'It is evident, Professor Franklin, that you are an expert in your field of practice, however, we are the experts in our field.'

Alice instantly took a dislike to this woman. Her dark bobbed hair was too severe and her suit overly masculine for her petite frame. Then there was the undertone to her voice; one Alice couldn't quite put her finger on but it unsettled her. 'No one can question your dedication. Because of you, the law is being changed. Now it's time for us to take the reins and get things properly up and running.'

Alice sat forward, resting her arms on the table and intertwining her fingers. *Two can play at this game.* 'I would love nothing more than to pass the reins over, however, you can't just add caveats and clauses left, right and centre. You will incite more rioting if you do.' Alice held the woman's stare, not prepared to be intimidated.

'Sam is right,' Curtis interjected, drawing Alice's attention away from the detective. 'We do know what we're doing. We need to ensure that we have a system in place which maintains the law. At the moment there are too many grey areas. We need to tighten things up or else it will all fall apart, and you don't want that now do you?'

Alice sat back in her chair. Her lips pressed into a thin line. They were all waiting, she could tell, for her to concede, to accept whatever path they chose. They were going to be sorely mistaken. 'This is the twenty-first century, there are thousands, if not millions of unmarried parents out there doing an absolutely superb job. Surely you don't think that you can turn the clock back and start dictating marriage as a stipulation for having a child?' She laughed, if not a little awkwardly.

'Why not?' Sam replied. 'If couples are married before they're able to apply to have a child then there won't be any room for dispute.'

'Room for dispute?' Alice repeated, confused.

'Yes.' The detective sighed loudly, clearly for effect. Thankfully she stopped short of rolling her eyes or else Alice wouldn't have been able to maintain her already-tested self-control.

Sam resumed talking to Alice as though she were a small child. 'What do you propose we do with the guy that finds out he's a father from a one-night stand only to be expecting with his new girlfriend. Or, how about the couple who go their separate ways and one of them gets pregnant again as they don't see their first child. Again, how do we police that? How are we supposed to manage the whole tirade of family dynamics if we don't demand order first?' She sounded so confident, so self-assured that Alice found herself fleetingly doubting her stance, before the absurdity of what was being planned brought her back to earth with a thud. 'We are less likely to walk into those situations if the couple are married before they apply.'

Alice understood what they were attempting to convey, and

she empathised, really she did. But from her perspective this wasn't that complicated. 'I can see how there may be some teething issues with getting this all into place, however, what we don't want is for any woman to not be granted the opportunity to have a child, or any man for that matter.' She raised her eyebrows a fraction awaiting some sort of bite back from the bobbed-hair woman.

Before it came, the conference room door swung open loudly making them all jump.

A middle-aged man, with thick bottle glasses and leathery-looking skin, pushed in a trolley holding several cups, a pot of coffee and a plate of stale-looking pastries. Silently, everyone around the table watched him as he completed his task. With the trolley positioned against the wall, he scuttled out again.

A senior officer, Smithers, who had contributed very little to the conversation, was the first one out of his seat. Alice watched as he greedily grabbed two sticky-looking pastries and placed them in a napkin before pouring himself a cup of black coffee. He sat back down, placing his snacks on the table in front of him.

'We do not want to deny anyone that right either,' the commissioner of police interjected. 'Nevertheless, some measures will need to be in place to prevent individuals from flouting the law, having multiple children with multiple partners. I agree marriage may be an archaic measure but it will be one that works, by allowing us to not only ensure that the one-child law is upheld but to also monitor the number of families having children.'

The realisation of what they were going to do unnerved Alice. Maybe she should have predicted this, an element of control being applied under the disguise of the law, but she hadn't. She had been too focused on finding a workable solution, that she had overlooked the snowball effect. She was no longer in control and she knew with unwavering clarity that she wouldn't be able to stop it now.

What had she done?

'That will be the only measure added, won't it?' she asked, almost helplessly. 'No one will be denied as long as they meet that stipulation?'

Alice watched as Sam and Curtis shared a look, Curtis nodding almost imperceptibly, a gesture so slight that had Alice not been watching, she would have missed it. *What did it mean?* she wondered, dread washing over her.

'DI Smithers and DI Wakley are experienced officers. They will be granted the necessary resources to enable a smooth transition for everyone involved. Rest assured we will do everything in our power to guarantee that individuals are not restricted any more than they have to be,' the commissioner said reassuringly, although it fell flat. 'We'd like to thank you for your input today and I hope that if we need any further advice that we can call upon you again?' she said firmly, standing up and holding out her hand for Alice to shake.

Surprised by the abrupt dismissal, Alice slowly rose to her feet and out of politeness, shook Gemima Curtis's hand.

It was only as Alice navigated her way back through the corridors of the police department and out into the crisp February air, that she stopped.

She drew in several deep breaths, her hand poised on her chest and her eyes wide in understanding. The wheels had been set in motion, she had set them moving, and now she had no control over the path that they took. She didn't know how this would be twisted or manipulated, but what she did know with utter certainty was that the law she had instigated, demanded of everyone, would not remain on the course she had originally foreseen.

12

ELSPETH

Efficiently, Elspeth pulled on the navy-blue ill-fitting scrubs. With her clothes neatly folded, she tucked them safely into her locker along with her handbag. Pocketing her pen, calculator and notebook, she slammed the small metal door shut and fastened it with a mini padlock, slipping the key into her top pocket.

When Elspeth had started her nurse training, she hadn't been sure where she wanted to go with it, what field she wanted to focus on, but after just one shift on the neonatal unit, her mind had been made up.

Usually she relished coming to work. This was the kind of job where you knew, undoubtedly, that you were making a difference, and she loved that feeling; that she mattered, that what she did mattered.

Today, though, she was going to throw that all into jeopardy.

Her stomach contorted into knots as she made her way to the staffroom for handover.

'Hey.' Rose, one of her colleagues, smiled.

Elspeth forced a grin. 'Hey.'

'You okay?' Rose asked casually as Elspeth sat down next to her.

'Of course,' Elspeth said, her voice a little too loud, a little too tense.

Rose stared at her for a moment, her eyes searching, before turning her attention to another nurse who had just arrived.

What's the matter with you? You haven't done anything yet.

She was struggling to act normal, the guilt of what she had planned already weighed heavily on her, like an iron chain around her neck.

Act normal, she reminded herself. She knew, however, that was going to be easier said than done.

Just then the night sister came bustling in. She looked exhausted as she sat down and pulled a sheet of paper out from her top pocket.

'Good morning.' She briefly looked around the room, doing a quick headcount of staff before she continued. 'All the babies are stable, we've had quite a peaceful night really. There are four in ITU all ventilated but stable, six in HDU and only three in special care, two of which are likely to be discharged home today.' She briefly referred to her notes before continuing. 'The transport team are bringing one in today from Southampton for ITU, but they'll call when they're ready to set off with all the details. And, down on maternity, there are two for midday antibiotics.'

'I'll do those,' Elspeth quickly volunteered, her smile fixed tightly in place. The sister taking charge of the day shift nodded lightly in thanks, making a note on her handover sheets.

Carefully, Elspeth glanced around the room. Had anyone thought her offer was out of place, or that she was acting strangely? She felt like every action, every expression was forced and exaggerated, she wouldn't have been surprised if everyone in the room was looking back at her, suspicious of her behaviour.

Thankfully, they weren't. Everyone had their attention turned elsewhere. Elspeth let out the breath she hadn't realised she'd been holding.

This was going to be an excruciatingly long and uncomfortable day.

With the handover completed, Elspeth headed to the high-dependency room, where she'd be working for the day, with two other nurses.

Her colleagues were chatting and laughing freely, which Elspeth envied. She didn't have that luxury, every nerve in her body was on high alert as adrenaline coursed through her veins. Fleetingly, she wondered if this was how actors felt before a live performance. Because wasn't that what she was doing herself, pretending?

Elspeth wasn't paying any attention to what they were saying, too preoccupied with what she intended to do.

Instead, she plastered a smile on her face and hoped it would suffice so that they wouldn't look too closely at her, wouldn't ask too many questions.

Finally, Elspeth headed down to the maternity unit.

The morning had crept past, all the while Elspeth felt as if she'd been working inside a thick fog. She hadn't been able to focus on even the simplest of tasks.

Unsurprisingly, her behaviour hadn't gone unnoticed. More than once, she'd been asked if she was all right, each time she repeated the same vague response, 'I've just got a bit of a headache.'

If they suspected, Elspeth didn't know. If they were watching her more closely, she couldn't tell, but each time she told the lie, a wave of nausea rolled over her; that feeling you get from riding a massive roller coaster, you know you won't vomit and yet it's there at the forefront. You can't ignore it, instead you have to breathe deeply and slowly just to get through it.

With the antibiotic glass vial in her hand, Elspeth took the back stairway to the floor below, a cold fear gripping hold of her insides.

Pushing through the heavy fire escape door, she trudged the length of the corridor, towards the reception desk at the front of the ward. Passing room after room of mothers with their newborn babies, Elspeth stared ahead purposefully, desperately trying to contain her racing thoughts.

Could I do that? Could I be a mother? The thoughts were so sharp and sudden, they startled her. With a faltering step, she blinked against the thoughts, fought to cast them out.

She had to remain focused.

'I've come to do your midday antibiotics,' Elspeth said, as casually as she could muster, to the receptionist.

'Great,' the woman replied, looking up from her computer. She stood, grabbing a set of keys. Elspeth's gaze gravitated towards them.

Those. Those are what I'm going to need.

'There are two due,' the receptionist chirped as she led Elspeth to the clinical room. 'Their names are there.' She nodded towards a large whiteboard. 'Are you okay to find out their drug charts, while I locate a midwife for you?' She indicated towards a metal filing cabinet.

'Sure,' Elspeth answered, eyes drifting back to the keys in the woman's hand.

The receptionist, unaware of Elspeth's growing anxiety,

searched through the bunch of keys. Locating the one marked with a green sticker which matched the one on the lock of the cabinet, she unlocked the top drawer for Elspeth. Then leaving the keys jangling in the lock, she gave Elspeth a quick smile before leaving.

A spark of fear made Elspeth hesitate. Was someone watching? Did someone know what she had intended? It all just seemed a little too easy.

Aware that the clock was ticking, she sprang into action.

Extracting the keys from the cabinet, Elspeth swivelled round to face the wall of cupboards. Unsure of which cupboard she needed, she quickly excluded two, already aware of their contents; needles, syringes and other such items she regularly accessed when in there.

That left three more.

With hands shaking, Elspeth fingered each key until she found the one matching the first cupboard. Her heart was racing and a bead of sweat had collected between her breasts. With a final glance over her shoulder to ensure the coast was clear, Elspeth guided the key into the lock.

Turning the key, she paused for a split second. She knew that once she opened the cupboard, there would be no going back.

Swallowing down her fear, her natural instincts, she pushed those thoughts to the depths of her mind and tugged the door wide open.

Taking care not to disturb the contents, Elspeth frantically searched.

It wasn't there.

Slamming the door closed, locking it and pulling out the key, Elspeth hunted for the next key. Her heart beat was thundering in her ears as her desperation escalated.

It has to be here somewhere.

Poised, ready to spring open the next cupboard, the main door burst open.

Elspeth swung around, swallowing the scream which was about to fly from her mouth, as a midwife backed into the room, pulling a small hospital cot in after her.

'I've brought the first one,' the midwife said, still without looking up.

Flustered, Elspeth pocketed the keys and swiftly stepped towards the filing cabinet, desperate to put some distance between her and the cupboards.

She busied herself with locating the drug charts, aware that her cheeks were flaming red and her eyes wide. Her guilt was written all over her face.

'We're bursting at the seams today,' the midwife continued, as she began unwrapping the blankets from about the sleeping baby in the cot. 'How's things upstairs?'

'We're actually quite quiet today,' Elspeth croaked, her mouth dry. Eyes purposefully fixed on the infant, so as not to meet the midwife's stare, Elspeth asked, 'So who do we have here?'

Taking in the small bundle wrapped in a rainbow blanket, a strange mix of emotions briefly descended on Elspeth. Her tummy fluttered lightly and her breath caught.

A small innocent baby, just like this one, could define her future, could change everything, that's if she was–

The midwife interjected, cutting off her thoughts. 'This is Harry Simmons.'

She proceeded to expose the white name tag secured around his tiny ankle and together they confirmed that his details corresponded with his drug chart.

Turning away, Elspeth took a moment to compose herself, before grabbing the necessary equipment and drawing up the antibiotic. With her heart rate settling, she administered the medication, all without Harry stirring.

'Okay, I'll be back with–' The midwife quickly referred to the whiteboard. '–Aimee in a sec,' she said over her shoulder as she carefully wheeled Harry, in his cot, out of the room.

Anxiously, Elspeth looked at the cupboards. Her fingers traced the keys which were still hidden in her pocket whilst debating if she had enough time to check another one.

Paralysed with indecision, she remained firmly rooted to the spot. She had nearly gotten caught last time, but her need to keep going, to know, was all-consuming. Her gaze darted between the cupboard and the door. *I can't get caught.*

Before she'd made her decision, the midwife returned. This time accompanied by not only another baby but also an extremely apprehensive-looking woman wearing a pink dressing gown.

'Will it hurt her?' the woman asked instantly, catching Elspeth off guard.

'No, it shouldn't do,' Elspeth mumbled, feeling uncomfortable under the weight of the woman's anxiety.

Whilst the woman fussed with the baby in the cot, Elspeth took her in. She looked exhausted, dark circles framed her eyes yet she was glowing at the same time. Despite her worry, she looked at her child with such love, such adoration that it made Elspeth want to cry.

Is that what it's like?

What's wrong with me? You need to get a grip.

Purpose dragged her back to the task in hand, she was there for a reason, one she had to see through. And until then, until she had a definitive answer, nothing was decided, nothing set in stone.

'No,' the midwife echoed, her voice so thick with reassurance and empathy, that Elspeth found herself glancing up. The midwife wore a hint of a frown, reprimanding Elspeth for her lack of sympathy. 'She won't feel a thing.'

Elspeth smiled tightly, then set to work calculating the drug dose, keen to be busy.

As she attached the syringe to the baby's cannula and administered the antibiotic, the mother took hold of her daughter's chubby hand, rubbing it carefully with her thumb. Such a small gesture, but the meaning was vast.

'Thank you, thank you very much.' The woman's relief was unmistakable and Elspeth's breath caught. It seemed so ironic to her that she was terrified of having what that woman so clearly cherished.

All she could do was offer a weak smile, as the midwife gently guided her and her infant out of the room.

'Can I leave you to clear up?' the midwife asked flatly, already halfway out the door.

'Yes, of course, no problem.'

'Brilliant, thanks.'

Elspeth waited for all of two seconds once the door had swung closed, before pulling the keys from her pocket. Hunting for the one she needed, she didn't even bother to check behind her this time when she found the right one. Instead, she shoved it in the lock, flinging the cupboard doors open.

The cupboard contained all manner of medicines, packets of pills, bottles of coloured liquid but no test.

Straight on to the next one.

Elspeth wasn't thinking. She was just acting, completely committed and unable to turn back. She had to find the test, to have her answer.

Focused, she yanked open the doors of the last cupboard.

More packets, more boxes, a record book and there – four white oblong boxes.

Pregnancy tests.

Grabbing one, Elspeth turned the box over in her hand.

That's it.

She didn't waste any longer looking at it before she slid the box into the depths of her scrub pocket and locked the cupboard. Somewhere in the shadows of her mind, she knew she had to be quick, knew it would raise eyebrows if she took too long, if she was still there, alone, without the midwife.

Turning round, Elspeth rushed to tidy up the debris from giving the antibiotics. With the rubbish disposed of and the drug charts tucked away in the filing cabinet, she exited the clinical room, then headed back round to the reception desk.

She was breathing like she'd been running, fast and shallow. A light film of sweat had formed on her brow. The keys, which were burning in her hand, an extension of her guilt, had to be returned. She had to face the receptionist again.

Her stride didn't falter as, with the palm of her hand, she wiped her damp brow and sucked in a deep ragged breath.

Act normal. Just act normal.

At Elspeth's presence, the receptionist glanced up.

In what she hoped was a casual manner, Elspeth dropped the keys on the desk and offered her thanks, before turning swiftly to leave. She desperately wanted to run, to sprint out of there, but with clenched fists she forced herself to walk, slowly and steadily.

'Did you lock everything up?' the receptionist called after her.

'Yep,' Elspeth replied over shoulder without slowing her stride. She powered down the corridor, through the fire escape door and halfway up the fire escape stairs.

Then she stopped.

A bout of queasiness overpowered her. With her hand pressed firmly against her chest, she closed her eyes and swallowed down several lungfuls of air. *It will pass.* She attempted and failed to reassure herself.

She remained motionless for several minutes until her panic slowly subsided.

There was no going back now, she realised with a heavy heart. Even if it was negative, she had changed, this had changed her.

Climbing the final few stairs, Elspeth slowed at the top. Peering through the glass panel in the heavy door, the corridor outside appeared empty.

She had one last thing to do, one more deceitful act to add to the accumulating list.

Swiftly, she slipped into the corridor and darted for the changing room, desperate to hide the stolen test in the depths of her handbag in her padlocked locker.

13

SAM

MARCH 10TH 2035

Sam had been pleasantly surprised to find an email from the ward sister waiting for her the next morning.

The list was certainly comprehensive, detailing staff members present on the shifts prior to the theft, inpatients on the ward during the allotted timeframe and all their relevant contact details. The only limited information Sam could see surrounded visitors.

A photocopy of the visitors log had been attached to the email. Frustratingly, it appeared to have been filled in by the visitors themselves. Some of the handwriting was indecipherable and it was completely possible that multiple people were missing from the log entirely.

Sam considered the effort it was going to take to compile a list of visitors herself from having conversations with each and every inpatient listed. Her annoyance flared. *This could have all been so simple, if only they'd kept a proper detailed inventory of all those attending the unit.*

She sighed loudly. This was turning, no, spiralling into a monumental piece of work. And even then, Sam comprehended the likeliness of people being forgotten, or purposely omitted was exceedingly high, especially if they had something to hide.

The potential gaps already present in her case didn't fill the detective with confidence.

Having influenced the stipulations within the law, Sam at least felt reassured that all the women, having clearly been through the approval process, had clean records. Also, they were either in the process of giving birth, or had recently given birth, so theoretically they shouldn't have needed a pregnancy test, which helped to limit her search somewhat.

A quick cross reference of all the names listed with the police database instantly identified two people of interest. The first; a midwife with a criminal record dating back to her teenage years with no convictions since. The second, and of particular interest to Sam, was a cleaner, Louisa Tanner.

The dossier on Louisa was extensive. She had a string of offences to her name including theft and deception, the most recent, only two years previously, for which she served six months in prison.

How the hell did she get a job at the hospital? Sam wondered, immediately suspecting a fraudulent application.

Thankfully though, it was something to start with, and fairly promising to boot.

Back in the main office, Sam approached a young suited man hunched over his desk, who was furiously typing at his keyboard.

'Hudson!' she said, self-assured.

Looking up, the young man, Detective Sergeant Robert Hudson, took in Sam's serious face looming over him and swiftly jumped up out of his seat, as though standing to attention.

'Yes, detective?' He pushed his glasses up on his exceedingly pointy nose with one finger, an air of nervousness evident in his demeanour.

'I need you to contact all these women,' she commanded, handing him a sheet of paper. 'I need to know who visited them during their stay in hospital: names, addresses, contact details.'

Sam was already striding back to her office when Hudson collected himself enough to reply, 'Of course.'

Sam heard him, but didn't feel the need to respond.

Knocking loudly, the detective stood to the side of the door, just out of sight.

Moulsecoomb, a north-east suburb of Brighton, was one of Sam's least favourite areas to visit. Who was she kidding, she hated coming here.

She'd made more than a few arrests from this area in the last couple of years. There seemed to be a distinct lack of respect for the law, with many unapproved pregnancies being shielded by the local community.

At one point, a rogue midwife had even been enlisted to support these women. Needless to say, said midwife was not only struck off but she was also serving time for aiding and abetting these criminals. Six years if Sam remembered correctly.

Sam listened as someone approached on the other side, their footsteps echoing against hard flooring. Reaching the door, there was a pause. *Peering through the door viewer*, Sam thought knowingly.

'Who's there?' demanded a female, her face likely still pressed against the viewer.

'I'm looking for Louisa Tanner,' Sam said, cautious to remain out of view. She knew her demeanour oozed a police vibe, often inciting an unfriendly welcome.

'Who's asking?'

'Are you Louisa Tanner?' Sam persisted.

'Depends. Who are you?' the woman asked again.

'Police,' Sam confirmed calmly, holding her badge up, so that it was visible for the woman to see.

When the female didn't initially respond, Sam suspected that she was currently debating her immediate options. She was likely to be considering whether to A: deny all knowledge of a Louisa Tanner, B: refuse to open the door and claim she was being harassed by the police, or C: open the door but pretend to be someone other than Louisa Tanner.

Eventually, having mentally run through her options, the chain on the door was unhooked.

Quietly, Sam exhaled the breath she'd been holding, in relief. This would certainly make things easier. With the suspect's picture on file, the detective would know instantly if this woman was her person of interest.

Slowly the door opened inwards, just enough for the woman to look out.

That's her, Sam thought confidently, taking in the middle-aged brunette. Although the same age as Sam, Louisa Tanner could easily pass as ten years her senior.

Her hard life was etched in her very skin, deep crevices framed her mouth presumably from years of chain smoking, her greasy limp hair hung lifelessly around her sallow face and her skin carried a jaundiced tone of someone who drank significantly more than they should.

'What do you want with Louisa?' Louisa asked, exposing a row of stained teeth.

'Can we talk inside?' Sam suggested, eyebrows raised in understanding. Louisa, however, remained unmoving.

Have it your way, Sam though indignantly. *If you want me to expose your dirty laundry on the doorstep that is just fine by me.*

'Several days ago, there was a theft from the maternity unit at the hospital, the unit you're responsible for cleaning. You wouldn't happen to know anything about that, now would you?'

Louisa's eyes widened and she looked anxiously beyond Sam. Sam couldn't help but turn to look as well.

Unsurprisingly, in such a tight-knit community, several neighbours were already standing in their open doorways, one had even moved into her front garden. Sam registered their hostility, arms folded across their chests, aggressive stares. In her fitted black suit, she knew she stood out. They will either be thinking copper or social worker. Either way, she wouldn't be welcome.

'You'd better come in before you create a scene.' Louisa moved to the side, hastily ushering Sam in, then slamming the door firmly shut behind her. 'They're nosy bastards round here,' she grumbled as a way of an explanation.

Sam's nose immediately wrinkled in disgust at the sight of Louisa's dingy flat. She clearly didn't bring her work home with her.

The compact lounge was littered with empty cider cans, half eaten pots of instant noodles and several ashtrays were overflowing with cigarette butts. The stench of stale smoke was overpowering. The detective stifled a cough. She was already itching to get out of there, convinced that every breath of nicotine-filled air would be shortening her life span considerably.

'You wanna sit down?' Louisa asked, indicating to a once-cream leather sofa, whilst she sat on a single high-backed fabric chair. Sam couldn't help but notice the large black circle soiling the fabric from where Louisa's oily head permanently rested. Her stomach rolled in disgust.

'No. Thank you.' Sam was keen to get this over with as quickly as possible.

'Suit yourself,' Louisa mumbled through pinched lips as she lit a cigarette.

'As I said outside, there was a theft–'

'I heard you. And you thought that seein' as how I've a criminal record n'all, I was your best bet. Well, it ain't me. I didn't take nothin'.'

Sam wasn't naive enough to believe that Louisa would simply own up, if it was her. Sam raised her eyebrows in undisguised scepticism. 'Are you telling me, you weren't aware that the maternity unit has a stock of pregnancy tests?' she persisted.

An indiscernible look, understanding perhaps or maybe even shock, flashed across Louisa's face at the admission of what had been stolen. Regardless, she seemed to grasp the severity of the accusation being made and answered firmly. 'No, I didn't.'

Sam watched with a frown as Louisa tapped the end of her cigarette over the edge of the chair, letting the ash fall onto the heavily stained carpet.

Sam changed tactics. 'What are your duties when you're at work?'

Louisa raised her eyebrows as if to say, 'what a stupid fucking question,' but realising that the detective was serious, she began reeling off her tasks.

'So you are responsible for cleaning the floors in both the reception area and the clinical room?' Sam repeated once Louisa had finished.

'I just said that, didn't I? I'm responsible for cleanin' all the floors.'

'Have you ever applied to have a child?' Sam asked, her tone casual.

Abruptly, Louisa burst out laughing. A laugh dripping with

so much hatred and loathing that the hairs on Sam's arms stood up. 'Like you lot would ever let me 'ave a kid,' she spat.

'Did you steal the pregnancy test for yourself or on behalf of someone else?' Sam demanded, pissed off with how long this was taking.

Louisa jumped out of her chair, startling Sam. 'How fucking dare you!' she snapped, finger pointing towards the detective's chest. 'I've had enough of you, you jumped-up cow. Who d'ya think you are to come into my home and accuse me of God knows what! I may not have a squeaky-clean record, but I didn't steal nothin'. Now, I want you to leave!' she ranted, her eyes wild. Louisa stomped back to the door. Pulling it open, she glared at Sam.

With jaw set, Sam took the not-so-subtle hint and went to leave.

'Oh and for what it's worth, I may not agree with how you police the laws, but I certainly ain't gonna help any of this lot to have a kid, they're not fit to be parents!' she yelled before slamming the door.

Unfazed by Louisa Tanner's outburst, Sam made her way back to her car. Call it a hunch or a gut feeling, but she wasn't convinced that Louisa was her culprit. In fact, she was sure of it. Unlocking her car and sliding into the driver's seat, Sam sighed loudly as she looked out of her windscreen to find half a dozen smashed eggs obscuring her view.

'Fucking marvellous,' she groaned, starting the engine and jabbing at the washer lever.

14

ELSPETH

Elspeth arrived on time for work. It had almost been a week since her last shift and yet the guilt of what she'd done still weighed heavily on her.

Like a robot, she walked through the morning routine. Carrying out daily checks, she ensured that each patient had the appropriate safety equipment, she reviewed the drug charts, jotted down times of medication before checking the IV drips and calculating the dosages of morphine to ensure they were correct, and all the while obsessing over her own dilemma.

She knew for sure she was pregnant, the test she'd stolen had uncategorically confirmed her suspicions.

Pregnant.

That word sent a spark of cold fear shooting down her spine and a sickening feeling rose in the back of her throat every time she thought of it.

Thankfully, the morning sickness had passed. But she was convinced that she was starting to show. The curve of her stomach had become more pronounced with each day and her breasts were growing almost as rapidly.

Elspeth had taken to hiding in the toilet cubicle to change

into her scrubs, fearful that her swelling body would give her secret away.

It was fair to say that she had been tormented as she frantically scrutinised every conceivable way out of this mess, and yet – she still didn't know what to do, didn't have a clue as to how to put this right, if that was even possible.

In her darkest moments, she'd hoped she would miscarry, solving the problem for her, and yet when this idea came to her, she felt both dirty and guilty.

She'd considered whether she'd be able to hide the pregnancy to the end. If she could, she could deliver the baby to a hospital to be adopted by an approved family, no one any the wiser that she was involved.

Or perhaps she could move, start over anew, with her baby, somewhere where she could pretend her husband had recently died, perhaps Scotland.

Or maybe she could tell Nick. Admittedly he'd be surprised at first, but once the initial shock had died down, he would embrace her, they'd get married swiftly and she would live happily ever after with her new family.

The only problem was, they were pipe dreams, visions through rose-coloured glasses. The reality that faced her was so much worse.

The scenario which she truly believed, the one which had her waking in the black of night, cold and shaking, involved the police. They would find her, and with unwavering conviction, she'd be arrested. She envisioned being thrown in a dank, dark cell, labelled as a criminal, where she would eventually give birth to her baby. The police would wordlessly remove her child from her, physically ripping it from her hands. She would then be left alone and forgotten, her broken heart rotting within her chest.

'Elspeth!' the sister in charge called from the door jolting her out of her thoughts.

'Hmm?' Elspeth responded.

'I need you to head down to maternity, they've just called. There's a baby that needs bringing up for low sugars and phototherapy.'

The colour instantly drained from her face, leaving her ashen. 'Okay,' she eventually croaked.

Elspeth hadn't ventured downstairs since the theft, too afraid that someone might put two and two together, that by seeing her face, a memory connecting her to the ward would be awoken.

Stop being ridiculous. They have no way of knowing it was you if you just act normal, she chided, as she took the main lift down.

At the main doors to the maternity unit, Elspeth swiped her ID badge, releasing the lock. With her hand clenched on the door handle, she sucked in a deep breath before yanking the door open.

For a brief second, she waited, as if anticipating an ambush. When nothing happened, she let out the breath she'd been holding and tentatively headed in.

The reception area was unexpectedly empty.

From somewhere further down the ward, a commotion drew Elspeth's attention. A woman was screaming, a guttural cry that gripped hold of her, and then in response the sharp, sweet holler of a newborn coming into the world.

Something stirred deep inside her. Anger perhaps, or was it jealousy?

Pursing her lips against her turbulent emotions, Elspeth idled at the desk, waiting for someone to appear. She didn't want to be in her own head, aware that her thoughts had been chaotic and unpredictable. Her hormones, she suspected.

Instead, she focused her attention on the posters, with curling corners, tacked to the walls. Breastfeeding, safe sleep, bonding. Her heart ached. It was an unanticipated raw ache that made her throat constrict and tears well in her eyes.

'Yes?' a woman demanded, having bustled around the corner. She looked flustered with unmasked irritation in her expression.

Elspeth blinked away her tears, as she schooled her features in to what she hoped was a neutral expression. 'I've come to collect the–'

'I called upstairs nearly fifteen minutes ago,' the woman rebuked. 'I'll inform the midwife that you've finally arrived.'

Elspeth flinched at the receptionist's sharp tone. She didn't notice, instead she stomped away muttering to herself.

'How rude,' Elspeth whispered under her breath, annoyance replacing the sadness she had felt only moments ago.

A young midwife Elspeth recognised strolled out from a side room. 'Hi, you here to take Poppy upstairs?'

'Low blood sugars and phototherapy?' Elspeth asked.

'That's the one, Poppy Barton. I'll just go and get her. Would you mind getting her drug chart from the clinical room?' The midwife held out a set of very-familiar keys.

Tentatively, Elspeth took hold of them. 'Of course,' she said, her voice strained.

Returning to the scene of the crime, wasn't there some unwritten rule about that? You don't go back, not unless you want to get caught.

Elspeth stalked round to the clinical room.

Poised at the door, hesitation rooted her momentarily.

She knew she'd have to go in there at some point, she just hadn't expected it to be so soon.

Get it over and done with, she thought sharply, shaking her head in an attempt to dispel her fear.

Entering the clinical room, Elspeth cast a glance around. Everything looked exactly the same.

What had she been expecting? A siren on the door, a poster of her face on the cupboard, a police officer with a badge and gun waiting for her.

She let out a nervous giggle. She was being ridiculous, she knew, and yet she was all too aware of the police's involvement, everyone had been talking about it, and that was what terrified her.

Focusing, she moved purposefully. Unlocking the filing cabinet, she grabbed hold of Poppy Barton's drug chart before slamming the drawer shut and relocking it.

Turning to leave, she let go of the door handle at the same moment that it was swung swiftly open.

A cry escaped Elspeth's lips and she stumbled backwards.

Three people were suddenly blocking her exit.

With relief, she recognised the first to be the ward sister, Judith. Behind her, however, was a woman who looked entirely out of place on the unit. Dressed in a serious-looking navy-blue suit, her black hair had been cut so bluntly that its edge appeared sharp, like a razor blade. What unnerved Elspeth most though, was her unsmiling face, her narrowed eyes were cold and her thin lips were pulled back in what resembled a sneer. Elspeth shifted her stare, uneasy. Beyond the two women, stood a young guy, he was unremarkable in every way were it not for his thick black-rimmed glasses which framed his eyes. He was shifting nervously from one foot to the other.

Elspeth's heart raced as a sense of dread washed over her.

'What are you doing in here?' Judith demanded, clearly startled.

'Just collecting a drug chart,' Elspeth said, trying and failing to sound cheerful. She held up the green chart as proof.

In the split second that followed, Elspeth watched as Judith took her in, watched as her eyes drifted to the drug chart before finally coming to rest on the keys in Elspeth's other hand.

A look of alarm flickered across her face, then as if without thinking, Judith glanced back to the suited woman. She hadn't appeared to notice, instead she was seemingly preoccupied by the small windowless space behind Elspeth.

The ward sister, regaining some control, cleared her throat. 'Right, well, I'm sure you have somewhere to be.'

Elspeth had been dismissed. Mumbling something indiscernible about needing to get back upstairs, Elspeth quickly excused herself.

As she squeezed past the human barrier, Judith's hand shot out and wordlessly she seized hold of the keys, before secreting them into her tunic pocket.

With her gaze firmly trained on the floor, Elspeth headed towards the reception area. It took all of her willpower to walk. Not for the first time, she had the overwhelming desire to run.

There was something about that woman, something acutely unsettling. Elspeth was convinced she could feel the stranger's eyes boring into her back as she moved further away.

Instinctively, Elspeth glanced over her shoulder.

She instantly wished she hadn't.

The woman's eyes were fixed, no, were burning into her, like she wanted to see into the depths of Elspeth's soul. A chill ran down her spine.

Elspeth was breathing heavily and her mind was reeling as she rounded the corner.

The woman had unnerved her. Who was she? Why had she looked so interested in Elspeth? A thought drifted across her mind, but before she could grip hold of its thread, the midwife returned.

'Here we are.' She smiled, before a frown creased her brow. 'Are you all right, you look like you've seen a ghost?'

'Hmmm. Yes, I'm fine.' Elspeth nodded.

The midwife didn't push her any further. 'I suggested parents wait ten minutes before heading upstairs, so you can get Poppy all sorted, I hope that's all right?'

'Yes, that's fine,' Elspeth responded, desperate to get off the ward.

'Okay, well... Thanks.' The woman turned away.

'Who's that? With Judith?' Elspeth blurted out without thinking.

Immediately she regretted saying anything. *What are you doing? You're going to draw attention to yourself.*

The midwife turned back then, a conspiratorial glean in her eyes. 'Hard to miss that one, isn't she? She's investigating the theft, I've not seen the guy before though. He's quite cute, don't you think? I don't usually like guys with glasses.' She lowered her voice to little more than a whisper. 'We've all been spoken to. I can't imagine it's going too well, or else why'd she come back? I don't think they've got a clue. I'm hoping she'll move on to something else soon, she's getting everyone in a fluster.' The midwife smiled lightly.

Elspeth didn't respond, couldn't comprehend the information quickly enough to form a response. The midwife, unfazed, shrugged dismissively, before striding off into a room further along the corridor.

They're police. Elspeth reeled whilst manoeuvring the sleeping baby in the cot towards the lift. *Shit! What am I going to do? Now they know what I look like. And that woman, does she know?*

Elspeth's thoughts were all over the place as adrenaline coursed through her body.

She considered going off sick, before hastily changing her mind, worried that it would only draw unwanted attention her way.

You need to calm down.

Stepping into the lift with the baby, she hit the button hard.

You're just going to have to carry on. Act as though everything is normal, after all the midwife didn't seem to think they had any solid leads.

As casually as she could muster, Elspeth returned to the unit with Poppy. She busied herself with settling her, all the while keeping one eye trained anxiously on the door, fearful that the police may turn up at any minute.

15

SAM

'Well? I haven't had your report on that hospital case yet. What's the hold-up?' Detective Chief Inspector Smithers enquired, glancing up from the newspaper laid out on the desk in front of him.

Sam cleared her throat nervously. 'I haven't yet narrowed down a solid lead.' There was no point lying, although she questioned his intelligence, even he would have been able to figure it out soon enough.

Smithers turned his full attention to her. Slowly, he took her in, one eyebrow half-cocked.

Prick, she thought. And yet, she tried desperately not to fidget under the weight of his scrutinising glare, to give him the satisfaction of seeing her squirm.

He laughed out loud, a cruel, humiliating laugh which resonated around the room. 'You've lost your fucking touch. A month behind a desk and now look at you, you can't even solve the case of the missing pregnancy test–'

Sam interjected, dangerously close to losing her barely tethered temper. 'The ward's security is non-existent at best, the staffing levels are abysmal and to top it off there were visitors coming and going all day long. There's more to this one.'

Smithers eyed her with a look of disdain. 'I'll give you two more weeks. Get me something concrete, otherwise you're off the case. Hudson's chomping at the bit to get his first case.'

'Hudson!' Sam stuttered. 'He's barely out of training.' *Let alone fucking nappies.* He didn't even look like he needed to shave.

'Yes, well, you'd better turn this thing around then, hadn't you? The department needs results, as you are well aware. I'm still trying to pick up the pieces after your last fiasco.'

She had known that Smithers would never let her live that down. He enjoyed lording it over her at every opportunity. She'd made one mistake, had one failure in her whole career and now he thought he was better than her.

I'll show you, she decided.

'On second thoughts, get Hudson in on this. He could use the experience and you could use another pair of eyes. I want this one solving.'

Sam's mouth fell open. He couldn't be serious.

She was about to protest, to stress her preference for working alone, when Smithers, clearly having finished the conversation, rudely returned his attention back to his newspaper.

Stupefied, Sam shut her mouth and stalked out of the office. It took every bit of her self-control not to slam the door behind her.

Sam strode back into the large office, her eyes scanning the room. She easily located Hudson hunched over his usual desk.

Let's just get this over with.

'Come with me, Hudson,' she instructed before he even had time to register her presence. Skittishly, he stood, following her into her small office without a word.

If Smithers is going to force me to babysit, the least I can do is make it appear as though it was my idea.

'Sit down.' She directed Hudson to a chair with a wave of her hand.

He did as he was told.

Sam shuffled through a few files on the desk, aware of Hudson's building discomfort. He pulled at his collar, then wrung his hands together.

Sam watched him, a note of satisfaction settling over her. Guiltlessly, she was playing with him, enjoying his obvious nervousness.

Eventually bored, Sam held out a file to him. 'I would like you to assist me on this case,' she began, taking in Hudson's astonishment. 'You've been in the department now for what? Seven months?'

'Fourteen,' he corrected nervously, taking hold of the file.

Oh shit. Sam was momentarily derailed by his admission. *How the hell had he sat at that desk for so long? Why didn't he demand a case sooner? I would have quit if Smithers dared to try that with me.*

'Well then, it's definitely time that we got you out from behind your desk, isn't it?'

Finally, having composed himself, he said, 'Yes, that would be... Anything I can do to help.'

'Great. We're going to head to the hospital in–' She looked down at her watch. '–ten minutes, I have a few unanswered questions for the ward sister. Have a read of the file and we can discuss it in the car.'

'Right.' Hudson smiled, getting up. 'I'll get straight on to this,' he said, shaking the file which was clutched triumphantly in his hand.

Sam raised her eyebrows. *He's going to be more of a hindrance than a help.* She sighed as she watched him leave, a definite spring in his step.

16

ELSPETH

APRIL 2ND 2035

Huddled in her coat, Elspeth waited impatiently for Brooke.

It was surprisingly cold for April but she was undeniably grateful for the protection the weather afforded her. She could still get away with wearing chunky knit jumpers and her winter coat without raising eyebrows.

Out of habit, she checked her watch again. Twenty minutes late. Brooke was never on time.

Elspeth hadn't even wanted to go out. In fact, it had been the last thing she wanted to do, preferring to stay curled up in her bed, hiding from the world.

But Brooke had been persistent, to the point of being irritating.

'You're turning into an old maid,' Brooke had teased. With a sigh, Elspeth found herself agreeing to dinner, simply to shut her up although her cravings may have also been a deciding factor in her decision.

The cravings had started a few weeks earlier. Initially, Elspeth found herself hankering for milk which soon encompassed milkshakes, before diversifying into all things unhealthy. And she could definitely eat a burger, with extra gherkins.

'Hey!' Brooke called happily, tottering down the road in very high heels. 'Have you been waiting long?' she asked, linking arms with Elspeth.

Elspeth raised an eyebrow as if to say, 'you're joking, aren't you?'

Not missing the look, Brooke laughed freely. 'Come on, you know I'm never on time, surely you've realised you should turn up later too.'

She had a point, Elspeth knew but she couldn't be late, that just wasn't her.

'So, where shall we go? There's a new burger place at the bottom of George Street, it's had some great reviews,' Elspeth suggested with a genuine smile.

'Actually, that's perfect.' Brooke grinned as she leaned into Elspeth for support. 'There's a gin bar up here I've been dying to try out. We can stop in there first, then go on for dinner after-wards.' She gave Elspeth's arm a little squeeze.

Elspeth opened her mouth ready to protest, but closed it again. What would she even say? I can't drink. I'm not supposed to drink. No, she couldn't tell Brooke anything or else it would inevitably lead to questions which she wouldn't be able to answer.

Instead, she let herself be led into a leopard-print themed bar, full of businessmen and women letting loose after work.

Brooke slipped so elegantly between several groups, that she could have been dancing. Elspeth trudged along behind her.

Claiming a newly vacated table, Brooke shrugged off her leather jacket to reveal a barely-there black lace top. Instantly she gained the attention of several guys and maybe a few girls too. She looked gorgeous and she knew it.

Self-consciously, Elspeth removed her coat, awkwardly

tugging at her heavy navy jumper, all too aware that she looked like the ugly sister.

'Didn't you have time to change?' Brooke asked earnestly, as she browsed the drinks menu.

Elspeth frowned lightly. 'I thought we were only going for dinner,' she mumbled into her own menu.

'Ohh,' Brooke squealed in delight, having already moved on. 'This one sounds delicious, apple flavoured gin, elderflower tonic and fresh lime. So does this one, passion fruit gin with orange and cranberry juice. Who knew there were so many flavours of gin.'

Frantically, Elspeth scanned the menu for an alternative, non-alcoholic, version, but there weren't any. A knot of panic started to creep in. She couldn't drink any of these, and yet she had to have a drink or else Brooke would know that something was amiss. After all, who goes to a gin bar without having gin?

'So, what's your flavour?' Brooke asked, wiggling her eyebrows happily.

'Um,' Elspeth's brow creased, 'I'm not sure, there's too much choice.' Just then, an idea started forming, a possible solution to her current predicament. Casually she pulled her purse out from her bag. 'I'll get these, maybe the barmen can give me a recommendation. What do you fancy?'

'Are you sure? They're not cheap.'

'Of course.' Elspeth smiled, already on her feet.

'Okay, I'll have the passion fruit gin with orange and cranberry, please.' Brooke put the menu back in its stand.

Having weaved her way to the bar, Elspeth was met by a bearded, tattooed barman with the most piercing blue eyes she'd ever seen. He looked like he should be gracing some magazine cover rather than mixing drinks.

'What can I get you?' He smiled kindly, resting both hands

flat on the bar and fixing Elspeth with a stare that made her heart flutter.

'Well,' she began nervously, 'my friend would like this one.' She indicated to the gin medley listed within the menu.

'Okay.' He collected a bowl-shaped glass from the shelf behind him. Expertly he poured colourful liquids into the glass and without looking up, asked, 'And what will you have?'

Apprehensively, Elspeth fiddled with the menu still clutched in her hand. 'Would it be possible to have an elder-flower tonic with a squeeze of lime?'

He placed Brooke's drink down on the bar in front of her. 'Of course. What gin would you like with that?'

Elspeth cleared her throat. 'Um, without gin actually, if that's okay?'

Unfazed, the barman replaced the empty gin glass which had been poised in his hand instead, picking up a small barrel glass. 'No problem.'

'Actually...' Elspeth interrupted, her tone urgent, 'would it be okay to still have it in the gin glass, please?'

The barman paused then, a quizzical look flashing across his features. Swallowing hard, Elspeth forced herself to meet his stare. *You don't know him, and you don't have to explain yourself.*

When she didn't offer anything more, he shrugged lightly before pouring her drink into a gin glass. Elspeth felt herself relax as she carefully returned to the table, drinks in hand.

'This is delicious.' Brooke grinned after taking a sip. 'How's yours?'

'Amazing,' Elspeth agreed with more enthusiasm than was called for. She hated lying to her friend but this tiny ruse would give her more time to... to what? The unanswerable question hit her hard. She was no further along in making any sort of decision, too consumed by her fear of getting caught. *Instead you've taken to burying your head in the sand.*

'You've been doing that a lot lately,' Brooke commented, pulling Elspeth out of her thoughts and back to the present.

'What?'

'Staring off into the distance. It's like you've disappeared somewhere else?' Brooke elaborated with eyebrows raised, inviting Elspeth to tell her.

Taken aback by Brooke's perceptiveness, she didn't know what to say. She had never known Brooke to be so observant before and it had caught her off guard.

Elspeth desperately wanted to talk to someone, to not be in this alone anymore. But... but she just didn't know who she could trust, not with something like this, something so significant. Then she had a thought, perhaps she didn't have to tell her the whole truth exactly, maybe she could sound her out.

'There's a lot going on at work,' Elspeth began cautiously.

'Like?' Brooke encouraged before taking another sip of her tropical-looking drink.

Elspeth narrowed her eyes slightly as she took her friend in. Her blonde hair was perfectly tousled, her make-up applied meticulously, and she was undistractedly focused on Elspeth. She was interested. Brooke had always been there for Elspeth before, hadn't she?

She finally relented to her inner turmoil. 'There was an incident, in the maternity unit.' Mindlessly she fiddled with her straw. 'The police are involved. It's as though everyone is a suspect.'

'What kind of incident?' Brooke leaned forward conspiratorially.

'There was a theft,' Elspeth blurted out before she could change her mind. 'A pregnancy test.'

Brooke's eyes widened in understanding. For a moment the

two women sat in silence, the weight of the situation resting heavily in the air, whilst the bar continued to hum with laughter and conversation.

Brooke glanced around, nervously. In a whisper, she asked, 'Do they know who took it?'

Keeping her expression blank, fearful of giving away the wrong emotion, of appearing too concerned, Elspeth responded. 'I don't think so.'

A frown disrupted Brooke's beautiful face then, the sort of frown which pulled on all her features. She was obviously troubled by this revelation, but why? Perhaps she was contemplating what kind of idiot gets herself into a situation where she needs to steal a pregnancy test, or perhaps she was considering potential culprit characteristics and how they could be ensnared. Elspeth's heart sank.

'I know that having the police there must be a nightmare for you but just imagine the living hell that that girl will be going through,' she finally said. 'You wouldn't steal a pregnancy test if you were allowed to buy one would you, which means she's unapproved. She must be so frightened.' Brooke sighed, the empathy unmissable in her voice.

Something caught in the back of Elspeth's throat. *Brooke got it, she actually understood.* Maybe Elspeth didn't have to do this alone, maybe she could confide in Brooke. Before she could say anything further though, Brooke continued. 'I hope that the good-for-nothing guy who put her in this situation is there by her side supporting her, cause I imagine they're in for a real rough ride.'

Abruptly, an attractive man in a dark grey three-piece suit sidled up to Brooke, oblivious to his horrendous timing. Surreptitiously, both women stopped talking.

At a glance, Elspeth disliked this intruder. He was exceedingly well-groomed, too well-groomed if you asked her, there wasn't a single hair out of place on his overly gelled head, not to mention his obviously plucked eyebrows. And besides all of that, his timing was atrocious.

With his attention entirely focused on Brooke and her reciprocating, Elspeth allowed herself to contemplate Brooke's words.

Why hadn't she considered him before. Yes, he had featured in her rose-tinted daydreams. And yet, she hadn't actually thought of involving him, not seriously.

Why should I be the only one to suffer? After all, this involves him as much as it does me. This is his baby too.

As if a light had just been flicked on in an otherwise-black room, Elspeth found herself smiling for the first time in months.

She was going to talk to Nick. He was a well-educated, caring man who dedicated his life to helping others. Surely he would want to know, to be involved. Wouldn't he?

A nagging doubt flew around the periphery of her mind. Elspeth chose to ignore it, instead focusing on the plan unfurling in her thoughts.

With a light smile, Elspeth sat back in her chair and enjoyed the rest of her alcohol-free drink.

17

ARTIE

APRIL 8TH 2035

Sipping his morning coffee at the kitchen table, Artie absent-mindedly scrolled through the news headlines on his phone.

He wasn't used to being up so early but sleep had eluded him, the adrenaline coursing through his body had made it impossible to switch off.

The previous day, he'd made a decision and today, he was going to act.

Elspeth padded down the stairs ten minutes later, already dressed but bleary-eyed. 'Hey,' she said, startled, 'you're up early.'

'Got a lot of work on today.' He pushed his guilt down. 'Coffee?'

'Oh. Yes please, that would be great. Can you tip it in here though.' She slid a travel mug across to him.

Silently, Artie set to making Elspeth's coffee just the way he knew she liked it. A heaped teaspoon of granules, half a teaspoon of sugar and a generous splash of milk.

They didn't talk, both too tired to force a conversation, but Artie's eyes followed Elspeth as she trudged around the kitchen gathering together her lunch. A breakfast bar, a banana and a creamy chicken ready meal thing, which looked revolting, not that he said as much.

'There you go.' Artie eventually smiled, holding out the full and lidded mug to her.

'Thanks.' She smiled in return. Despite her smile, she still looked so unhappy.

His heart ached. She really was very unhappy. Maybe it was him? Perhaps living with him was too stressful for her. A knot twisted tightly in his stomach. He couldn't stand the thought of not seeing her every day, but... perhaps she'd be happier being away from him.

'Busy day?' he asked quickly to distract himself from the path he was heading down. He knew it wouldn't do either of them any good.

'Not particularly.' Elspeth took the mug from him. There had been a time, not that long ago, when he would watch her practically skip out of the door to work, even at this ungodly hour. Now, though, she looked as though she was literally dragging her feet.

'I hope you have a good day.' Artie's voice was soft, if not a little sad. He had a thousand things he wished he could say, so many words of encouragement and support and love, and yet he said none of them.

For a moment, she looked at him, really looked at him. He forgot to exhale the breath he was holding as she drew nearer. Without warning she leant in and hugged him. Her arms slipped around his waist, so comfortably, so perfectly, it was as though they were meant to be there.

For a second she held him so tightly that he couldn't help thinking that she was scared of slipping away without an anchor to hold on to.

Artie could tell that for Elspeth, that embrace was her way

of saying whatever it was she needed to say and couldn't. Was it a goodbye, or an apology? He didn't know. Whatever it was, it frightened him.

Her head came to rest gently against his chest.

As if waking up, Artie quickly wrapped his arms protectively around her, laying his cheek lightly on the top of her head. He wanted to be present, he wanted to be there for her.

Elspeth seemed to sink into him even further. Artie breathed her in. She smelt of roses and chocolate. Such a familiar and comforting smell.

They remained like this for what was only a few seconds. He didn't know what it meant, didn't want to read into it, but he already was. Desperately, he tried to rein in the torrent of emotions threatening to overwhelm him.

Hope, desire, fear.

All too soon, Elspeth pulled away.

With her mug in her hand, she grabbed her bag. All Artie could do was watch. Even though she wouldn't look at him directly, Artie could see the tears glistening on her eyelashes.

'See you later.' Her words were so solemn, so final.

She disappeared out of the door, leaving him alone once again.

With renewed purpose, Artie bounded up the stairs two at a time. He headed into his room and straight to the window.

Pulling the curtain aside a fraction, he cautiously peered out. He watched Elspeth as she climbed into her car, started the engine and drove away. Only when he was sure she wasn't about to turn round, did he let the curtain fall back into place.

She should be gone all day, that gives me plenty of time.

Heading back to the hallway, he paused at Elspeth's door,

his ear turned towards Brooke's room. Silence. Without hesitation, he let himself into Elspeth's bedroom.

Her room was so... her. Mismatched furniture filled every inch of space, with splashes of pinks and yellows. Knowing exactly what he was looking for, Artie didn't linger, instead he scanned the obvious places.

There, on her bed, was what he wanted.

Her laptop.

Grabbing the device, he tucked it under his arm before turning to leave, making sure he closed the door after him.

Disappointingly, Elspeth's computer was easy to get into, too easy in fact. Three guesses at her password and the screen had blinked into life as if offering up all her secrets.

His annoyance at her lax security melted away almost instantly as her home screen filled with a familiar picture.

He smiled lightly. There was a similar picture Brooke had tacked to the fridge. The three of them at the beach the previous summer. He remembered that day as if it were yesterday, of course, as that was the night...

Concentrate.

Efficiently, he pulled up Elspeth's search history. Empty. Alarm bells instantaneously sounded in his head.

Why has she cleared her history? What is it she doesn't want anyone else to see?

Artie had worked for enough criminals, enough desperate individuals, to know how they operated and this was terrifyingly familiar. Her actions were starting to fit a pattern, a picture which sent a cold chill down his neck.

What was she trying to hide? He had already checked the police database and the nursing council for any issues relating to Elspeth. There had been nothing. But that had been several weeks ago.

An assault of worst-case scenarios barrelled into his mind.

Had she hit someone with her car? Had she accidentally injured a patient? With each new idea, Artie was trying to consider routes out, how he could cover her tracks, what he could do to make it disappear. But until he knew, it was all speculation. He needed something concrete.

Moving on, Artie navigated to her deleted files. That too was empty. Dread settled into the pit of his stomach.

With a few more clicks, Artie accessed the hard drive.

There, unguarded, were the most recently deleted files, hidden in plain sight for those who knew where to look.

If she had truly wanted to obliterate her files, she should have used a wiping programme, he thought knowingly.

For a moment, the cursor hovered over the file, Artie's finger poised to tap the button.

He hesitated, just for a moment, as he contemplated what he was about to do. There would be no going back, he realised, once he'd crossed that line. This wasn't some paying customer, some low-life who had sought him out in desperation, this was his friend, the one person who he cared about most in all the world.

And that was why he needed to know.

He clicked on the file.

Artie's mouth fell open.

His eyes scanned the contents, wildly. His fists tightened into balls. His breathing quickened.

He pounded his fists against the desk.

Pushing himself to his feet suddenly, he moved away from the borrowed laptop, fearful that he might punch his fist through it.

Anger wrapped in despair flooded through him. He dragged his fingers through his hair and looked up to the ceiling.

She was pregnant.

She had been with someone else. She was having someone

else's baby. He knew she wasn't his, that Elspeth could do whatever she wanted with whoever... but it hurt like hell.

A hole opened in his chest. A black, empty nothingness.

Perhaps she had never cared for him the way he cared for her, perhaps he hadn't been enough for her, or perhaps it had all been some big joke and he was the punchline?

He knew his thoughts were selfish and in that moment, he didn't give a shit. Deep down, he had hoped for a second chance, that there was still a chance that they could...

Not now.

He pressed his fists into his eyes and sucked in a deep breath. It was as though all his hopes and dreams were crashing in around him. He clamped his teeth together to stop the growl threatening to explode from his throat.

He didn't know what to do.

He knew now that he shouldn't have looked. Elspeth hadn't told him because it was none of his business. Because she had moved on and he hadn't.

He needed to put her computer back, to forget that he knew. But so many thoughts were raging through his mind. Who was the guy? How had she been able to keep it all a secret? How long had she been planning this?

Brooke must have known, Artie realised then, his anger flaring again. Elspeth would have talked to her about it, would have wanted to celebrate her news. Had they been laughing at him all along?

Slumping in his chair, he was about to shut down the file when something caught his attention. Artie leaned in closer to the screen.

He opened an article.

Absorbing every word, its meaning, he opened the next file, then the next one.

It didn't take a genius to see the pattern, for understanding to settle in.

Her pregnancy was illegal. It was an accident. The realisation hit him hard, she hadn't planned this, hadn't been laughing at him.

'Oh, Ellie, you stupid girl,' he murmured.

As Artie's anger began to ebb, his mind cleared, he was able to think more rationally.

To be approved you firstly had to be married and Elspeth was unequivocally single. In the legal sense of the word, at least. He had been wrong and foolish to jump to such conclusions. How could he have doubted Elspeth, their friendship?

She was therefore in a dire situation, one even more serious than Artie could have conceived.

He had so many unanswered questions. What was Elspeth planning on doing? What had she already done? Who else knew?

He had to know more.

Artie looked back towards her laptop. Knowledge was power, he reminded himself before he delved back into the files, determined to get his answers.

———

Exhausted, Artie erased the deleted files from Elspeth's computer before switching it off and returning it to the middle of her bed.

He had managed to piece together what he could from her files.

She was pregnant, maybe as far as three months considering the dates of some of her earlier searches.

The police were involved somehow, but Artie wasn't yet sure

how. Elspeth had been obsessively searching about an investigation, but hadn't appeared to turn up anything solid. It was possible that what she was looking for wasn't yet public knowledge.

And finally, there was a protest. This Saturday. Artie suspected that Elspeth was planning on attending. It would make sense, he knew. She was illegally pregnant and the protest was about revoking *The* Law. But it would certainly complicate matters further, especially if she were arrested, which wasn't unheard of at these events, and he should know, having worked behind the scenes in promoting these gatherings. Illegally of course.

Back at his desk, Artie rested his head in his hands, and sighed loudly. He knew inexplicably that he would do whatever he could to help her, to keep her safe, no matter the cost. Artie just had to figure out how.

Turning to his own sophisticated computer set-up, he huffed. 'Let's find out what this police investigation is all about.'

He knew that if he was to be of any use to Elspeth, he would have to firstly know what the police knew.

With purpose, Artie deftly tapped at his keyboard, determined to find something, anything, that could help.

18

SAM

APRIL 10TH 2035

Sam and Hudson were sitting at their makeshift desk in the poky storage room, on the neonatal unit, surrounded by all manner of medical equipment; infusion pumps, drip stands and what Sam presumed to be ventilators.

With Hudson's keen terrier-like attitude, he had managed to ascertain the names of several nurses who had cause to attend the maternity unit during the suspected timeframe that the theft occurred.

Today they were pursuing this new line of enquiry by questioning several of those identified.

With a mix of admiration and annoyance, Sam had begrudgingly admitted that Hudson had opened up what was starting to feel like a dead-end case. Not that she was planning on sharing this information with him, of course. Nor would he be leading the interviews. She was the senior officer and it was necessary to maintain some sense of order. That being said, if there was a confession to be extracted, then Sam wanted to be the one to do it, this was, after all, her case.

The first nurse, Veronica Anderson, was one of the ward sisters, in her mid-sixties, awaiting the time when she could comfortably retire and pack in working long days and night shifts, the detective suspected, taking in the tired-looking woman.

Veronica had attended the maternity ward during her shift to support with the delivery of a premature baby, she had explained. It was blatantly obvious from their brief interview, that this was not a credible suspect. Veronica had either been in the delivery suite surrounded by multiple witnesses or with other medical staff responsible for transferring the infant for care. They would clarify her story just to be thorough, but she would be discounted from further enquiries.

Sam couldn't help the note of smug satisfaction she felt, not to mention the relief. Had Hudson walked onto the case and immediately identified the suspect that she could not, that would have certainly spelled the death of her career.

They were now patiently awaiting the arrival of an Edward Reed.

Hudson had suggested that this too may be a dead line of inquiry, hedging his bets perhaps. Sam, however, was silently optimistic. She had enough experience to know that sometimes the culprit was not the most obvious of choices. Reed could have stolen it for a girlfriend, or sister even, she wasn't going to write this one off too quickly.

A tentative knock sounded at the door.

'Come in,' Sam called quickly before Hudson could open his mouth.

Sam had been on the force long enough to know that male officers elicited different responses to their female counterparts. Perhaps more intimidated by men, or they simply didn't take women seriously but suspects often presumed that the male was superior. *Well not in this instance*, she thought, radiating confidence and what she knew was an air of authority.

A young man, in his mid to late twenties wearing the unit's

uniform of navy-blue scrubs, cautiously peered into the room. 'You wanted to talk to me?'

'Yes. Please come in and take a seat,' Hudson responded, indicating to the uncomfortable plastic chair opposite them. Sam shot Hudson an indignant look, he didn't notice, however, too absorbed in his notes. She wanted to put him in his place, to remind him that she was the one leading. With a frown, Sam made a mental note to pull him up on this later.

Turning her attention back to the nurse, she fired off her first question, her irritation audible. 'You were working a night shift on the sixth of March, is that correct?'

Edward answered after a moment's consideration. 'Yes.'

'And during that shift, you went down to the maternity unit, didn't you?' Sam had fixed him with an uncomfortable stare, which he wouldn't or more likely couldn't meet.

'Um, yes, I think so,' he mumbled, his attention turned to Hudson. *Less intimidating*, Sam decided, triumphantly.

'And why was that?' she continued.

Again Edward paused to think, all the while Sam scrutinised him. She watched for the merest hint of deception, any sign of hesitation which may indicate a lie. 'To do their evening antibiotics,' Reed finally offered, his response measured. He fidgeted slightly in the hard seat then, crossing his legs.

'And am I correct in thinking that this is done in the clinical room?'

'Yes.' Edward nodded once.

'And to access the equipment necessary to give the antibiotics you need the unit's keys, is that right?' Of course she knew the answer to all of these questions, but she wanted him to say it, to admit he had the opportunity, the means to commit the crime.

Edward again glanced at Hudson, perhaps searching for

some camaraderie between men or at the very least an explanation.

Hudson thankfully remained impassively silent, other than the occasional encouraging smile or jotting down of some vital thought or consideration.

This wasn't necessarily good cop, bad cop, rather superior, single-minded cop and novice cop. Hudson had been schooled on his place already, he was to watch, to listen and *if* invited, to contribute. To Sam's relief he didn't intervene, or offer anything further to Edward. Sam would not tolerate being undermined in her investigation.

'Yes,' Edward said, resigned. Having realised that Hudson was not his ally, Edward kept his focus firmly fixed on the table between them.

The corner of Sam's mouth twitched slightly at his admission to having the unit's keys. *Right place, right time, now I just need motive.*

'Are you in a relationship, Edward?' Sam asked, softening as she changed focus.

Instantly, Edward scrunched up his face, confused by the interest in his personal life. 'Excuse me?'

'A relationship... are you in one?' Sam repeated evenly.

'Um, no, I'm not, but what does that have to do with–'

'When was your last relationship?'

Lightly, Edward shook his head. Perhaps she had touched a nerve, delved a little too closely to the truth. If Edward knew, if he was responsible for the theft, he may well be considering how far to go before he demanded a lawyer.

If he asked for legal representation, if he felt that answering these questions incriminated him, then he obviously had something to hide, Sam decided whilst Reed continued his internal debate.

'Answer the question,' Hudson interjected firmly.

Aware that they might be on the verge of losing Reed's willingness to co-operate, Sam didn't halt Hudson's input. They didn't have anything concrete to justify bringing Reed into the station, she knew, and nor would they if he clammed up now.

Edward sighed. 'About a year ago.'

'Their name?' Sam pushed, not missing a beat.

Notably flummoxed, Edward's mouth fell open slightly and his eyes darted between the two officers. 'Why is that relevant?'

Interesting. Why doesn't he want to tell us? Is he trying to protect someone?

'It would really help if you could provide their details, in case we need to corroborate what you've told us.' Hudson smiled.

'Fine. It's Christopher Francis,' Edward huffed, visibly deflating at the admission, 'but really we didn't end on very good terms, so he might be a bit frosty if you turn up mentioning me.'

Sam's jaw visibly tightened. She gave Hudson a sideways glance, he caught it and lightly shook his head. This wasn't their guy he was telling her.

No. This could still be their suspect. Ignoring the note of desperation in her thoughts, she considered her next line of enquiry. She wasn't ready to give up on this one, not yet. After all, he could have stolen it for someone else.

'Do you have any siblings?'

'Siblings?' Edward blustered. 'No I don't, nor do I have any pets if that answers your next question.' His frustration was palpable.

Sam sucked in a deep breath.

Damn it.

Aggressively, she struck a line through her notes, knowing that Hudson had been right. Another fucking dead end.

A glance, unnoticed by Edward, as he didn't react, passed

between the two detectives. Sam conceded. This was not who they were looking for. There was no point wasting any more of their time, despite her rising despair, she wasn't stupid enough to keep flogging a dead horse.

With a single firm nod, Hudson understood.

'Thank you for your time, Edward. If we have any further questions, we'll be in touch,' Hudson offered, standing up.

'What? Is that it?' Reed asked in confusion, although he mirrored Hudson and rose to his feet.

'That's it,' Hudson confirmed and promptly showed Edward out.

Sam slammed her notebook down on the table, her fury bubbling to the surface. They had spent most of the day in this uncomfortably clinical hospital, chasing up new leads and to no avail. They had crossed off all but the last two nurses on their list, who weren't working today.

Sam desperately needed this solving. Smithers was breathing down her neck, pressing hard for results. Failure was not an option. Her reputation was on the line and that pissed her off.

'Don't worry, we've still got another couple of leads to follow up tomorrow,' Hudson said, the empathy and sincerity in his voice rubbing Sam up the wrong way.

No one should be so fucking nice.

She needed to get out of the hospital, aware it wasn't helping her mood.

'I need a drink,' she groaned. Gathering up her stuff, Sam strode out of the room in search of a bar and a double vodka and Coke, Hudson left open-mouthed in her wake.

19

ELSPETH

APRIL 11TH 2035

Elspeth had taken to wearing scrubs which were a size bigger, in an attempt to conceal her ever growing bump. She knew she'd put weight on, that her face was looking fuller. To her relief, no one had commented.

She was finding working on the unit increasingly difficult; constantly being surrounded by babies, precious little ones, when she couldn't even stroke her own belly. It was torture. She had to keep reminding herself not to do it, even though it felt so natural. Not to mention the toll the night shifts were having. Elspeth was exhausted as it was without throwing back-to-back nights into the mix.

Sleepily, she sat through the morning handover, jotting down the occasional note, although her mind kept drifting back to Brooke's words in the bar.

Brooke, with her black and white view on things, had managed to confirm what Elspeth had struggled to conceive. She shouldn't be doing this alone.

To her surprise, the night sister, Rose, finished handing over. She hadn't heard any of it. Everyone stood and began shuffling, in a sea of blue uniforms, out of the room.

Rose, however, remained standing by the door. As Elspeth approached, she felt Rose's nervous gaze fix on her. Instinctively, her heart beat a fraction faster.

What does she want?

She began to panic, her face taut with fear. Elspeth averted her eyes downwards, hoping to walk past unseen.

No such luck.

Rose gently put her hand on Elspeth's arm and casually guided her to the side, until the room had emptied out.

'I'm afraid the police are here to talk to you.' Rose motioned solemnly.

'Me?' Elspeth whispered, her breath catching. Her eyes widened with fear.

Do they know? How have they found out?

'Don't worry,' Rose said reassuringly, perhaps noticing Elspeth's obvious alarm. 'It's just routine, I think you're one of the last ones on their list to be interviewed about the theft.'

Managing to regain an infinitesimal amount of composure, Elspeth asked where they were.

'In the equipment room,' Rose said, sympathetically. 'Take as long as you need, I'll get Leticia to watch your babies.'

All Elspeth could do was nod in response. Words had failed her.

Instead of heading straight to the staffroom, positioned at the end of the corridor, Elspeth ducked into a small toilet en route.

She needed to compose herself before walking into the lion's den. She had known that they were interviewing staff from her unit, but she had hoped, no, prayed that she wouldn't be one of them. She didn't do well under pressure, not when she had everything to lose.

There was so much at stake. If it was just about her she

would have faced her fate head on, defiant and determined, but it wasn't just her. She had to think of her baby, the person growing inside of her. She had to do everything within her power to keep that vulnerable tiny human safe and secure.

Stood over the sink, Elspeth ran the cold water and splashed her face. She tugged a paper towel free from the dispenser and lightly dabbed it against her wet skin.

Everything will be fine, she assured herself, although the sentiment was lacking conviction.

Elspeth wanted to believe that it would all come out in the wash, a phrase her mother was so fond of using. But Elspeth was yet to see a way out of this that didn't result in her going to prison and her baby being lost to her.

'Don't give them anything,' she told her reflection forcefully. *This is just routine. You're not actually a suspect. Yet.*

Carefully, she rearranged the items in her scrubs pocket. She removed her notebook, aware that its weight pulled her top down, flattening it against the swell of her bump. Instead she held it tightly in her hand.

With her free hand, she brushed back a few strands of hair which had escaped her hairband.

Finally, she took several slow breaths to steady herself. She had never been so terrified, but she was not going to let them see her fear.

You can do this.
You have to do this.

At the door, Elspeth was greeted by a pleasant face she recognised from the maternity unit.

Detective Sergeant Hudson introduced himself, a light

smile on his lips, as he showed her into the room. Elspeth swallowed down the lump in her throat and tried not to overanalyse his smile. But she couldn't help it.

Why is he smiling? Does he know something? Do they suspect me?

The room which had once been so familiar to her, now felt foreign. A desk and chairs had been arranged purposely in the middle of the compact space. Behind that desk was a sight which immediately unsettled her, her resolve wavering.

The serious female detective, the one who had sent a chill running down her spine, was sitting, straight-backed behind the desk.

Slowly, Elspeth sat down as the unsmiling woman introduced herself as Detective Inspector Sam Wakley.

Elspeth fidgeted self-consciously, acutely aware of how her top clung to her body. Nervously, she crossed her arms.

The room felt stuffy, like there was barely any air, and the light pouring in from the large window behind the detectives was far too bright. Elspeth squinted against it.

'Are you aware why we're here, Miss Adams?' Detective Hudson asked gently, perhaps reading the anxiety she was struggling to keep hidden.

He sat forward and laid his hands out, open, on the table between them. He seemed... nice, Elspeth thought before silently scolding herself. *That's what he wants you to think. He would just as easily send you to prison.*

'You're investigating a theft from the maternity unit,' she replied honestly.

'Yes, that's correct. And do you know why *you're* here?' he asked with a small friendly smile.

Was that a trick?

Elspeth began to panic. Instinctively, she glanced at the

female detective. She remained silently stony-faced. Unrestrained thoughts ran freely through Elspeth's mind. All she could do was shake her head in response.

'You were reported to have been working a day shift on the sixth of March, is that correct?' he asked evenly.

She responded without hesitation. 'I believe so.'

'And during that shift, you were tasked with undertaking the antibiotics on the maternity ward, is that also correct?'

'Yes.'

'I would like you to tell us what you remember from that day, please.'

'Okay. Well–' She paused briefly, wondering how much she needed to say. Like any pivotal moment in your life, you remember every detail with extreme clarity. Elspeth had revisited that day over and over again, obsessively dissecting every tiny element and evaluating it in-depth to ensure she hadn't incriminated herself. But of course, she didn't need to offer that much information. Perhaps less was more.

'Tell us about when you went down to the maternity unit.'

'Right, of course. Well, there were two babies for antibiotics that day. I can't remember their names off the top of my head, I'm afraid,' she said, trying to sound apologetic. A little lie.

When neither officer interrupted, she continued. 'I'm pretty sure that the second baby was accompanied by the mother.' Elspeth observed both detectives scratching notes in their notepads. *What have I said? Why are they writing? Have I given something away?*

The precariousness of the situation wasn't lost on her. She was sat face to face with her pursuers. One wrong word, one misguided look might inadvertently give her secret away.

'And can you tell us where the antibiotics are prepared and given?' Detective Hudson pressed, bringing Elspeth back.

'In the clinic room.' She shifted in her seat, careful not to expose her bump. The sun was starting to give her a headache, or perhaps it was the adrenaline coursing through her veins.

'Okay.' Hudson smiled, before looking down at his notebook. Elspeth watched with keen interest as he searched back through a few pages, the rustling of the paper deafening in the awkward silence of the room. Finally, he settled on a page crowded with notes. Elspeth couldn't help but look, her eyes were drawn to those words. She couldn't make sense of what was written.

'Can you tell me about the process of administering antibiotics, what you need, what you do, that sort of thing?' he eventually asked.

Elspeth felt as though she was being walked, eyes wide open, straight into a trap. The way the detective framed his questions, so specific, purposeful even, that she suspected a hidden agenda.

With trepidation, she talked him through each step, conscious not to say any more than was absolutely necessary.

'So,' he began once Elspeth had finished, 'you need drug charts, syringes, needles, sterile water, etc. to enable the administration of one antibiotic?' He used his fingers to count out the items.

'Yes.' Elspeth agreed.

'And where is all this equipment kept?' he asked innocently without missing a beat.

There it was.

The place he had been leading her.

There was no point in denying what he already knew. 'In the cupboards,' she confirmed as evenly as she could manage, but even she noted the rumble of fear lacing her voice.

Detective Hudson nodded casually. 'And the cupboards, are they easily accessed?'

Elspeth looked over to the other detective again. She was sat a fraction further away from the table than Detective Hudson, like an observer. So far, she had remained silent. Elspeth wondered if it was all part of some plan.

As their eyes met, a shock of fear sparked down Elspeth's spine. The detective already had Elspeth fixed with an unwavering stare, like she was trying to look inside her, to see the truth beyond her words.

Elspeth looked away, her eyes settling on the tabletop between them. 'They all have locks on them, you need to have the keys.'

'So you had the keys to get into the different cupboards?'

Elspeth was breathing faster. 'Yes.'

'Elspeth?' Hudson said to gain her attention. 'Do you know what was stolen from the maternity ward?'

She resisted the urge to roll her eyes. Of course she knew, everybody knew. It was all anyone talked about. It was no longer simply a crime, it had become a scandal.

It was fair to say that the gossip mill had been working overtime on this. Understandably, Elspeth's least favourite theory to date was the one closest to home, stolen by an unapproved pregnant midwife. 'A pregnancy test.'

She watched Hudson's eyebrows arc just a fraction, surprised by her admission. More notes scribbled down.

'Everyone has been talking about it,' Elspeth added quickly, for clarification.

He only nodded once, an acknowledgement. With a steely stare, he then asked, 'Elspeth, did you take the pregnancy test?'

Elspeth barely heard the words over her violently beating heart. It was as though all the air had suddenly been sucked out of the room.

Both officers appeared to be leaning further forward, as if waiting to pounce on her if she admitted her guilt.

She looked between them, swallowed down the absolute terror building up in the pit of her stomach and lied. 'No.'

20

SAM

The air con was whirring loudly as it threw warm air at them, yet the car still felt cold. The traffic through Brighton town centre was heaving, even for a weekday.

Fucking day trippers, Sam moaned inwardly.

She had moved down to Brighton almost ten years earlier when the department was founded. At the time, she would have preferred to stay in London, but then she knew that would have been career suicide. Now, though, she loved the city. In fact, she couldn't imagine living anywhere else. It was her home. The traffic, nevertheless, was always a fucking nuisance.

Sam and Hudson had been sat, unmoving, for over ten minutes.

There was a silence, an oppressive, awkward silence which hung between them. Sam could sense it, but she couldn't seem to muster up the enthusiasm to make small talk.

There was something about the nurse that they'd just interviewed, something that didn't sit quite right. Sam couldn't put her finger on it. It was like an itch she couldn't scratch.

Elspeth Adams had appeared co-operative, she'd answered

all their questions appropriately and there wasn't anything glaringly obvious, but perhaps that was the problem.

She'd had an answer for everything but without really telling them anything. Or maybe it was just her... her sweetness that irked Sam. Even her name, Elspeth, irritated Sam. That didn't make her a suspect. But still...

'Well?' Sam blurted out, her frustration finding an outlet. Hudson visibly jumped. 'What do you make of that one? There's something off about her, don't you think?'

He gave Sam a sideways glance, perhaps worried about pissing her off further. 'You could be right,' he finally agreed, Sam detecting a hint of scepticism. She suspected that Hudson was annoyed that she'd called it first.

Sam had believed that Hudson was going to dismiss Miss Adams completely, just like the one before and the fact that he hadn't outright rejected her, was workable.

'What makes *you* think that?' Sam enquired, keen to know if their thoughts overlapped because really, she didn't want to let this one go, all too aware that they had no other leads.

Sam wouldn't admit it, but she wanted, no, needed the reassurance. Her confidence had been battered by the last case, the humiliation lingering. And she couldn't afford another fuck-up. Her wounded pride still healing.

'Well, she was in the clinical room at the right time with access to the cupboards, and she did seem nervous, although I'm sure that's not unusual given the circumstances.'

Sam nodded in agreement, relief washing over her.

Hudson, perhaps unsure what to make of Sam's silence, continued talking. 'What do you think? I mean it could be another dead end?'

Finally the traffic ahead began moving.

Sam started the engine, put the car in drive and pulled forward, following the line of vehicles in front of her circling the large roundabout before taking the second exit. Then they were stationary again.

'No, I think there's more to Miss Adams. We should dig a little deeper before we write her off completely,' Sam eventually said, the sudden eagerness in her voice noticeable, 'her responses were too concise, like she was reading from a script. I definitely think that she's worth investigating further. Let's see what we have on her, shall we?'

Sam was unconcerned that Hudson didn't respond, that he didn't appear as eager as she did. She was too focused, too preoccupied with her own thoughts.

Sam had always loved this part of the job, the excitement and anticipation that came with a new lead. The sense of pride she felt, when she'd connected all the dots, not to mention the thrill of getting cuffs on a suspect. There was nothing like it.

Don't get ahead of yourself. She attempted to rein in her building emotions, aware that unless they had concrete evidence the CPS would never approve a charge.

Nevertheless, she was thankful to finally have something to report back to Smithers. At the very least it would keep him off her back a while longer. 'If her record's clean, we could consider surveillance.'

The words escaped her lips unintentionally. She had been mentally working through all possible avenues, all the resources at her disposal. The force had experienced funding cuts practically year on year and resources were scarce to say the least. But Sam wouldn't hesitate at throwing everything she could at this woman to secure an arrest. To secure *her* reputation.

'Surveillance?' Hudson repeated sceptically.

Sam narrowed her eyes. 'She doesn't exactly strike me as the criminal type,' Sam began tentatively, vocalising her thoughts as they came to her. 'It is exceedingly unlikely that she's in this on her own. I imagine she's had help, an accomplice. Or else I suspect that we would have known about her sooner. We also have to consider the possibility that she's considered, if not undertaken an illegal termination.'

That could complicate things, Sam knew, but it wouldn't necessarily mean game over.

Hudson interrupted, a frown creasing his forehead. 'Where do we stand if she has had an abortion?'

Sam turned in her seat, fixing him with a serious look. 'In exactly the same place.' She didn't want to contemplate the extra red tape that would be involved if she had, she was going to try to stay positive. 'As long as we can prove that that's what she's done, then we'll have cause to charge her for theft of a controlled item, illegal conception of a child and the illegal termination of a child. She'll get at least ten years,' Sam declared.

She was feeling more confident than she had been earlier, and yet it wavered, buckled slightly under the weight of uncertainty. She needed something solid that she could build her case around. Until she had that crucial piece of evidence, it was all speculation.

Hudson fell silent, perhaps mulling this over, then as the traffic shifted, he pointed out of the window. 'We're moving again.'

Sam righted herself and edged forward.

'Can I ask you about your last case?' Hudson enquired.

Of course he'd want to know, she realised. It was like the giant elephant in the room. Fine. If he wanted to know then she'd tell him, at least he could have a good laugh at her expense.

But what was there to tell? She knew she had followed procedures to the letter, knew that the woman was guilty but had no way of proving it and even if she did, she had no one supporting her. She had been shut down, her hands tied.

126

Let's just get it over with. 'Okay.'

'How do you think she did it?'

Sam whipped her head round sharply.

Hudson didn't miss the look of shock mixed with relief etched across her face. 'I've been through the files,' he clarified. 'She was definitely an illegal. Do you think her papers were fake?'

Sam blew a long steady stream of air out of her nose. He believed her. The feeling was almost euphoric, after having been silenced for so long, at her lowest point, she'd even started questioning herself, her actions. She shook her head, a smile finding its way to her often down-turned lips. 'Most definitely. However, the government system corroborated her story. And that's what I couldn't work out. The first thing I did when the case came in was to check the system. There was nothing. She hadn't been approved.' Her words trailed off, as though she was repeating this for herself as much as for Hudson.

That was the conundrum which kept her up at night. How had she done it? Everyone Sam had spoken to had said the same thing. Jessica Anderson had been unsuccessful in her application to become a mother. She had told anyone who would listen, usually over several bottles of wine in the pub, no doubt drowning her sorrows. Sam was certain that when Jessica had fallen pregnant, she was unapproved.

The department had received an anonymous tip-off. Jessica had been seen buying baby clothes, she was off the booze and she had a glow. *A glow, what does that even mean?*

It goes without saying that Sam had checked the system as a matter of routine, needless to say there was nothing there. But then how, a matter of weeks later, was it there, flashing mockingly at her on the screen?

'Maybe she knew someone on the inside? You know, who

could have forged the papers for her. Did you have any leads?' Hudson chipped in, clearly interested.

Sam would never have expected to find an ally in this young, inexperienced, gangly man, and yet some of her disdain for him thawed in the confinement of her car. Not that she would be telling him as much, she was still his superior after all. 'I looked at that possibility, but they just didn't mix in those circles, not to mention the firewalls on those systems are practically impenetrable. There wasn't a common link.' She sighed loudly. 'And then the press got hold of it. It became a fucking circus and well Smithers didn't want the bad publicity. So, he shut it down. I don't think I'll ever know.'

'Hmm,' Hudson muttered but then became brighter. 'I'm sure if you'd had more time, you would've solved it.'

Sam smiled. 'So, I've told you my story, what's yours?' Sam asked, happy to move on.

Hudson let out a nervous laugh. 'Oh... Well, mine is a story of big fish in a little pond before becoming a little fish in a big pond.'

Sam's eyebrows arched, a silent enquiry.

Now it was his turn to sigh. 'I was from a small rural team in East Sussex. I'd been working on some leads, dealers targeting the local kids, that sort of thing. Anyway, I made a couple of busts, turned out I'd inadvertently arrested one of the biggest county line dealers. Had concrete evidence that sent him down for fourteen years.' Sam noticed his cheeks pink. 'I was recommended for the transfer. Special branch, I mean, I couldn't turn it down. First day on the job with The Enforcers and I was assigned to desk duty.'

'Why?' Sam blurted out.

'Did you want to be partnered with me?' he asked without malice.

No, she hadn't. Her lips thinned at the realisation. He had

been stuck behind that desk because no one had been willing to work with him, to show him the ropes. That included her.

'I could have pushed harder for a case,' Hudson said as if sensing her guilt. 'I guess that the longer I sat there, the more of an issue it became. But I certainly have learnt a lot, reviewing old cases and supporting with admin.' He shrugged dismissively.

Sam, not knowing what to say, asked, 'So, you married?'

Yes, this was a poor attempt at small talk, and yes it was likely in an effort to make up for her culpability in Hudson's office confinement.

'Yep, six years now.'

'Kid?' Sam was beginning to feel uneasy, this was uncomfortable and unfamiliar territory for her and she knew she wasn't well versed in making idle conversation. If anything this felt as though it was quickly turning into an interview.

Hudson didn't reply instantly, instead he paused as if considering his response. 'Not yet, but we will. When the time is right.'

That was that. She was all out of chat.

With her attention focused on the road ahead, Sam said, 'As this is your first Enforcers case, we'd best make sure we get a good result.'

21

ELSPETH

APRIL 12TH 2035

Elspeth had been sitting at the bus stop for the past thirty minutes. She had lost count of the number of buses which had pulled in, just for her, only to realise she had no intention of moving.

Brooke's words at dinner the other night had resonated with her. *Why should I be in this alone, after all this was his baby too,* she had told herself, over and over like a mantra. So, having checked and rechecked Nick's work schedule, scrolled through all his Facebook and Instagram posts, she was as sure as she could be, that he would be at home.

With conviction Elspeth had walked all the way, certain about her actions. And yet, somehow she hadn't quite made it to his flat.

Instead, she found herself sitting on the uncomfortable plastic bench in the offensive defaced bus shelter on the opposite side of the road.

She couldn't seem to persuade her body to move any further. Unsure, she'd been staring up towards the closed curtains of what she believed to be his window. If she were being honest with herself, Elspeth was terrified that Nick would reject her, her baby, that he wouldn't want to help, denying any involvement, or worse still that he would call the cops.

Elspeth checked her phone, perhaps hoping for an excuse, a reason to leave. Nothing new. Turning it off, she slid it back into her bag. Again, she looked up to the window. A frown creased her brow, something was different. The curtains had been opened, she realised. Her pulse quickened.

She was on her feet, as if being drawn in by some magnetic pull she couldn't see.

Standing at the building's entrance, a single door with several square glass panels down its centre, Elspeth pulled the long silver handle. Locked. To the left, Elspeth located an entry panel. She ran her index finger over all the buttons. A loud sigh escaped her lips as she realised that she couldn't get in without a code. Shamefully, she couldn't recall Nick's flat number.

A tentacle of uncertainty wound its way into her mind. Maybe this was a sign, perhaps this was fate's way of stopping her.

Ready to retreat, a heavy clunk of metal scraping against metal startled her. The door had unlocked. With an uncomfortable nervousness, Elspeth peered through the glass panels. An elderly woman seemed to be struggling to pull open the door.

'Here, let me help you,' Elspeth called out.

In acceptance, the woman backed away a few steps. Elspeth shouldered open the hefty door.

'Thank you, dear,' the small lady said, a smile crinkling her already-wrinkled face. 'I don't know why they had to choose such a ludicrous chunk of wood.' She shook her head. 'I'm eighty-two, you know.'

Elspeth grinned, her own dilemma receding momentarily. The elderly woman, with her immaculately set grey hair and dressed neatly in a cream knit cardigan, grey trousers and sensible black shoes, could be her grandma, she realised.

'It is very heavy,' she agreed.

'You don't live here, do you?' The old lady looked right at Elspeth, the way only the older generation seemed to do, with real intent and interest.

'No. I was just going to surprise my friend.' Elspeth found that she hadn't wanted to lie to this lady.

'Oh, isn't that a lovely idea. Well, I hope they are surprised.' She patted Elspeth lightly on the arm as she shuffled past, her black square handbag swinging on her forearm as she left.

It definitely would be a surprise, Elspeth knew, apprehension seeping in again.

At the top of the staircase, Elspeth wandered to the end of the corridor. Retracing her steps from a night so long ago, that it felt as if it had been a dream, she found herself standing outside flat four.

Nick's flat.

Mindlessly, she ran her hand across the swell of her stomach, reminding herself of the reality of her situation.

Unexpectedly, a vision of herself, slamming that door with tears streaking her face, sprang into her mind. She had been so naive, she knew, swept up in a blur of desire and alcohol.

Shame blushed her cheeks; it had been a sordid one-night stand. She didn't doubt that she'd become another notch on his bedpost, they'd barely said more than two words to each other since – Elspeth ashamed, Nick blithe.

Swallowing down her memories, Elspeth moved closer.

Before she could change her mind, she knocked firmly.

She waited, her nervousness obvious as she wrung her hands together. The corridor was still except for the muffled cries of a child from within another one of the flats.

After a minute, he still hadn't appeared. Elspeth, heart pounding, looked back behind her, along the hallway. He hadn't left, she was sure of it. She would have seen him, wouldn't she?

Purposefully, she knocked again, this time with more force, the sound resonating around her.

Equal measures of both relief and dread stirred in her gut as a sound from behind the door told her Nick was approaching. She tucked her hair behind her ears just to have something to do with her trembling hands.

The door opened.

Nick appeared, shirtless and with his hair ruffled from sleep. Registering Elspeth, a mixture of emotions flicked across his face; surprise, confusion, curiosity, it was as though he was an actor warming up for a performance. Finally he regarded her warily, as though anticipating her to strike out at him. When it didn't happen, he relaxed, taking on his more familiar air of arrogance, a persona which seemed to fit him like a well-worn glove.

'Hi,' he said with a tentative smile.

Elspeth cleared her throat. 'Hi. I was wondering if we could talk?'

Caught off guard, he hesitated. 'Um.' He glanced back into the flat. 'Yeah, I could meet you in the coffee shop down the street,' he said sheepishly, pulling the front door closer to his body.

What's he hiding? Elspeth wondered. Then it dawned on her, her eyes widening in understanding. He had a girl in there, another one. The bastard.

Reading her expression, Nick shrugged, an air of smugness rolling off of him.

'Maybe this was a mistake,' Elspeth mumbled, her voice barely a whisper.

This wasn't right. This wasn't what I envisaged.

Panic started to creep in. How could he be with someone else when she had been so very alone? A bubble of hurt surfaced unexpectedly and tears blurred her vision.

'Elspeth!' Nick said, reaching out to touch her. Instinctively, she stepped back. 'I said, just give me five minutes and I'll meet you in the coffee shop on the corner, okay?'

You've come this far. He needs to know. You have to tell him.

'Okay,' she responded flatly.

Elspeth ordered herself a decaffeinated tea. With the large cream-coloured mug in hand, she sat down at a small table nestled in the corner of the coffee shop, with a view out on to the street.

In any other situation she would have appreciated this perfect people-watching spot. She could have spent an entire afternoon observing the shoppers strolling by; admired an elderly couple wandering leisurely along the road, hand in hand, cooed at a cute puppy on its daily walk. Today, however, she didn't notice anything, instead she stared glumly at the window, not seeing anything beyond the glass, too preoccupied by her thoughts.

They cycled round and round as though stuck on a continuous loop; her alone with the baby, her in prison without the baby, Nick happily married to someone else.

Perhaps she was being unfair, after all he didn't know, yet.

What had she expected? She should have known, should have guessed that he would've found a new play thing soon enough. It's not as if they had been dating. Then why did she feel so angry?

Elspeth released a slow, steady breath through her nose, whilst her foot tapped furiously against the floor.

Calm down.

Punching him in the face the moment he walked in would admittedly be very satisfying, but not helpful she realised begrudgingly.

She smiled fleetingly at the thought nevertheless.

Slowly Elspeth sipped at her drink, the comforting hum of chatter from the other occupied tables flitted around her.

'Elspeth?' Nick interrupted.

'Oh, hi,' she said. She hadn't seen him come in. That annoyed her.

'You all right for a drink?' He looked at the cup still clenched in her hands. She nodded.

She watched him as he strode confidently to the counter. He was dressed in dark skinny jeans and a crisp white T-shirt showing under his jacket, his hair was damp as if he'd just been caught in a light shower. He looked great, it pained her to acknowledge, especially when she knew she looked like shit.

Eventually, he returned with a cappuccino and sat down opposite her. He placed his cup on the table, sat back and crossed his legs. He waited silently, perhaps expecting Elspeth to fill the void.

She frowned.

Why him, Elspeth? She sighed internally. *Why did it have to be him?*

She ran her index finger around the rim of her cup as she carefully considering her next words. She wondered then what he must be thinking, what explanation he had given to her unannounced visit. No. Maybe it was better if she didn't know, it would probably do little to endear him to her.

'Are you all right?' Nick asked, disrupting her tangled thoughts, clearly uncomfortable with the silence. 'You look pale.'

On the surface, Elspeth suspected she appeared calm, although tired, when in reality she was in a state of sheer panic, the state she'd been in for months.

'Do you remember the night,' she began hesitantly, 'the night we spent together?'

From the Cheshire cat-like smile which twisted his face, he remembered. Elspeth sagged. He had clearly misinterpreted her intentions and how wrong he was.

'It was a great night, wasn't it?' Nick grinned, with an arrogant tilt of his chin.

You've got to be kidding me. Elspeth frowned, completely unenamoured by him.

Having relaxed, he picked up his coffee and took a sip. His demeanour altered then, a cocky confidence seeming to replace what had been apprehension.

Returning his cup to the table, a thin layer of froth coated his top lip. Elspeth looked at it. Focused in on the white foamy cream and wondered if she would have found it alluring. Maybe, in a different life. Perhaps she would have leant across and gently wiped her finger across his lip to remove it. No, she found it disgusting, repulsive even.

'Um, you've got some foam–' She indicated to her own lip and pointed in his direction.

'Oh.' He blushed and quickly wiped his mouth with the back of his hand.

'As I was saying, that night... I think it's fair to say that we'd both had a lot to drink and got caught up in the heat of the moment–' She paused, eyebrows arched, waiting for him to nod in agreement or to hold his hands up to the fact that they hadn't been careful. He didn't. Instead, he just stared blankly at her as though waiting for the point. For the punchline.

Elspeth bent forward, closing the gap between them. 'We didn't use any protection.' Her voice just loud enough for him to hear.

As the realisation of her words settled in, Nick's eyes opened wide. 'But I thought–' he sputtered loudly, sitting so far forward he was almost out of his seat.

'Shhh!' Elspeth panicked, motioning with both hands for him to sit down.

She scanned the coffee shop, worried that they were drawing attention to themselves. Her eyes locked with a well-dressed middle-aged couple who were looking over. *Shit.* She smiled apologetically.

'Keep your voice down,' she demanded to Nick once the couple had returned to their conversation.

'I can assure you, I haven't got anything. Anything you've got you caught from someone else!' he blustered in a harsh whisper.

Shock registered on Elspeth's face as she acknowledged his meaning. 'I haven't got a freaking STD, if that's what you think.'

'Well what is this about–' She watched as a flurry of emotions played out on his face, before settling on confusion. 'I thought you were on the pill,' he said without understanding. Elspeth didn't miss the accusation in his voice.

'What made you think that?' Elspeth retorted, mimicking his tone. 'If I recall correctly, we did very little talking.'

Nick raked his fingers through his hair, several strands shooting out in all directions. *Now that is attractive*, Elspeth thought fleetingly.

'So what exactly are you trying to tell me?' he asked, leaning towards her with his forearms resting on his knees and his hands clasping so tightly together that his fingers were turning white.

Elspeth glanced around the room. Satisfied that no one was eavesdropping, she too leaned further forward.

Looking straight at him, she whispered, 'I'm pregnant.' The steadiness of her voice surprised her.

He stared at her. Then as the truth of her words started to take root, he threw himself heavily back in his chair as if he had just been wounded. He blew his cheeks out before exhaling loudly.

He sat forward again, shaking his head. 'Are you sure?' His voice was hoarse.

With immense control, Elspeth suppressed the humourless laugh which seemed a fitting response for such a ridiculous question. Instead, she rolled her eyes. 'Of course I'm sure.'

'But... how can that be?' His eyes were wild with fear. 'It was, what, almost four months ago. That would mean you're–' He hesitated, his eyes falling on Elspeth's stomach.

'Almost four months pregnant.'

Again he sat back in his chair, rigid. The tension in his posture, his shoulders, visible. A haunted look disturbed his features.

She waited. She had been there herself when she found out. She sympathised with the torrent of emotions Nick was suddenly experiencing. Strangely, he looked so vulnerable, so small, all his arrogance having dissolved.

'How can you be sure it's mine?'

Annoyance simmered below the surface of her calm exterior. Elspeth had anticipated this, of course he would question his part in all of this, why wouldn't he, it's not as though a baby comes with a certificate of parentage that she could hand to him. 'Because you're the only person I've slept with in the last year.'

An image of Artie unwelcomely flitted into her mind. She forced it back down. She hadn't lied to Nick, her night with Artie had been the previous summer.

Nearly a year earlier, she realised, a heaviness in her chest. Elspeth had believed that it would lead to more, that it had meant more. She had been sorely mistaken.

Nick nodded slowly, as though moving any faster would disrupt his thought process. 'Who else knows?' he eventually asked.

'No one,' she spat, her irritation flaring. 'I'm not a complete idiot. I know how serious this is, Nick.' She took a breath. *Calm down, he has a right to ask.* 'I've been too scared to tell anyone, not even my closest friends. But the pregnancy test was the one stolen from work, the one the police have been investigating,' she added for clarity, a pained expression marring her soft features.

Worry flashed behind his eyes. 'Do you think the police suspect you?'

Elspeth shook her head. 'I don't think so. They interviewed me yesterday. They didn't seem very interested in me and they haven't said that they want to talk to me again. But I certainly don't want to do anything that could draw attention to myself.'

'Okay, good. Good.' He appeared to be reassuring himself more than Elspeth.

An awkward silence hung between them. She could tell that Nick was thinking, but what, she didn't know. For all she knew, he could be wondering how quickly he could relocate.

Eventually, he reached across the table and to Elspeth's surprise, he took her hand in his. His expression was unreadable as he said, 'I'll sort this out, Elspeth, I promise. You won't have to go through this alone.'

In that moment, words failed her.

Yes, she'd hoped for his help, his support, but never truly believed he'd offer it. He wasn't smiling, but that was understandable. What they were going to face would be difficult and potentially dangerous. But she wouldn't be alone.

Relief engulfed her. She felt lighter than she had in months.

Maybe everything would be all right.

22

ALICE

APRIL 14TH 2035

Hundreds of bodies were crammed side by side, creating a living, breathing human blockade. Brighton seafront was impassable.

Car horns blared. Hot, frustrated drivers protesting their own plight, whilst police shouted, forcefully attempting and failing to reason and cajole the mass to move on.

Stood in the very centre, her distinct silvery shoulder length hair carefully hidden beneath a summer hat and large dark sunglasses obscuring her features, Alice took it all in. Revelling in the power, the purpose of these individuals who had come together as one unit, one force to be reckoned with. Women and men, young and old, stood together. It was inspiring. She was inspired.

They had been failed, no, betrayed, by the system. They were entitled to be enraged, to demand to be heard. Alice, at least, had given them that, a platform and a voice. Placards were being thrust high into the air and chants rang out, like a church bell being chimed for all to hear.

She was anonymous amongst them, another activist fighting for justice.

To Alice, this was so much more than a fight for choice, for the freedom to choose. This was personal.

Perhaps, this was an act of defiance against those who had taken her words, her research and twisted it into something so distorted and cruel that it discriminated against all but a tiny few privileged individuals, or maybe this was her atonement. A necessary fight to make right some of what had gone so horribly wrong. Either way, she knew this was another cut marring their impenetrable armour, one of many which had already happened and there were more yet to come. Eventually, they would fall, they would yield, the voice of the masses would have to be heard. She hoped.

Really it hadn't taken a lot to organise. An anonymous social media account here, a few well-placed messages there. Alice had anticipated depleted numbers nevertheless, the last two protests had barely made the papers, their message seemingly losing its impact. To her delight, however, their numbers seemed to have swelled.

Pushing up onto tiptoes to survey the crowd, she guessed at five hundred, maybe even more.

With a little guidance from a computer whizz, who remained nameless, Alice was causing a ripple and she liked how it felt.

'END THE LAW!' the crowd sounded with one unanimous voice. Alice joined in, shouting as loud as her lungs would allow her.

Like navigating her way through a complex and winding maze, she slowly moved through the crowd, eager to see how far word had spread.

The protest, thus far, had been a peaceful demonstration, much to Alice's relief. She knew that bad publicity would not help to turn the tide on this cause.

A tide I caused, she thought, saddened.

Lightly, she shook her head, dispelling her dark thoughts, aware that she was trying to change it.

Just look around you. You are not alone in this.

Without warning, a cry echoed out from within the crowd's centre.

It only took a second for Alice to register the cause of the ripple.

The prime minister.

Alice had known that the prime minister was scheduled to stay at The Grand Hotel, on Brighton seafront, as part of her Conservative campaign. She was, after all, the audience that mattered most.

Without hesitation, Alice pushed her way forward through the waves of people, keen to see her response to Alice's 'little' demonstration.

Carefully, she elbowed her way past as many of the demonstrators as she could, before being met by a solid wall. Everyone had had exactly the same idea.

They all wanted to get their message across, to be heard. Everyone here had a story to tell, one of rejection and misery, of loneliness and desolation.

The woman currently in front of Alice shouted so loudly it bordered on screeching. In her hand, was a piece of paper which she brandished like a weapon. A letter of refusal, the loss of a dream, Alice realised, catching a glimpse of the emblem heading the letter. A lump caught in her throat.

'It's my right as a woman. I want to be a mother!' the young woman screamed through her tears, her voice hoarse. A man, probably of similar age, wearing black-framed glasses and an expression filled with grief, gently placed his hand on the woman's lower back. The gesture was so subtle, yet it spoke volumes, more so than the woman's screams. They were in it together, her pain was his pain.

Alice's heart went out to them, this childless couple. She understood, she really did.

With renewed determination Alice gently shouldered past the pair and their grief, pushing closer to the front.

She didn't have a plan, she would figure it out as she went, but she had to get to the edge of the crowd, to stand in front of the woman in charge and be heard. She knew her hat and glasses would only provide her with a thin veil of anonymity. She would just have to take that risk.

The crowd swayed unsteadily with people shoving, trying to get to the front. Alice struggled to stay upright against the tidal wave of motion. Those at the front were also pushing back as they demanded more room with outstretched arms emphasising their opinions.

Beyond the crowd, the prime minister in her expensive black suit, leather briefcase in hand, flanked by several bodyguards, was attempting to placate the increasingly disgruntled mob in front of her. The wary bodyguards were trying to usher her away to safety, but she was too caught up in arguing her point, a point which had once been Alice's, the overpopulation of the world.

Unexpectedly, a man flew forward out of the crowd, slipping through the wall of police keeping the protesters at bay. He was heading straight towards the prime minister. Alice's eyes widened, 'No!' she called, her voice swallowed by the din of the crowd.

Without missing a beat, a suited bodyguard with an earpiece and tattooed knuckles stepped in front of the prime minister and as if swatting away an annoying fly, swiped out towards the running man, striking him across the chest. He fell awkwardly to the floor, hitting his head with a thump loud enough to be heard over the shocked intake of breath from several protesters.

Alice's mouth fell open. It was going to fall to pieces. This was no longer the peaceful protest she hoped for. In that one moment, it had instantaneously taken a frightening turn towards rioting, towards rebellion.

The crowd reacted spontaneously, as though a firework had unexpectedly been set off amongst them. Several people dashed to help the injured man up, whilst other, more angry, demonstrators charged at the police, the bodyguard, fists raised.

In the background a terrified-looking prime minister was being hurried away into a waiting black car as the police descended more forcefully, with riot shields and batons, on the protesters.

Alice watched in horror as chaos ensued.

Large numbers attempted to flee, fearful of the repercussions were they to be caught and arrested, however, unbeknownst to them, they were being hemmed in, like sheep to the slaughter, by a swelling number of police officers. Only a few managed to escape.

Panic swiftly descended on those trapped. No longer were they standing together, united. No, it was now every man or woman for themselves. Protesters were jostling in all directions, desperate to find a way out.

'Calm down!' Alice called to the frantic swarm. 'Don't panic. It will be all right.' But no one was listening.

Coming to her senses, Alice realised that she too needed to get away. She didn't doubt that the paparazzi were already there filming the debacle, the last thing she wanted or needed was to give them any further ammunition by getting arrested herself. This was already going to be front page news, she knew, just not for the right reasons.

Moving swiftly, she turned away from the front of the group, where the police were grappling demonstrators to the ground before slapping handcuffs on them.

The promenade. She realised that may be her only option, it may afford her the chance to slip away, unnoticed across the pebbled beach.

With hands out in front of her, Alice moved cautiously through the ever-changing flow of scared people.

The protesters were being pressed in, forced into a bottleneck by the police who were advancing on either side. She didn't know what lay ahead. She couldn't see past the sea of bodies overwhelming her.

The crowd had slowed to a walking pace when heavy hands shoved Alice roughly from behind. Looking back, a middle-aged couple holding hands were attempting to run past her, oblivious to Alice. They squeezed ahead, but couldn't get any further. There was nowhere to go, no room to breathe.

Briefly, Alice wondered what had brought them here. It didn't take much of an imagination to realise that like so many others, their hopes of parenthood had been stolen from them with a single letter saying *Denied*.

A cry of pain to her right yanked Alice back to the present, to the mayhem engulfing her.

A young woman, wearing jeans and a burgundy hoodie had fallen to her knees. She was desperately trying to push herself back up, to regain her footing, but the weight of the crowd swarming around her kept knocking her back down.

She was being trampled.

Eyes wide with panic, Alice reacted instinctively.

Diverting her course, a path which would have led to the promenade and to safety, Alice turned towards the young woman and began forcing her way against the tide of bodies.

Alice propelled past the fearful and scared, the angry and enraged. People around her were reacting to their uncontrollable emotions, decent individuals thinking of nothing and no one except themselves.

Hands pushed, bodies collided, feet became entangled. Several times Alice stumbled amongst the commotion, barely managing to stay upright herself.

Reaching the injured protester, she didn't hesitate, Alice reached out, grabbing her under the arm with firm hands. With all the strength she could muster, Alice attempted to heave her up, the woman allowing herself to be hauled upwards. Before she could find her feet, however, a surge of terrified protesters descended upon them, blind to their plight.

The woman fell again.

As she went down, her right hand instinctively curled around her stomach. A protective shield.

Alice couldn't miss the movement, couldn't pretend that she didn't understand it.

'Come on,' she demanded loudly to be heard, 'we really need to get you out of here.'

This time, she successfully aided the woman to her feet.

Alice's eyes swept over her. She was probably in her early twenties. Her deep brown eyes, wide with fear, looked haunted, Alice thought. Long brown hair had escaped from its hiding place under the hood of her jumper and was cascading down her chest in thick waves. Her jeans were ripped and her knees bloodied but otherwise she appeared uninjured.

She continued to cradle her stomach.

'Let's try this way,' Alice suggested, taking charge, as she guided the woman towards the edge of the swarm.

Unsurprisingly, the woman allowed herself to be led, her hand never leaving its place from her belly. Alice supported her around the waist, attempting to use her own body to shield that of the woman's.

Propelling them ahead, Alice forcefully pushed past strangers, people who she may have connected with at any other time, in any other place, but at that moment, she couldn't worry about them.

They reached the edge of the distorted mass of bodies.

A row of police officers were right there, in front of them poised behind transparent riot shields and beyond that were several ambulances and the paparazzi.

An idea infiltrated Alice's mind, like a lightning bolt striking.

'Stay with me,' she said into the woman's ear, her voice surprisingly steady when in reality she was petrified. Alice's heart was pounding so ferociously, she had to resist the urge to put her hand against it.

Alice diverted the woman straight towards an officer, whose face was obscured by his helmet and shield.

With steely determination, Alice met his enquiring stare. Was he wondering if she was familiar? She didn't give him long enough for the thought to take root. 'My daughter!' Alice yelled loudly to the officer. She could feel the woman in her embrace try to pull away from her. She held her tightly. Alice knew what she was doing. Didn't she?

Letting all the fear she had been suppressing free, it instantly surfaced in her voice as she shouted at him. 'Please! You have to help us. We got caught up in these riots whilst out for a walk.'

Cautiously the officer lowered his riot shield a fraction. *This might just work.* 'She's been injured and needs attention!' Alice pleaded, her eyes purposefully drifting to the ambulances behind him.

Unmoving, the officer eyed them more closely. He didn't seem convinced. His face remained blank, perhaps hardened by experience, impervious to the distress of civilians.

Alice knew then that she would need to give him something

more, something he couldn't ignore. A final plea. 'Please, she's pregnant! She needs medical attention immediately!'

In her peripheral vision, Alice could see the woman's head whip round as though she'd been slapped. She could just make out the horrified expression distorting her pretty features, grey suddenly colouring her cheeks.

Yes, she had just announced what Alice now knew was a secret, but she had to, to get them out of this. Surely she had to understand that were she arrested and her pregnancy exposed then her fate would be sealed.

Alice wanted to tell her it would be all right, to offer her some sort of comforting reassurance but the officer was watching them with hawk-like eyes. With unfaltering determination, she met his eyes, her look pleading.

With silent resolve, the armoured officer turned to the side then, creating a small opening. Their freedom exposed behind him. He tilted his head, indicating for them to pass.

Without hesitation, Alice tugged at the woman, desperate to get them out before he changed his mind.

'Thank you,' Alice said once they were beyond the barrier of his shield.

They'd done it, they'd made it out.

She released a slow, steady breath as a firm hand curled around Alice's upper arm, holding her still.

Looking back with what she hoped was a neutral expression, the officer was regarding her seriously. Alice's mind raced. He had that look again, as if there was something buried deep in his memory that he was trying to find, to pull back to the forefront. 'Do I know you?' he asked.

'I don't think so,' she lied with a practised ease. A bead of sweat nevertheless formed at the edge of her brow. She tilted her head forward slightly, hoping to obscure more of her face with the rim of her hat.

'Thank you so much, we need more good men like you in the services,' Alice said.

His grip loosened and Alice took the opportunity to gently extract her arm from his fingers. With much less haste than she would have liked, Alice walked straight ahead, forcing the woman along with her towards the queue of ambulances.

When they were at what she hoped was a safe distance, Alice risked a glance over her shoulder. The officer had turned his attention back to the raging disorder, having forgotten all about them.

With strong hands, Alice continued to steer her companion, but rather than heading straight towards the waiting ambulances and flashing cameras of the press, she diverted her towards the safety of the promenade.

Wordlessly, they walked together for a full minute before Alice finally felt able to release her grasp on the woman's jumper. Interestingly, she didn't move away, didn't run.

With the danger at a distance, their fear ebbed slightly. They slowed their pace to that of a gentle stroll.

'I should thank you for helping me,' the woman eventually offered, her voice quivering as she lowered her hood. Her hand, which hadn't moved from its protective position across her stomach, finally fell to her side. 'But what you did, what you said back there,' she inclined her head but her eyes didn't stray from the path ahead of them. 'That was risky.'

'I know,' Alice said without apology. She did what she had to, and it had worked. Thankfully. She didn't want to consider what would have happened if she had got it wrong. 'How far gone are you?' Alice asked softly, wanting to be distracted from her own tormenting thoughts.

She removed her sunglasses and hat. Both women now without disguise.

Those dark eyes glanced at her suspiciously, and yet she

didn't attempt to deny it, perhaps aware that it would be futile at this late stage. 'You're not approved, are you?' Alice probed gently, encouraging, when the woman didn't answer.

She noticed as her mouth opened, as if on the cusp of saying something, before she shut it again having thought better of it. 'Why were you at the demonstration?' she finally asked Alice, deflecting.

A sorrowful smile found its way to Alice's face. 'To right a wrong,' she said honestly, 'and you?'

'I was curious, I guess. I wondered if it would make any difference.'

She appeared lost, Alice thought, as a wash of emotions barrelled through her. Sadness, guilt and something else, something so deep and unfamiliar that she couldn't put a name to it.

Suddenly, the woman stopped walking and turned to face Alice. 'I don't think anything will change,' she said flatly, her face an unreadable mask. 'Thank you for your help.' She smiled weakly before turning to leave.

'I could support you, assist you,' Alice blurted out desperately. If she left, Alice knew she'd never see this young woman again, she'd never know what became of her and her baby. The thought suddenly seemed unbearable. She dug around in her bag.

'I doubt that,' the woman responded, not unkindly. She started walking away.

'Here,' Alice pleaded, following her. She pressed a business card into her delicate hand. 'Please take it. I... I want to help.'

The woman didn't look at the small white rectangular card but tucked it in her jeans pocket nevertheless.

Alice remained motionless long after the woman had gone.

It was only as she persuaded her feet to start moving again that she realised what that unknown feeling had been; it was her maternalistic instinct rising up from the depths of her gut.

She wanted to protect that girl, to comfort her, to take care of her, all feelings Alice had locked away a long time ago, with the memories of her own child.

She didn't know if she could push them back down again. She didn't know if she even wanted to.

All she could do now was wait and hope.

23

ARTIE

Artie had extracted all the information he could from accessing the police mainframe, which had been sparse at best. Until a report was submitted, there would be little to go on there.

Against his better judgement he had ended up reaching out to one of his previous contacts.

Gary, a middle-aged overweight copper, had been desperate when he'd sort Artie out the previous year. He had been cruising through his last few years of service, when he unfortunately found himself captured in some very regrettable footage. It was a rather unflattering still of the man, not to mention the plethora of drugs and prostitutes also visible.

Gary had begged Artie to erase the humiliating and career-destroying evidence from the hotel surveillance system. Had this most heinous content ever come to light, Gary would have lost his career, his pension, not to mention his utterly devoted wife.

At the time, Artie had hesitated. Obviously working for a police officer when your own activities were firmly outside of the law could be seen as foolish. Still, Artie had realised that at some point having a copper on your side might have its benefits.

So, he'd agreed, for a very substantial fee of course, to make Gary's little misdemeanour disappear. What Gary had failed to consider, however, was that Artie did occasionally like to check in on old friends, to ensure they were keeping their noses clean.

Unsurprisingly, Gary's first transgression was not to be his last.

It was fair to say that Gary had been less than thrilled when Artie contacted him, out of the blue, to negotiate the dissolving of some new footage. Even so, Artie had gotten what he needed, information, crucial information which meant that he could help Elspeth. Now all that he had to do was tell her that he knew.

Artie had been waiting for the right moment to talk to her, but it had seemed to him as though everything was against him.

He'd tried several times to broach the conversation. He knew he needed to be delicate, to let her know that he was on her side but every time he tried there would be an intrusion, an obstacle which he couldn't seem to overcome; Brooke would come sweeping in like a whirlwind or the bloody gas man would turn up to read the meters or Elspeth would return home late from work only to disappear wordlessly to her room.

Artie didn't have the heart or the courage, it would seem, to corner her. Instead, he promised himself that he would broach the subject tomorrow. He would definitely talk to her *tomorrow*.

Only, tomorrow soon became today and today was the day of the protest.

Artie had been pacing the house like a caged animal all morning. He'd woken up to find that Elspeth had slipped silently out of the house before even the birds were singing. He'd hoped to dissuade her from going, to give her enough of a reason not to venture to the protest. But she had gone, and he'd missed his opportunity. He'd said nothing.

As though serving penance for his cowardness, all he could do was wait for her to return. That was, if she did return and wasn't arrested first. Artie intermittently scoured the local news channels, then the police records, keeping watch for any glimpse of her.

To his relief, it didn't come. She had remained invisible, stayed below the radar. That was something at least.

Finally, a key scraped in the lock. Artie jumped to his feet.

Quickly, he moved to the already-full kettle and turned it on.

'Hi,' he called from the kitchen door, with feigned nonchalance, as Elspeth removed her trainers.

'Hey,' she murmured in return.

'I've just put the kettle on. Tea?' Without waiting for a response Artie turned back to the kitchen and purposefully gathered mugs and milk.

Elspeth hobbled into the kitchen, sat awkwardly on the edge of a chair, resting her hands, palms up, in her lap.

With unmasked concern, Artie took her in. Her jeans were ripped and bloodied and her palms were scraped raw and filthy. She had been crying as well, he could tell from her red-rimmed eyes and blotchy nose. 'What happened?' he demanded. In three quick strides, he had crossed the room and was bent down in front of her. Carefully, he assessed her injuries.

'I fell over,' Elspeth answered, her voice wobbling as though she was struggling to contain her tears.

'Where?' He turned her hands over in his.

She sniffed. 'I was on the seafront.'

Artie looked up to meet her stare whilst still holding her hands. She hadn't lied to him, he knew, the protest was being held on Brighton beach, but she wasn't telling the whole truth either. 'Let's get these cleaned up.' He smiled tightly, letting go of her.

Artie could feel Elspeth's eyes following him as he grabbed the first aid kit, a bowl of water and a clean cloth.

Perhaps she's going to tell me, he hoped, knowing it would save him the uncomfortable yet inevitable task of telling her he already knew.

'How did you fall over?' Artie was keen to keep her talking.

Returning to the table, he set about opening plaster packets before adding a few drops of tea tree oil to the water. 'This may sting a bit,' he said, wetting the cloth before lightly dabbing it against her palm.

She winced. 'Someone bumped into me.'

When he spoke, his voice was serious. 'I hope that they at least had the decency to help you up again.'

She didn't respond this time. With one hand clean, Artie applied a plaster, patting it down against her skin. Then he moved on to the other one. 'What happened, Ellie?' he asked with a sigh. She wasn't going to tell him, and he wanted to get it over and done with. He needed to hear the truth.

'I told you—'

'What you told me was that someone knocked you over on the seafront and didn't help you up again.'

She opened her mouth to speak, but whatever words she needed appeared to have abandoned her. She closed her mouth.

'Why were you on the seafront?' he pushed.

She wouldn't, or couldn't meet his stare. Instead she looked off towards the front door, perhaps hoping to find an answer there, or a way out.

'Ellie, were you at the anti-law protest?'

He watched as her eyes widened in fear.

'Why would you ask that? What a ridiculous question,' she blustered without true conviction. She never was very good at lying. Artie withheld the disappointed sigh which threatened.

He finished cleaning her hand, the sudden tension between them unmistakable. He wanted to keep pressing her, to ask more questions, but her body language was screaming with unease. She was sitting rigidly, back straight, stare fixed on the floor, the fingernails of her free hand were digging into her thigh, her knuckles whitening under the strain.

With sagging shoulders, he smoothed down the edges of the plaster.

The second he released her hand, Elspeth pulled away from him, as if she'd been burned. She stood, the chair scraping loudly against the hard floor.

'Thank you.' She went to move past him but without thinking, Artie reached out.

His hand landed lightly on her shoulder. 'Ellie,' he pleaded.

'What?'

'I know.'

There. He'd said it.

He hadn't meant to blurt it out, not like that, not when she was already so petrified, so defensive. But the words had just... rushed out.

Before Elspeth had a chance to ask *'what?'*, Artie deliberately looked at her bump, which was only mildly obscured by her baggie burgundy hoodie. He watched as her hand instinctively moved, shielding her swollen belly.

'Please don't lie to me,' Artie said, his voice hoarse. 'I know you're pregnant.'

He watched as her eyes glazed over with tears and she paled.

She slumped back down on the chair. She was so small and helpless, Artie had the overwhelming desire to wrap her in his arms and hold her. He concentrated all his willpower on suppressing that urge and instead forced himself to sit opposite her. His hand did find its way to her knee, however, where it rested lightly.

'Talk to me, Ellie. Tell me what happened, tell me how to help you.' His voice was thick with emotion.

To his surprise, she nodded. She was going to tell him.

'Okay,' Artie began nervously. 'How far gone are you?'

She wiped a tear from her cheek. 'Nearly four months.' She couldn't seem to bring herself to look at him as she made her admission.

'I won't ask how,' he said, attempting and failing to defuse the tension, 'but what do you want to do?'

A look of shock flashed across her face, as though she hadn't expected to be asked that question, then just as quickly, it was gone. Artie waited as Elspeth seemed to collect herself, her thoughts.

'The funny thing is...' she began, almost as though she were talking to herself, 'at first, when I realised, I was so afraid that the only logical option seemed to be a termination. But I didn't know where to look or who to go to for that, not without drawing attention to myself or getting caught, and before I'd realised, too much time had passed and well...' She shrugged and looked up at him. His breath caught at her vulnerability. 'Then that was no longer an option. But now, now that's the last thing I want. I can't believe I'd even considered it. This is my baby,' she said defiantly, running her hand lovingly across the swell of her stomach, 'and nobody is going to take it from me.'

Deep down, Artie already knew that Elspeth wouldn't want to give the baby up, but that wasn't going to make things easy. 'So what do you plan on doing?' He was testing the water to see if Elspeth already had an idea, a plan that they could work with.

Her cheeks blushed. 'I've just told the, um, the dad. He said he would help us.'

Irritation instantly flared. *The guy hasn't earned that title yet.* Not that Artie voiced this opinion to Elspeth, he knew he needed to tread cautiously, to keep Elspeth from shutting him out again. 'How is he going to do that?' The scepticism in his voice, his words was unmissable, however.

Elspeth noticeably bristled. 'You don't need to worry. He said he'd sort it out and I believe him.'

Artie's eyes narrowed. There was something she still wasn't telling him, he realised. Perhaps this guy didn't want to help, perhaps she was alone in this... but then why wouldn't she say? 'I can help you, Ellie, I want to help you. If you'll let me.' *Please let me.*

'Thank you, Artie.' Her tone was resigned, hollow almost. And as if a switch had been flicked, he saw the shutters go up behind her eyes. 'Really. I should have known I could count on you. But–' She stood, a resolute expression settling on her face. '–the less you know, the better. I'm putting you–' She shook her head lightly. 'This is my baby and my problem. Thank you for your concern though.'

With that, Elspeth walked out of the kitchen before Artie could think, or could say anything further.

For a while, he sat motionless in the kitchen, a torrent of emotions overwhelming him. He listened as Elspeth stalked upstairs, he heard the bath running, the echo of music, and finally the bathroom door shutting.

'Fuck!' he growled, flinging his arm out aggressively, swiping everything off the table. He barely registered the glass bowl of water as it smashed to the floor, shattering into tiny pieces. A mirror image of how his heart felt in that moment.

This wasn't going to end well. There was a burning sense of dread in his stomach.

Why was Elspeth putting all her faith in this guy, a guy who was stupid enough to get her pregnant in the first place, a guy who up until then clearly hadn't come up with any sort of plan to protect her?

*She may not want my involvement, may not think she needs it, but that doesn't mean that she won't. Especially when **he** fucks up, which he will.*

Defiantly, Artie resolved to be ready, to have a plan. He would not allow her to be separated from her child, to suffer at the hands of those in charge, those who he already despised with every fibre of his body.

No, he would find a way out of this for her.

With determination, Artie set about picking up the pieces of glass, a new idea solidifying.

24

ELSPETH

APRIL 14TH 2035

E lspeth moved swiftly and deliberately. She pushed the plug into the bath and turned both taps on full.

For a moment, she stood motionless, eyes closed, listening to the rushing water. She focused on her breathing, whilst ignoring the torrent of emotions threatening to swallow her whole. Her chest rose and fell rhythmically.

When she felt able, she opened her eyes and shifted her attention back to the rising bath water. Choosing a pretty pink bottle from her shelf, she tipped a small amount of lavender bubble bath into the stream of water, before striding to her bedroom.

Grabbing her phone from her bag, she swiped through her playlists until she found the one she wanted.

Arms ladened with comfortable clean clothes, her thickest towel, and her phone which was playing Nora Jones, Elspeth returned to the bathroom, shutting and locking the door behind her.

Placing everything on the floor, she swiftly undressed.

Looking down, she could still see her toes, although she wasn't sure for how much longer, her bump seemed to be growing quicker than she'd expected, her body obviously embracing the change. She wiggled them, a sad smile finding its way to her lips.

Carefully, she climbed in. The water was hot, which was exactly what Elspeth needed. She felt cold, numb even, like ice had crept into her body and frozen her bones. She sunk in slowly, letting the bubbles wash over her.

When the water was deep enough to cover all but her island-like bump, which appeared to be floating in the sea of white froth, she turned off the taps.

Resting her head back, she closed her eyes.

Despite her stillness, Elspeth's thoughts were spiralling so furiously she feared that she might lose control of herself completely. The police interview had thoroughly unsettled her. She had been petrified ever since, fearful that she had somehow given herself away, said something incriminating which would be enough for them to arrest her. She was struggling to sleep, unable to concentrate and she startled every time the door or phone rang. But they hadn't requested to see her again, hadn't indicated any further interest in her. She hoped that was a positive sign, grabbed on to it with both hands in an attempt to ease her fears. Now, though, Artie knew.

How had he found out? What must he think of me? Why didn't I accept his help? Sadness twinned with fear engulfed her, her heart turning heavy.

Once she had hoped that there might have been something more between them. She bit her lower lip, remembering the way he pressed his lips against hers, the tenderness of his touch. A shiver shot down her spine.

She shook her head, dispelling the memory. That would never happen again. Not that he had wanted to explore anything further with her last time. No, he had snuck out, probably embarrassed and regretful. She had woken up, alone and humiliated. How had she got it so wrong? Why did she keep getting it so wrong?

Anyway, I'm used goods now, she thought savagely. *He will never want me. He probably only offered to help out of some misdirected sense of loyalty, or pity.*

She sighed loudly, all her sorrow evident in that one sound.

What if Artie tells someone? she panicked, aware that even telling Brooke could be disastrous.

No, he wouldn't, she told herself, answering her own fears. *He may not want to be with me, but he's a decent, honest man.* She felt confident that, for now at least, he would keep her secret.

Her thoughts changed course abruptly, turning to Nick.

It had only been a couple of days but there had been no word from him.

Elspeth had hoped to see him at work the previous day, in fact she had attempted to seek him out. The thought of being able to talk to someone openly, to share this with someone who was as invested as she was, was dizzying. She wasn't stupid, though, she knew Nick had been with someone else. Besides, she didn't feel that way about him. She just wanted to feel supported, to know she wasn't alone. She wanted someone who she could share this experience with. Nick might not have been her first choice, but the thought of doing it alone terrified her. She wanted a companion, someone to help her through the difficulties, and she didn't doubt there'd be many along the way. And who better to share it all with than the baby's father.

Piece by piece she was starting to knit together some semblance of a life she could live with, she could accept if it meant she could be a mother.

She would make it work, whatever it took, she mused.

But he'd been absent from the ward. Elspeth had eventually gotten up the nerve to ask one of the other nurses who gave her a cheeky 'I know why you're asking' kind of smile before she told Elspeth that he had been moved to the accident and emergency department as part of his rotation.

He said he would help you, you have no reason to doubt that, she reassured herself, doubt sitting in the periphery of her mind. *It will take time, whatever he's planning. Obviously, he'll need to be careful, so as not to draw any unwanted attention.*

Elspeth had started looking at emigrating, but to do it properly would have taken months, and time was not on her side. She knew she could board a plane and go anywhere in the world, but it was what happened when she got off the plane that petrified her. Where would she live? How would she provide for herself and a baby? What would she do about medical care? These were all things she knew she would have to figure out, was prepared to face head on, she just felt calmer knowing she would have Nick to support her in those decisions.

But she understood and accepted that she would be leaving her life behind.

Her thoughts returned to Artie once again.

What would he do now that he knew? Elspeth didn't have that gut-wrenching anxiety, the type that would tie her stomach up in knots, which was a good sign. She trusted him to keep her secret. Yet, simply knowing put him at risk, even if she hadn't accepted his help, he could still be prosecuted for not turning her in. She would not involve him further, she decided, resolute. She couldn't have that on her conscience as well.

Her mind continued to wander further off track. *Would it have been any different if Artie was the father? Would he have been there for me? Supporting me, loving me, even?* She shook her head wistfully. That was pure fantasy, a pipe dream which would never be reality.

Everything was such a mess, she knew as she shifted awkwardly in the water.

Her words to Artie came back to her. Of course, she wanted to keep her baby. Admittedly, she wasn't sure at first, fear and terror overshadowing all other emotions, but it hadn't taken long for her to realise that what she already felt for this baby was indescribable. There wasn't a name which encompassed the unconditional, overwhelming love she felt when she thought of the tiny person growing inside her.

Every bone in her body already loved this child.

Which is why I will do whatever I have to.

But really, how had Artie found out? She worried that she hadn't been careful enough, that she hadn't been concealing her bump as well as she thought she had. What if someone else suspected? She began considering other ways to hide her changing body. Not that she wanted to leave, but she knew she didn't have long until everyone she knew would start to notice.

Surprisingly, a very noticeable fluttering from within her drew her attention to her stomach. Her hands automatically followed. She sat a little more upright in the cooling water.

For a moment, she wondered if she imagined it.

Then it happened again.

Was that her baby moving?

She couldn't help it, tears pooled in her eyes. 'Hi,' she whispered gently, as she rubbed her hands over her belly. She hadn't ever comprehended the unbearable bond she'd feel. And yet it was there. In the way her hands encircled her bump, the way she knew she would do whatever it took to protect her son.

A son.

She didn't know why, but the image of a little boy filled her thoughts. Her son. Maybe all women unwittingly knew, or maybe she was wrong. But for now, he was her little soldier.

25

ALICE

MAY 3RD 2035

A lice was escorted through the grand hallway, her kitten-heels clicking loudly on the well-polished parquet flooring.

She was led into an ostentatious waiting room, off from the large corridor.

'Please take a seat,' the middle-aged man instructed as he gestured to a mahogany and blood-red leather chair. Alice did as she was told, her large black handbag resting on her lap.

Surreptitiously, she observed the man, in his tailored suit and brogues as he strode, straight-backed, towards an antique desk on the opposite side of the room. Surprisingly, he sat down and began efficiently tapping away at the computer. Call her old-fashioned, but that gentleman, which he presently appeared to be, did not strike her as the receptionist type. But then, she knew she was old and probably outdated. Plus, he probably wasn't called a receptionist, perhaps he was a personal assistant, or a personal organiser of all things important.

She was nervous.

Silently, Alice took in her surroundings. Large portraits of previous leaders hung in gold gilded frames covering the off-white walls. There was a closed solid-looking wooden door inlayed into the wall to Alice's left. Several well-kept potted plants were dotted strategically around, in an attempt to soften the otherwise-uninviting room.

Alice was used to waiting, she had been involved in countless meetings with all manner of officials over the years. Some more memorable than others, of course.

This meeting, however, was different and that made her apprehensive. The uncomfortable silence of the room doing little to ease her worries.

Each slow minute was marked by the heavy clunk of the clock hand in an ancient-looking timepiece hung high on the wall.

Finally, a small light on the man's desk began flashing red, catching both their attention.

Alice waited impatiently as he stood, straightened his suit jacket and walked round from behind the desk. 'Juliette will see you now,' he instructed formally, as he moved towards the closed door.

Alice rose and moved behind him.

After a single firm knock, he swung the door inwards without awaiting a response. 'Alice Franklin to see you.' Having introduced Alice, he stepped to the side, allowing her to pass.

'Thank you,' she said politely as she entered the prime minister's office. The door closed quietly behind her.

No turning back now.

'Good afternoon.' Prime Minister Juliette Marshall smiled confidently, her arm extended across her desk, hand poised for a handshake.

Alice shuffled forward, somewhat clumsily, her heel snagging on the edge of an awful-looking rug.

The prime minister's handshake was firm and swift.

'It's a pleasure to meet you,' Alice said.

'Shall we take a seat?' Juliette indicated two comfortable looking high-back chairs placed either side of a low wooden table.

Alice nodded. 'Yes, of course.'

'Tea?'

'That would be lovely.' Alice was all too aware that her mouth was suddenly dryer than the desert.

Juliette picked up her telephone, pressed one button and requested a large pot of Earl Grey, she then moved out from her desk coming to sit opposite Alice.

Alice couldn't help feeling a little enamoured by this woman, she exuded confidence. Even the way she walked was powerful.

It was fair to say that Juliette Marshall had broken the mould when elected prime minister, in a landslide victory at the last election. A black single woman running office. A woman to inspire women. *And hopefully one to be receptive to my plight*, Alice hoped.

'I have to say I was delighted to receive your meeting request. Your work in the field of epidemiology has been groundbreaking.'

'Thank you.' Alice smiled, her cheeks colouring slightly.

A tap on the door paused conversation. A silver tray of tea was brought in and laid on the table between them.

With adept hands, Juliette poured the tea into china cups, handed one across to Alice and indicated to the milk and sugar. Alice noticed Juliette adding two spoons of sugar and no milk to her tea whilst she only added a small drop of milk to hers.

'So, tell me. How can I help you today?' The prime minister was direct without being brusque before taking a sip from her cup. Alice smiled lightly, she liked this woman, straight to the point without the need for mindless chit-chat. She could feel herself relax.

'Well...' Alice placed her untouched drink back on the table. She reached into her bag, pulling out a thin black file. 'I wanted to talk to you about the SCF Law,' she said pointedly whilst gripping the file.

'*The* Law?' Juliette clarified.

Originally it was named the SCF Law, single child family, but as with everything the tabloids quickly shortened and mocked it, and soon it was known nationwide as *The* Law, with the emphasis firmly on the '*The*', as if this was the only law that had ever been passed.

Alice nodded in confirmation.

'All right.' The note of scepticism in her tone was unmissable.

Alice passed the file to the prime minister. Juliette carefully put her cup down and took it.

Alice remained silent whilst the information was digested and absorbed, having learned years ago to allow them this time. She knew that if she interrupted prematurely, she could risk derailing the individual from their thoughts. The only movement she dared make was to quietly sip her tea.

After several long minutes, Juliette closed the file and looked at Alice. Had she been wearing glasses, it would have been one of those disbelieving glares over the rim of her spectacles. Thankfully she was not, therefore it was merely a questioning if not confused stare. Alice could handle that.

'I know what you must be thinking,' Alice began in the hope of allaying any fears, but the prime minister jumped in.

'I can assure you that you don't.' Her voice was unreadable. With the flat of her hands she patted the file, which rested on her lap. 'If I am not mistaken, this was your achievement, the fruition of what must have been years of hard work. Why?'

The woman opposite her was right, but this was not what Alice had expected at all. She had been prepared for the sell, she had readied the statistics, the figures, the data. But '*Why?*', well that was personal. It was such a simple question really. But Alice couldn't seem to find the words to answer. She opened her mouth, yet nothing came out, it was as if the words had abandoned her. She closed it again. Frustratedly, she wrung her hands together. Her skin was exceedingly dry, she noticed absent-mindedly.

'You're right,' she finally agreed. 'This is, was, my life's work, all there in that little file.' Her voice wobbled with emotion. *Pull yourself together*, she thought harshly, *you can't afford to get emotional.*

'I wanted to change the world, to make it better, to protect it, to allow it time to heal.' She sighed. 'But it would seem that here, in England, it has had completely the opposite effect.'

'How so?'

'The theory base,' Alice indicated towards the file still laid on the woman's lap, 'demonstrated that by limiting each family to one child, we would eventually be able to stabilise the world population. And as you'll see it is making a difference already, only ten years in.'

Alice noticed Juliette's eyebrows arch, just a fraction, but the implication was loud enough, *where are you going with this?*

'However, what I had not anticipated was the snowball effect. *The* Law has been revised and altered so dramatically that it no longer serves the purpose for which it was agreed upon. Do you know that we are the only country in the world who deny families the right to have a child? The only country to handpick which families are good enough to be parents? The only country where a mere one in every ten are approved?'

The prime minister shuffled, uncomfortably, in her seat. But Alice was on a roll, she wanted to hammer her point home.

'In Scotland, France, Spain, Australia even, they all signed up to the same programme,' she was gesticulating fervently with her free hand, 'and they have all been successful in the implementation and maintenance of *The* Law, without a single woman being refused. But our version has become a dictatorship, favouring only those with enough money, the right education, the right job even, to qualify them for parenthood. This oppression on women, on our choices, our rights is unquantifiable. And the damage we're doing is irrevocable.' Her words were pleadingly passionate.

'I am not asking you to revoke *The* Law, it is serving its purpose. The numbers are beginning to slow and I do believe in what I, what we, set out to achieve. But what I am asking is that you reinstate it to its original objective, one child to every family who wishes to have one.'

Alice sagged back in her seat, spent.

This woman was the key to change, and perhaps more diplomacy should have been used, but Alice knew that this was her one opportunity to right this wrong, to rectify what had gone so horrendously wrong. Diplomacy was a necessary casualty.

For a while the two women sat silently, Alice praying she hadn't overstepped, Juliette likely considering how best to respond.

'I agree with you that things appear to have deviated down an incidental path,' the prime minister confirmed diplomatically. Alice could feel the knot in her stomach relax at the response, her jaw slacken, her taut muscles loosening. Juliette agreed in some part, whatever came next, Alice hadn't been shut down immediately. There was room to negotiate, room to beg if she had to.

'However, I feel it is extremely important that I emphasise to you the achievements that we have made. We have been successful in fulfilling our role as a country to look after the planet and our resources, and not only that, the effects have been even further reaching than I imagine you intended. With a more manageable population there is more available housing, unemployment is at a record low, school class sizes are down, the NHS is no longer at threat, waiting times are much quicker and well, people seem happier.'

'I don't disagree that those are all wonderful achievements,' Alice said. 'However, if we continue to restrict the birth rate in this way, we will find ourselves in an economic crisis of our own making. In another ten years' time, with so few people, the housing market will stall, every sector of the workplace will dwindle, skill-sets will be lost, there will be another recession.'

The prime minister seemed to flinch against the word recession, the country had barely recovered from the last one.

'Also,' Alice continued, once again reaching into her bag and pulling out a newspaper, she handed it to Juliette, 'those are not pictures of happy people.'

Juliette looked at the front sheet, a multicoloured image of protesters with their placards and signs, clashing with police.

Alice continued. 'We are the only country where protests are still prevalent. And you'll have to excuse me for being so forward, but it appears that nothing is being done to address this in a meaningful way, apart from the execution of brute force to quell this uprising.'

Juliette sucked in a deep breath. Alice was speaking the truth, not that she anticipated Juliette admitting as much but the demonstrations were a thorn in the prime minister's side, a smear on her otherwise-successful term in office.

The protests had never actually stopped, they had continued year after year although some with dwindling numbers. Alice, however, had stoked that particular flame in the past year, keeping the issue in the public eye. She, of course, remained behind the scenes, hidden from sight. It would not serve her purpose to be exposed now as the organiser of such gatherings.

Perhaps Juliette had attempted to ascertain the root of the revolt, without success it would seem or else Alice wouldn't be sitting there. She swallowed hard, pushing the thoughts out of her mind.

'So, tell me what you propose?'

'I propose that you continue to uphold *The* Law, that you continue to reiterate its pertinence to the survival of our planet. You simply acknowledge that you have heard the people, that following consultation with your advisors, an amendment is feasible,' Alice suggested with a light shrug as if it should be that simple.

The prime minister once again looked at the newspaper. 'I can't promise anything. After all, I will need the agreement of cabinet ministers to make any alteration. However, the voices of the people should be heard, should be considered and, if appropriate, acted upon. I will see what can be done.'

26

SAM

MAY 6TH 2035

'I managed to get us a couple of paninis and drinks,' Hudson announced triumphantly as he climbed into the passenger seat of the car, carrier bag in hand, startling Sam.

He had been apprehensive when Sam announced that some surveillance of their suspect was in order. But two days in it was fair to say that his mood had not improved. She couldn't blame him, of course, she was bored herself, but then she was being driven by something deeper, something personal. She would sit there for as long as it took to get something tangible.

'Here.' He smiled for what Sam suspected was the first time that day as he handed her a polystyrene box. 'Ham and cheese.'

'Thanks,' Sam murmured, taking the box. Greedily, she bit into the hot toastie.

'Any movement?' Hudson nodded in the direction of the house.

Finishing her mouthful, Sam shook her head lightly.

This was the reality of surveillance, hours and hours of nothingness. Just sitting and watching. It was nothing like the movies made it out to be.

In the past two days, they had followed Miss Adams to

work, where she had remained for the entirety of a twelve-hour shift. The previous day she had ventured to the supermarket. Hudson, in his civvies, had tailed her. She had bought all the usual: milk, bread, cheese, crisps, chicken. No alcohol, interestingly. Hudson had reported that she'd walked through the baby clothes aisle, although this was on the way to the checkout, and she hadn't stopped to browse.

They still had nothing conclusive, and yet Sam knew with quiet confidence they were on the right track. She felt comfortable with her decision to concentrate all their efforts on this one suspect. Even if she was their only viable lead, Sam didn't have the feeling that she was missing something. She felt at ease.

The guv'nor had quizzed her extensively, sceptically, of course. She had held firm though, assuring him that she would secure an arrest within a week, but she needed resources and resources cost money.

Eventually, he relented, his fear of further embarrassment for the department outweighing any apprehension he had about Sam's decision-making ability.

Now the clock was ticking.

At two, Elspeth appeared. Sam couldn't help but notice how overdressed she was for the mild May weather, in a thick green coat, heavy knit jumper, jeans and boots.

Silently, they watched her, an air of apprehension filling the car.

Elspeth headed straight towards them. Instinctively, the detectives sunk into their seats. Had she seen them? Did she know they were there watching her every move?

Elspeth stopped before she reached them, by a blue Ford. Her car.

They observed as she swung the boot open, deposited a black leather overnight bag in it and shut it. Without so much as a glance in their direction, she climbed into the driver's seat.

Sam and Hudson shared a conspiratorial look. Silently acknowledging the significance of her movements, of her overnight bag.

A tingle of excitement ran down Sam's spine. This could be it. What they had been waiting for. The concrete evidence they needed for an arrest.

As their suspect started her car, Sam in turn started hers. Sam had enough experience of tailing cars to understand the importance of hanging back slightly, allowing one or two cars to slot in between them, to shield her from sight. This wasn't like being in a patrol car, which was like wearing a neon jacket on a dark night, she didn't want to be seen.

Sam mirrored every turn Miss Adams made, at a safe distance of course. Quite quickly, Sam realised that they were going north west, out of Brighton.

'Where do you suppose we're heading?' Sam said into the silence of the car.

'Hmm, not sure, but we'll soon find out,' Hudson answered flatly.

They travelled for thirty minutes, passing several small villages, which Sam decided she would like to visit on a day off. Not that she often took them. She also didn't tend to leave Brighton, she didn't have cause to, but these quaint villages with their chocolate-box cottages and antique shops were strangely inviting. She made a mental note to get out of Brighton more, to widen her horizons.

Sam followed Elspeth as she pulled into a car park, positioned behind Storrington high street. Slowly, she drove beyond the blue Ford, which had pulled straight into a vacant space.

Strategically, Sam passed several cars, deftly following the one-way system as it turned right, then manoeuvred into the first available space. From here they could see Miss Adams' car without her easily noticing them. Perfect.

Elspeth purchased a parking ticket, placed it in her car window, then headed off back towards the high street, her overnight bag left in the boot.

All the while, Sam and Hudson scrutinised her every movement.

'You follow her, I'll get a ticket and catch you up,' Sam announced decisively, digging around for some change in the well of the car's armrest.

'Okay.' Hudson at last seemed more animated; he practically jumped out of the car before setting off with a light jog to maintain a visual of their suspect.

Sam's heart was beating a little faster. Call it instinct, call it a gut feeling, whatever it was, she was convinced that Miss Adams was about to unwittingly reveal herself to them. And Sam planned to savour every moment, to bask in that feeling of righteousness.

With a ticket displayed in the windscreen, Sam strode out of the car park. Pulling her phone from her pocket, she hit the call button. 'Where are you?' she demanded when Hudson answered.

She followed his instructions which took her along the high street. Briefly, she registered a beauty shop, pub and café as she carefully darted in between the window shoppers.

At a set of traffic lights, she waited impatiently, as the ever-steady flow of cars forced her to stop. Her foot tapped fervently against the pavement in time with her beating heart.

Eventually, the cars ground to a halt, allowing Sam and an elderly man to cross.

Sam could see where she was heading, a small tea room set

back from the hustle and bustle of the main high street, but close enough to draw in the customers.

As Sam neared, Hudson waved, catching her attention.

He was sitting at a small garden table with two chairs, in a makeshift garden, to the side of the tea room.

Sitting down, Sam automatically looked through the large windows, into the tea room. 'She's down the far end,' Hudson confirmed quietly.

Sam discreetly turned in her seat. There. Sam relaxed a fraction as she spotted Elspeth sat at a small table tucked away in a corner, a menu in her hand.

'What can I get you?' an overly made-up waitress inter-rupted, notepad and pen poised in front of her, pulling Sam's attention away from where it wanted to be.

'Latte, please,' Hudson responded smoothly.

'Coffee, black,' Sam added abruptly, eager for this girl to go away. She wanted to talk to Hudson, to glean from him anything of importance that had happened in her two-minute delay.

The waitress continued to hover for a moment. perhaps waiting for Sam's manners to kick in. If that was the case, she'd be waiting a fucking long time. She was about to throw the woman her best 'fuck off' glare when she exhaled loudly before turning and stalking away.

'Did she stop at all? Talk to anyone?' Sam quizzed her part-ner, nonplussed by the waitress' rudeness.

'No, she headed straight here. She obviously knows this place–' Sam looked at Hudson as he stopped mid-sentence.

She was beginning to recognise the mild nuances in his demeanour, presently there was a distant expression etched on his face, as he delved into the depths of his memory. It was like watching the hand on a clock ticking; you know it's going to move but each small movement is eked out, stretching out for longer than is necessary. She wanted to rush him, but managed to bite her tongue, aware of his extraordinary ability to retain and retrieve snippets of information. Sometimes inconsequential, other times insightful and vital.

'Her parents,' he eventually blurted out. Before he could elaborate though, the obviously disgruntled waitress unceremoniously plonked a tray, containing their drinks, onto the table between them. The drinks sloshed aggressively out of the cups, thick brown liquid pooling on the tray.

'Thank you,' Hudson responded, maintaining a level of politeness which dumbfounded Sam. They had just lost half of their drinks and he was playing nice. He had a lot to learn.

Taking their cups, the waitress snatched away the tray, droplets of coffee flicking across the table. Sam swallowed down a sneer. She couldn't draw attention to them, she knew, but she'd love to drag that girl down a few pegs.

'Her parents live in Storrington,' Hudson finally confirmed, once the waitress was out of earshot.

Sam's face fell slightly. *Don't tell me, we've just followed her all this bloody way to watch her have afternoon tea with her parents.* She sighed heavily to herself.

Automatically, Sam looked over her shoulder again. Miss Adams was still alone, attention turned to her phone.

The detective brooded over the potential false alarm, whilst stirring her coffee. In the back of her mind, she knew she only had one week to come up with something concrete or she was off the case. This was becoming a joke, a huge embarrassing joke.

After a moment, Hudson rapped on the table, gaining Sam's attention. With a slight tilt of his chin, he indicated in Miss Adams' direction.

Casually, Sam swivelled in her seat. Sat opposite Elspeth was a man. From her vantage point, she could tell that he was young, with a thick head of sandy blond hair.

Not her dad then. Relief settled in.

Glancing back to Hudson, he had his phone held up in front of his face. 'Say cheese,' he smiled with fake enthusiasm.

Sam didn't oblige, aware that this was simply a ruse whilst he snapped pictures of Elspeth's companion. Hudson had a clearer view.

Sam doubted that anyone would have considered his photo-taking odd anyway, people were always taking pictures of random things these days: food, flowers, signs, anything to make their otherwise-ordinary lives seem a tad more exciting.

'This one's a good one,' Hudson indicated a little too loudly, passing the phone across to her. Accepting it, Sam glanced around at the other customers. No one was paying them any attention.

Turning to the picture, she was amazed at its clarity. She absorbed every detail of this man, noting the lighter shades of blond streaking his hair, his strong yet straight nose, the green hew of his eyes and the very taut expression fixed on his face.

Annoyingly, she didn't recognise him. Sliding the phone back to Hudson, Sam shook her head lightly. In understanding, Hudson shrugged once. He didn't know either.

This was very exciting. Perhaps he was her boyfriend.

Regardless of their relationship, this guy was another lead.

Sam desperately wanted to switch seats with Hudson. She wanted to watch how Miss Adams interacted with her companion. Was he a friend, or a boyfriend? Could he be involved? Did he know about the theft? Sam fidgeted frus-tratedly.

'They're ordering,' Hudson whispered, having leaned forward.

Silently the detectives waited, occasionally sipping their drinks. Hudson busied himself on his phone whilst Sam skimmed through her notebook, looking for something she may have missed, a small detail which might give some indication as to who this guy was.

After a few minutes, Sam couldn't help herself, she turned to look once more. Miss Adams appeared stony-faced. Her companion was bent forward towards her, talking intently. His hands were clenched into white balls. An argument? A lovers' tiff?

'Not a happy meeting then,' Hudson whispered, seeing what Sam saw.

'Can I get you anything else?' the waitress asked nonchalantly, startling them both.

'No thank you,' Hudson replied, this time his voice lacked civility.

Sam jumped to her feet. 'She's going!'

Behind them, they watched the hurried image of Elspeth Adams exiting the tea room and striding back towards the high street, her companion abandoned at the table, with two untouched plates of food.

'For our drinks,' Hudson indicated, thrusting a ten-pound note at the waitress who was still idling beside their table. 'Keep the change.'

Both detectives moved to follow their suspect, when Sam stopped abruptly, hand shooting out to holt Hudson.

'What is it?' he asked but his eyes didn't leave Elspeth as she continued stalking up the high street, back in the general direction of the car park.

Sam tilted her head back towards the tea rooms. 'I think we should take the opportunity to find out who our guy is, don't you?'

Hudson looked at her then, understanding blossoming on his face. Sam couldn't help but smile.

In sync, they turned, walking deliberately into the tea room and right up to the table.

Sam slid into the seat opposite the very handsome-looking young man.

Before he had a chance to protest, she held out her badge. 'Good afternoon. I'm Detective Inspector Sam Wakley and I think we need to have a chat.'

27

ALICE

MAY 6TH 2035

Alice and her colleague Mark were working side by side, analysing the data from their latest research study, bee restoration in England.

The programme had of course been successful, but to ensure future funding, the results needed to be simplified and cohesive to present to their funding panel. Alice couldn't focus, however. Her thoughts were annoyingly preoccupied.

She had yet to hear anything from the prime minister's office. Alice knew it would take time, the wait nevertheless was still unsettling. She couldn't determine if she should be reassured by the silence or not.

Focus. With her head resting in her hands, she diligently reread the same data notes which had been sat in front of her for the past twenty minutes.

She still couldn't make sense of what she was reading, unable to absorb the numbers.

It's no good. Frustrated, she pushed herself to her feet.

Mark eyed her warily. 'All right?' Genuine concern filled in his voice.

As her closest confidante, Mark understood Alice's growing

unrest at *The* Law. Although she had not divulged any details, he knew that she was, in part, responsible for the swelling discord. He was, however, fully informed of her meeting at Downing Street. 'Still no news?' He'd guessed as to her cause of distraction.

'No,' Alice answered meekly.

If only it were that simple.

For the hundredth time she looked at her phone. Nothing. Alice had been unable to stop herself from worrying about the girl from the protest as well. Something else she had hidden from Mark.

The same questions circled her mind. Could she have done more? Was she all right? Would she actually be able to help were she to call? Alice wanted the woman to call, desperately wanted to assist her and yet she wasn't convinced that she could help, that she could change anything. Especially if she didn't hear back from the Prime Minister.

Seeing that woman, concealing what was so natural, had been like a slap in the face. Her work in action. Alice couldn't quash the sorrow she felt for the woman's situation.

There was no denying that ten years ago, the young woman's situation would have been vastly different. She would have flaunted her growing bump proudly in fitted dresses, she would have celebrated with an elaborate baby shower and most of all she would have talked endlessly about her hopes and dreams for the little one. Instead, she was hiding and scared and probably alone.

Alice felt tears spring into her eyes. 'Just going to go for a walk,' she announced stiffly, unable to look at Mark. 'I need to clear my head.'

She darted out of the office before the tears fell.

Outside, Alice pulled a tissue from her pocket to wipe away the stray tear which had streaked a path to her cheek.

She headed for the park, seeking fresh air.

Once there, she slowed her pace. Breathing deeply, she turned her face to the sky, letting the sun warm her skin.

Unintentionally, she found herself sitting down on a bench, opposite a small park.

She watched as two children chased each other around the sad-looking play area. She wondered why she'd sat there. Perhaps her conscience hoped to seek solace from being reminded that all was not lost, children were still being born, some women were still gifted the joy of motherhood.

Her phone's shrill ringtone sounded from within the depths of her pocket, startling her. The number withheld. Alice answered regardless, aware it could be important.

'Hello, Alice speaking,' she spoke softly.

'You said you could help me, how exactly?' a whisper of a voice demanded.

For a split second, Alice didn't comprehend. *Who is this?* was poised on the tip of tongue when realisation hit her, like a ray of sunshine illuminating the path ahead.

'Yes,' Alice mumbled, her mind whirling quickly. 'Well... Um...' She tripped over her own thoughts which were swirling in a disorganised mist.

She heard the woman sigh softly, sadly, as if disappointed.

Alice had imagined this conversation a thousand times already, and none of them started like this. She had to do better if she was going to make any sort of meaningful impression on this girl. If she didn't want her to hang up.

'I am very well connected indeed,' Alice continued, this time more confidently. 'I don't fully understand your situation or what you would like to do?'

'I want to keep my baby!' The voice was fiercely resolute.

'Okay,' Alice responded. The woman was clearly scared, Alice noted, not unkindly.

'As I was saying, I'm very well connected. If you need somewhere to stay for a while, I can arrange that, if you need a passport, I can procure one, if you need money, I can give you that.' Alice would find a way to give her any or all of those things if it would make a difference, improve her situation.

For a moment there was an overwhelming silence. Alice was desperate to offer more, to pledge herself to this woman, but she held back, aware that she must be considering her options.

'I may need all of those things.' She sounded cautious.

'Of course.' The smile on Alice's face was evident in the tone of her voice. 'Shall we meet?'

Surprisingly, the woman agreed.

Unsurprisingly, she chose a very public space, which concerned Alice somewhat, although she didn't question it. The woman didn't know Alice was trustworthy, would pretty much risk anything if she believed that she could secure a happy future for this mother and child.

With arrangements made, the woman spoke slowly. 'Why do you want to help me?'

Of course she would want to know why I would be willing to risk everything to help someone I don't even know. 'To make amends,' Alice said earnestly, aware she had said something similar when they had first encountered one another.

The woman didn't ask any further questions, perhaps content with Alice's repeated sentiment, or perhaps she would demand to know more when they met in person.

Long after their call had ended, Alice sat, contently, on the bench in the middle of the park. She continued to observe the children, their laughter warming her heart, a smile eventually pulling at the edge of her lips. She felt reassured and confident. She would make this right, even if for just one person.

28

ARTIE

MAY 6TH 2035

Déjà vu tugged at Artie's conscience in an unsettling way. He was waiting impatiently for Elspeth to leave the house. He needed access to her room, again. Artie didn't like sneaking around behind her back and invading her space, but if she wouldn't willingly accept his help, then he had to do it this way for now. *She'll understand*, he tried to convince himself meekly, although the guilt he felt was unmissable.

They had barely spoken since Artie confessed to Elspeth that he knew her secret. He suspected that she'd been avoiding him, rushing out the door without breakfast, coming back late when the house was silent, barricading herself in her room.

Artie sighed loudly. This was not what he had imagined. He knew that deep down, he had hoped for something more, something else. Elspeth opening up to him, he supposed, seeking solace in his embrace, loving him back even.

'Stop it,' he hissed to himself.

She had made it clear that she didn't think that she needed him, but when had that stopped him before. Better to be prepared, he reminded himself.

He wanted to make sure that Elspeth had a back-up plan.

She may never need it, may never even need to know the lengths that he was going to for her safety but he couldn't just sit by idly.

The morning stretched out for what seemed like an eternity. Artie worked on a misdemeanour that he was being paid handsomely to make disappear. Honestly, sometimes he felt like he should tell people that he was a magician, as that is what he often did, made things vanish.

Finally he heard Elspeth leave her room, closing the door firmly behind her. He listened, ear turned to the hallway, as she padded downstairs, grabbed her car keys from the sideboard before slamming the front door behind her.

He ran to the window.

There it was again, that feeling that had been there before.

He shook it off, instead focusing his attention on Elspeth. He watched from behind the curtain as she trudged down the street, to her car. He noted the thick coat she'd been wearing, it had become like a suit of armour for her, protecting her from unnecessary stares. Then he noticed the overnight bag in her hand.

Where was she going? A tendril of worry creeping in.

He couldn't help her if he didn't know where she was. She hadn't said that she was staying away, not that she had said anything to him these past few days. A cold dread swept in, obscuring his initial worries. What if she wasn't coming back? His eyes widened in fear.

Think rationally, he reasoned with himself, she'd need more than what was in that bag and she would have said, even with things the way they were between them, she wouldn't leave without saying goodbye.

Feeling a little calmer, he continued to watch Elspeth as she stowed her bag in her boot before climbing, a little awkwardly, into the driver's seat.

As she started the car, he couldn't help but notice a set of headlights flash into life a little further down the street. His brow furrowed. Eyes trained on the other car, Artie didn't miss its purposeful cruising, how it pulled away slowly, how it crawled forward all the while maintaining its distance.

As the car passed below his window, Artie could just make out a passenger. That meant there were two of them, two people who he hadn't seen walking to their car, two individuals who must have already been sat, waiting patiently in their vehicle.

From the beating of his heart and the hairs standing on end on his arms, he knew who they were.

'Shit.'

The police.

It was only going to be a matter of time, he understood, until they narrowed in their focus. He had just been hoping that they had other lines of enquiry to keep them busy a while longer.

Artie watched helplessly as the surveillance car followed Elspeth. Soon they had both turned out of sight.

For the briefest moment he considered calling or texting Elspeth, to warn her. But what if she panicked, what if she got arrested for looking at her phone?

No, he couldn't risk it.

Artie growled in frustration, pacing aimlessly in front of the window. His hands balled into tight fists. He pressed them firmly against his closed eyes.

'Think,' he snarled at himself.

If the police had anything concrete, and last time he checked they didn't, they wouldn't be following her. No, they would have arrested her. But where was she going? The not knowing was excruciating, she could be walking into a trap.

Brooke. The thought sprang to him.

Running downstairs, he found Brooke curled up on the sofa, watching crap daytime TV.

'Hey,' he said breathlessly. He leant against the doorway in what he hoped was a casual stance.

'Hey yourself,' Brooke replied without looking away from the screen.

'I was thinking I might treat us to a takeaway tonight, you know seeing as how we all missed Sunday night?' Artie would gladly buy Brooke a takeaway to find out if she knew where Elspeth had gone.

'Ohhh, lovely,' Brooke purred, turning to smile at Artie.

'Do you know if Ellie will be in too?' he asked, forcing his voice to hold steady.

'She won't. She's gone to Storrington,' she said with an absent wave of her hand. 'But we can still get a takeaway?'

'Of course.' Artie nodded, a genuine smile lighting up his face as a sense of relief settled in.

She'd gone to her parents. Artie let out the breath he hadn't realised he'd been holding. 'You can choose,' he called back as he began his retreat upstairs.

'Let's have Chinese,' Brooke shouted after him.

Upstairs, Artie darted straight into Elspeth's room. Hunting through every single drawer, every hiding place, he searched. Eventually, in a filing box, tucked in the base of her wardrobe, Artie found what he wanted. Her passport.

With the document in hand, he made one final sweeping glance of the room, to make sure nothing looked out of place. Satisfied, he edged out the room, closing the door behind him.

In his room, Artie couldn't help turning to Elspeth's passport photo. The grainy image showed her serious-faced, just the edge of her mouth turned up the smallest amount, as though she was desperately trying not to smile.

God, she even looks beautiful in her passport photo.

The innocence of her face suddenly infuriated Artie. She didn't deserve this.

His thoughts automatically turned to a previous client, someone whose situation wasn't vastly different from Elspeth's. He had been able to help her.

He recalled how easy it had been to hack the government system, to plant the documents, to forge the certificate of approval. But she had been married, he reminded himself. There was no way to do the same for Elspeth, he couldn't forge a marriage, the police would only have to scratch the surface, would only have to talk to her parents, her friends, to see the deception.

His client had caused quite a storm, he remembered. There had been a huge news circus surrounding her story. The innocent mother whose pregnancy had been overshadowed by a bogus police investigation. She had made such a fuss, and threatened to sue the police department. Genius move really, they were never going to touch her after that. But – that was not Elspeth.

Working swiftly, Artie scanned the passport. With the copied image on the screen in front of him, he took a moment to consider his actions. One passport wasn't going to be enough. The police surveillance had clearly spooked him.

Elspeth will probably have to move around, to hide, he realised sadly. No, three identities would be better.

Expertly, Artie began editing the details he was going to need to procure the documents. He was uncomfortable about outsourcing this, but he needed them flawless. He knew exactly who to go to though. It would cost him handsomely, but he didn't care.

Pulling the burner phone from his drawer, Artie dialled a number he knew by heart.

'Hey, it's me,' he said when the phone was answered.

'Yep,' a husky voice responded.

'I'm sending you some information, I need three sets of documents, the whole works.'

A loud whistle sounded from the person at the other end of the phone, indicating the expense of this job.

'And I need them in forty-eight hours.'

'Gonna cost ya,' the deep voice informed Artie.

'Just make sure they're perfect!'

Without any further conversation, the phone went dead, leaving Artie with a sick nervous feeling.

He just prayed that the documents didn't come too late.

29

ELSPETH

MAY 6TH 2035

S he didn't know where she was going. She was just driving, following the twisty country lanes which spanned out ahead of her.

A mixture of emotions were bubbling just below the surface. She didn't want to think, she didn't want to feel, she just wanted to drive.

In an attempt to drown out the thoughts demanding her attention, she turned up her music, its beat blasting from the speakers.

Elspeth wasn't paying attention to the speed of her car. The trees and hedges were a blur at the edge of her vision. All she knew was that she wasn't going fast enough. She wouldn't be able to outrun her thoughts for much longer if she didn't speed up. Her foot pushed harder against the accelerator.

The afternoon sun was blinding and the car was warming up like a greenhouse. It was suffocating. In her coat and jumper, Elspeth felt flushed, but she didn't want to pull over, wouldn't risk stopping. She opened the window wide. The cool air rushed in around her, whipping her hair into long tangled curls.

Elspeth could feel the sting of tears and her breathing hasten. Hopelessly, she tried to force it back down. To ignore it. She bit her bottom lip hard enough that the distinctive metallic taste of blood filled her mouth.

Hurrying round the next bend, the unexpected sight of a large dirty green tractor taking up the entirety of the lane, shocked Elspeth.

She jammed her foot on the brake. Hard. The tyres screeched loudly against the road and the car pitched forward as it wrestled to a stop.

She screamed.

As the car halted, her body slammed back into the seat.

Her bumper had stopped mere inches from the rear end of the gigantic mechanical machine.

For a moment, Elspeth was unmoving, shock paralysing her. *Stupid. Reckless. Idiotic.* She grasped at these words whilst the tractor continued rumbling on ahead, utterly unaware of the near miss behind it.

Gradually, she managed to steady her breathing, whilst behind her, a red Mini driver lightly tapped their horn, letting Elspeth know that they were there waiting, the lane too narrow for them to pass.

With exaggerated caution, Elspeth raised a shaky hand to indicate that she'd heard them, before pulling away slowly. Suddenly thankful for the slow amble of the tractor ahead, Elspeth carefully followed the road as it curved to the left before pulling into the first layby she spotted. Her car rocked and jolted against the uneven ground as she left the road. She didn't notice.

Turning off the engine, she closed her eyes and let the swarm of emotions overtake her.

Sucking in ragged breaths, sobs soon escaped her mouth.

She had never felt so alone or so afraid. It was as if a black, empty void had opened up inside her. She wrapped her arms tightly around her middle, desperately trying to hold herself together, to keep herself from falling apart entirely.

In the stillness of her car, the unwanted memories hit her hard.

'I've sorted everything out,' he had told her. At the time, Elspeth had sensed a note of pride in his tone, now though she realised that it was probably relief.

'That's fantastic,' she'd replied idiotically, unaware of what was to come next.

'Did you bring a bag? You know, with your things.' He had indicated with a nonchalant wave of his hand. One that said he didn't really care what she had brought as long as he didn't need to think about it.

'Yes, it's in my car. Where are we going?'

The tears cascaded down her cheeks, like little rivers running south. How could she have been so naive? She had looked at him, sat in that tea room opposite her, and she genuinely hadn't seen it coming.

'I found a guy.' Nick had smiled proudly, leaning across the table towards her. Before she could question this, he'd continued on arrogantly. 'It wasn't easy. I mean, obviously I didn't want to advertise what I was looking for. But he comes with, well, recommendations.'

She had sat unmoving as he'd carried on, his true colours shining brightly. 'It isn't exactly cheap either, but how do you put a price on our futures, right? Anyway, he said, the guy, I mean, that if we are there tomorrow morning then he'll do it.'

Nick had looked at her so expectantly, as if awaiting her praise, like a cat who'd brought its owner a disgusting dead mouse. But she had just stared, blankly at him.

'Do what?' she'd eventually asked.

'The termination,' Nick had said like a diamond ring on a plate, full of sincerity and hope. He had whispered the words of course, afraid that someone might hear him, but to Elspeth it was as if he'd shouted them. They seemed to resonate to her very core, slicing on their way in.

She remembered how her mind had been spinning. What the hell had made him think that was what she had wanted? Had she suggested that she had wanted an abortion in her words or her body language? No, she knew she hadn't, but then why? All these unspoken questions were quickly answered by Nick.

'I know it's a lot to take in,' he'd said, 'but really it's the best thing for both of us. I mean, we could go to prison for this. My career would be over, my reputation in tatters. God, what would my parents say,' he had rambled on. Misreading her silence, he had taken her hand. 'I know it's late for this, but well if you'd come to me sooner, never mind. What I mean is, this guy, he assures me it will be okay, you'll be okay afterwards.'

The shock of realisation had been like a snake bite, sharp and painful and lasting.

She relived the moment she'd yanked her hand out of his, suddenly sickened by his touch. The look of disgust which had twisted her face. The words she'd spat, through gritted teeth so full of hatred and sincerity. 'Is that what you think I wanted from you? You arrogant, self-absorbed arsehole. I would never terminate my baby. Do you hear me? Never! I will do it without you if I have to?'

She hadn't meant it to sound like a question. Nick, however, had jumped on it like a get-out clause.

'I will not lose everything for a one-night stand. I want no further part in this,' he spluttered, his face wiped of all emotions. She wasn't foolish enough to try and change his mind. It was made, as was hers.

She had walked out, determined to leave before a single tear was shed.

Thinking about it, Elspeth understood that her tears weren't for that prick. No, she would have likely tired of his ego soon enough, aware that what hid below the surface of his handsome face was shallow and selfish. She was crying out of regret. This should have been an amazing, life-enhancing experience for her, shared with someone who loved her. An image of Artie flashed into her mind. She shook her head lightly, dispelling the picture, aware this wouldn't help. Instead she was going to have to do this alone.

Slowly, the rasping sobs subsided. Her eyes, red and puffy, drying.

The word 'alone' resonated within her, cracking open the void in her chest even further. She tightened the hold she had on herself. Slowly and purposefully she breathed in and out. This couldn't be good for the baby, she told herself firmly.

Finally, a facade of calm settled across her face, even if there was still a gaping hole inside of her. She had messed up, spectacularly so, and she knew that from now, from this very minute, she needed to make better decisions.

She would, never again, allow herself to be so meek and pathetic. Never again would she be vulnerable at the hands of others.

No, from now on she needed to be stronger. To be determined. If not for herself, then for her child.

But... She still didn't have a solution, didn't have a way out, unless—

At first the thought crept in gently, then with more strength.

She didn't have much time, that was obvious, a couple of weeks, a month perhaps, after that it would be impossible to hide the swell of her stomach. She wasn't foolish enough to believe that she could do this all alone, she had tried and quite quickly found herself up against a wall. She needed help, but not the sort of help she'd hoped for from Nick, the sort that relinquished all control, but rather someone with means who could enable her departure. Support her in starting a new life outside of this country.

Elspeth couldn't, no, wouldn't involve Artie, she cared too much about him to implicate him further. Him knowing was dangerous enough. But what about that woman, the one from the protest?

Elspeth hesitated for a moment, torn. She didn't know this woman from Adam, she might not be who she presented herself as or she might be exactly who she said she was, in which case, it would be another person in jeopardy because of Elspeth.

Her choices were non-existent and yet this was her decision. Call or don't call.

With sad determination, Elspeth dug frantically in her bag. She knew she'd chucked the woman's card in there, hoping she'd never need it but too afraid to throw it away.

At the bottom of the bag, she found it.

Elspeth studied the card. It was expensive, she realised. 'Professor Alice Franklin' it read in an embossed black font. A mobile number was printed underneath.

Without hesitation, Elspeth grabbed her phone and dialled the number. But found herself hanging up almost immediately.

Holding the cool material of the phone against her forehead, Elspeth paused, doubt taking hold of her like an iron fist.

Think, she told herself.

Okay, this woman said she could help me, but she could also report me. She seemed genuine, but clearly I'm not the best judge of character.

Perhaps meeting in a public space would be wise, an opportunity to sound her out without being cornered. Yes, she liked the sound of that, somewhere busy and open. No need to leave anything else to chance.

She redialled the number, this time ensuring her number remained withheld.

Elspeth waited as the phone rang. *What if there's no answer?* Elspeth panicked briefly, before a gentle voice answered. 'Hello, Alice speaking.'

30

SAM

MAY 7TH 2035

Sam felt lighter than she had in weeks, if not months. It was as if a weight she didn't know she had been carrying had suddenly been lifted from her shoulders. She couldn't help it, she was grinning. A big, stupid grin.

Grabbing the plastic cup of lukewarm coffee, she sauntered back to interview room one, barely registering the sticky linoleum under her feet. With her free hand, she knocked. Even her tapping sounded jovial.

With some effort, she wiped the happy look from her face, replacing it with a straight, if not slightly terrifying, look.

Hudson opened the door. He moved aside to let her in.

Both detectives took their seats opposite the petrified-looking suspect and Sam, wordlessly, slid the coffee cup across to him.

The ominous silence was all for effect of course, she wanted him to be worried, he should be worried.

With trembling hands, he accepted the drink. Both hands circled the flimsy plastic, as if he needed the heat, before he drank deeply. As the bitter-tasting liquid registered, his mouth twisted in distaste. Cheap instant coffee, Sam thought knowingly, probably not up to his usual standards. She watched as he put the cup on the table, pushing it away.

Hudson broke the silence. 'Right.' He looked at his watch, registering the time. He turned on the recording. 'It is May 7th, 2035 at 10:12am. Present are DS Robert Hudson and DI Sam Wakley interviewing Doctor Nicolas Russo.'

Sam had allowed Hudson to take the lead in the interview. He'd deserved it, she had decided, aware that the case had stalled before he'd joined her team.

From her seat, she could see that he'd sketched out a list of questions in his notepad. She remembered doing something similar for her first interview.

'Can you please confirm for the record that you have declined to have a lawyer present at this time,' Hudson requested.

Nicolas cleared his throat. 'That's correct.'

Sam took Nicolas in. His clothes were crumpled from a night in the cell, the skin around his eyes appeared sallow, probably from lack of sleep, and his hair looked flat and lifeless. She didn't need to check his record to know that this was his first time in a station. He had that dazed, wide-eyed look about him.

'Can you please tell us how you know Miss Elspeth Adams?'

'We worked together at the hospital.'

A small smile pulled at the edge of Sam's mouth. It was so refreshing when a suspect talked; so often on the advice of their lawyers, they resorted to 'no comment'. She understood that his co-operation was superficial, he wanted to save his own skin. The previous day, when confronted in the tea room, Dr Russo had pretty much offered up Miss Adams on a silver platter in exchange for a pardon. He wouldn't get it of course, Sam thought, not that she had said as much to him. His co-operation remained vital.

'Can you explain the nature of your relationship?'

Nicolas blew out his cheeks, then ran his fingers through his hair. 'Well, we were colleagues, on the same unit,' he paused for a moment, then added, 'but we also slept together.'

'So you were in a relationship with Miss Adams?'

Sam didn't miss the cocky tilt of Nicolas's chin as he replied, 'No, she was just a one-night stand, a bit of fun, you know.'

Hudson ignored Dr Russo's inappropriateness. 'And when was that?'

'New Year's Eve.'

Sam sighed inwardly. *What did Elspeth see in this guy? He's an absolute cock*, she thought whilst trying her damnedest to keep a neutral expression.

Sam caught Hudson jotting something down, before he then angled the pad in her direction.

4 months pregnant, it read.

Sam blinked unbelievingly. How is it possible that no one had noticed, no one suspected? Unless they did. Perhaps there were more people involved in this than they had initially thought.

'Was that the only time?' Hudson asked for clarity.

'Yeah, it was fun and all but she's not really my type, I generally prefer blondes,' Dr Russo said innocently.

Sam had to bury the sudden urge to lean across the table and punch him hard in the face. His lack of respect for women was astounding and that was saying something, as Sam had worked with some sexist pigs in her time.

'Please tell us about the pregnancy?' Hudson pressed, a sense of urgency creeping into his questioning.

'Okay.' Their suspect sighed, all bravado disappearing. 'So, Elspeth turned up on my door, several weeks back now–'

'When?' Hudson interrupted.

'Hmm, end of March, I think, or beginning of April. I don't

remember the exact date. She asked if we could talk. I couldn't let her in, you see, I had an, um... a friend staying so I met her in the coffee shop on the corner of my road. And that's when she told me she was pregnant. Honestly, I wasn't expecting her to drop *that* bombshell.'

'What exactly did she say?' Hudson pushed, irritation evident in his voice. *That would've pissed me off too.* Who tells a story like that? She said she was pregnant, the end. No, there was much more information to glean from this dickhead and Hudson knew it, thankfully.

Russo thought for a moment. 'She said there had been a bit of a mix-up about contraception. I thought she was on the pill. Turns out she wasn't. Obviously I asked if she was positive that it was mine, she said she hadn't been with anyone else. I mean,' he shrugged, 'it wasn't as if we could get a DNA test. She wanted help and I wanted the nightmare to be over, so I said I would help her.'

'And how did you plan to do that?' Hudson asked, clearly frustrated.

'I found a guy, who could, you know, get rid of it.' At least Russo had the decency to look sheepish, Sam thought, disgusted by this poor specimen of a man.

'We'll come back to this guy later. I'm going to want all his details,' Hudson indicated, making a few notes on his pad again. 'So you made all the arrangements for the termination of the baby?'

'Yes,' Russo confirmed.

Gotcha.

Sam allowed herself to smile. They had enough to prosecute him on the attempted illegal abortion of a baby if nothing else. And they might be able to get the abortionist to boot. Sam and Hudson exchanged a conspiratorial look.

'Did you see any evidence of the pregnancy?' Hudson then inquired.

Nicolas wrinkled up his nose in confusion.

'Pregnancy test, growing stomach, that sort of thing?' Hudson confirmed.

'No,' Russo replied flatly. 'Come to think of it, she was wearing a really unflattering baggy jumper yesterday. I assumed it was to hide the bump.'

'And so when you met Miss Adams yesterday, that was to take her to the appointment?' Hudson asked, moving the interview along naturally.

'It was actually arranged for this morning, I'd booked us a B & B for the night. But she flipped out.'

'Flipped out?' Hudson repeated.

'Apparently she didn't actually want to, you know, have a termination. She said she wanted to keep the baby and would do it alone. Can you believe it? I honestly don't think she realises she's gonna get caught.' He shook his head.

Sam noticed the light frown creasing Hudson's brow. *What's he thinking?* He made a few more notes, then sat motionless staring at what he'd written.

The silence stretched out, almost uncomfortably so. Sam waited calmly. This was Hudson's interview and she wouldn't jump in, but it was torturous.

Eventually ready to continue, Hudson tapped his pen on his notepad and cleared his throat. 'So, let me make sure I have understood the situation clearly. Miss Adams approached you several weeks ago identifying her pregnancy. However, you have no proof?' Hudson glanced up for confirmation. Nicolas nodded once. 'Okay, but you agreed to help. You arranged a termination. But on informing Miss Adams of this yesterday, she declined your support?'

'Yep.'

'Okay, that's everything for now,' Hudson said, startling both Sam and Nicolas. 'Interview terminated at 10.46am.' Hudson stopped the recording, motioning to Sam to follow him as he exited the room.

Stood, heads bent together in the corridor, Sam asked, 'What's going on?'

'Honestly, this might all be some sort of twisted revenge situation.' Hudson pressed his lips tightly whilst pinching the bridge of his nose with his thumb and index finger.

'What do you mean?' Sam wasn't ashamed to admit she was lost.

He looked a little uncomfortable, she realised, instantly becoming concerned with where this was going. Briefly, she considered whether she should have led the interview, perhaps the pressure had been too much, before he spoke again.

'He's clearly a dick but what if it wasn't just a one-night stand for Elspeth? What if it meant more to her than him and when he didn't reciprocate, she made up this whole thing to get back at him?'

For a moment, Sam didn't grasp Hudson's words, her brain not willing to acknowledge their meaning.

'Think about it,' her partner said gently. 'We have no proof that she's pregnant. He hasn't seen the test or her bump. Maybe the reason she flipped out yesterday was because she knew that if she went to the appointment, then the "doctor", if that's what we're going to call him, would have quickly realised that she'd been lying, exposing her secret.'

Sam instantly felt the lead weight settling back down on her shoulders.

This could have all been some elaborate hoax. She started to panic, her palms becoming sweaty and her breathing quickening. Then a thought jumped into her mind. 'But then why steal a pregnancy test if it's all a ruse?'

Hudson paused for a moment, thinking this through. 'Well... What if she genuinely thought she was pregnant at the beginning? She might have stolen the test, had a negative result, but the seed had already been planted in her mind.'

'Shit!' Sam cursed. *He's right.* This could have all been some fucking wild goose chase. She was only just keeping a lid on her mounting anger, her fury.

'Okay,' she breathed, ideas swirling furiously within her mind, 'let's say you're right. She still stole the pregnancy test which is a controlled item, conviction one.' She held up one finger. 'He arranged an illegal abortion, conviction number two.' She added a second finger. 'And if we get our abortionist, that's conviction number three.' Three fingers extended in front of Hudson's face. 'And that's worst case, she could of course be pregnant.'

Sam realised that she was holding on to this investigation by her fingertips. It didn't take a genius to work out that with a reasonable lawyer both Miss Adams and Dr Russo, having no previous convictions, would walk away scot-free.

And yet, she wasn't ready to give up. Sam needed a good result, she needed *this* result, to redeem her reputation. But... what if it all backfired. A bubble of fear was beginning to build. She couldn't take further humiliation.

Think, she told herself sharply, determined to salvage something.

They could go after the abortionist – that would definitely be a great bust. But there was a nagging doubt flashing away in the periphery of Sam's mind telling her that there was something still in this. They hadn't disproved Miss Adams' pregnancy yet and until then, Sam didn't want to leave any opportunities, any possibilities, unpursued. She had to, no, she wanted to believe that they still had a workable case.

Sam was thankful for Hudson's silence whilst she worked

through this. When she finally met his waiting stare, he asked, 'So? What do you think?'

'You may be right, but I just have this feeling.' She struggled to find the right words. 'I think we go after Miss Adams, and we'll just have to determine whether she is or she isn't pregnant later.'

Hudson didn't seem convinced but he was as invested as she was. Eventually he sighed. 'Okay, let's find out where she is and bring her in for questioning.'

31

ALICE

MAY 9TH 2035

Alice waited nervously on the hard concrete seating outside Churchill Square. She watched the bustling crowd scuttling like ants around her. For a moment she envied them, these unhampered strangers, with their mediocre problems, never truly appreciating how fortunate they were. Some of them at least.

Eyeing the crowd carefully, Alice was looking for one face in particular.

Even now, she could picture her with absolute clarity. Her long, wavy brown hair escaping from underneath her hood, the roundness of her cheeks, and those large chocolate brown eyes, so full of fear. What if she didn't turn up? Alice worried unexpectedly. This idea didn't sit well, she shoved it away.

'Hi,' a quiet voice whispered from over Alice's right shoulder making her jump.

Alice turned. The young woman was perched on the raised seating behind her.

'Hi.' Alice smiled, what she hoped was a warm, kind smile, although she had to will her heartbeat back to its normal pattern.

Why am I so nervous?

'Do you mind if we go for a walk?' There was something different in her tone, something more commanding than when they had first met.

'Yes, of course,' Alice said, pushing up to her feet.

Alice let herself be guided away from the busyness of the shopping area. As they neared the promenade, the crowd began to thin out somewhat.

Alice watched as the tight set of the woman's jaw relaxed slightly.

'I haven't properly introduced myself yet, I'm Alice Franklin,' Alice offered in an attempt to fill the silence.

'Yes, your card told me as much,' the woman replied, not unkindly, before continuing. 'I'm Elspeth.'

'Nice to meet you.' Alice smiled again, keeping her gaze firmly fixed ahead. Elspeth. It suited her, feminine yet strong. She would need to be, to weather the storm coming.

'I looked you up,' Elspeth added seriously, shoving her hands into the pockets of her oversized jumper, her bump barely obscured beneath the swath of heavy material.

A look of surprise flashed across Alice's face but just as quickly it was gone. She should have expected that and yet she hadn't. Strangely, though, Elspeth had still decided to meet her. The direness of her situation became more apparent.

'I'm sure you found some interesting reading,' Alice said honestly.

'Yes, I did. I read that you're responsible for *The* Law,' Elspeth said, a note of determination or was it defiance to her voice. 'Is that true?'

Alice knew that it would be futile to gloss over the truth. Elspeth had clearly done her research. Alice inhaled. 'Yes, to some extent. My research was the cornerstone for changing the law, that much is true.' She exhaled before continuing. 'The evidence for change was overwhelming. The numbers didn't stack up.' How many times had she had to recite this speech, to substantiate her research? 'Our population was growing at an exponential rate and resources were going to run out. I lobbied for a change, one which I genuinely believed would be fair for everyone.'

Elspeth stopped mid-step and turned to face her, anger burning behind her eyes, her arms wrapping tightly around her middle. 'How so?'

Of course she only knew *The* Law as it was, not as it was supposed to be.

'The Law that I recommended was designed to allow every woman or every family the opportunity to have one child. It didn't discriminate, it was simple and it was fair. In the majority of countries around the world, it has worked, you could even go so far as to say it's been a success. Unfortunately, a very small handful of countries, including ours, opted for a more-controlled approach, one which I never imagined or would have agreed to.'

Alice searched Elspeth's eyes for the glint of hatred which she had grown accustomed to. It wasn't there. What she saw, though, was worse. Her anger had dissolved to what looked a lot like pity. Alice didn't want this woman's sympathy, she didn't deserve it. She had long since accepted her part in all of this, and she was working furiously to atone for it.

'So what changed?'

Alice managed to withhold the cruel laugh which threatened to erupt from her chest. 'Politics. Power, perhaps? I had no say, no control in how it evolved. They did with it what they wanted.' Her sadness was palpable. She tried to pull it back in, to keep it within her. Elspeth did not need to contend with her regrets on top of her own worries.

Thankfully Elspeth didn't offer any words of condolence, didn't try to offer forgiveness for what Alice had done. Forgiveness was a gift, one which Alice could not accept until she had put right what had gone so terribly wrong.

'Shall we keep going?' Alice gestured with a wave of her hand.

Elspeth nodded. 'So, *The* Law...'

'Is a much more selective and oppressive version of what I imagined, what I recommended,' Alice confirmed, anticipating her question.

They walked away from the busy centre, soon reaching the less-crowded promenade. It didn't escape Alice's attention that this was the place where they had first collided, their fates unequivocally twisting together.

Alice felt herself relaxing as a soft breeze tousled her silvery hair. Only now, did she take the opportunity to look at Elspeth. She had dressed for necessity, Alice realised, in trainers, leggings and an oversized deep green jumper, which was just starting to cling to the curve of her stomach. Her black baseball cap was pulled low, casting a shadow over her already-tired eyes, perhaps in an attempt to conceal her identity, and her long brown hair had been swept into a plait which trailed over her shoulder. She was very pretty, Alice acknowledged, and young, younger than she'd first imagined, maybe only twenty-two.

'So, is that why you offered to help me?' Elspeth interrupted Alice's thoughts.

A sad smile stretched across Alice's face. 'I never wanted anyone to suffer, but they have. There is a whole generation who have been denied the right to be parents because of me, because of my research. I have tried to have *The* Law reviewed, to reinstate it to its original purpose, but so far, I haven't been successful. I would really like to set things right and I hope that for you, I can go some way to achieving that, if you'll let me, that is?' That was it, the truth.

For a moment it hung there, precariously dangling

between them, as they continued moving at a slow pace. When Elspeth didn't respond immediately, Alice considered that Elspeth may well turn her back on her offer, that the instrumental role she played in *The* Law proving too significant to overlook. That her attempt at redemption would be denied.

'Do you mind if we sit for a moment?' Elspeth indicated a bench.

'Of course not.'

Sitting side by side, both women stared out towards the sea. Alice watched the waves as they crashed angrily against the pebbles. It was relentless yet calming, she noticed, as the water swept back out to join the vastness of the ocean before another wave pounded the stones.

A movement drew her back to the present. Elspeth had moved her hand purposefully to cup her stomach.

This time a genuine smile lit up Alice's face. 'May I?' she asked, eyes fixed on Elspeth's bump.

With a hint of hesitation, Elspeth nodded.

Carefully, Alice laid her hand on her belly. Beautiful.

'Oh,' Elspeth gasped, eyes wide. 'Did you feel that?'

Alice shook her head. Elspeth spontaneously moved Alice's hand to the side and they both waited. A light fluttering soon pushed against Alice's hand.

The baby. Kicking.

An overwhelming sense of awe and joy filled Alice's heart. 'Please, let me help you both,' the words spilled out from her.

'Okay,' Elspeth agreed, her voice full of sorrow. 'I'm afraid I don't have much time though.'

Reluctantly, Alice withdrew her hand. 'I think it would help if you tell me everything, then we can work out what you're going to need.'

She didn't miss Elspeth's hesitation, the pause which

allowed her time to weigh up her options, then slowly Elspeth began her story.

Alice wasn't sure if Elspeth had told her everything, yet it felt complete.

Elspeth sagged back into the bench. She looked... different all of a sudden, lighter perhaps, Alice mused. With a renewed sense of purpose, Alice rifled round in her handbag before pulling her phone. She tapped away for a moment, then turned to Elspeth.

'You do realise...' she began, 'that until things are changed here, once you leave you won't be able to come back?'

Elspeth's eyes glistened with tears as she said, 'Yes.'

Such a lot to deal with and to do it all alone must be unbearable, Alice acknowledged sadly, her heart going out to this young beautiful girl.

Offering a little encouraging smile, Alice said, 'I know that will be difficult for you, but once you're out of the country, somewhere safe, you'll be able to truly enjoy your pregnancy.'

Alice turned her attention back to her phone, not because she needed to, she had already found what she was searching for, but because she sensed that Elspeth required a moment.

Finally, when she was sure Elspeth was ready, she held her phone out to her.

Taking it, a look of confusion quickly creased Elspeth's face. Her eyes darting from the picture to Alice and back again. 'That is my house in Italy,' Alice clarified, 'and it is yours for as long as you need it.'

Elspeth's eyebrows arched high and her eyes widened in disbelief. 'Are you sure?'

'Of course. In fact, you would be doing me a favour. I do

worry about it, sitting empty for most of the year. Some years I don't even manage to get out there.'

Elspeth took Alice's hand, grasping it between her own. 'Thank you,' she offered, her voice barely a whisper. 'Obviously, it would only be temporary, until I find us somewhere more permanent to stay.'

'As I said, it's yours for as long as you want it,' Alice reiterated, swallowing down her own tears. She was finally able to help. 'Now,' she said, squaring her shoulders, 'getting you out of the country, that could be the tricky bit if the police are still interested in you, but it just so happens that I might know someone who can help.'

32

ARTIE

MAY 10TH 2035

The sound of Alexa playing in the kitchen pulled at Artie's attention, like an invisible string being tugged.

Curious, he padded downstairs.

In the kitchen, he was greeted by the sight of Elspeth, her back to him, swaying happily to the upbeat sounds of Bruno Mars as she stirred a pan on the hob.

Like ships passing in the night, Artie had barely seen Elspeth for several days. He had wanted to tell her about the police, to warn her that she was being followed, but as obviously as they had been there, they were now gone. Artie suspected that they may have found another lead, a reason to suspend their surveillance of Elspeth. And even though he should tell her, even though he knew it was information she needed, he couldn't burst whatever happiness she was clearly experiencing at this moment. This rare and wonderful moment.

Instead, he had to swallow down the overwhelming urge to move behind her, to lay his hands on her hips and kiss her cheek. His face flushed red from the intimacy of his thoughts.

He waited, not wanting to disturb her.

'Hey! You made me jump,' she scolded him playfully,

turning to see him leaning casually against the door frame. 'How long have you been standing there?'

'Not long,' he lied. 'You seem happy?' he said, unmoving, wary of dispelling the atmosphere.

'I am.' She smiled, resting with her back against the kitchen counter.

Her burgeoning bump took him by surprise. In her clingy summer dress, he could see the full swell of her stomach.

'I know, he's growing quickly,' Elspeth said, reading his expression. He watched as she ran her hands in circles all over her bump.

'He?' Artie repeated cautiously, fighting the urge to go and place his hands on top of hers. Pregnancy suited her. She was stunning.

'I think he's a he.' Elspeth shrugged lightly, her cheeks reddening. 'Is that silly?'

Moving forward, as though being pulled by a magnet, Artie found himself standing shoulder to shoulder with her, his stance a mirror image of hers. He smiled. 'No, that's not silly at all.'

She beamed up at him, her lips lush and full. He desperately wanted to kiss them.

'So why are you so happy?' he asked, trying to distract himself from his inappropriate thoughts.

'Because I've got a plan.' Elspeth turned back towards the bubbling pan.

Artie stiffened, his face instantly unreadable. 'Really?' he asked, his voice low and steady, in contrast to the whirling of his mind. *The father?* Anger was rolling off of him in waves. He suspected that if that was the case, it would be a flawed plan. He would likely be putting Elspeth and the baby at risk.

'Yes,' she reassured him, her voice overly bright. 'A friend has offered us a place to stay for a while.'

'I would have helped you.' He forced the words out, his gaze fixed on the wall.

She turned to him. He felt her body press against his side, her hand resting on his upper arm. His body tingled in reaction to the contact, like fireworks crackling under his skin. 'I know you would have.' She looked up at him, a note of sadness creeping into her voice.

'Then let me, please,' he pleaded, his eyes meeting hers, his hand encompassing hers on his arm. The heat was almost unbearable, her closeness dizzying. Her face was mere inches from his.

Artie's instincts kicked in, demanding him to move away, that he put some space between them, he didn't listen. He leant in closer. The warmth of her breath was intoxicating. He drank her in. Desire took over, he couldn't fight it any longer, not if he was about to lose her.

Tentatively, his lips brushed lightly against hers.

When she didn't pull away, he pressed harder. Her other hand suddenly came to rest on his chest, above his heart, as she kissed him back, softly at first but then with such urgency. A moan escaped her lips then and her mouth parted, her tongue searching for his. His fingers wound their way into her hair. Every fibre of his being felt suddenly alive, it was like being woken from a long and heavy sleep. He never wanted it to end.

'Hello?' Brooke's high-pitched voice called from the front door.

'Shit,' Artie growled as Elspeth pulled away guiltily.

He followed her with his eyes as she quickly grabbed at her jumper on the counter, swiftly tugging it on to conceal her secret. Artie didn't move, didn't trust himself. Instead, he savoured the lingering taste of her on his lips.

He eyed Elspeth, anticipating the telltale signs of regret, for a flicker of emotion that told him it was a mistake. Nervously, she tucked a strand of hair behind her ear before she looked up at him from under her long lashes. He held his breath and she held his stare. Then she smiled.

His heart skipped a beat. And he exhaled. He breathed out all his fears, all his anxiety, all those confused feelings. She felt the same.

'There you two are,' Brooke chirped, poking her head into the kitchen. 'Ellie, you look hot, you should get that jumper off.'

Her cheeks were definitely flushed. *Did I do that?* he wondered excitedly.

'Um, Artie, can you give me a hand with my bags, please?' Brooke asked before turning away, not waiting for his response.

Sighing loudly, he pushed himself away from the counter. *Damn Brooke.*

He moved into the hallway to find several shopping bags dumped by the front door.

With hands laden, Artie swung Brooke's shopping onto the kitchen counter, his eyes instantly searching Elspeth out. She was sat at the table, her gaze already trained on him.

'Town was heaving,' Brooke moaned, hanging her bag on the back of a chair.

For a moment, Artie wondered how it was that Brooke was completely blind to Elspeth's pregnancy, it was so obvious, wasn't it? Elspeth was practically glowing.

Then he realised. *Clever girl.* He chuckled. Elspeth was using the table as her camouflage, she was leaning forward with her chin resting on her upturned palms. Artie grinned. Her bump was completely hidden like that. Maybe it was only obvious because he knew, because he was looking for it.

But his joy, his happiness, was short lived as the reality of Elspeth's words sunk in, settling heavily on his heart. She was leaving.

Surely, after their kiss, that changed things, didn't it?

Perhaps he could go with her, or at least know where she was going? He could join her?

He knew that she had to leave, especially with the police sniffing around, but he'd still been holding on to the idea that he would be the one to assist her, the one to take her away.

He had so many questions to ask her, so much that needed to be said, shared.

'Can you pop these in the fridge,' Brooke asked, thrusting some packets at him. Distracted, he did as he was told.

'What's the matter?' Brooke was looking at him with a frown.

'What?' Artie asked.

'Your frown, what's wrong?' Brooke clarified.

Swiftly his eyes flicked to Elspeth, her face etched with concern too. 'Oh, I was just thinking about my work project,' he lied easily.

'Having problems?' Brooke enquired, a note of interest in her voice.

For God's sake. Normally she doesn't give a shit about my work, but of course today she's bothered. 'I have a client I want to help, but they're not very receptive. But I'm hopeful that I can convince them to let me guide them,' he finally responded, his gaze purposefully drifting to Elspeth. This time she didn't meet his stare, understanding that his words were meant for her ears.

Surely she knows that she can trust me. But... what if that's the issue, trusting me? Or perhaps she doesn't want it to be me who helps her? He replayed their kiss in his head.

No, I didn't imagine it, she kissed me back. He had felt her need, her desire, it had mirrored his. Then why was she being so difficult?

'Do you want to talk about it?' Brooke persevered.

'No, but thanks. I'm sure with time, they'll realise how useful I can be.'

From behind the table, Elspeth stood suddenly. 'I forgot, I said I'd give my mum a call. Can you turn my sauce off, please,' she said to no one in particular, her gaze firmly fixed on the floor.

'Okay,' Brooke replied, moving to the hob.

With Brooke's back turned, Artie watched as Elspeth made a quick retreat. Her name was on his tongue, he wanted to call after her, but stopped himself, not wanting Brooke to see, to know. Elspeth didn't even glance back.

After a minute Brooke headed upstairs too, leaving Artie alone.

A snake of doubt unexpectedly slithered into his thoughts. *Should I have kissed her? Did I take advantage? But she kissed me back, didn't she?* Soon, what had been the most perfect of moments for him, had been tainted by his worrying. *Maybe I overstepped with the kiss, but she can't leave, not like this.*

He thought about her new identities, which were stored safely in the false bottom of his desk. *Old habits die hard.* He smiled weakly to himself.

They were some of the best forgeries he'd seen, and he'd seen his fair share. *Maybe I should just give them to her now, that way she will be able to move around unseen. But who is helping her? Can she really trust them? Where is she going? Does it even matter?*

His thoughts soured. *Elspeth may not want me involved but it's likely that she'll need a new identity, that she'll need the anonymity that a different alias would afford her, at least until she's out of the country.* He knew he was going to give her the brown envelope filled with three new lives. Even if in allowing her to escape, she disappeared from him too.

But, just perhaps, she'd change her mind.

33

SAM

MAY 12TH 2035

S am and Hudson stood proudly at the front of the briefing room, picture-covered whiteboard behind them. Eight uniformed officers sat eagerly before them, awaiting instruction.

Sam had pressed hard for the warrant, which she had tucked securely in her pocket. She hadn't been sure Smithers was going to come through, but Hudson had really worked some magic, appeasing whatever reservations Smithers had, which she knew were likely to be more about her than the case itself.

'Right. Listen up,' Sam shouted across the din of voices. The officers quietened down. 'I'm sure you've read the brief, but just to clarify... This is a multi-occupancy house. We are to apprehend only Miss Elspeth Adams,' she pointed to a blown-up picture of Elspeth taken from her Facebook account, 'however, the whole house is to be searched.'

Her eyes swept over the officers. Sam registered that half of them were women, which pleased her. Men had dominated the profession for far too long, besides women were more than capable of doing this job, in fact Sam would bet that they were even better in many circumstances.

'In terms of evidence, I want anything indicating a pregnancy or a baby. I also want all her devices seized as her search history may yield something vital.'

Sam looked at Hudson, eyebrows raised. She was silently granting him permission to take over, to add anything he felt was imperative at this stage.

He cleared his throat. 'Miss Adams is believed to be pregnant, so please do treat her with care.'

Good point, Sam acknowledged. The last thing they needed was a complaint being made.

Again Sam looked to her audience. 'Any questions?' When no one responded, she clapped her hands together sharply. 'Right then, let's get ready.'

At six thirty in the morning, the odds of Elspeth being at home were tipped in their favour and that helped Sam to relax. She wasn't nervous exactly, more excitedly on edge, like all the fibres in her body were positively charged.

Hudson had insisted on driving, probably to keep himself occupied, which left Sam sitting idly in the passenger seat. Although she was aware that this was his first raid in her team, Sam couldn't bring herself to make pointless chat on the journey. She was focused, her mind surprisingly calm and she wanted it to remain that way.

The silence in the car was palpable, Sam ignored it.

Within minutes, Hudson was pulling up behind the police van and two patrol cars.

The sun, already high in the sky, illuminated their presence. There were no shadows to mask them. Thankfully, the road was deserted. The last thing Sam wanted to deal with was an audience or a social media frenzy.

Huddled together around the police van, Sam spoke in rushed whispers. 'You two, take the alley down the side and cover the back gate. The rest of us are going through the front door.'

'Rammit?' a sturdy-looking officer asked, a glint of excitement in his eyes.

Sam nodded. He turned to the back of the van and hauled out the scratched, solid battering ram.

'Right, let's do this.'

Like a black mist, the police, flanked by Sam and Hudson, descended on the unremarkable terraced house, squeezed between a row of other unremarkable houses.

The large officer with the battering ram took his position in front of the pale blue front door. He looked back to Sam for confirmation.

She dipped her head slightly.

With a splintering crash, Rammit smashed against the front door with such force that the reverberating sound echoed like thunder in a summer storm.

Wood fragments burst out like rain, littering the floor. The door was hanging on its hinges. With a final, strategic blow, the door collapsed.

'POLICE! We have a search warrant.' Several officers hollered warnings as they pushed through into the hall, Hudson hot on their heels.

Sam, however, halted in the doorway, as her team infiltrated every room of the house, savouring the moment. Her heart was pounding and her breathing had quickened from the adrenaline coursing through her body.

This second, this uniquely rare second, epitomised why Sam loved what she did. This job was her everything. Without it, she wouldn't know what to do, or who she was.

Sam sucked in a deep breath, dispelling her thoughts, then stepped carefully over the splintered remains of the door.

'What the fuck's going on!' a blonde woman, wearing an oversized T-shirt, demanded as she was marched down the stairs by a female officer. 'What the fuck have you done to my door?'

she shrieked, seeing the wooden remains scattered across the floor.

Sam motioned towards the doorway leading into the lounge with a nod. The officer guided the protesting blonde into the lounge and indicated for her to sit on the sofa.

'I'm not sitting down, not until someone tells me what's going on!' she yelled, her eyes wide with anger and confusion.

'Take a seat for a minute, then someone will come and speak to you,' the officer said, her experienced calmness rolling off of her in waves. The woman, although still irate, obeyed.

Sam strode further along the hallway and into the kitchen. She rocked back on her heels, scanning the room. She didn't know what she was looking for, she was just... looking.

She took in the family-sized dining table, the full fruit bowl on the counter, the pictures of nights out and nights in pinned to the fridge door. Lightly, her fingers tugged at a photo of all three housemates. Miss Adams and Miss Russell smiling, glassy-eyed at the camera, Mr Jones smiling at Miss Adams. *They have to know, how could they not?* She folded the picture in half and tucked it in her back pocket.

'Stop resisting,' a stern voice barked.

Sam turned to see two of her biggest coppers, battling to restrain a shirtless male. With his tattooed arms already cuffed behind his back, he twisted and pushed against his restraints, his tight muscles straining.

Sam couldn't ignore the look of absolute hatred burning in his eyes as he was forced into the lounge. A cold shiver ran down Sam's spine, like he had just danced on her grave.

She knew the occupants of the house, had meticulously checked their backgrounds, neither had a record, but that look, that loathing...

'She's not here.' Hudson marched towards Sam with his

hands shoved deep in his trouser pockets and a perplexed expression twisting at his features.

'Damn!' Sam had been so confident, had been sure that they'd get her. 'Get everyone to search the property. We'll find out what those two know.'

Sam stood in front of the leggy blonde, Brooke Russell, and the shirtless man, Artie Jones.

Everything about her demeanour was designed to be intimidating, from her squared shoulders to her pinched lips, which was just what she wanted. She wanted them to be on edge, she wanted them to talk.

'Where's Miss Adams?' Sam asked directly, her focus currently on Brooke.

'What?' Brooke responded but her attention was turned towards the officer rummaging through her cupboards. Sam clicked her fingers in front of her face. 'Pay attention, please. Miss Adams. Where is she?'

Before Brooke had a chance to answer, Artie cut in. 'I want to see your warrant!' he spat, venom lacing his words.

Sam's eyes narrowed. *One too many cop shows?* she wondered, but then doubt crept in. He was too self-assured, too prepared, for her liking. He had a confidence which came with knowledge, experience even... *Who is this guy?*

Slowly, she reached into her pocket, her mind still whirling with confusion. Her fingers grasped hold of the folded piece of paper bringing her back to the moment.

Don't overthink it. He's clean, you checked.

Sam pulled it out and opened it. She gazed over the words, all for effect of course, she knew that every t had been crossed and every i dotted. Finally, she held it in front of Artie's face. 'I'm sure you'll find everything in order.'

She kept it there for the briefest of seconds, before whipping it away dramatically. She didn't have to look at him to know that pure rage continued to burn there. Sam, however, couldn't meet his stare, not yet. The coldness was still thawing from her spine.

'Miss Russell, where is Miss Adams?'

'Elspeth? Why? What's this about?' Brooke stuttered, looking up at Sam.

'We have reason to believe that Miss Adams was involved in a theft from the local hospital, do you know anything about that?'

Sam watched the rainbow of emotions pass across Miss Russell's face: confusion, shock, disbelief then... understanding. She knew something, Sam realised.

'Theft?' Brooke mimicked.

'Yes. Tell me what you know.'

Brooke's gaze nervously slid to her housemate, but he was looking ahead, at Sam. She could feel his hostility boring into the side of her face.

'Well,' Brooke began apprehensively, 'I don't know anything, not really but...' She bit her lower lip.

Sam watched as the pretty woman internally debated whether or not she should continue. Finally, she released her lip. 'Elspeth did mention that there had been a theft. Not that she said she had anything to do with it, of course,' she added quickly. 'She said a pregnancy test had been stolen, but surely all of this,' she waved her hand, indicating to the disarray caused by the team of unwanted officers in her home, 'isn't all about a stolen test, is it?'

'Have you noticed anything unusual in Miss Adams' behaviour recently?' Sam pressed, ignoring Brooke's question.

'No!' Mr Jones hissed, too quickly.

'No,' Miss Russell agreed, although the uncertainty in her voice was unmistakable.

Sam waited, she didn't fill the silence. Sometimes, silence was the most powerful weapon she possessed.

'I mean, she has been... well... withdrawn. I don't know, she's such a bubbly person normally, but recently, she had seemed so...' Brooke put her head in her hands, 'isolated.'

Because she's been hiding a mighty big secret from you, Sam thought. She turned her attention to Mr Jones. She met his hostility head on, but flinched. She cursed herself for it. *What is it with this guy?*

'Mr Jones, have you noticed anything unusual? A change in routine perhaps, or as Miss Russell has indicated, a withdrawal?'

He scowled, his hands still fastened behind his back. He shook his head just once.

Sam's brow creased. *Fine, if that's how you want it.* 'I have reason to believe that not only is Miss Adams responsible for the theft, but that she is also illegally pregnant.'

Miss Russell stilled, her eyes widening.

Okay, she didn't know, but Mr Jones, his face remained unreadable, like a book of empty white pages.

'Pregnant,' Brooke said, stunned.

Sam spotted Hudson step forward. 'Mr Jones, were you aware of Elspeth's pregnancy?' he asked, his voice coaxing.

'If she didn't know,' he growled indicating towards Brooke, his eyes never leaving Sam, 'then what makes you think I would know. Now unless you're planning on arresting me, get these handcuffs off me.'

The two detectives exchanged a look. Sam dipped her head slightly. Hudson stepped forward and deftly removed the cuffs from Mr Jones' wrists.

Sam watched as Artie rubbed his wrists, as if he were trying to rub the memory of the cuffs away.

She pursed her lips tightly. 'My team are currently searching the house for evidence. If you know of anything, then I suggest you say now.'

Sam noticed Artie's attention flicker towards the doorway,

then just as quickly it was back on her again, leaving her wondering whether she had imagined it. But... what if he was hiding something? Did he know, or was there something else? Drugs perhaps.

'Stay here with them,' she instructed Hudson as she marched out of the lounge.

Hand braced against the stair bannister, she sucked in a deep breath, trying to clear her head. His relentless stare had unnerved her, it was like he was trying to burn a hole into her very core.

Come on, focus. You have a job to do.

She headed upstairs, following her instinct. There was something off about Mr Jones and she wanted to know what it was. Fury, probably more than was warranted, fuelled her.

Once at the top of the stairs, she passed the first two bedrooms, girl's rooms, with little more than a glance, before moving on to the one obviously belonging to Mr Jones. Two officers were already searching the sparse room.

'Anything?' she demanded, announcing her presence.

'Nothing yet, guv.'

'I'll finish off here, you two can help downstairs.'

Alone in Artie's room, Sam sat on the edge of his small double bed. Apart from a decent-looking computer set-up, which was to be expected for a web designer, the room left little to be desired. With only a chest of drawers and a lonely book on the small nightstand, the room was devoid of all personality.

If he wanted, he could just disappear without a trace, Sam realised, an edge of nervousness creeping in.

'Don't wait for your world to change. Change it yourself,' Sam read out loud, his book in her hand. 'Self-help shit,' she huffed, throwing it back on the nightstand.

With meticulous haste, Sam set to searching.

Firstly, she hunted through the drawers, running her hand

along the underside and rear of every drawer. Then she threw back his duvet and pillows, her hands pressing firmly against the mattress, feeling for anything unusual.

Nothing, there was nothing.

Slowly, she moved to his workstation. Expensive, she appreciated.

Sam wasn't up to date with all the latest technology, preferring her twelve-year-old laptop which did everything that she needed a laptop to do, but even she knew this was good quality equipment.

She started in the two drawers. Aside from a few pens, some blank CDs and a couple of notebooks filled with sketches of what she presumed were website logos, both were barren. With more care, she fanned out the small stack of papers on his desk. Designs, more logos and a few sketches.

'Useless,' she hissed, her hand lashing out. The papers slowly fluttered to the floor, like oversized snowflakes.

She stalked out of Artie's room and strode back to the middle room.

'Have you found anything?' she demanded of no one in particular. All three officers paused their search to look up at her.

A clear plastic bag was then dangled in front of her face by a young male officer who Sam hadn't worked with previously. 'Laptop,' he confirmed.

'Anything else? Baby clothes, nappies, pregnancy vitamins, anything like that?'

The officer slowly turned his head from side to side, as if conscious of receiving a tongue lashing. 'There was a suitcase, stowed under the bed. Few items of clothing in it. Do you want us to bag it?'

'Yes.'

Shit, shit and double shit. Was she planning on absconding?

Or was that her labour bag? Sam whirled, heading back downstairs.

I want some fucking answers and I'm going to get them.

'Right,' she said with false confidence as she entered the lounge. 'We're starting to bag up our evidence.' Sam observed Miss Russell's nostrils flare in surprise, as though she had just had a whiff of something rather unpleasant. 'I appreciate that Miss Adams is your friend, and helping a friend in need is commendable,' she continued smoothly, 'however, in this instance, your friend is a criminal and that would make you an accomplice,' she said slowly, allowing the truth of her words to settle in. Sam turned to Hudson, who was standing in front of the large bay window. 'How many years would they get for aiding and abetting?' she asked, waving her hand with a flourish, as if she were conducting an orchestra, towards a suddenly-ashen-looking Miss Russell.

'Oh, five minimum,' Hudson replied unfalteringly, understanding Sam's tactics.

Sam waited, eyebrows raised.

'Honestly, I didn't know,' Brooke said, her voice barely audible.

Sam sighed dramatically. 'Well, can you tell me where she is now?'

Miss Russell's face lit up. 'She's at her parents. She stayed there last night,' she said brightly, as if she were pleased to be helping, unaware that her information could lead to Miss Adams' arrest.

Mr Jones tore his gaze from Sam to stare in disbelief and contempt at his housemate.

Sensing his glare, Sam watched as Miss Russell shrugged in response.

'What? I don't want to go to prison,' she mumbled, although an edge of guilt had obviously crept in.

Sam, eager to move, turned her attention to Hudson. She jerked her chin towards the window, indicating that they should get going if they wanted to catch their suspect before she evaded them again.

He nodded.

'My colleague here,' Sam indicated to a serious-looking officer, 'will take all of your details. We may need to talk to you again. Thank you for your co-operation.'

Without looking back, Sam walked out of the lounge and towards the front door. She knew that Hudson was right behind her as she left the property, Miss Russell's irritating demands for compensation drifting away on the breeze.

34

ELSPETH

MAY 12TH 2035

The baby was screaming. A persistent shrill cry which was slowly boring a hole into her exhausted brain.

Nothing Elspeth did seemed to soothe the baby.

'Please stop crying,' she begged, jiggling the fractious bundle in her arms.

The baby's breaths were ragged and the screams were becoming increasingly hoarse. Elspeth bounced up and down on the balls of her feet, whilst incessantly shushing the irate infant.

She was silently praying, wishing for some divine intervention to stop the baby's wailing but instead those little lungs gulped down more air, ready for the next onslaught.

It didn't come.

The heartbeat of silence stretched out, the emptiness of sound deafening. With cold fear, Elspeth stilled. In her arms, the baby's mouth was open in a scream that didn't appear, the bright blue eyes lifeless...

The baby was dead.

Her baby was dead.

Elspeth woke instantly, a sob escaping her lips.

Her T-shirt, damp with sweat, clung uncomfortably to her body. Her hair hung in matted tangles around her clammy face. It was just a nightmare, she reassured herself, although the ghost of her dream lingered.

On the bedside cabinet, her phone rang loudly. Dazed, she reached for it. Unknown number. She didn't answer. Finally it stopped, the screen revealing eight missed calls and a text message, all from the same number. She clicked on the message.

It's me. Answer your phone. Artie x

Her nightmare started to recede into the recesses of her mind as she focused on the kiss at the end of his message. She couldn't help but wonder what it meant. A year ago – shit had it really been that long? A year earlier, he had walked away not wanting to pursue a relationship, not wanting to even acknowledge what had happened between them, what Elspeth believed to be the most natural of steps for them to take.

Now, though, it was as if he had changed his mind, as if he wanted something more from her. He had kissed her. She sighed loudly.

She knew that their kiss was the reason she'd decided to stay with her parents. She knew she couldn't resist him, couldn't deny her feelings for him. But she also couldn't face any further heartache.

She looked at the 'x' again.

Had he added it purposefully or was it accidental, finger memory taking over when he wrote the text? She pictured him debating his decision, his finger poised over the screen. Had he erased it before adding it again? Her heart fluttered.

The ridiculousness, no, the childishness of her thoughts didn't escape her. Here she was nearly five months pregnant, facing a lifetime in prison if she got caught and she was scrutinising the meaning of a text.

'Just call him back already,' she chided herself, scraping a stray hair out of her sleep-heavy eyes.

Before her finger could hit the call button, the phone rang again.

The same unfamiliar number as before.

'Hello?' she croaked, answering the call.

'Ellie,' Artie's silky voice sighed, heavy with relief.

'Artie, it's...' she quickly checked the time on the old-fashioned alarm clock next to her bed, 'it's five past seven, is everything all right?'

'No, no it's not!' The sheer terror coating every word he said had her sitting straight. 'I need you to listen to me very carefully–'

A cold dread crept into her body. 'What's happened?'

'They're coming for you, Ellie.'

'Wh–'

'The police. They were following you the other day, but I wasn't sure... They've raided the house, they know you're pregnant and they know you're at your parents.' His voice was tight, as if he was battling to keep his emotions from boiling over. 'Ellie, you need to get a few things together and leave. Right now.'

Elspeth covered her mouth with her hand to stop the panic from bursting out of her, like a swarm of locusts ready to devour everything. They were coming. Here. The thought of her parents, her hard-working, honest parents... A sob escaped.

'Ellie,' Artie's voice came quickly, breaking through her spiralling terror, 'I know you're scared but I need you to focus. You're going to need to move quickly. Can you do that?'

'Yes,' she choked, trying to pull herself together.

'Okay, good. You'll be okay. I want you to write this number down, then turn your phone off. Take it with you but don't turn it on again. Grab your things, whatever you have with you. Get in your car and drive west,' he instructed calmly yet firmly.

'West?'

'Yes, head to Southampton. Whatever you do, do *not* stop unless you absolutely have to. Do you understand me? I mean it, Ellie, don't stop and don't turn your phone on again. When you get to Southampton, you're going to need to buy a new SIM card, just get anything cheap, anything. Then call me on this number.' She was struggling to focus. She was a criminal and she was about to go on the run, to hide, but...

'Then what?' Elspeth said, more to herself than Artie.

The reality hit her, she doubled over on the bed, like she'd been punched in the stomach. Who was she kidding? There was no way out of this, she had been so naive to think she could get away with this. What kind of life could she offer her baby? They would always be on the run, she would be forever looking over her shoulder. She would never be able to register her baby's birth, could never take him to the doctors, would never be able to send him to school.

'Ellie? I need you to start moving,' Artie encouraged, when she didn't respond. She was petrified. 'Please, Ellie, if not for me, do it for your baby, your baby deserves to be with you and you want to be with your baby, don't you? Think of that, okay. You can do this, I know you can. Please, Ellie.'

The pleading in his voice, his words, cracked through the veil of ice holding her. 'Okay.'

Artie sighed with what sounded like relief. 'Okay, good. Now go!' He hung up.

Slowly, Elspeth climbed off the bed. Her limbs heavy and her head foggy, she felt as though she was wading through water. Every movement taking twice as much energy.

Pulling on the previous day's clothes, she grabbed together the few belongings she had brought with her. A weekend with her parents, probably the last weekend she would spend with them before she left for Italy.

With everything bundled back into her overnight bag, Elspeth hunted through the desk for a pen and paper. She tried not to think about the hours that she'd spent sat at this very desk, whilst revising for her exams, for her future. She had always known what she wanted to do with her life and she had worked damned hard to get there too. She couldn't afford to go down that road now, she didn't know how much time she had.

In the next drawer, she found what she needed. Carefully, she copied down two phone numbers. She buried the scrap of paper in her pocket, before turning off her phone and throwing it in her handbag. Then she scribbled a note for her parents; brief but heartfelt. There was no point lying, she realised, the police would be there soon enough and would no doubt tell them everything.

With one final sweeping glance of her bedroom, Elspeth crept downstairs, placed the note beside the kettle, then left.

Tears were running freely as she climbed into her car. Would they be disappointed with her, disown her, or would they understand? Elspeth hoped that, one day, she would be able to explain, to tell her parents how the love she felt for her child had been more important than anything else, had been worth risking everything for.

Cowardly as it may seem, she was running, and she would continue running, for as long as was necessary to keep them both safe and together.

Briefly she touched her bump, and sighed through her nose. 'It's just you and me.'

Starting the car, Elspeth cautiously drove out of her parents' cul-de-sac.

On high alert, she sat rigid as she turned onto the next road, fearful that at any moment a police car would appear. At the next junction, Elspeth turned right.

She exhaled loudly through her nose. With a final glance in her rear-view mirror, the village soon disappeared into the distance, along with everything she had ever known. There would be no going back now, or ever.

The small life inside of her, pressed firmly against her side, a comforting reminder of what she was fighting for. Determination spread through her body. She would go to the ends of the earth for her baby, to hold him tightly in her arms.

Never again will you allow yourself to be vulnerable. The promise she'd made herself, echoed in her mind, like a reassuring mantra.

You can do this. You are doing this.

With the endless road laid out in front of her, Elspeth turned on the radio, an unexpected calmness washing over her.

Nearing Southampton, the traffic slowed to a crawl as miles of roadworks disrupted the rush-hour flow of cars. The sun, high in the cloudless sky, was burning brightly.

Elspeth had the air con on, a stream of cool air blowing directly on her to counteract the already stifling heat of the car. Her T-shirt, wet with sweat, clung to her back. She sat forward slightly to avoid resting against the seat.

The journey had been smooth, so far, allowing Elspeth time to consider her next move.

She was hoping to find a superstore on the outskirts of Southampton. Reluctant to drive into the city, she was aware that there would be more cameras and she didn't want to leave a trail for the police to follow if she could help it.

Elspeth had also been thinking about Artie. She had

followed his advice, driven the way he'd told her to, too dazed to think of anywhere else to go. But she had to start thinking for herself now. She couldn't rely on him, couldn't afford to be so vulnerable, not if she was going to protect herself and her baby. She also reasoned that the fewer people who knew her plans the better.

Once she had a new phone, she would call Alice. She had already accepted her offer of a place to stay. Now all she needed was to work out how she was going to get there. She would drive all the way to Italy if that's what it took. Yes, she'd have to call Artie at some point, to explain, but she didn't want to think about that just yet.

A movement to her right caught Elspeth's attention. The sleek black estate idling next to her, in the stationary traffic, was edging away from her slightly. Its bumper creeping closer to the Mini in front of it. Then a flash of blue in her rear-view mirror had Elspeth turning in her seat. Behind her, the two lanes of cars were parting, as though undertaking a synchronised dance, to allow a gleaming police car, with flashing lights adorning its roof, through.

Elspeth's heart leapt into her throat. Fear ripped through her body. How had they found her so quickly?

Eyes scanning the road ahead, Elspeth was stuck, like a rat in a trap, with no way out.

She knew she looked like a deer in headlights, knew she had to calm herself down.

Sucking in big deep breaths of air, Elspeth forced her racing heart to slow.

Although her body was rigid, her eyes were frantically searching, scanning for a way out. The cordoned-off lane to her left was deserted, likely in preparation for maintenance work. But it would provide her with an escape route. Up ahead, she was confident that she could make out the curve of a slip road. If she could reach it, she might just stand a chance.

With another glance in her mirror, the police car was ever nearing.

Cautiously, Elspeth mirrored the surrounding vehicles, edging her car to the left, in the hope of blending in. The siren wailed loudly as it crept closer.

Keeping her hands braced firmly against the steering wheel, Elspeth's knuckles whitened under the pressure.

She could easily read the licence plate of the police car as it continued to close the distance. She shifted her car into drive, the engine ticking over silently, her foot poised above the accelerator, ready to flee.

Elspeth fixed her gaze on the cruiser in her mirror.

It closed in.

Her foot touched the rubber of the pedal.

The officer in the passenger seat seemed to look right at her reflecting stare, their eyes meeting briefly. Elspeth's heart paused. The oppressive heat in the car suddenly swelled, a bead of sweat ran down between her breasts.

The police car, siren still blaring, pulled level.

She swallowed hard.

Then with morbid curiosity, she found herself turning her head a fraction. To look.

The officer closest to her was listening intently to the radio pinned to her chest.

Then, as if feeling the weight of Elspeth's stare, she looked up. Their eyes locked. A flicker of something, recognition perhaps, flashed across the officer's face. She opened her mouth as if to say something, words forming on the edge of her lips.

Elspeth couldn't look away as her foot quivered against the accelerator, the engine purring slightly, when the officer's partner said something, drawing her attention away. The officer's words were instantly forgotten.

A brief exchange occurred between the two coppers, the female officer leant forward, pressing a button on the dashboard.

The screeching siren instantly changed. A more violent, persistent screaming was emitted as the police car pulled forward with as much speed afforded to it by the narrow path. The officer didn't so much as glance back at Elspeth.

With the coppers' rear bumper in front of her and getting further away, a bubble of nervous laughter burst out from her.

'They weren't here for you, it was a false alarm.' She giggled uncomfortably. Time to get off the motorway, she realised, her heart still thumping fast.

The car park was busy, which Elspeth considered, eventually deciding it was probably better that way. She didn't know what she was doing, not really, but had watched enough police programmes to be reassured by the bustle within the shop.

With a baseball cap, retrieved from the back seat of her car, pulled low over her eyes and her hair tucked within its confines, Elspeth strode swiftly into the supermarket.

Get in, get out, she told herself.

Heading into the depths of the store, bag strategically held in front of her blossoming bump, she weaved past the casual shoppers.

Tucked away in the furthest corner was a section dedicated to all things electronic. Elspeth's eyes darted across the rows of televisions, sound equipment and sports watches before settling on a selection of mobile phones.

Perfect. Her shoulders relaxed a little with relief.

With her head down, she quickly scanned the choice of

phones and SIM cards. There was too much choice. Did it matter which one? Were any of them traceable? *Just pick one*, she scolded, conscious that the minutes were ticking by whilst she was debating her choices.

Her fingers circled round a card at random, when a high-pitched voice from behind startled her. 'Can I help you with anything?'

Elspeth jerked around to find a greasy-looking teen with severe acne smiling broadly at her.

Misreading the look of worry which flashed across her features, he continued talking. 'There are a lot to choose from, aren't there? What do you need it to do?'

No, no, no. Her brain whirled. She didn't need this, someone who might be able to identify her. She held up the card in her hand. 'I'll take this one.' Her tone was intentionally clipped, hoping he'd get the message.

He looked at her choice, a frown wrinkling his raw-looking forehead. 'That is our most basic SIM card,' he said, patronisingly. 'The data package is very limited, if you regularly access the internet you'll end up getting charged.' He reached past her to unhook an orange card from the shelf. 'Can I recommend this one, it's a little more expensive but the data allowance is much better.'

For a moment, Elspeth considered yelling at him, an unnatural and unexpected fury suddenly building up in her gut, like molten lava in the belly of a volcano threatening to spew out. She wanted to scream at him, to shout that she didn't need his fucking help, that she wasn't some helpless little girl who didn't know what she was doing, even if that wasn't entirely truthful.

What would he do if she yelled that she was a criminal, on the run from the police, that in all likelihood the SIM card would only be used a handful of times whilst she attempted to evade the police before eventually skipping the country.

But... thinking better of it, she managed with some effort, to smother the burning embers inside her. Humiliating and terrifying this boy would only make her more memorable, she knew. Instead, she blew out her cheeks in surrender, replaced the SIM card in her hand and took the one the boy was still holding out to her.

'Thanks,' she said flatly. 'Where do I pay?'

Smiling wider than a Cheshire cat, probably at his inflated commission, he indicated to the till behind him. 'Just here.'

He scanned her purchase whilst Elspeth dug around for her purse. She was about to tap her bank card against the card reader, when she paused. *Would they be monitoring my bank accounts? Waiting for me to use them? Could they trace me to this location by a single purchase?*

With her doubt weighing heavily and the risk too significant, she slid the card back into her purse and instead paid with cash. The only cash she had.

'Have a great day.' The shop assistant smiled as Elspeth snatched up her purchase and quickly departed, keeping her head down until she reached the safety of her car.

With her old SIM card discarded in a bin, and the new one in its place, Elspeth dialled the first number on the scrap of paper.

35

ALICE

MAY 12TH 2035

'Hello?' the voice said after several rings.

'Hi, it's Elspeth.'

'Elspeth! Hi. Um... just give me a minute, hang on...' Covering the speaker of her mobile, Alice motioned to Mark that she was stepping outside. He raised his eyebrows. Alice pretended not to notice.

She hadn't found the courage to tell Mark about Elspeth and the promise she'd made to help her. She knew he'd disapprove. Besides, she had already considered all of the elements of the lecture he was sure to have given her and still decided that her actions were justified. So she'd decided not to involve him.

'How are you?' Alice asked gently, in the solitude of the coffee lounge.

'I've run out of time,' Elspeth said, the urgency in her voice unmissable.

'What's happened? Are you all right? Where are you?' The words tumbled out of Alice, a maternal instinct long since forgotten, rising to the surface, like a flower blooming after a harsh winter.

She listened intently as Elspeth sucked in a deep breath and then recounted her last few hours.

Only when Elspeth fell silent, did Alice speak. 'I think it's fair to say that things have just become more complicated. I wouldn't be surprised if they have already taken steps to prevent you from being able to leave the country.'

Alice was thinking out loud, she wasn't trying to frighten Elspeth any more than she already was, she was simply trying to work through the problem, taking into account all the variables. The raid indicated that the police knew something, that they had evidence perhaps to link Elspeth to the theft or worse, her pregnancy. They had enough to have issued an arrest warrant. If they hadn't already, they would soon realise that Elspeth had fled. She would be wanted.

'Any news from your guy?' Elspeth asked hopefully, breaking into Alice's thoughts.

'Not yet, but he hasn't failed to deliver before.'

Alice had provided her contact with everything he would need to supply a new passport for Elspeth, one which should allow her to travel, but Alice recognised that they couldn't wait too much longer, not least because of the increased risk for heavily pregnant women to fly.

'I guess I'm going to need to find somewhere to lie low then.' Elspeth sighed, her frustration evident. 'I can't use my bank cards or else they'll be able to find me. Alice, you have already offered me so much, done so much for me, but can you... will you...'

'Of course, whatever I can do to help,' Alice jumped in to save Elspeth the humiliation of having to ask. She would give Elspeth whatever she could to keep her and her baby safe, to give them a fighting chance of escaping. And really, what she had offered was so small, so insignificant in the grand scheme of things.

Alice had amassed wealth beyond that which she would ever have needed for herself, and she had no family to spoil, no partner to enjoy it with. No, she wanted to use her ill-gotten gains to enable a family to remain together, to cleanse her tarnished soul for all the pain she had caused.

'Thank you,' Elspeth said. 'I truly don't know what I would have done without you. And I will pay you back, every penny. I have savings, I just can't risk accessing them right now.'

'Please, Elspeth, don't worry about that,' Alice quickly retorted, uncomfortable with her praise. 'So we need to find you somewhere to stay for a day or two.'

'Yes. I'll look for a B&B, somewhere that I can keep myself tucked away, out of sight of prying eyes.'

'Actually...' Alice said slowly, her mind trying to keep up with her mouth. 'I might know somewhere you can stay. Let me look into something and I'll call you straight back.'

'I don't want–'

'You won't be putting me out, Elspeth.'

Elspeth simply said, 'Thank you.'

***

Mark raised his eyebrows again, as Alice walked back into the office. Or maybe they had remained like that since the phone rang, Alice mused, smiling to herself. Despite the urgency of the situation, she felt... hopeful. And really what else did she have, if she let them rob her of hope then they had already won, there would be nothing left to fight for. Alice was not the type of person inclined to giving up, to admitting defeat easily. No, she would rather stick two fingers up at them, the police, the government, the lot of them and battle through, finding another way. And that was exactly what they were going to do now.

'What was that all about?' Mark asked directly when he

realised that Alice was ignoring his first and more subtle attempt at questioning her.

Alice hadn't wanted to involve Mark, in part because of the headache it would cause, but also to protect him, her dearest friend. Now, though, she had little choice in the matter. She needed his help, or rather the keys to his lodge. In reality it wasn't as grand as it sounded, it was more of a static caravan than a lodge, but it was remote and empty, and that was the best way to protect Elspeth.

'Well,' Alice began a little sheepishly, 'I have been assisting a young lady who has recently found herself in difficulty, and that was her.'

'Assisting her how?' Trust Mark to be direct, she thought, not unkindly. Alice couldn't lie to him, couldn't even omit information, he knew her too well, recognised when there were gaps in her stories. That's what came from having known someone for longer than she cared to recall.

She wrinkled her nose up, preparing for a telling off.

'That bad?' Mark groaned.

'Her name is Elspeth,' Alice began, resigning herself to the fact that she would tell him everything. 'She's pregnant. Illegally.'

She watched as Mark's eyes widened and his mouth fell open. Alice felt her heart beat faster.

'I know what you're thinking, but–'

'No, Alice, you don't,' he said in a low growl. 'Even for you, this is a step too far. You do know that you'll go to prison for helping her, don't you?' he spat as he rose from his seat. 'Orchestrating the occasional protest is one thing, that's not necessarily illegal, but this, this definitely is. Do you understand that?' he demanded, his voice rising an octave as he paced in front of her.

Rarely had Alice seen Mark so riled and especially not with her. She put her hands up in mock surrender. 'I do understand, really I do,' she said calmly. She lowered her hands until they rested on her lap and Mark seemed to collect himself a little, enough that he sat down again. 'Please, let me explain?'

He nodded once, clearly not trusting himself to speak yet.

Alice didn't hold back, there was no point. She told him all she knew of Elspeth's story, and everything of her own overlapping story. She told him how she felt guilty and responsible, although he already knew that, and how helping Elspeth made her feel... better, like a better person. She wasn't sad as she explained nor did she cry but she couldn't miss the sympathetic tilt of Mark's head as she spoke earnestly, as she ran out of words.

He sighed before he spoke. 'Alice.' He placed his hand affectionately on her knee. Once upon a time she had selfishly wished he wasn't gay. It wasn't that she was necessarily attracted to him, although she couldn't deny that he was a handsome man. No, it was because she could be herself with Mark and he hadn't ever shied away from her. He had been there by her side even in her darkest days, in her ugliest depressed lows, when she couldn't even stand to look at herself and he had never walked away, never turned away from her, not once. *I hope now won't be that time.*

'I know that this has been a burden for you,' he continued, 'one that you've carried for too long, but...' He paused, trying to find the right words. 'But this is like hitting the self-destruct button, Alice. Yes, it was your, our, research which founded *The Law*, but those leaders, they are the responsible ones. You know that.' Mark sighed, aware that this was well-trodden ground between them.

'That may be, but she still needs help, Mark, now more than ever, and just because things have become... complicated, doesn't mean I should walk away.'

He blinked slowly whilst thinking. 'Okay, let's say for one

minute that I condone what you're doing, which I don't, but there is currently a pregnant girl in Southampton who is on the run from the police. The plan, correct me if I'm wrong, is to smuggle her out of the country on a forged passport which you are supplying, hopefully before the police track her down?' He raised his eyebrows, silently questioning if he had understood so far.

Alice nodded grimly. It sounded so much worse when he summarised it like that, she realised.

'So, as you are unsure how much longer the fake identification will–'

'Only a couple more days,' Alice interrupted, trying to inject some optimism into this bleak scenario he was painting.

'My apologies,' he said humourlessly. 'So until the passport is ready, where do you propose to hide the girl until she can escape to safer shores?'

It was Alice's turn to raise her eyebrows. 'Well...' she cleared her throat nervously, 'you know how you have that lovely lodge, in Dorset...'

'No! Absolutely not!' Mark was back on his feet again. 'Have you not heard a word I've been saying? Prison, Alice, that's where I'll end up for concealing her. Can you imagine me in a prison cell? I couldn't survive without my memory foam mattress and don't they sleep in bunk beds? No, definitely not. Also, what would I tell John? Do you mind if we house a fugitive in our holiday home, somehow I don't see him going for it, do you?'

Alice couldn't help the smile which had bloomed on her face. Mark's tantrums always amused her, even now, it wasn't the act of helping her which was the issue, it was the potential second-class bedroom facilities at Her Majesty's prison block that offended him.

'What are you smiling for?' Mark demanded, Alice's grin unmissable.

'I was just thinking what a wonderful, amazing and supportive friend you are, and how I'm lucky to have you in my life,' she said earnestly.

All the steam seemed to leave Mark as he sat back down opposite her. 'No, I am the fortunate one.' He smiled. 'So what am I going to tell John?' Mark asked with an exasperated sigh.

Alice reached across and squeezed his hand. He would never truly understand how much she appreciated his friendship. 'The truth.' She wouldn't ask him to lie for her on top of everything else. 'Tell him that I'm going to stay there for a couple of days, which will be the truth.'

That shadow of anger crept across Mark's face again at the realisation of her words. Alice jumped in quickly to stave it off before it became a storm. 'She'll have to stay inside, to stay hidden, but she'll need things, like food and toiletries. And besides, I could use the break, you're always telling me I work too hard.'

Mark's brilliant blue eyes were fixed on her. Like windows into his soul, Alice could see his internal battle as his emotions swirled like a mist, each one vying for dominance. Eventually, the fog cleared and he nodded solemnly, his decision to help her made.

'When do you intend to leave?' he asked her, although she could tell from his slumped demeanour that he already knew the answer.

'Today. As soon as I've grabbed a few things. That is, if you don't mind?' she added quickly, her hand sweeping across the mound of paperwork covering her work space.

Mark smiled tightly. 'You know as well as I do, we're weeks if not months ahead of our deadline,' he said dryly. 'John's working from home, I'll text him to tell him you'll stop by in a bit for the lodge keys.'

Alice jumped up, suddenly eager to get going. She swept up some of the papers, tucking them away in a drawer, whilst another stack she carefully folded and eased into her handbag. 'A little light reading,' she said, aware that Mark was watching her every move.

'Right, well I'm sure that it will only be a few days, so I should be back well before next week's board review...'

'Just take care of yourself, please!' he said, pulling Alice into a firm embrace before she had even registered him moving.

'Of course I will.' She hugged him back briefly. 'And don't worry. Everything will be fine.'

Alice had never been overly fond of unnecessary human contact, she couldn't get on board with all the cheek kisses that acquaintances seemed so comfortable with these days, surely a good handshake should suffice. Or was it just that she was so out of practice. Mark on the other hand was very tactile, he seemed to relish any opportunity for physical contact.

Slowly, so as to not offend him, Alice detangled herself from his embrace. Then with a fleeting smile, she breezed out of the office.

'I hope so,' Mark said as the door shut quietly behind Alice.

36

SAM

Sam scrutinised Elspeth Adams' case notes, for the fourth time that weekend.

She was supposed to be off, using up some of her untouched leave, but it was impossible to switch off after everything had gone to shit at the raid. There had been nothing, Sam thought angrily. Absolutely fucking nothing to work with. Her laptop history had been wiped clean, she hadn't bought anything incriminating, Hudson had ensured Sam that her phone record hadn't yielded anything either, not to mention it was now dead and to top it all off her suspect had gone to ground.

All of this was suspicious in itself, but they had nothing to go on. They couldn't trace her whereabouts, she hadn't used her bank accounts. It was as if she'd literally fallen off the face of the Earth, which Sam knew was practically impossible these days. And yet she'd done it. She must have a bolthole somewhere, but where? And who was paying for it?

Sam blew out her cheeks. They had been so close, having only missed her by minutes.

Sam recounted the mad dash they'd made to Storrington,

the tense and uncomfortable silence, the air thick with desperation, in the hope of catching Elspeth before she got word. Sam had barged into Elspeth's family home, without so much as an explanation, leaving Hudson to mollify the home owners, only to find her gone. Her bed, still warm, only recently vacated.

The parents had denied all knowledge of their daughter's pregnancy, of course, professed her innocence even. Not that Sam believed a word that they said, obviously they wanted to protect their only child.

But where had she fled to? That was the conundrum keeping Sam from sleeping, the mystery gnawing at her insides, like a rat chewing through rope.

She had to have someone helping her surely, or how else had she managed to evade them all this time? She just didn't strike Sam as the criminal mastermind type, but then she thought back to Elspeth's interview. She had sat in front of them during their first round of enquiries, innocently, like butter wouldn't melt, and denied everything. A bare-faced lie.

Sam leant back, head resting against the sofa and stared blankly at the ceiling. This case was starting to slip, like grains of sand, through her fingers. Smithers had already hauled her ass into his office, looked down his pointy nose at her as he reddened with anger. He had raged, spit flying everywhere, as he demanded that she sort out this mess before threatening her with desk duty again.

She closed her eyes and tried to clear her mind, but her head ached, like someone was pressing firmly against the side of her brain, muddying her thoughts. The two bottles of wine she had sunk the previous night were the cause, she knew. Maybe eating something would help.

Grabbing her phone, she found the number of the local Indian takeaway and dialled. She ordered her usual before turning her attention back to the disorganised sprawl of paper covering her coffee table.

'Come on. Concentrate.' She growled at herself in frustration.

Spontaneously, she picked up the top sheet and held it in front of her face. Dr Russo's interview transcript. Sam could practically recite the conversation from memory. As she was about to discard the sheet, deeming it useless, a thread of a thought drifted into her mind.

He believed that he was the father; Miss Adams had told him as much, Sam thought with more conviction. She was desperately pulling at the thread, trying to follow it to its end.

Sam found herself pacing backwards and forwards in her modestly decorated lounge, the piece of paper gripped in her hand.

Where are you going with this, Sam? She tried to order the pieces, to find a logical conclusion, there was something she wasn't seeing, yet.

Miss Adams has disappeared, which if nothing else confirms her pregnancy. She needs drawing out... we need something tangible to offer her, something she'd risk exposing herself for...

Like a firework exploding in a multicoloured cloud in front of her eyes, it hit her. The answer. She knew what they had to do to draw Miss Adams out.

Without a second thought, she called Hudson.

He answered on the third ring. 'Hey. How's your weekend off?' he asked lightly, she could almost see the smile on his lips.

'Yeah good,' Sam said dismissively. 'You working today?'

'No. Day off. Just about to sit down for dinner.' Sam could hear several voices in the background, or maybe it was the television. Of course he wouldn't be sat obsessing about the case like she was, she thought sharply, unfairly. He had a life, a wife. Quickly, Sam dismissed her negativity.

'I've been thinking about the case...'

Hudson laughed lightly. 'Now that doesn't surprise me.'

'I know what we need to do to find her!'

37

ARTIE

MAY 16TH 2035

Artie threw together a sandwich. He wasn't really hungry but he needed to occupy his time, to occupy his hands. No, what he needed was to see Elspeth. But she didn't want to see him.

When she had finally called, hours after she'd fled, she'd been... different, detached even. Having reassured him that she was somewhere safe, that she would be all right, she informed Artie that she didn't want him involved any further, that she wouldn't be in contact again.

Her words had stung, like he'd been pierced through the heart. He wasn't ashamed to admit that he pleaded with her, begged her, but she had cut him off, her final words crushing.

Artie had replayed their conversation over and over, heard the hardness of her voice, the coldness of her words. And yet, he knew she hadn't meant it, knew it wasn't of her own volition. Artie could hear the tears burning in her eyes as she spoke, as she told him that their kiss was a mistake, that they could never be together.

He hadn't been able to concentrate since.

Knowing it would be futile, he found himself calling her, repeatedly, but true to his advice, she had kept the phone off.

Where is she? Is someone still helping her? Is she really all right?

He could feel himself getting wound up, his blood starting to bubble with frustration. It wasn't that he wanted Elspeth to need him, if anything, it was the complete opposite. He needed her. Artie knew he would give up everything, in a heartbeat, for her. He would happily follow her lead, let her make all the decisions, he just wanted... to be with her, to support her, to care for her, to love her.

'Argh!' he growled, throwing his untouched sandwich in the bin.

'Woah!' Brooke said, walking into the kitchen and throwing her hands up in the air in mock surrender. 'What did the sandwich do?'

Artie knew she was trying to lighten the mood. She'd been beyond annoying the past few days. He sensed her guilt, knew she was trying to make amends for blabbing to the police. Perhaps she needed to hear that she had done the right thing, that he understood. But she hadn't and he didn't.

'I'm not hungry,' he mumbled, turning to leave.

'Artie. Wait, please?' Brooke called after him.

For a split second he debated pretending that he hadn't heard her, and yet his conscience wouldn't allow him to take another step, aware that she was clearly remorseful. Instead, he stopped in the doorway, his back to Brooke.

'Okay,' she began tentatively, 'I know you're mad at me...'

Artie rolled his eyes. Perhaps he should have continued walking, he really didn't want to deal with this now, he had plenty of his own misery to contend with.

'I was scared, okay,' she shouted at his wall of a back. 'The police had just burst through my front door, told me my best mate had been keeping this massive secret from me and that if I didn't help them I could go to prison too.'

Artie turned round, untethered anger burning in his eyes. 'Oh cut the self-pitying crap, would you. Do you think any of this has been easy for Ellie? She was trying to protect you, to protect us both, to keep us out of it for that very reason and you sold her out, just like that.' He clicked his fingers loudly.

'You knew!' It wasn't a question, more a realisation.

Brooke's acknowledgement was like pouring water over his burning fury, it seemed to instantly fizzle out. His shoulders sagged as he nodded.

'Who's the dad?'

The question hurt more than it should have. Yes, he was jealous, of course he was, but it was more than that, there was regret too. Regret that he never said anything, never acted on his feelings. 'I don't know.'

Artie found himself slumping into a kitchen chair, opposite Brooke.

'It feels like she hates me.' He sighed dramatically, not knowing where that honesty had come from.

Brooke snorted. 'No, she doesn't.'

'Maybe that was an exaggeration, but it's not like it used to be. She...' he shrugged deflated, unable to find the right words for his feelings, 'she won't talk to me anymore, won't confide in me.'

'Did you ever tell her?' Brooke asked softly.

'Tell her what?'

'That you love her.'

Artie met Brooke's stare, his eyes wide with horror. *How does she know? Is it that obvious?*

'Come on, I might be self-absorbed sometimes, but I'm not blind. When she came to look at the room, I knew then. You had this look...' Brooke smiled sadly. 'It was like everything else had disappeared and she was all you could see. I wish someone would look at me like that. Anyway, you know she loves you too, don't you?'

The words hit him hard, like an arrow piercing his already-fractured heart. He didn't believe Brooke, although he desperately wanted to. If that were true Ellie wouldn't be shutting him out, he reasoned.

'Well she does. Ever since the night, you two... you know. What happened? I was positive that I was going to wake up as a spare wheel–' Brooke trailed off, noticing the glum expression casting a shadow over Artie's face.

Artie shifted in his seat, he wasn't entirely comfortable with this sort of conversation, and yet, he wanted to talk about it, about her.

He shook his head. 'I honestly don't know,' he began, talking openly. 'We had a great night, an amazing night, it was... Then in the morning, I went out to get us breakfast, I thought it would be romantic, you know, breakfast in bed. Only by the time I got back she'd gone, not just to her room, but left the house completely. And then later,' he sighed, 'it was as if nothing had ever happened, she wouldn't even look at me. I thought she regretted it and that was how she wanted to deal with it.'

Artie couldn't miss Brooke's shocked expression.

'What?' he said flatly, worried about where this was going.

'If only you'd grown some balls and talked to her, then maybe none of this...' She stopped herself from finishing her sentence. She started again. 'Artie, Elspeth thought that it was you who had gotten cold feet. She told me that she'd woken up and you'd gone without so much as a word, and you were gone ages. She thought it was you who had the regrets. She was trying to make it easier for you.'

Artie felt the lump rise in his throat, he swallowed hard as Brooke's words sunk in and took root.

It had all been a misunderstanding.

Had he let his male pride come between them? The answer, he knew, was staring him in the face. He'd been afraid of the rejection, the let-down, no matter how gently she'd done it. He'd avoided the conversation, silently agreeing to the pretence.

Brooke was right, he should have grown some balls.

If only he'd stayed with Ellie that morning, wrapped his arms firmly around her, then none of this...

'Do you know where she is?' Brooke asked, breaking through his thoughts.

Artie's eyes narrowed, automatically.

'Please, give me some credit. I'm not about to go running to the cops. Jesus, Artie, is that really what you think of me?'

'Sorry,' he mumbled, 'no, I don't.' Even though he didn't know, Artie wasn't sure he would have shared that information with Brooke anyway, she clearly didn't do well under pressure and he wouldn't do anything to jeopardise Elspeth's safety.

For a moment, they sat in silence, lost in their own thoughts. Finally Brooke spoke. 'I take it you've tried calling her?'

Artie nodded.

'Me too, her phone's no longer connecting.'

He didn't know why, but Brooke's attempt at contact surprised him. He thought he might just like her a fraction more than he did before, maybe.

'What about social media?' Brooke suggested.

Artie raised his left eyebrow.

'Have you looked to see if she's checked in at all?'

Artie opened his mouth, ready to shoot her down, to tell her that that would be a rookie mistake, when it dawned on him, he hadn't said anything about social media.

Without another word, Artie was on his feet and scrambling down the hallway.

'Didn't think of that, did you?' Brooke called triumphantly behind him as he took the stairs two at a time.

Please don't have been on social media, please don't have posted anything. Shit, shit, shit. I should have been more explicit, I should have told Ellie, he panicked. These thoughts were barrelling through his mind as he waited impatiently for the computer to fire up.

He knew the police would be monitoring all those sorts of accounts, a single post could lead them directly to her. She would know, she would have worked it out, he reassured himself as he hit the buttons, logging into his own account.

His breath caught as her beautiful face stared back at him from her profile picture. He blinked hard and focused on the task. He searched her history and her most recent posts.

Nothing new.

He leant back in his chair, fingers intertwined behind his head and let out a long stream of breath, as though trying to expel all his anxieties and worries.

His eyes once again fixed on her beaming smile.

How did I fuck this up? How did I lose her? The anger was both raw and terrifying at the same time. *I could have had everything, everything I'd ever dreamt of, but I threw it away.*

He had loved her from the moment they'd met and now he knew, she had loved him too. His eyes glistened as his heart broke. It was too late, she was gone and he'd let her go so easily.

Why didn't I...? Why did she...? It could have all been so different.

A faint beeping, like a distant alarm, dragged him back to the moment. He looked around, momentarily confused.

It was the burner phone, the one he used for work, the one he'd called Elspeth on.

Quickly, with his heart in his mouth, he yanked open the drawer, hooked his fingernail in the corner and lifted out the false bottom. It could be Elspeth. She could be in danger. Just as he grabbed hold of it, the phone stopped ringing before he could answer it.

It wasn't Elspeth. It wasn't her number. But it was familiar, a number he recognised.

Reluctantly, Artie skimmed through several messages; all from the same number with the last one directing him to his email.

He pursed his lips, trying to think through the fog that had been clouding his mind. Then it came back to him. A complete set of new identification. The client was a regular, requesting fake social media accounts, untraceable campaigns, that sort of thing. This request, however, had seemed out of character, but he hadn't asked questions, she was reliable and paying hand-somely, so Artie had accepted. Only, he had failed to deliver.

His head dropped. *You can't get anything right*, he thought viciously. With some effort, he forced himself to navigate away from Elspeth's sunny smile and opened his unregistered email account. A frown creased his brow at the sight of three unread emails.

Clicking the newest one, he skim read the message. The urgency was evident. She needed the documents and she needed them now.

Artie skipped the middle email, instead choosing to open the oldest one. He scanned it; confirmation of payment, request for prompt delivery and an attached photo.

He recalled the conversation. The client had seemed on edge, not unusual in itself, working on the wrong side of the law goes hand in hand with apprehensive and cagey clients, but there was something... unnerving about her tone. It had struck a chord with Artie. She had sounded desperate and he had let her down too.

Artie straightened his back. He would get this sorted. Now.

He opened the attachment.

His mouth fell open at the sight of the captivating woman staring back at him.

Ellie.

But how? His brow furrowed whilst his brain struggled to keep up. Elspeth had said that she had someone supporting her, but he'd been convinced that she meant the baby's father and hadn't wanted to tell him. He never imagined that it would be one of his clients.

Laughter, filled with relief and disbelief, suddenly escaped his lips. Two minutes ago he had been sure that he wouldn't see her again, wouldn't ever get to hold her again and now... unbeknownst to her, he had been tasked with aiding her disappearance.

As his laughter gradually subsided, Artie recognised the precariousness of his situation. If he did anything out of the ordinary, anything to alarm the client, or Elspeth, he could lose her all over again... but he couldn't ignore this unexplainable turn of events.

Artie didn't believe in God or fate or anything he couldn't explain through science and maths, but this, this he couldn't fathom. Surely this wasn't just chance, was it? The one person that Elspeth chose to trust, was not only one of Artie's clients but she was also the most unlikely of candidates.

The client, he knew, was a well-established epidemiologist, who had previously advised the government on environmental issues and had been instrumental in establishing *The* Law. The very law which was behind Elspeth's arrest warrant.

Artie was meticulous when considering his clientele, ensuring that he knew exactly who he was dealing with, even if he assumed an air of ignorance.

Professor Alice Franklin was one of his most interesting clients. All the work she had requested had been in an attempt to sabotage and bring *The* Law she had helped to shape into disrepute. At the time, Artie had believed that this was an act of retaliation, maybe a partnership turned sour but now... now he wasn't so sure. This didn't serve that purpose. Helping Elspeth was another level entirely. But could she really trust this woman? And how was it that they knew each other?

Artie turned his attention to the brown envelope, visible in the exposed compartment of the drawer. The identification was ready, Alice had only requested one set but Artie was already in possession of three for Elspeth, so she could disappear without any trace being left. He knew he was going to hand them over, he had planned to give them to Elspeth anyway, but the police had shown up, scuppering his plans before he'd had the chance. An edge of anger seeped into his thoughts as he pictured that arrogant copper woman.

No, don't get distracted.

Now, Artie realised, the question was, how would he get the envelope to Elspeth?

He knew that with one message he would know where she was. But she hadn't wanted him involved, hadn't wanted to see him again. Perhaps he should send the documents via courier, to honour her wishes. That was the right thing to do, but... Who was he kidding? He couldn't, no... wouldn't pass up the chance to see her again.

Yes, there was a real possibility that Elspeth would slam the door in his face, she might even scream and shout at him, tell him she didn't love him. But that was a chance he was willing to take, a sacrifice he would make just to see her again, especially if there was a shred of truth in Brooke's words.

Decision made, Artie typed out a brief text message. The only thing he had left to figure out was how he was going to lose the undercover cops he knew had returned and were stationed very inconspicuously outside.

38

ELSPETH

MAY 17TH 2035

E lspeth stood on the wrap-around veranda with a decaf coffee in her hand.

The view from the lodge was breathtaking. With acres of forest and greenery to get lost in, it offered an unimpeded view of the horizon. Elspeth stood watching the tendrils of orange light snake through the sky as the sun rose. She could have been anywhere in the world.

Elspeth exhaled loudly, she had barely travelled, and soon she'd be calling another country home, a shiver of fear mixed with excitement ran down her spine.

Every single bone in her body wanted to leave, to be safe with her baby, but there was an anchor pulling her back. The sound of Artie's hurt voice broke through into her thoughts. She pictured his face, heard his pleading words. He had asked if he had done something wrong. Didn't he know that he hadn't done anything wrong, nothing at all. It was all her. She was the one who had done the irreparable damage. She had slept with a guy who now repulsed her and was pregnant with his child. How could Artie still look at her the same way? She loved her child unconditionally, but how could Artie feel the same?

Her eyes glistened as she tried desperately to put a lid on that box. If she thought about Artie much more, leaving would become insurmountable. She knew she would find herself staying, talking herself out of going and she couldn't risk that.

'Hey,' said a soft voice from behind her.

Elspeth wiped away the tears that had escaped, trying to hide her regret. 'Hey.'

'It's beautiful, isn't it?'

'Yes.'

'How are you this morning?' Alice asked, coming to stand next to Elspeth, her own drink in her hand.

Elspeth smiled what she hoped was a happy smile. 'I'm fine thank you. It's such a wonderful place. Your friend is so lucky to have this,' she said, turning her attention back towards the overwhelming expanse of wilderness in front of her.

Alice had explained, when they arrived, that her dearest friend had lent her the property, knowing that Alice was helping a woman 'in trouble'. Elspeth hadn't asked what extent of disclosure was made to insinuate 'in trouble'. Maybe she should have, after all, knowing that someone else knew about her made Elspeth uneasy, but she trusted Alice. She had, after all, kept her secret and kept her safe thus far.

A wisp of worry flickered across Alice's face. 'Did you sleep okay?' she asked, clearly seeing through Elspeth's forced smiles.

'The baby comes alive at night, I think he might be a night owl,' she responded, delicately running her hand over her bump. Really, Elspeth had spent the night wondering... and worrying about her car.

She had abandoned it, choosing what appeared to be a busy residential road, in a nondescript town just outside of Southampton. The recurring thought that it had been reported was playing on her mind. Would the police realise that she had continued west? Would they somehow connect Alice's car to

264

hers? Elspeth had been careful to ensure that the meeting point with Alice had been as far away from the car as possible. But what if…?

'I've got some great news,' Alice said, true excitement in her voice. Elspeth looked at her again. 'My guy, with your new passport, he's going to deliver it tomorrow.'

Elspeth contorted her face to present a mask of happiness, hiding the sudden sinking feeling. 'That's fantastic news,' she lied. The calm she had felt watching the sunrise, drifted away with the morning breeze. The next day, a whole new and completely alien life was going to be handed to her.

'Would you like me to start looking at planes and ferries?' Alice asked, her eyes expectant.

'That would be wonderful. I'll be in in a minute.'

'Okay.'

Elspeth hadn't anticipated saying anything further, didn't even know if Alice was still there and yet words, desperate to be spoken, to be heard, unexpectedly started tumbling out of her. 'I know that it's completely inadequate, but I wanted to say thank you, for everything you've done, that you are doing for us. I honestly don't believe that I could have got this far without you. You see, I'm not particularly brave. If I'm being completely honest, I never dreamed that my life would end up like this.' She swallowed a breath of air and continued. 'The consequence of choice, of my decision has been so unbelievably extreme, so far reaching. Of course I would have always wanted my baby, but not like this, not running from everything and everyone I care about.'

Elspeth didn't look back and if Alice had heard, she didn't respond, perhaps aware that they were just words which needed to be voiced so she could let go of them.

After a moment, Elspeth blew out a long, slow breath and a lump rose in her throat. Don't cry, she willed herself. This is what needed to happen. *No*, she thought more fiercely, *what I need is to be allowed to have my baby here, surrounded by those I love, in a world where it isn't a crime to have a child, to be a mother.*

The injustice of her situation, the anger she felt towards a system she couldn't do anything to change, boiled inside of her and spilt out in the only option available to her, tears.

Angrily, she wiped them away. She hated her tears, they made her look weak and sad, she wasn't weak, nor was she sad, she was strong, and powerful, and above it all she was angry.

She wanted to defy them, to prove that a piece of paper with a government stamp wasn't what made you a good mother, nor was it what job you had or the amount of money in your bank account. No, it was the love you felt, the decisions you made, the drive you had to teach your child right from wrong, to encourage them, push them, hold them, be proud of them, that was what made you a good mother.

And yet, Elspeth knew that none of that mattered.

She had broken the law, no one would listen to her now, her story wouldn't be heard, at least not from the viewpoint that mattered. She had no choice but to leave and she would, of course she would, but still, it didn't mean it was an easy decision.

Finally, the tears stopped as her anger waned. Gently, she caressed her bump. 'I'm sorry little one,' she spoke gently. 'I just wish things were different for us.'

Alice had found several possible options for Elspeth's departure, which she presented professionally over a lunch of cheese sandwiches. Elspeth's latest craving.

The fact that Alice hadn't presumed to make the decision for her meant more to Elspeth than Alice would know. With so much out of her control, Elspeth often felt that she was holding on to little more than sand when it came to her life, so the chance to make a decision for herself was refreshing, if not unnerving. The risk of making the wrong decision wasn't lost on her either.

They had spent several hours weighing up the risks of each route. Flying would obviously be quick and direct but security would be tight and it was more likely that she'd stand out amongst a crowd. Elspeth's bump was unconcealable now.

Driving, although seemingly a safer option, still wasn't without risk. The journey itself would take her several days, she would have to factor in frequent rest breaks, and Elspeth was highly aware of her lack of experience driving in another country. That was all before she'd even considered the risks posed by hiring a car and the ferry crossing itself.

She was leaning more towards the swifter, if not riskier option, of flying. The thought of driving all that way to Italy, alone, brought her out in a cold sweat.

'It's a bit of a minefield, isn't it?' she eventually said, rubbing her temples firmly to stem off the headache which was threatening.

'You don't have to decide right at this minute,' Alice said kindly. 'I'll make us some tea.'

Elspeth half-smiled in response, because she knew she had to decide and she needed to do it today. Now.

Whilst Alice bustled around in the kitchen, Elspeth took a moment to clear her mind. Her hands rested gently on the top of her bump and she breathed in and out slowly, her eyes closed. Under her fingers, she could feel the gentle movements of her son as he turned inside her. The reassurance that those little nudges offered her was like finding a shining star in an otherwise cloud-covered sky. He was real, her little soldier, and he needed her to be strong.

Make a decision, she told herself sternly. Elspeth knew she couldn't afford to lose any more time. Once her passport arrived the next day, she had to be ready to leave.

Reluctantly, she opened her eyes to find Alice standing by the table, a mug of tea in each hand and a sad look on her face.

Alice rearranged her face into a light smile so quickly that Elspeth found herself wondering if she had imagined her haunted look. With a light shake of her head, she cast the thought away, she had more pressing concerns.

Alice slid one of the cups towards her and sat down.

'What would you do, Alice, if you were me? Well I doubt that you would have gotten yourself into this sort of situation but... you know–' As much as Elspeth appreciated the respect and space Alice had offered her to make this decision herself, she really couldn't decide, or rather she was afraid that she would make the wrong decision.

Alice struck Elspeth as a methodical yet thoughtful woman who made sensible decisions based on fact rather than emotion. *Heaven knows why she's helping me then.* Still, Elspeth trusted Alice's judgement.

Alice didn't answer immediately, instead she sipped at her tea, perhaps collecting her thoughts, Elspeth considered.

Finally, Alice spoke softly but firmly. 'I would drive. I won't pretend that it isn't a long journey or that it will be easy, however, weighed against the difficulty of getting through airport security who will likely be on high alert, I honestly believe that it is the safest choice.' She held Elspeth's gaze confidently, 'But ultimately it is your decision. And I will support you, whatever you decide.'

Elspeth reached across the table and gave Alice's delicate hand a gentle squeeze. It amazed her how adept Alice was at cutting through the crap straight to the core of the issue. As though she had read Elspeth's innermost thoughts and voiced them aloud so that they had to be acknowledged and dealt with.

Driving was the right decision, she knew, she was just procrastinating, hoping for a quicker, easier solution. Of course, there wasn't one. Nothing had felt uncomplicated for Elspeth lately.

'I think you're right,' she finally replied, her words sounding heavy. 'I just–' She blew out her cheeks, unable to find the right words for what she was feeling, words that would capture the tornado of emotions that seemed to ambush her at every turn.

'I know.' Alice waited a few moments before speaking again, this time in a much brighter tone. 'Let's look at ferry times, then we can plan our route. I've driven it once before, several years ago now, but I remember a few lovely places we could stop along the way.'

Elspeth's eyes opened wide. 'We?' She tried, and failed, to hide her surprise. It wasn't that she was against the idea, especially not when faced with days of driving, but could she allow this woman to put herself at even more risk than she had already, and besides she had already refused Artie's help. Why should this be any different? 'I couldn't ask you–'

'You're not,' Alice interjected. 'But for one thing, I'm not prepared to send you on a week-long journey across Europe all by yourself, besides I haven't had a holiday since... well, I can't even remember so I am definitely due one. And secondly, I'd be so worried about you, wondering if you were safe, that it might well induce a heart attack, so really you'd be doing me a favour by letting me tag along.' She smiled brightly.

Although Elspeth found herself smiling in return, she still wasn't sure she was prepared to put Alice at risk, even though she desperately wanted her company. It wasn't right, she couldn't be selfish. What kind of person would she be if she repaid this woman's kindness with a criminal record?

'Elspeth,' Alice said, pulling her out of her thoughts, 'you're not doing this alone. If you were my daughter, I would hope that someone would want to help you. Please, let me be that person.'

Elspeth's breath caught.

To fill the silence of their first night together, Alice had shared her story, her past, with Elspeth. How she had lost her own child, how she hadn't been brave enough to try again and how her husband, desperate for children had, with some persistent nudging from Alice, walked away from her.

Elspeth had cried, whilst protectively holding her bump, unable to comprehend the heart-rendering despair that Alice must have felt. She couldn't fathom how Alice had carried on, woken up each morning, with that kind of pain. But she had. And here she was, offering her help, how could she possibly say no?

Elspeth opened her mouth, then closed it again, unable to find the right words to express her inexpressible gratitude. Alice had become not only her saviour but also her friend, a friend she had not realised she needed so desperately. 'That would be wonderful,' she finally said, 'but only if you're absolutely sure.'

Alice beamed at Elspeth. 'I wouldn't have offered if I wasn't. Now we've got some planning to do.'

I t was unusual for Hudson to be the one pacing, but he was and had been for the past ten minutes. Sam had found herself watching him from underneath the sharp cut of her black fringe. She was waiting, for what, she wasn't sure. Perhaps for him to have an epiphany of sorts, as long as it wasn't a breakdown.

He was putting her on edge, she realised, making a concerted effort to relax her clenched jaw. It was... distracting.

Backwards and forwards he trudged, treading down the already-thin carpet of the training room, his head bent, his hands buried deep in his pockets.

Elspeth's car had turned up, spotted by traffic police on a routine patrol, outside of Southampton. Miss Adams, however, had apparently disappeared.

A door-to-door enquiry in the immediate vicinity had turned up nothing. A review of local security cameras and public transport were also void of any useful information. It was as if she had vanished. They had contacted every possible transport service they could think of. Airports, trains and ferries, she hadn't boarded or attempted to board any of them.

And to top it all off Sam suspected that Smithers had just read Hudson the riot act.

She could imagine exactly how that meeting had gone.

Smithers would have started off all smiles, requesting an update, but quickly turned sour at the lack of leads and very circumstantial evidence. He would have questioned the additional resources recently allocated to the case bemoaning the financial implications and strain this would have put on other cases. Then, getting into the swing of things, Smithers would have likely hinted at the repercussions were the press to get hold of the story, how the unit couldn't take further embarrassment before he subtly indicated a black mark marring Hudson's record were the suspect to continue to elude them.

She also knew that Smithers would have also relished the opportunity to bad-mouth her, disguised as a friendly warning, of course.

Hudson hadn't said as much, he was too... kind to share the burden, but she had been on the short end of Smithers' temper often enough lately to recognise the haunting look in Hudson's eyes, the desperation in his voice as he attempted to grasp at the smallest of possibilities. But with nothing viable, he had fallen silent, and commenced his plodding from one side of the room to the other.

Finally he paused. 'What about the housemates?' he asked, his voice husky.

Reluctantly, she shook her head. Hudson winced as if pained by the news, before resuming his to-ing and fro-ing.

Sam had been convinced that Mr Jones was aiding Miss Adams somehow, they both had, but he hadn't left the house for days, hadn't done anything to arouse their suspicion. The surveillance unit posted outside his house hadn't moved at all and so had been called off by Smithers.

What they needed was a carrot, Sam realised, something or someone who could draw Miss Adams out of hiding.

Sam had originally broached Elspeth's parents confident that they would be able to draw her out. Sam had suggested an appeal to ensure their daughter's safety. Sam had hoped to put them in front of a camera, desperate and distressed, their pleas drawing Elspeth out of hiding.

Much to Sam's frustration, they had point-blank refused, however. Whether they had seen through the ruse or they were simply too pissed off with their only offspring for getting herself illegally up the duff, Sam couldn't be sure. But either way, they needed new bait and quickly.

Hudson's relentless shuffling was starting to grate on her last nerve. She was as worried as him, but they couldn't let this defeat them. Miss Adams was guilty, her abscondment was as good as a confession in Sam's books.

'Do you have to keep doing that?' Sam finally demanded, her tone harsh.

'Hmm?' Hudson paused, his brow crinkling in confusion. 'Doing what?'

Sam indicated with a wave of her hand to the path Hudson had been trampling.

'Oh,' he said, coming to sit next to her. 'I didn't realise...' He let out a long slow breath. 'I just can't believe she's slipped through our fingers, I mean, are we missing something?' he growled. 'This should have been an open and shut case, but it's like she's running rings around us and we're still stuck at the starting line trying to tie our fucking shoelaces.'

Sam turned to Hudson, giving him her full attention. As his mentor, his senior, she was supposed to guide him through the stumbling blocks which inevitably arose in most cases, to steer his thoughts to more productive paths. However, instead of words of reassurance leaving her lips, she found herself agreeing with him wholeheartedly.

'I'm convinced she's not in this alone. Either we need to work out who's helping her, or we need to draw her out.' Sam shuffled a few papers on the desk to keep her hands busy, before speaking again. 'Who has the most to gain, or lose from her pregnancy, apart from Miss Adams that is?'

Without an answer, they fell back into silence. Their desperation palpable.

'Doctor Russo,' Hudson murmured to himself after a minute.

Sam pursed her lips, not wanting to go down that route again. They had already exhausted all avenues relating to that sexist pig.

Russo, they knew, hadn't attempted to contact Miss Adams. Considering his laissez-faire attitude towards their suspect, that wasn't a big surprise. Having cleansed his conscience by throwing the mother of his child under the bus, the good doctor seemed to have recommenced what Sam presumed was his normal behaviour. He had been out with several different women in little over a week and at least one was observed to scurry away in the early hours of the morning after, looking dishevelled and a little embarrassed.

Sam didn't see the appeal, she really didn't. She preferred her men to be... honest. But partners for her had been few and far between. She was a stereotypical copper, married to the job, and she liked it that way, usually.

A wisp of an idea floated around her then, her thoughts about Russo developing into something substantial, workable even.

'Okay, I've got an idea,' Sam said cautiously, startling Hudson who had been lost in his own thoughts. 'I'm not sure if it's got legs that we could run with yet, but hear me out.'

Sam couldn't help but notice as Hudson raised his eyebrows, aware that even she didn't sound convinced about her pending proposal. And to be honest, she couldn't believe she was about to make this suggestion, not when she would have shot Hudson down if he'd so much as thought about pulling that prick back in. But to hell with it...

'I think we were on to something with the parents...' she paused as though carefully considering her next words, 'but maybe we've been thinking about this from the wrong angle. I think we need to be thinking more like Miss Adams. We're fairly confident she hasn't left the country although it is unlikely that she's been sat idly by either. But what's keeping her here? Perhaps she's still hoping that Russo will have a change of heart. To want to run away with her? Maybe *he* is our carrot?'

Hudson looked as though he was suppressing the urge to roll his eyes. Dr Russo didn't want to be involved and Sam knew that, but if he could help, then Sam would damn well make him.

'I think he could be the perfect bait. We could use him to lure her out,' she said with more conviction.

'You know as well as I do that he has no interest in anything but saving his own skin,' Hudson responded flatly.

'Exactly. We could offer him that deal he's so desperate to have, or at least appear as though we will consider it.'

Hudson mulled this over for a moment.

Russo would be easy to manipulate, Sam knew. It was worth trying, after all they had little to lose at this stage apart from their reputations. Although they'd have to be careful, a lawyer would be quick to use violation to have their evidence overturned.

'Okay,' Hudson eventually agreed, if not a little hesitantly. 'Let's give it a try.'

'Excellent. You set up a meeting with Russo, today, and I'll talk to Smithers.'

Hudson nodded once, then turned to leave, his shoulders still sagged in defeat.

Sam was silently confident that this would work, that this case was salvageable, they had to pull Elspeth out of her bolt-hole by whatever means were available to them.

40

ELSPETH

MAY 18TH 2035

'I think I'll go lie down,' Elspeth said softly.

Shutting herself in the cosy bedroom, she lowered her heavy body onto the bed and raised her swollen feet up. Inspecting her legs, she turned them from side to side.

Who knew pregnancy gave you fat ankles?

The last couple of days, Elspeth had felt safe, safer. Concealed within the thin veil of protection that the lodge afforded her, she was overwhelmed with a curious desire to finally get to know her changing body. Yes, it had been there, developing and swelling under her very nose, and yet she had covered it up, masked it not only from those around her, but perhaps even from herself.

Alongside her swollen ankles, she had also discovered a few stretch marks scored across the tops of her hips and around her breasts.

She had examined every inch of her skin. She was amazed by what her body was capable of, felt proud that she was able to do this, and perhaps she even felt a little more able, a little braver.

Getting comfortable, Elspeth's thoughts returned to their

impending visitor. She was profoundly intrigued by the phantom lawbreaker. Who was this man that Alice trusted implicitly, yet had never met? She was dying to know more about him, what he looked like, why he did what he did, and yet she wouldn't. She would remain stowed away, her new-found sense of caution keeping her hidden.

Although she had come to the realisation that she preferred not to spend too much time on her own, her thoughts often wandered to places she didn't feel strong enough to explore.

Mindlessly, she grabbed the phone on the compact bedside table and turned it on. She wasn't stupid enough to call anyone, aware that the police would likely be waiting for her to make that sort of mistake, but surely checking the internet couldn't hurt?

She needed a distraction.

Elspeth found herself logging in to her social media account. She just wanted to look at her photos, she told herself, to remember happier times, easier times, to hold on for a moment longer to the life she was about to walk away from.

Pictures of Artie and Brooke filled the screen. Scrolling down, she knew the exact one she was looking for. It wasn't difficult to find. She soon stopped on the image of the three of them at the beach.

With treacherous tears stinging her eyes, she zoomed in on Artie. His brilliant blue eyes weren't looking at the camera but were instead focused entirely on her, as though there was no one else in the world at that moment. How had she never noticed that before? His smile was the mirror image of hers.

She sucked in a deep ragged breath.

Stop doing this to yourself, she silently roared. She shook her head, dispelling the thoughts. Nothing good would come from going down this road. And yet she couldn't help herself. She didn't want to let go, didn't want to accept that it was over, not really. But she had to, had to force herself to.

As Elspeth was about to close the page down, to put the lid back on a box she shouldn't have opened, she noticed the blinking mail sign in the corner.

Without thinking, she clicked on it. Two messages were waiting for her.

The first from Brooke, was short and sweet.

```
I know you're pregnant, the police raided the
house, looking for you. I understand why you
kept it a secret. I don't know if I could've
helped you but I would have tried, if you'd
told me. Artie misses you. When you get where
you're going, let me know you're safe. B x
```

Elspeth sighed through her nose. That was Brooke, straight to the heart of the matter. Confident that she would be forgiven, Elspeth made a mental note to contact Brooke once she had settled into Alice's Italian home. *If you ever make it.* In the recesses of her mind, the negative remark loomed, threatening to smother the hope that had been blooming in her chest.

Quickly, she moved on to the second message which was anything but straightforward. After their last meeting, Elspeth had been resigned to the fact that Nick had no interest in the baby. She'd made the difficult decision not to look back, after all she wasn't going to beg. But this message... Elspeth had read through it twice to make sure she hadn't misunderstood it.

```
'Hello Elspeth. Last time we met, I came
across as very crass, and for that I would
like to apologise. I have had some time to
think your situation through. If, as you have
```

279

stated, this child is mine, then I would like
to be involved. Can we meet, please? I would
like to prove to you that I am sincere. Call
me. Nick.'

She frowned. *Arsehole,* she scoffed silently. *If the baby was his.* Why the hell would she lie about it? Her initial thought was to ignore his message, to chalk it up as another aspect of her life she was leaving behind, and yet... Didn't her baby deserve to know who he was, warts and all? Elspeth was under no illusions that sooner or later Nick would tire of them, leaving her to pick up the pieces. But still...

Damn. She knew she was going to regret it and yet she found herself tapping out a brief message regardless. 'I can meet you tomorrow. I'll contact you in the morning.'

She sent the message before she could change her mind. She had made the effort, she reasoned, if he chose to be unavailable, then that was his problem. Now all she had to do was convince Alice to make a brief detour on the way to the ferry.

Elspeth heard the unmistakable knocking at the door. Automatically, she moved to sit on the end of the bed. Her curiosity piqued.

After a long pause, she heard the faint voices of Alice and the stranger.

There was something unusually familiar about the tone of that voice, something she couldn't put her finger on.

Elspeth found herself stood with her ear pressed to the door. She didn't recall moving and yet she had. She listened.

The male voice spoke again, she couldn't make out the words but a spark of recognition ignited.

No, it couldn't be. She almost laughed out loud at the ludicrousness of her thoughts. *Don't let your feelings confuse you. It couldn't possibly be him. How would he have tracked you down?*

Holding her breath, her hands were braced against the door. She willed him to speak again. Then she'd know it had been a mistake, her twisted emotions playing cruel tricks on her.

There it was again. That voice. A voice so familiar to her, she would have known it in a crowded room.

Without another thought, she swung the door open.

Artie.

Elspeth's mouth fell open at the sight of him, of Artie, sitting on the sofa of the lodge.

How?

He turned to look at her, a wary smile finding its way to his lips. 'Ellie.' His voice caressed her name as he slowly rose to his feet, hands raised as though afraid that she might bolt like a frightened animal. 'I can explain.'

As her initial shock dissipated, she longed to close the small distance between them, to tell him how much she had missed him, how she was sorry for her harsh words. But the look of caution in his eyes, the tightness around his mouth, stopped her.

'How did you find me?' she asked, her confusion obvious.

'You two know each other?' Alice's surprise was unmistakable as she interrupted the charged atmosphere.

Elspeth's gaze slid to Alice, as though remembering she was there, before settling on the unmissable pile of documents spilled across her lap. She tried and failed to make sense of the situation. How had Artie found her and when had the documents arrived? Why did Alice have them all out in front of him? And why did he look so... guilty?

Looking back, she stared, uncomprehending, into his eyes.

'I know what you must be thinking,' he offered, hands still raised.

'I doubt that,' Elspeth retorted, aware she wasn't thinking anything.

She saw his throat bob, as he swallowed hard. Slowly he lowered his hands. 'Okay,' he croaked, 'where to begin?' he said more to himself than to her.

Alice rose in the periphery of her vision, the papers rustling loudly. 'Why don't you sit down, Elspeth.'

With a small nod, Elspeth moved, eyes remaining fixed on Artie as she sat where Alice had been perched moments earlier.

'I think I'll give you two some privacy,' Alice whispered tentatively. She pressed the array of documents into Elspeth's hand, before she left the room.

'Sit down, Artie.' Elspeth sighed when he remained statue-like in the middle of the tiny lounge.

Why does this feel so weird? And what's going on?

Sitting down, Artie exhaled almost sadly. 'You've grown.' He was taking in the swell of her stomach. She hadn't been hiding her pregnancy here, away from intrusive eyes. And it had been enjoyable, freeing even. She knew that her dress clung to every curve, accentuating her bump, not to mention her breasts, which seemed to be growing almost as quickly as the baby.

'You need to tell me what's going on, Artie. How did you find me?' she pressed, her voice even.

If he found me, the police might not be far behind. Panic was starting to take root, drowning any sense of calm and peace she'd felt.

Artie wrung his hands together, then sighed. 'When you left – when you called,' he corrected himself, 'I honestly didn't know what you had planned, or where you were. You said you were safe but I didn't know. What if the police...' He stopped mid-sentence, sucked in a deep breath and shook his head unhappily. 'That isn't what I wanted to say... The truth, I want you to know the truth, Ellie... I brought your new identification, I'm the one your friend Alice came to for the forgeries.'

He had brought the forgeries. The words repeated themselves in her mind. It was only now that she looked at the papers in her hands. Passport, medical passport all signed and dated with vaccinations she hadn't had, birth certificate and driving licence. All in triplicate, all bearing her face and each set featuring a new name. Hannah Matthews. Natasha Green. Florence Davidson.

But if that was true, if this is what he did, then everything that had come before had all been a lie. He had been lying to her all this time. Did she even know him at all? The truth of his confession stung sharply.

'You've been lying to me?'

'That was never my intention.' He offered her a placating smile. 'My line of work was never something I could publicise, I've been pretending for so long, Ellie, that after a while it doesn't even feel like lying.'

'You could have told me the truth, you could have trusted me.'

The smile he gave her was so sorrowful that she almost reached out to him. But she didn't. Her anger at his deceit was too fresh, too raw.

'Ellie, you have no idea how many times I wanted to tell you, I did, and yet I knew that telling you would put you in danger. I couldn't do that...' he trailed off.

Elspeth watched as his gaze drifted to the window. She didn't interrupt, even though a succession of questions burned in her mouth, she could tell he had more to say.

It was only as she waited that the irony of the situation hit her. He hadn't told her his secret to protect her. Hadn't she been doing exactly the same thing, pushing him away, forcing distance between them, to protect him?'

Artie eventually continued, the words rushing out of him. 'I genuinely didn't know you were here, not to begin with. I've been going out of my mind with worry. I thought I'd lost you, that you'd left, that I'd never get a chance to say all the things that I wanted to.' His eyes came back to her. 'And then Alice contacted me. I don't know if it was coincidence or serendipity, and I don't even believe in all that stuff. But what are the chances... the person helping you came to me? I couldn't have written it even if I'd had the imagination to. Alice inadvertently told me where you were. You see, I had everything you needed, I'd put it all together weeks ago, only I never got the chance to give them to you.'

Artie moved out of his seat. Sliding onto his knees in front of Elspeth, he reached for her hand, but paused. When she didn't pull away from him, he grasped her left hand, holding on to it so tightly, it was as though she was his lifeline, saving him from sinking.

Elspeth exhaled slowly. Artie's face was mere inches from hers. She drank him in. He smelled of coffee and home.

'I know you told me not to come after you, to leave you to live your life, but you are my everything, Ellie. Being without you has been torturous, it's like I've been trying to breathe underwater, I just can't do it. I made a mistake last time, I shouldn't have gone to get breakfast.'

'Breakfast?' Elspeth interrupted.

'I never left you, I never regretted a single moment that we'd spent together. That night was like all my wildest fantasies coming true.' He smiled at her, a real breathtaking smile and then it faltered. 'I went to get us breakfast. I wanted to surprise you, to let you know... But it took ages and when I came back... I never left you.'

There were no words for the swarm of emotions overwhelming Elspeth. She sat rigidly as his words sank in. Was he telling her the truth or just spilling out the words he thought she wanted to hear?

Artie wasn't who he said he was, wasn't who she believed him to be. Could she trust him now? All this time, he had been keeping a giant secret from her, but then, had she not done worse? She had lied to him too yet he was still here, still trying to help her.

She looked at him, really looked at him. His ocean-blue eyes were unguarded, the smattering of freckles on his cheeks, the angle of his jaw, all so familiar to her, it was like coming home, he was like coming home.

This was her Artie, exactly as he'd always been. Artie who made her stomach twist in knots and her heart flutter. Artie, who she had loved from the first moment they'd met and been too afraid to say.

All the time she had spent thinking the worst, believing she wasn't enough for him, believing he hadn't wanted her, that he had never felt that same way.

How foolish she had been. How foolish *they* had been.

An urge deep inside her stirred, a bud of hope perhaps. She tried to force it away, to pretend it wasn't there.

She had come so far, too far to drag him into this now. *That's why you have to make him leave.* Everything she had done so far had been to protect him. She knew what she had to do.

'Say something, please,' Artie pleaded.

'I wish things were different, I really do,' her voice was hard. She watched as he flinched slightly at her coolness. *You have to keep going*, she told herself, as she pulled her hand free from his. 'I don't need you, and I don't want you.'

She pressed her lips tightly to quell the sob which threatened to escape. She knew she was hurting him, causing him more heartache, and yet she knew it was for the best, it would keep him safe. She had to forge on, to ignore every fibre in her body which wanted to curl into his arms.

Crestfallen, Artie sat back on his heels.

She was intentionally hurting him, she knew, and yet Elspeth hoped that the damage wouldn't be irreparable, that one day, when the dust had settled, he might forgive her.

'Okay,' he said slowly. 'I'll go, if that's what you really want?'

Elspeth didn't trust herself to speak, instead she nodded only once, tears blurring her vision.

'Say it!' he growled, his voice raw.

She opened her mouth, the words poised on her lips, but she couldn't force them out, couldn't voice them. As she closed her mouth, he leant forward, his hands cupping her face, so gently as if she were a delicate flower. His eyes searched her, desperately looking, perhaps for the truth in her words. It wasn't there.

With sudden urgency, he pressed his lips against hers. She could taste his desire, his passion. She let it engulf her, let it wash over her. She drowned in him. Her lips moved against his.

No, you have to let him go.

The thought was so jarring, she pulled back. Artie's eyes flew open, despair visible.

It was too late for them. So much had happened, she knew, so much had changed since then.

Her eyes unintentionally drifted to her blossoming belly. She would never regret her baby, but surely he couldn't feel the same? Not when another man's child grew inside her.

As if reading her thoughts, he gently placed his hands on her bump. 'I love every part of you. You don't have to do this alone, not if you don't want to. If you'll let me, I'll be there for you, for both of you.'

With those words, it was as if the chasm she'd been trying to force between them, to keep in place, melted away.

She couldn't fight it any longer, didn't want to fight it.

She gave into her heart's desires.

Now, she was the one closing the distance between them. Furiously, she crushed her lips against his. Her hands buried themselves in his hair. Artie pulled her towards him. She opened her mouth, his tongue urgently searching out hers. The salty taste of her tears mingled with the warmth of his breath. The sweetest of tingles ran the length of her spine and her head swam, awash with him. With Artie. Her Artie.

'Ahem.' A farcical cough sounded from somewhere outside of the moment, dragging Elspeth back to the present. Alice.

Detangling herself from Artie, Elspeth couldn't help the shy smile which lit up her face, especially as she looked at Artie, his smile the mirror image of hers.

Cheeks already flushed, Elspeth was at least saved from looking embarrassed. 'Alice, this is Artie.' Elspeth grinned stupidly. She knew that this feeling couldn't last forever, reality was outside the door, like a wolf prowling in the woods, waiting for her. Decisions, tough and likely impossible, were going to have to be made and sooner rather than later.

'Well, Artie, it's nice to be properly introduced. Am I to presume...?' She raised her eyebrows in question as her gaze fell to Elspeth's bump.

And there was the first hurdle. The flame of happiness Elspeth felt was extinguished almost immediately.

'No, I'm not,' Artie answered, 'but I hope to play a significant role, that is if Ellie will have me?'

He was looking at her again, eyes burning with desire. Hope rose in her chest, before being swiftly smothered by guilt. Elspeth desperately wanted to say yes, but how could she, not without him knowing it all.

'You know I have to leave,' she said, lightly waving the documents in her hand. 'How would that work? I can't ask you to give up your life here, not for me. I don't know where I'll end up, or if I'll ever be able to come back.'

There, she'd said it. The complicated, unchangeable truth of her situation hung heavily between them. It was like being precariously poised on a knife's edge. She couldn't see a way out, not one where she got to have them both.

'Ellie.' He sighed. 'I will go anywhere with you, as long as you are both safe, that's all that matters.'

'But...'

'But what? I can work from anywhere in the world.' He smiled sheepishly. 'I rent a room in someone else's house and besides, without you there it's going to feel very empty. There is absolutely nothing tying me here.' He looked at her, eyebrows raised, inviting her to disagree.

She couldn't.

'We're leaving tomorrow,' Alice said gently, filling the silence.

'Ellie?' Artie encouraged.

Her face split into a wide smile. 'Are you really sure?'

'Yes, I am,' he said, deadly serious, before returning her smile. She could have sworn her heart missed a beat. In that moment, she had no words to convey how she felt, a lump had formed in the back of her throat. Lightly, he squeezed her hand. He understood.

Artie turned to Alice. 'So, what's your plan?'

41

ARTIE

MAY 19TH 2035

The roads were surprisingly quiet. Initially Artie felt uneasy, exposed even, without a camouflage of vehicles to hide within. Eventually as he settled into the journey, he concluded that it was probably for the best, they were making good time, even though he didn't want to rush the journey. No, he was happy, content just being sat next to Elspeth.

Glancing over at her in the passenger seat, she was dozing lightly, head resting against the window.

A smile graced his lips. *What actually happened yesterday?* he wondered, still in disbelief. At best, he'd hoped to be able to talk to Elspeth, for her to accept his help. At worse, thankfully that hadn't happened, in truth he didn't know what he would have done if she pushed him away again.

What he got instead, what she'd given him, was so much more than he had imagined. She'd accepted him, every part of him, without judgement.

He didn't deserve her, couldn't fathom how he'd gotten so lucky, but he wasn't going to ask. He was going to treasure every moment of what she offered him for as long as she wanted him.

An image of Elspeth from the previous night, or was it that

morning, filled his mind. Curled up in bed together, having talked late into the night, he remembered with perfect clarity how her hair felt running lazily through his fingers, how her eyes, heavy with sleep, had fluttered closed and her lips curled up just a fraction, in what he suspected was contentment.

That was how it should have been last time. So much time together had been wasted. *No*, he thought angrily, *don't spoil these memories with your negativity*. He knew he couldn't change what had already happened, but he could certainly help to shape the future.

With more resolve his thoughts turned to their plan. Artie had to acknowledge Alice had certainly been thorough in her planning and for that he would be forever thankful. Alice had kept Elspeth safe, given her somewhere to hide and been someone to turn to when she needed it and more than that she was as devoted as he was to getting Elspeth and the baby out safely.

They'd had to alter the plan slightly the previous day to allow Artie to dump his hire car, which they had done early that morning, choosing a busy multistorey car park. He had everything else he needed, passport, laptop, a change of clothes and Elspeth.

He sighed, a mixture of happiness twinned with anger.

They still had Elspeth's request to navigate.

A brief meeting with the father, en route to the ferry.

They'd reluctantly agreed to it, but Artie didn't like it, not one iota. His knuckles tightened on the steering wheel and his jaw set. That waste of space didn't deserve a minute of her time, he didn't care whether he was the baby's biological father. In Artie's opinion he'd relinquished all rights to that title when he left Elspeth to deal with this alone. Hatred flared in him.

'Artie?' Elspeth's sleepy voice said.

He glanced across to her. Her dark brown eyes were fixed on him, worry evident.

'I don't like it,' he mumbled.

He didn't need to say any more, she understood. She shifted in her seat, turning to face him. 'I know. I'm not particularly thrilled about it either. But–'

'You don't have to explain to me.' Artie exhaled, his shoulders sagging slightly. He knew he was jealous, it didn't take a genius to work that one out, but he didn't want Elspeth to feel that she always had to explain herself to him. Her motivations were understandable, commendable even. She should be able to make her own decisions. It didn't mean he had to like them but he would begrudgingly accept them.

'No I don't, but I want to.' She smiled at him and some of the anger melted. 'I know this might be difficult to understand, but it feels like the right thing to do.' She paused as if searching for more of an explanation. 'I'm taking the high road. He may be a dickhead, he may not have been there but in years to come when my little man asks me, I can put my hand on my heart and tell him that I did everything I could. That I wasn't the one responsible for preventing him from having a relationship with his father. Does that make sense?'

'Yes,' Artie acknowledged heavily. His left hand released the wheel, coming to rest on Elspeth's leg. He liked that he could touch her, just to have that contact with her, that he didn't need to find a reason to be close to her.

'You have nothing to worry about, you do know that, don't you?'

He swallowed hard. 'I know,' he said with unwavering conviction. And he did. He had always known that she loved him the way he loved her, he had just been too naive to see it for what it was. He had let his fear of rejection blind him. That still didn't mean that he had to like it though.

She ran her hand across the back of his neck rhythmically as they fell into silence. There was a nervous energy building in his very core which he couldn't ignore, no matter how hard he tried. He knew why they were stopping and he loved her for her compassion, for the desire to see the best in people, but he wouldn't relax until they were boarded on that ferry and there was a good distance of water between them and Dover.

'Ten minutes,' Artie grumbled flatly as they neared their destination.

Elspeth wiped the tiredness from her eyes as she yawned. 'I must have dozed off again.'

Alice cleared her throat, then leant forward. 'Elspeth, not that I want to add any extra pressure to you right at this moment, but...' Artie saw Elspeth's face harden a little, as if preparing her defences for whatever Alice was about to throw at her. 'We might have some traffic to get through near to Dover, so we don't have that long if we're to make our ferry.' The apologetic tone was obvious in her voice.

Elspeth visibly relaxed. 'I won't be long, I promise. Ten minutes tops. I plan to hear what he has to say, if he seems genuine then I'll contact him when we're settled. If not, well it will be more like two minutes.' She offered a half-hearted smile.

Artie not only disliked this guy, he absolutely loathed him. How could he not see what a lucky bastard he was or could have been, he corrected himself? Well, his loss was Artie's gain and he sure as hell didn't plan to let her down.

Following the satnav, they pulled into a large housing estate full of row after row of identical houses. A characterless development which was perfect for waiting in.

Parking amongst several cars, Artie nervously sucked in a breath.

'I'll be fine,' Elspeth said, picking up on the waves of tension rippling off of him. He sensed that she wanted to roll her eyes but thankfully she didn't. Yes he was likely overreacting, he didn't care though.

'Ten minutes,' he reminded her, 'or else I'm coming in to get you.' He meant it as well.

She nodded.

'Do you remember which way to go?' Again Elspeth nodded. 'Good. Remember when you're ready to leave, take the first path from the car park, that will bring you out there,' he said pointing to a small gap in between the indistinguishable terraced buildings.

Artie had used this pub himself once before for a drop-off. The multiple exits afforded him some reassurance. After all, you never knew who you could trust in this line of work. *Scratch that*, he thought, *you can't trust anyone in this line of work.*

Elspeth followed his gaze. 'I'll be back before you've even had a chance to miss me.' She smiled trying but failing to alleviate some of his agitation. As she opened the door, Artie reached out and caught her hand in his.

'I...' he began to say, then stopped, catching sight of Alice in his peripheral vision. A pinkness crept into his cheeks. Damn, he wanted to kiss Ellie. If they had been alone... 'If anything doesn't feel right, then walk away,' he found himself saying. She did roll her eyes at him that time.

'I will,' she replied, gently pulling herself free of his grip.

Artie watched Elspeth as she walked away from the car.

His mind was reeling. Should he head to the pub? He could wait at the edge of the path. She wouldn't even be able to see him, he reasoned, but he would be able to see her and that would make him feel so much calmer. He could also do with stretching his legs.

'She'll be fine,' Alice, who Artie had completely forgotten was in the back of the car, offered as if he had just said his thoughts out loud. 'She's a very strong woman.'

'It's not Ellie who worries me. It's the arsehole she's meeting.'

42

ELSPETH

MAY 19TH 2035

Elspeth followed Artie's directions, taking the long way round. Turning the final corner, she spied the pub.

It was just how Artie had described, tired and old-fashioned but it suited her intentions. Artie had wanted to make sure she had options, although Elspeth hadn't truly believed she was putting herself at any additional risk. She hadn't said as much, aware that these extra precautions made Artie feel better and really, it didn't matter to her where she met Nick.

The sooner this was over with, the sooner she could be back with Artie and they would be on their way, a new life within her grasp.

She smiled lightly at the thought of Artie. A rush of warmth heated her body as she recalled how they'd laid cocooned in each other's arms the previous night.

Come on, she chided herself, *you need to focus.*

Reaching the pub's front door, she squared her shoulders and inhaled deeply. 'Let's get this over with.'

Walking in, she was surprised by its busyness. Her eyes darted across the many faces of the patrons, who had all fixed her with inquisitive, if not unfriendly, stares. She held her chin high. No one knew her, she reasoned, and therefore she had nothing to hide. Although she was wearing a billowing dress which obscured her bump, at nearly five months pregnant it was impossible to hide completely. For all anyone knew, though, her pregnancy was fully above board and legal.

She could feel all eyes on her as she moved further into the room.

It's not because you're pregnant, she attempted to reassure herself, *it's because you're a new face.*

She repeated this over and over in her mind as she scanned the bar for him. He wasn't there. Doubt and annoyance flared. She would check the garden, if he wasn't there then she would leave. She certainly wasn't going to sit around waiting for him, he'd had months to turn up and repeatedly he'd let her down.

Following the chalkboard sign, Elspeth found herself leaving the oppressive low ceilings of the mock-Tudor pub and entering a well-maintained spacious beer garden. Cautiously, her eyes swept across the numerous occupied benches.

There.

Tucked in the furthest corner was the father of her baby. Nick gave her a half-hearted wave.

As she neared, she couldn't help noticing his gaze which had already gravitated to her blossoming bump. She didn't miss the way he recoiled slightly as if disgusted by her, before settling on a hardened, unreadable, expression.

This doesn't bode well.

'Hi,' he said as she sat slowly on the opposite bench.

'Hi.'

She took him in. He looked like shit. Dark circles framed his tired eyes and his hair hung limply, obscuring part of his face. He was alarmingly dishevelled, as though he hadn't slept well for weeks.

Nick cleared his throat, in an almost nervous gesture. 'How are you?' he asked stiffly.

'I'm fine. How are you?' she responded, mimicking his tone.

'Okay, I'm okay,' he said without enthusiasm, looking down at the half-drunk pint in his hand. What the hell was going on? He was the one who wanted to talk but it was like he couldn't even bear to look at her.

Nick pursed his lips, as if trying to think of what to say.

Unable to stand the awkwardness further and well aware that she didn't have the time nor the patience, she spoke curtly. 'Nick, you asked to meet me? Why?'

He looked up to meet her waiting stare. A look she couldn't put her finger on flicked across his face, then just as quickly it was gone, replaced by a cold indifference.

'Yes... Yes, I wanted to talk about the baby.' He practically spat the words as if they burned in his mouth.

She didn't know where this was going, but she didn't like it. As calmly as she could manage, Elspeth raised her eyebrows in a silent question. She wouldn't make this any easier for him, he didn't deserve that. He clearly had an ulterior motive for asking to meet, she realised.

'I've had time to think about things–'

'You said that already, in your message,' she interrupted childishly.

'How... I mean, when. Yes, when are you due?' he asked, eyes drifting back to his hands.

'That isn't why you asked me to meet, is it? To talk about due dates? Nick, be honest with me, what do you want?' Anger flared in her voice. Searching Nick's face, she desperately wanted to find a sliver of the father her child deserved. She was both disappointed and perhaps relieved to find it was absent.

He squirmed, his hand subconsciously rubbing his chest.

His eyes darted to somewhere off to the side of her, before returning to meet hers.

'That is why I wanted to meet,' he said, his tone defensive. 'You've told me nothing about the baby other than that it's mine.'

Elspeth supressed a groan. 'I'm sure you could've figured that one out for yourself,' she retorted, 'besides, it's not as though you've shown any interest before. Why the change of heart?'

She watched as Nick pursed his lips, and his hand went back to his chest. Rubbing, backwards and forwards, like a nervous tic.

'I told you, I've had time to think.' He stared at her as if trying to look into her soul, to see something that wasn't visible. She didn't look away, she had nothing to hide. 'Elspeth, are you really pregnant?' he pressed impatiently.

'Is that what you think? That I made it up?' she growled. Her anger was about to boil over. In an effort to stay calm, she clutched the edge of the table with such force she thought the wood might splinter between her fingers.

His gaze flicked over to the side again as that chest tic worked overtime. 'Just tell me, Elspeth, are you really pregnant?'

Cautiously, Elspeth found herself following Nick's stare. What was he looking at, a pretty girl perhaps? One who hadn't trapped him with a child he didn't want?

What she found was so much worse, it sent a bolt of ice, so cold down her spine, that she had to stop herself from visibly shivering.

Two men were sitting awkwardly together, as though they were strangers. One of the men caught her looking. Swiftly he averted his eyes, his hand involuntarily coming to his ear. To the ear piece barely concealed.

She whipped her head back round, as unadulterated fear

seized her as suddenly as if she'd been grabbed, rendering her motionless. Words failed Elspeth as the realisation of what was happening took root. And there in front of her, Nick was still scratching mindlessly at his chest. As his hand moved down, the collar of his shirt shifted, exposing something small and black, attached to his skin. *What's that?*

It hit her then, he was wearing some sort of device, a microphone perhaps, probably recording every word she'd said, waiting for her to confess.

What had he done?

He had set her up. This was a set-up and they were the police.

'Well?' he pressed, his voice sounding whiny and obnoxious. Her mind whirled. She needed a way out, but those men, the police, were sitting right there, next to her exit.

She was trapped.

'Elspeth? Did you hear what I asked?'

His voice broke through her terror. She had not come this far, had everything she dreamed of within her reach to have it ripped away, by him. No, she would not let him do this to her.

As she looked at him, really looked at him, the oddity of their situation hit her. Here she was bulging with his child, and yet she didn't know anything about him, not really. She didn't know when his birthday was, if he had any siblings, where he grew up. Nothing.

In that moment a scrap of an idea came to her.

Regaining a fraction of her composure, she smiled, too sweetly. 'Do you know what I've just realised, Nick?' She didn't wait for a response before she continued. 'We don't really know very much about each other, do we? Don't you think that's unusual, given our situation?'

He opened his mouth to speak, probably to lead her into a confession, but she carried on. 'I need the bathroom and to get a drink, when I come back I think we need to rectify that. Let's get to know each other better before we move forward.'

Without waiting for him to say anything, she hauled herself up as swiftly as she could manage, her body suddenly feeling twice as big as it had five minutes earlier, and strode back towards the pub.

It was only then that she realised what that look had been in his eyes... Guilt.

Once inside, her eyes darted frantically looking for the way out. She'd bought herself some time. Only a few minutes. Would it be enough? She didn't know but she had to try. She had wanted to be able to hold her head high, to have some semblance of pride left when she walked away from Nick, but that was slipping out of her grasp. He had deceived her.

Now all she could hope for was to make it out of there without being arrested.

Walking quickly, but not wanting to draw any more unnecessary attention to herself, she swallowed down the desire to run.

The door was mere feet away, when a voice, urgent and low, caught her attention. A woman, eyes trained on her, hand to her ear, was staring directly at her.

Police.

Elspeth halted.

She was trapped.

Briefly, she wondered what would happen if she tried to run for it. Not that she believed for one minute she'd be able to get very far, but if they were going to arrest her, she at least wanted to make it more difficult for them. To put up a fight. To be able to say, *I never gave up*. Perhaps there were even more officers waiting outside for her?

'Can I get you something?' an old man asked from behind the bar.

Elspeth turned to him. 'Oh, where's the toilet, please?' Her voice was surprisingly level considering how hard her heart was beating.

He pointed to the side of the bar. 'Follow the corridor round, then you want the first door on the right.'

'Thank you.'

Elspeth walked, in what she hoped appeared to be a casual manner, down the corridor. With her hand poised to push the bathroom door open, something caught her attention. A fire escape.

'Thank God,' she breathed.

Elspeth took a step towards it, but paused. How far would she get? Perhaps to the main road? Even though every fibre in her body wanted to escape, to run through that door, she forced herself into the toilet.

With trembling hands, she dug around in her bag. Grabbing her phone, she called one of only two numbers she had.

After a single ring, Artie answered. 'What's the matter? What's happened?'

'I've been set up, Artie. He set me up,' she rushed to tell him.

'Shit. Where are you?' he growled, his voice thick with fear and anger.

'I'm in the toilet. There are undercover police here, I'm sure of it.' She bit back the tears threatening to spill over.

Don't cry, she told herself, determined to remain composed. She had to keep it together, to get herself out of this mess which she had walked eyes-wide-open into.

That was what infuriated her more than anything, she had been the one to agree to the meeting, against both Artie's and Alice's advice. She had demanded this, to be the better person. *Look where that's got you*, she thought bitterly.

Elspeth knew that Artie was thinking from his silence, but

she didn't have time to spare. If she wasn't back in two minutes, she suspected someone would come looking for her.

She knew she only had one chance. 'Artie. There's a fire exit, at the side of the building, by the entrance to the car park–'

'We'll be there in one minute.'

The wait was agonising. Each second seemed to last for minutes. Elspeth paced the small space afforded within the confines of the bathroom, her nervous energy preventing her from standing still.

It must be a minute, she reasoned, unable to wait any longer.

With trepidation, she eased the door open a fraction.

She peered outside. Relief washed over her at the sight of the empty corridor. She'd half expected to see a swarm of officers, ready to pounce.

Supporting her bump, she pushed through the door and darted for the emergency exit.

With a loud groan, Elspeth put her weight on the substantial door, heaving it open. Terror instantly engulfed her at the emptiness of the drive.

Artie wasn't there.

'You won't get away,' Nick sneered behind her.

She whirled round to see him looming closer, a look of hatred burning in his eyes.

'Do you know what you've done?' she spat at him.

'You brought this on yourself, you know that don't you? If you'd just got rid of it like I told you to–' Disgust dripped from his voice as his eyes bore into her stomach. It was as though he was trying to kill the baby with his hatred.

'It?' Elspeth repeated, rage filling her words.

'You have no idea how hard this has been for–'

The screeching of tyres cut him off mid-sentence. Relief washed over Elspeth as Alice's familiar car came into view, stopping at the base of the stairs in front of her.

Artie.

Reassured by their presence, Elspeth turned back to Nick. 'You bastard. You're not fit to be a father,' she hissed, her voice so level, so cold that Nick flinched. 'What *you* have been through is nothing compared to what we've endured, what you've done to us.'

She stumbled down the stairs to the waiting car conscious of Nick following her.

Artie, suddenly there at her side, righting her with a firm and reassuring hand on her elbow. With swift ease, he guided her towards the passenger seat.

'Who's this? Another mug you've conned with your lies. Is he the father too?' Nick goaded, having regained his usual obnoxious confidence. He was closing the distance between himself and Artie. 'Mate, a word to the wise. She's not as innocent as she makes out–'

Nick didn't get to finish his sentence. Wordlessly, Artie stepped forward, away from Elspeth, hand balled into a fist as he lunged effortlessly at Nick.

A bone-splintering crack sounded as Artie's knuckles connected with Nick's nose. Elspeth watched from her safe position within the car as red ooze spilled down Nick's face, coating his chin and T-shirt.

He screamed.

Elspeth wanted to feel sorry for him, she wanted to feel remorse, but she didn't. She felt satisfied.

Artie darted back to the driver's side. As he did, the discernible face of DS Hudson filled the doorway of the emergency exit. He ran, then skidded to a stop next to a blood-covered Nick.

For a moment, Hudson's eyes locked on to her.

Elspeth had the urge to scream, and yet not a sound passed her lips. She had been rendered immobile with sheer panic. If

303

he reached out, he would be able to yank the door open, to pull her free from the car.

And yet he didn't move.

At her side, Elspeth felt Artie dive into the driver's seat.

She didn't look, though, couldn't turn away from her assailant. She watched as Nick shouted at the detective, arms frantically waving in Elspeth's direction as blood-filled saliva splattered across the floor. And yet the detective stood statue-still.

She wanted to look away, but she couldn't tear her gaze from him. What was he doing? What was he waiting for?

And then as if she had voiced her thoughts out loud, as if she had shouted them at him, Hudson mouthed one word. 'Run.'

It was unmistakably clear.

Artie, in that moment, put the car into reverse, expertly careering back down the short drive.

Hudson's eyes never left hers, not as they pulled out care-lessly onto the main road, not when the tyres screeched in protest as Artie yanked the steering wheel to the side, not as the car slammed into drive, hurtling them away at a speed Elspeth couldn't comprehend.

Only then, when she could no longer see Hudson, did she suck in a deep, gulping breath of air.

He had let her go. He hadn't even tried to stop her.

Why?

Elspeth didn't have any answers, couldn't grab hold of a suitable conclusion.

As they hastened away, Elspeth's mind reeled. She turned to Artie to tell him, only out of the window she caught sight of DI Wakley, darting out from behind a large white van, a look of horror on her face.

Wakley saw them, each and every one of them as they rushed past her.

Elspeth wanted to apologise to Artie and Alice for putting them in danger with her stupidity, with her naivety, but as she turned in her seat, the image of the female detective running behind them, silenced her.

From the ashen look on Artie's face, he had seen her too.

'We could be in trouble,' he said, fear coating his words.

43

SAM

MAY 19TH 2035

As the car sped away, Sam ran. Her feet moving automatically as she chased her suspect, her case, her reputation.

How?

Her mind worked slowly, as though fog clouded her thoughts. She struggled to piece together the events that had just unfolded. How it was that she had ended up running after a car containing not only her suspect, Miss Adams, but also Mr Jones *and* a third party.

The woman in the back was someone she knew, yet couldn't place. She racked her brains, tried to find the face, the context which fitted that woman, but Sam was drawing a blank.

She stopped running, aware that her efforts were futile. She had to get back to the surveillance van, to her team. They had to get after them.

Somewhere in the haze of confusion, Sam acknowledged that she had been right all along. She'd known, had that gut feeling about Artie Jones. His loathing for the police was founded on something deeper than being pulled out of his bed in the early hours of the morning. He had been helping Elspeth all along. A note of satisfaction rose within Sam, before it was extinguished by her rage.

'What happened!' an urgent voice called from the pub door as she jogged closer.

'That car!' she directed, gesticulating furiously after the car that was about to disappear around the corner. 'After it. Don't let her get away!'

All the officers, having abandoned the pub, were darting to their patrol cars, whilst Sam came to a stop beside the van.

Hudson appeared at her side, a smattering of blood covering his face and shirt.

Sam's eyes widened in alarm, Hudson reading her stare quickly offered his reassurance. 'It's Russo's.'

Russo. His name was like a slap in the face. She should've known they couldn't trust that snake. Should've guessed that he would rat them out at the first opportunity.

A sneer distorted her face.

'We don't have time for that. Get in, quick!' Hudson interrupted, shoving her into the front seat of the van. She would have time to consider how to make that prick suffer later, something excruciating, she decided, not to mention humiliating.

Both patrol cars, sirens hollering, passed them. The van, however, moved at an achingly slow pace, likely weighed down by all the high tech equipment stowed in the back.

As they pulled away from the curb, something in Sam's periphery vision caught her attention. There, reflected in the wing mirror was Nick, covered in his own blood, arms flailing frantically. He was attempting to wave them down, to stop them.

Hudson, seeing the same thing, spoke first. 'Leave him.'

Sam nodded. Hudson knew as well as she did that this was all his doing. Russo was to blame.

She focused on the road ahead.

They raced in the van which seemed more a hindrance than a help, their suspect already out of sight. Hudson's radio crackled continuously, directions being relayed from the cars up ahead.

A ringing rose in Sam's ears and her heart pounded. They were getting away and there was nothing she could do about it.

She tried to claw at the pieces of information she had, to glue them together. She wanted answers but had none.

'She had help,' she spat. 'Jones was in that car along with another woman. I want to know who that woman is!'

'We're getting an ANPR,' Hudson answered, his ear pressed close to his radio.

The radio finally provided an answer. 'Vehicle registration identified the present owner as one Alice Franklin.'

For a moment, that name meant nothing to Sam. It wasn't an offender known to her, wasn't a lead previously discounted. She replayed the passing car in her mind. There was something strangely familiar about her hair, its silver-grey colour, the way it hung immaculately.

Sam's eyes shot open in understanding. '*Professor* Alice Franklin,' she said in disbelief. 'She's the founder of *The* Law.' She was about to demand they check if the car was registered as stolen, but Sam stopped herself, already knowing the answer.

That *was* Professor Franklin in the car.

'You sure?' Hudson asked, clearly confused.

'Positive.'

She couldn't comprehend this turn of events, couldn't make sense of how Professor Franklin had been dragged into this mess. And yet she had, she was somehow involved and was in as much hot water as Miss Adams and Mr Jones. Sam didn't even want to start considering the publicity, the damage this would do to her team if Franklin's involvement got out to the press. It could be the final nail in their coffin.

'What happened, when you got to the pub?' Sam demanded then, turning to stare at Hudson.

When Elspeth disappeared to the bathroom, Sam had felt uneasy, a sense of dread had seeped in. The conversation between Russo and Adams had been stilted and, to be frank, rather uncomfortable to listen to. He hadn't even attempted to present as the apologetic ex. She would have had to be stupid to not have questioned their meeting.

Sam had sent Hudson in, conscious that Elspeth was out of sight for too long. Had Russo tipped her off? Given her some sort of clue, some sign despite his general pissed-off demeanour?

Hudson didn't answer immediately which only infuriated Sam further. It was all she could do not to verbally lash out at him. Her emotions were overwhelming. She was losing. She did not lose. She would not lose.

'By the time I got there,' Hudson began, 'Russo was already screaming. I found him outside, they'd gone through a fire escape. He was bleeding all over the place and Miss Adams was already in the car, I couldn't get to her in time.' It sounded to Sam as though he wanted to add *I'm sorry,* but didn't.

Sam knew this wasn't his doing, knew he had at least tried to reach her. Nevertheless, none of this helped her to understand what had happened nor how the professor fitted in.

Sam swallowed down the growl of frustration burning in her throat. It wouldn't help for Hudson to see how close she was to losing it.

Just then, Hudson's radio hissed again.

'Dover, they're heading to Dover.'

A glimmer of relief – or was it hope – passed silently between them. 'We have to salvage this.'

44

ALICE

MAY 19TH 2035

Alice sat silently in the rear of the car, a kaleidoscope of emotions demanding her attention.

Seeing that horrendous detective had sparked an element of fear she hadn't previously felt, her hands gripping her own thighs. She had developed a distinct dislike for her from the moment they met all those years ago. Evidently her feelings had not subsided over time. Perhaps she should have considered Sam Wakley's continued role within the department, contemplated being hunted by that woman, a woman whose reputation preceded her. She hadn't, of course, and perhaps it was for the best.

She pushed the fear aside, boxed it up and swallowed it down, instead choosing to focus on the unexpected conundrum also puzzling her.

That man, presumably another detective, of sorts, had very definitely let them escape. *Why would he do that?* But more than that, Alice was convinced she recognised him too, had seen those hollow eyes before. But from where? She couldn't remember. She had met so many people over the years, in so many different situations. And yet she did remember him, he had left some imprint on her, enough for her to have noticed.

She rubbed her temples lightly, focusing on the road ahead. Artie expertly sped the car through the outer villages of Ashford, the almost-indecipherable sound of sirens whispering in the distance. It was no good, she couldn't place him, couldn't remember where she had seen those empty eyes before.

No one had spoken a word since they left the pub. Not one. Perhaps unable to find the right ones, or more simply afraid of saying the wrong ones. After all, what do you even say in a situation like this? Nothing seemed fitting.

Alice had gone into this knowing the consequences if they were caught and she would accept whatever came her way. If they didn't make it, she knew she had done the right thing. This was the first action against *The* Law which felt like it meant something, felt like it would make a difference. She had tried going through official channels, to no avail. Perhaps, if they were caught, she could somehow use the publicity to hammer home the injustice of it all. Although she couldn't think about that, couldn't yet admit defeat.

Her thoughts found themselves turning to Mark. *Would he understand?* She desperately hoped so and yet she knew there would still be a storm to weather. If she was arrested, their funding would be withdrawn, the company's reputation destroyed and her dearest friend would be out of a job. All because of her. That was a lot to ask someone to forgive. And still, she suspected that after it all, he would.

Despite everything that had happened and was yet to happen, Alice refused to regret helping Elspeth, helping herself.

With determined resignation she settled into her seat.

Alice's gaze slid from the road to Artie. She watched him as he frequently glanced over at Elspeth, it was as though he couldn't help it, his eyes drifting of their own accord. She recognised that look, one of awe and something else, fear perhaps. He seemed to be trying to memorise every detail of her face. Likely worried about what was to come, that having only just come together they may soon be forcibly separated.

Alice had known, from the first moment she'd seen them together, that he would go to the ends of the earth for her. *And so he should*, she thought. In the face of adversity, Elspeth has stayed strong, she was focused and determined. To be honest, she was a little in awe of her.

Fleetingly, Alice wondered if her child would have been as brave as Elspeth. Yes, she decided silently, she would have encouraged them to be headstrong, to be courageous even when all hope seemed lost. A sigh escaped her lips.

Elspeth peered over her shoulder at the sadness of Alice's exhale, a sorrowful expression on her face and offered what was unmistakably an apologetic smile.

Alice wanted to tell her that all would be well, that they would make it, but she didn't want to lie to Elspeth. She knew as well as Alice did that the threat was real, that the wolf was clawing at the door.

The sirens were getting louder.

Alice refused to turn and look. Refused to let alarm consume her.

They reached the motorway, the road stretching out in an endless straight line before them, as Artie pushed the car to its limits, the engine whirring loudly as they weaved in between the increasingly congested traffic.

Elspeth's hand reached across and rested gently on Artie's tense arm, his hands straining against the steering wheel. The look that passed between them was utterly heartbreaking.

In that moment, Alice felt like an intruder. She wished she could give them some privacy, to say the things that needed to be said.

Instead, she diverted her eyes, a single tear rolling down her cheek.

'Artie—' Elspeth said softly, carefully.

'No! I'm not giving up.' Artie's grave voice echoed in the small space. 'Don't you either.'

'There's no way out of this, Artie. I'm so sorry for dragging you both into this.' She glanced back to include Alice. 'I never meant to hurt anyone else. I think you should pull—' The despair in Elspeth's voice was crushing.

'Stop that,' Artie growled, cutting her off.

'You have nothing to apologise for,' Alice said and she meant it. 'Come on now, all's not lost yet. Look.' She indicated in front of them with a single nod.

There, up ahead, was the sign for Dover.

Maybe they would make it.

Maybe there was still hope.

45

ARTIE

MAY 19TH 2035

'Artie–' Elspeth's voice broke through the tirade of thoughts swirling round his mind. It was careful, tentative. He glanced at her. She looked apprehensive, as though she was on the edge of...

'No!' he said sternly. 'I'm not giving up. Don't you either.' His voice came out harsher than he meant, but that look, that haunted look in her eyes petrified him.

'There's no way out of this, Artie. I am so sorry for dragging you both into this. I never meant to hurt anyone else. I think you should pull–'

'Stop that!' he demanded. He didn't want to hear it, didn't want to hear those words come out of her mouth. She couldn't surrender, couldn't give up, not now, not when she had come so far and was so close to freedom.

How could she even think to ask that of him? He would rather die than let the filth lay a hand on her. Surely, she knew what she meant to him, the lengths he'd go to, to protect her.

Alice said something then, infiltrating his brooding.

There up ahead was the sign for Dover.

They were nearly there.

With a glance in the rear-view mirror, Artie could see the flashing blue lights of not one but two cop cars. They were like flies to shit, he thought angrily, his knuckles whitening as his hand grasped the steering wheel tighter.

For a moment, hope swelled in his chest. He risked another glance at Elspeth. From the look of anticipation which had filled her features, he knew she felt it too.

Could they make it? Could they continue to outrun the police? The possibility hung there like an unanswered question. Safety was so tauntingly close and yet so far out of their reach.

In that moment, Artie promised himself that no matter what, Elspeth would make it out. He would make sure she got the life she deserved with her baby. He wouldn't let her down. Not now, not ever.

Elspeth's hand moved from his arm, coming to rest on his thigh. The casualness of the gesture, the familiarity of it was crushing.

This is some twisted fucking fate you've been dealt, to get the girl, only to face losing her in the same breath.

He shook his head. *Concentrate!*

As they progressed, more signs appeared. They were getting closer. And yet, it still felt like they had a marathon to run. The traffic was slowing, cars beginning to come to a standstill, bumper to bumper, making it damn near impossible to navigate at any sort of speed.

At least, he realised, the police would have the same difficulties. Even they couldn't sail their way through the traffic.

Artie was thinking ahead, or at least trying to. If by some miracle they could get through the traffic, get through Dover's checkpoints, they still had the process of boarding the ferry to navigate. If there was even a minute delay once they drove up that ramp, that would be all the police needed to storm the ferry, to drag them back off, hands cuffed like criminals.

Artie was starting to see red, the image of Elspeth, beautifully pregnant, in handcuffs, humiliated and defeated was more than he could bear.

They needed a diversion, a distraction, something that would buy them some time, or at the very least, impede the cops. But what?

'Artie! Look out!' Elspeth screamed, her nails digging into his leg.

A gigantic lorry had swerved precariously close to them, to Elspeth, in an attempt to bypass the queue of cars for the slip road.

Instinctively, Artie yanked the steering wheel.

In response, the car swerved sharply to the right.

The lorry narrowly missed colliding with them but they were careering dangerously into the outside lane, Artie no longer in control of the vehicle.

A thunderous metallic crunch echoed around them as they sideswiped another car, a BMW, forcing it into the central barrier. As it ground against the concrete blocks, sparks of metal and fire rained down around them.

Artie's window exploded, into tiny shards of glass, against the pressure.

He flung his right arm up, to act as a barrier. Unavailingly, pain blistered in his cheek as several pieces pierced his skin.

Elspeth and Alice were screaming.

Artie wasn't thinking, he was just reacting.

He wrenched the wheel the opposite way. They ricocheted violently back into the central lane.

His heart pounded in his chest.

He just about managed to regain control of the car when, in his mirror, Artie watched in horror as the BMW spun out of control.

In a clash of glass, rubber and smoke, it barrelled head on

into another car. The ear-splitting smash reverberated all the way to Artie's core.

What had he done?

His eyes were wide with terror, he desperately tried to focus on the road ahead, but he couldn't not look, his gaze impulsively reverting to the collision behind him. What if he'd killed someone? What if he'd killed them?

'Are you both all right?' the words burst out of him at the thought of Elspeth and Alice.

He glanced at Elspeth. Understandably, she had wrapped herself protectively around her bump, tears running down her face.

'We're okay.' Alice smiled weakly, although Artie could see in his mirror that she was pale and breathing hard.

'I'm so sorry. I didn't see that lorry. I could have killed us–'

'But you didn't,' Elspeth cut him off, her voice hoarse from screaming. She had unravelled herself and was leaning back in her seat.

No, he hadn't, by some miracle. And he couldn't stop, no matter the cost. He had to keep going, he knew.

And yet, he found himself looking back again.

There, clambering awkwardly out of where the window should have been, was the driver, perhaps injured but not dead. Relief washed over Artie.

He hadn't killed anyone.

He was shaking, he knew and he didn't want Elspeth to see. He tried to steady himself, he forced his limbs to still. A sheen of cold sweat coated his brow. Roughly, he wiped his hand across his face, only for it to come away bloodied.

'Artie, you're bleeding.' Elspeth gasped.

'It's nothing, I'm fine.' He could feel the trickle of blood running down his cheek but he couldn't pause to think about it.

'I think you may have just inadvertently provided us with a

distraction,' Alice said, her voice strangely light considering the near miss they'd just had.

Artie forced himself to focus on the road ahead, on traversing the precariously busy motorway. 'What?'

'The cars are blocking most of the road. Look, the police can't get through.'

Elspeth turned in her seat and Artie risked another glance in his rear-view mirror.

Alice was right.

The police were stuck, the wrong side of the accident. Artie could see that one car had stopped to help whilst the other was continuing to try and force its way through, sirens incessant.

The smallest of smiles graced his lips.

That was not the distraction he wanted, had intended on creating, but it would certainly do.

Up ahead was their exit. The ferry, almost in sight.

From memory Artie knew that the port was large, affording several lanes of waiting cars as well as several checkpoints. He needed to bypass them all. But how?

He took the slip road off the motorway, followed the ramp down to the port before finding himself stuck behind a wall of cars all waiting, all desperate to escape for just a tiny pocket of insignificant time.

'Shit!' he growled, startling Elspeth and Alice.

They were hemmed in.

Like a caged animal, Artie furiously scanned his surroundings. He was in lane three of what appeared to be six lanes and up ahead was the first of two checkpoints.

Painstakingly slowly, each car was having its details examined, passports studied by an attendant, before a barrier was then raised permitting them entry.

He couldn't wait that long, they were like sitting ducks if he didn't do something. And soon.

He was sure he could hear more police sirens. Artie didn't doubt that they would have forced their way through the accident by now, eager to close the distance between them.

It wouldn't have taken a genius to work out where they were heading.

To his left, a row of tourist-packed coaches and heavy-duty vehicles idled, large gaps spaced between each one as they rolled forward in an orderly fashion.

Decision made, Artie knew what he had to do.

Edging ahead, he started drifting Alice's car to the left, encroaching on the next lane. Several horns were blasted aggressively as pissed off drivers were forced to halt against Artie's recklessness. He didn't care, dismissed it all instantly. He forced his way into that lane. He was almost where he needed to be.

The barrier was right there, Artie could clearly make out every detail of the attendant. The badge hanging around his neck, the radio pinned to his chest, the stubble on his chin.

He knew he would only get one shot at this, at timing his next move perfectly. He wanted a million more nights with Elspeth, to hold her, to caress her, to love her. He had to get this right. No, he corrected, he *would* get it right.

Neither Elspeth nor Alice questioned him, perhaps understanding what he was attempting or maybe just too petrified, too drained to form words. He would apologise to them again later, would replace Alice's wrecked car, when they were safe.

Now, though, they had to act.

In one swift, timed advancement, Artie hit the accelerator and diverted left again, swerving expertly into the space between two coaches, the first one pulling forward to drive through the open barrier.

With Alice's bumper up against the rear of the coach, they were going to go through with it.

Artie ignored the endless queue of traffic, the angry shouts of those watching him in disgust. He kept his eyes focused forward and hands gripped on the wheel.

He didn't stop for the attendant who half-heartedly moved as if to prevent his entrance, but changed his mind at the last second. He didn't stop when the coach paused, instead he sped around it, accelerating down a recently emptied lane towards the waiting ferry. He kept going. He wasn't going to stop until their car was tucked safely on that big fucking boat.

A growl escaped his lips.

They were so very close.

Then, as if from nowhere, another attendant appeared, moving to stand in their path, preventing them from passing the final checkpoint, the checkpoint with the barrier already raised, invitingly. This one acting without a single doubt, without concern for his own safety, stood statue-like, hands raised to stop them.

For a split second, Artie considered driving on, ploughing straight into the unknown man, his desperation consuming him, making him irrational. But with his conscience weighing in, heavy and oppressive, he knew he was many things but he was not a murderer.

Artie slammed on the brakes.

The car screeched to halt.

'Fuck!' he yelled into the stunned silence of the car.

Behind them, the wailing sirens could still be heard.

A sob escaped Elspeth's mouth. She looked petrified, like she'd lost all hope.

The ferry was there, its ramp metres away and they weren't going to make it.

But she has to make it.

It was as if he'd been struck by lightning. The solution to their problem, the answer that he needed. It was suddenly so obvious, practically staring him in the face and yet he hadn't seen it, hadn't wanted to see it. But now he knew how to protect her, how to save her.

The attendant was approaching, shouting orders and gesticulating frantically, but Artie ignored him. The unceasing call of the sirens were growing louder still, but Artie ignored them too.

Instead, he leant towards Elspeth, his Elspeth. His lips searching out hers.

She hesitated, worry and confusion evident, before giving in to him.

He kissed her deeply.

Reluctantly, he pulled away and forehead resting against hers, he breathed her in.

He wanted to remember this.

'Alice. See that she gets on the boat,' Artie demanded, desperately trying to unsee the raw fear shining in Elspeth's eyes as he pulled away from her.

Then he climbed out of the car.

46

ELSPETH

MAY 19TH 2035

E lspeth watched in stunned silence, as Artie exited the car and marched towards the attendant.

Too slowly, she found herself reacting. She raced with fumbling fingers to undo her seat belt, to get to Artie. She didn't know what he was about to do but she had a sinking feeling, one which left her empty and afraid.

There was an unmistakable urgency burning deep within her. She needed to reach him, to stop whatever it was he'd convinced himself to do.

The attendant's hands remained raised, no longer in an attempt to stop their car. They were now raised to stop Artie, to placate him, as he strode, back rigid, shoulders taut, towards the obviously fearful man.

Her cumbersome body, awkward to manoeuvre, hindered her moving quick enough. As she finally extracted herself from the car, she was barely in time to see the unmissable nod of agreement pass between the two men.

What's he just done? What's been agreed?

Artie turned, his face paling at the sight of her out of the car.

'Ellie. What are you doing? Get back in the car. You have to go. Now.'

Realisation hit her.

He wasn't going to go with her, she knew, her heart fracturing.

That isn't what I want. How could he decide that, how could he make that sort of decision without involving me, without talking to me?

'No!' she yelled, her voice strangled. 'I'm not leaving without you. Please, you don't need to do this.' Her eyes pleaded with him. She couldn't lose him, not now, not after everything.

He looked behind them. She followed his gaze. In the distance, the flashing lights of the police were indisputable. They had made it through. They were closing in.

'Yes, I do,' his voice strained.

'Please,' she sobbed, 'I don't want to do this without you.'

She thought she saw his emotions waver, just a hint, before being replaced with steely determination.

'You don't need me there. You're so much stronger than you give yourself credit for. Look at everything you've already done. Don't forget, Alice will be there with you, she'll look after you. I promise.' She knew the words weighed heavily on him, could see them crushing him as he forced them out.

But you won't be, she thought, her chest aching.

Elspeth rushed to him. The need to hold him, to touch him overwhelming her.

Her lips pressed against his firmly, her arms encircled his neck. She held him tightly to her, knowing she wouldn't be able to let go.

He kissed her back, the passion devastating.

How can he leave me?

All too soon, Artie tore himself out of her grasp, gently

prising Elspeth's arms from around his neck. 'Go,' he said, kissing each of her hands before letting them go.

From behind her, firm hands settled on Elspeth's shoulder. Alice, she knew without turning.

Artie spoke to Alice, his urgency undeniable. 'If you don't go now, you won't make it.' His words were cold and detached.

Elspeth allowed herself to be led, pulled by Alice. Tears she hadn't known she was crying obscured her view.

It was like being torn in two. She had to go, she had no choice but to leave. And yet her feet didn't want to obey. How could she leave him behind?

'We don't have much time,' Alice whispered into her ear, pushing her with gentle force towards the car.

'Ferry's going!' the attendant called, the indifference in his voice unmistakable.

Now Elspeth understood what Artie had done. He'd made a deal with the attendant, a man who didn't care if they got on or not. Didn't understand the knife edge Elspeth was resting precariously on.

She wondered what that stranger deemed Elspeth's freedom to be worth, what price he'd demanded to allow her to be a mother.

The sirens, blaring, dragged Elspeth out of her thoughts.

'Artie!' she cried, her voice ragged, as Alice guided her into the passenger seat.

He looked at her, hearing her despair. His eyes were filled with such adoration and love, that her heart shattered. 'I love you.'

Before she could respond, before she could tell him that she felt the same, he turned away from her.

'And I you,' she sobbed, her words lost to the breeze.

She desperately hoped that he knew the depths of her feelings for him, feelings she had hidden for years, too embarrassed to voice.

All her composure, her strength, seemed to disappear.

A body-wracking sob escaped from her.

The sirens were ear-piercingly loud, and the lights, hews of red and blue, were unavoidable. Elspeth couldn't hear anything above them, couldn't focus on anything as the car began moving.

Turning in her seat, her eyes found Artie.

She watched him as, with back turned to her, he squared his shoulders and walked away. Facing their enemy head on with such bravery, such courage.

Without hesitation, Alice drove the car straight at the ramp. They bumped uncomfortably up the incline, Elspeth barely registering the motion as they slotted into the last space at the rear of the ferry.

She'd left him behind. She'd left Artie there.

As if she had been hit full force by that thought, struck by its meaning, she once again clambered out of the car.

Elspeth ran, ignoring the weight of her body, the discomfort of the movement, to the back of the boat.

The rising ramp was already obscuring her view as the ferry's engines roared to life, a whirlpool of water being spun around them.

On the dock, the police were now exiting their cars.

Artie was quickly surrounded.

She watched in horror as he was forcefully shoved to the floor, officers swarming him like he was a criminal.

His name erupted from her lips, but he couldn't hear her, couldn't see her as she raised herself up on tiptoes to see over the ever-rising ramp which soon hid him from view, separating them.

Then he was gone.

She wrapped her arms tightly around her middle. Desperately she tried to hold herself together from the feeling of numbness which was beginning to overwhelm her, threatening to drag her down to a dark and miserable place.

She had lost him, again. Had let him leave her.

Her baby kicked firmly.

The physical reminder of what she was fighting for, would continue to fight for, was immense, and was exactly what Elspeth needed, it was like a lifejacket stopping her from sinking, from drowning under the weight of her sadness.

She had to hold it together, for him, her son. 'I know, little one, I miss him too.'

Only then did she realise just how deep Artie's love for her ran, recognised the sacrifice he'd made for them.

Artie had gifted her the ungiftable, her freedom and her family.

47

ARTIE

MAY 19TH 2035

A rtie finally had everything he'd ever dreamed of and he had given it all up. And yet, he didn't feel afraid.

Puffing out his chest, he walked forward. He wanted to head them off.

From behind him, he heard the heavy clank as Alice's car mounted the ferry's ramp swiftly followed by the final call ringing out clearly. Once that ferry had departed, it wouldn't return, couldn't be forced to turn round in neutral waters.

They're going to make it, he thought, a wave of relief engulfing him.

Artie didn't dare look back for fear that he wouldn't be able to stop his feet from carrying him to where he really wanted to be. Beside Elspeth.

With immense difficulty, he kept moving, forced one foot in front of the other.

The lights of the impending police cars were blinding, as three sets sped towards him.

The whirring of the ferry's engines drowned out all other noise.

Artie continued walking away from the dock, putting as

much distance as he could between himself and Elspeth. Two police cars and a van swarmed him, halting with precision in front of him. Artie instinctively raised his hands above his head.

A calming warmth settled over him. He'd been here before and he had nothing to be afraid of, he reminded himself.

He knew too many secrets, had too many friends in very high places. Besides, it didn't matter what happened to him, because they were too late. She was gone and was never coming back.

A blur of officers engulfed Artie. Each one shouting, their anger and adrenaline palpable.

Artie let himself be shoved to the ground. He didn't put up a fight, not when his arms were twisted painfully behind his back, not when his wrists were bound tightly, not when his already-lacerated face was ground into the hard concrete floor.

He would suffer it all, blissfully accept his fate, so long as they couldn't reach her.

Despite the weight of those holding him down, he found himself twisting. He needed to see, wanted the reassurance of seeing for himself.

There.

The ferry.

It had made more progress than he could have hoped for. There would be no turning back. The police didn't have jurisdiction over the crossing. Nor would the French co-operate with any request made to detain Elspeth once she reached safer shores. They had always been strongly opposed to the draconian approach the British had taken to *The* Law. They wouldn't stop Elspeth.

She'd made it.

He wanted to laugh, to shout, to celebrate.

If anyone was going to do it, it was always going to be her.

'I knew you were involved! Where is she?' DI Wakley demanded, her face coming within inches of his.

Artie didn't reply, just let the relief spread throughout every nerve, every particle in his body.

'I said, where the fuck is she?' Desperation evident in the copper's voice.

'Gone!' Artie growled triumphantly. 'She's gone.'

There was a pause, a moment's realisation when the copper looked around, took in the scene, eyes settling on the ferry sailing out of view.

'Fuck!' the woman screamed. 'Fuck!' she hollered again, feet practically stamping on the ground.

Artie smiled broadly as he was hauled to his feet.

'I wouldn't be so fucking pleased with yourself,' the detective spat. 'Someone's going to pay for this whole fucking fiasco and it isn't going to be me.'

Artie smirked. 'I wouldn't be so sure about that.'

48

ALICE

OCTOBER, 2035

Alice sat at her desk, computer on, papers spread out in front of her and yet she found herself staring out the window.

The view was unspectacular in every way, a grey slab of concrete car park surrounded by a ring of high-rise buildings, but she wasn't attempting to admire the scenery.

The morning's interview, the last of a series of interviews she'd participated in over the past week, was vexing her. As were the astonishing events of the last month.

That day, for the first time ever, she had walked away from what typically ended up feeling like an interrogation with a surreal sense of satisfaction, of being understood and perhaps even admired.

They had genuinely listened to her, and more than that, they had heard her. And that did not happen often.

A knock at the door pulled her gaze back to the room.

'Come in,' she called, sitting a little straighter in her chair.

A young suited man, wearing thick black-rimmed glasses, who Alice recognised instantly, walked into the room.

Confidently, he held out his badge. 'I'm Detective Sergeant Hudson, I wondered if I could have a few minutes of your time?'

Alice rose. 'I know who you are, detective.' She smiled. 'Please, take a seat.'

Sitting back down, Alice breathed through her nose. She'd been expecting a visit, had been almost on edge waiting for it and now that he was here, she felt surprisingly calm whereas the young detective appeared somewhat nervous. He fidgeted with the cuffs of his shirt sleeves before subconsciously wiping his hands across his trouser legs.

'Do you also know why I'm here?' he asked.

'Why don't you tell me, although if I'm being honest, I had expected your partner,' Alice responded carefully.

'DI Wakley is taking a sabbatical,' he answered dismissively. 'I wanted to talk to you about your recent involvement with Miss Adams.'

Alice raised her eyebrows, encouraging him to continue. She knew it was too late for them to do anything, knew the tide was turned considerably in her favour, yet she found she didn't want to confirm anything, didn't want to say any more than was necessary, anything that might add fuel to a fire she hadn't anticipated.

He cleared his throat. 'We– I mean, I, have reason to believe that you aided her abscondment from the country when she was illegally pregnant.' Now it was his turn to raise his eyebrows. His question, which wasn't a question exactly, more of a statement, hung between them for a moment. 'Is that true?'

Alice pursed her lips as she thought about how best to answer. 'Did you know, detective, that as of Monday, *The* Law will have been amended? It will no longer be illegal for a woman to do what her body allows her to do.'

'Yes, I might have heard something of that nature.' He

smiled, then sighed tiredly. 'As of Monday, Miss Adams' case will no longer be active. Her file will be closed.'

'Why then, may I ask, are you here?'

'Can I be frank with you, professor?' He waited for Alice to nod. 'I have a vested interest in this case, I spent a lot of my time,' he paused, as if carefully considering his next words, 'contemplating how best to pursue this case. I guess I am just at a loss as to some of the finer details. And I know that if left unanswered, these uncertainties will plague me.'

Alice genuinely smiled at him, perhaps understanding what he wasn't saying rather than what he was saying. 'I know exactly what you mean. You see I found myself very recently perplexed by a conundrum of sorts. That was until a dear friend of mine aided me in ascertaining the solution. May I tell you about it?'

Hudson frowned lightly but agreed, humouring Alice.

Alice leant forward, arms resting on the table. She was toying with him, she knew, and she shouldn't. Not when he had been so instrumental in their escape. She made the decision to tell him everything.

'Very recently, Detective Hudson, we came face to face. Do you remember? I am not sure if at the time you even noticed me, in the rear of the car?'

Hudson's eyes widened a fraction in understanding. He nodded. He had known she was there.

'Well, there were two things that puzzled me about that encounter. Firstly and most importantly was why you didn't apprehend Elspeth then, when you very clearly had the opportunity. And secondly, I knew I had seen you somewhere before. The fact that I remembered you, meant you must have made an impression on me previously, as I have met many people over the years, and yet I couldn't for the life of me work out where or even when.'

Alice readjusted herself in her seat. The detective remained still, perhaps it was the admission that he had obviously let his suspect go which had him so rigid, or was it that Alice was beginning to tell him what he wanted, to answer his questions.

'I did ponder both of those points, all the way to Italy. That is where Miss Adams is now, although I suspect that you may have already connected those dots for yourself.' She didn't pause long enough for Hudson to offer any comment. 'As you can imagine, these things were soon forgotten. I had more pressing concerns such as Elspeth's baby and ensuring Elspeth received all the care and treatment she required.'

The detective interjected. 'Boy or girl?' He almost appeared sheepish, as if he regretted asking, but desperately wanted to know.

Alice tilted her head, considering whether she should tell him or not. Relenting, she answered, 'A beautiful boy.'

And he was beautiful, with a full head of brown hair and chocolate brown eyes, just like his mother. Elspeth had of course been a natural with him and it was fair to say Alice was understandably smitten. In fact, she couldn't wait to fly back to Italy the following week, to be with them all. With her family.

This appeared to satisfy Hudson, so Alice continued. 'But once Mr Jones had rectified the unfortunate incident which occurred on the motorway, and joined us, he was able to help me answer my questions.'

She thought of Artie then, the memory of him arriving in Italy.

The police had, of course, detained him for much longer than was necessary, threatened him with incarceration for the pile-up if nothing else. And there was nothing else, as they had never had anything more than circumstantial evidence regarding Elspeth's pregnancy. Although he was released pending further investigation, Artie was told not to abscond. Artie, of course, had set to work contacting anyone and everyone he could to make the incident disappear, to dissolve any lawsuits against him. His desperation barely concealed in his daily calls to Elspeth. And he had, eventually. At what cost, though, Alice wasn't sure.

Artie had seemed heavier somehow, an air of moroseness to him Alice hadn't noted previously. At the time, she had suspected that it was anger, having been forced to miss the baby's birth, that he had not been there to support Elspeth. But it had lingered.

Perhaps the brief yet undeniable time he had spent in a cell, considering a future locked up, away from Elspeth, haunted him. With time and the distraction of a baby, it eventually faded, replaced by a happiness Alice believed that he deserved.

These were thoughts she did not plan to share with the detective, she pushed them aside. 'I'm so very glad that those involved saw sense and dropped all charges, by the way. After all, it was just an unfortunate accident and nobody was seriously injured. Anyway, isn't it funny how things are so often interconnected, woven together like the roots of a tree. By solving one puzzle, the second sometimes resolves itself.'

'Why don't you tell me where you're going with this?' Hudson said firmly. Was that a note of anger, or frustration in his voice? Alice couldn't blame him, the police had come away from the whole thing looking less than competent. Apart from Russo's minor charge, for which he received community service, their case had all but hit a stone wall.

'Yes, of course,' Alice responded with a light smile. 'Well, Mr Jones, Artie was kind enough to do a little digging, shall we say. And what he found answered not only my first question but, in turn, it allowed me to solve the second conundrum. You and your wife were unapproved, weren't you?'

Hudson's face reddened instantly, his anger flaring. Alice was being forward, she knew, but she wanted to get the truth out there.

'How did... Those records were restricted. You had no right...' Hudson blustered. He made as if to stand.

Alice raised her hands, calming. 'I don't intend to share that information with anyone else,' she said gently, 'but like you, I wanted to understand it, to have all the pieces.'

Hudson halted, resuming his seat, his desire to have answers outweighing his instinct to leave.

Alice wouldn't humiliate him further by admitting that she also knew it was his wife's mental health which had been the crux of the issue, the reason for their refusal. It appeared that she had had a few troubled years as a teenager, all long before she ever wished to be a mother. But that information damaged any hope they had of being approved.

'You see by understanding your personal plight, I was able to appreciate your actions, why you allowed Elspeth to slip away. Was that the only time you let her go or were there others?'

Hudson blinked slowly. 'I'm not sure I know what you're insinuating, but were I to go along with this ludicrous theory of yours, it would be reasonable to consider that I had many opportunities to place hurdles in the path of the investigation. Not that that is what I did, of course.'

Alice grinned, really grinned.

At the acknowledgement of Hudson's rejection, Artie had done a little more digging. It would seem that Detective Hudson had *requested* a transfer to his current department, following their second refusal to be parents. Alice now knew why Hudson had been hindering the case all along. He longed to be a father. Like her, he had been fighting back, had been silently attacking *The* Law by whatever means were at his disposal.

'My second quandary, the where I had seen you. Once I knew your story, it all fell into place. It was at an anti-law protest, a protest *I* organised. You were supporting your wife's pleas for a change.'

This obviously startled the detective as his eyes widened.

Once Alice had remembered, she couldn't believe that she had ever forgotten.

In the midst of the rally, he had made the subtlest of gestures, placing his hand gently on his wife's back, a movement so indistinct and yet it had spoken volumes. It wasn't in an attempt to quieten her, or to comfort her, it was a motion of solidarity, an indication to their partnership. He was supporting her, he too felt her pain. And yet, it was his expression which Alice could recall with such clarity that it was as if she'd only seen him the previous day. He had looked so lost, so desperate, knowing he couldn't take her pain away, couldn't give her what she wanted, what she desired. But he was there, by her side, whilst she demanded change, her screaming just a drop in the ocean then.

'It seems to me, Detective Hudson, that we have both been on the same page all along. Every woman deserves the opportunity to be a mother.'

They stared at each other for several long minutes, the truth out there for them both to see, before Hudson finally rose to his feet.

'Thank you for your honesty. It would seem that without me asking, you have answered my questions, although I do still have one more–'

'Yes?'

'How did you meet Miss Adams?'

Alice laughed lightly. 'Just some chance meeting,' she responded earnestly.

Hudson was by the door. 'Well, I hope Elspeth knows how lucky she is to have you.'

'No, Detective Hudson, I am the lucky one.'

THE END

ACKNOWLEDGEMENTS

Firstly, thank you to all you readers who have made the decision to pick up this book. It has been years in the making and knowing that it is out there, being enjoyed, only makes this experience more real and more exciting.

I would like to thank Bloodhound Books for seeing the potential in my story and for making this dream into a reality. Betsy Reavley, our first phone call was both nerve-wracking and exciting but one that I am so glad we had. To the rest of the fantastic team at Bloodhound Books – thank you all for your time and support.

To my editor, Morgen Bailey. What would I have done without all your guidance and advice? Probably had a book filled with pursed lips, frowns and clichés. You have helped to shape this into a novel I am truly proud of. Thank you.

My two beta readers, Jane Chase and Barbara Harwood, it was your words of encouragement and your excitement that helped push me towards realising my dream. I will be forever grateful.

And last but by no means least, to my wonderful husband,

Dean, and amazing son, Heath. You have both been there through the long hours bent over my computer, providing not only encouragement but also useful and interesting words. I love you both.

A NOTE FROM THE PUBLISHER

Thank you for reading this book. If you enjoyed it please do consider leaving a review on Amazon to help others find it too.

We hate typos. All of our books have been rigorously edited and proofread, but sometimes mistakes do slip through. If you have spotted a typo, please do let us know and we can get it amended within hours.

info@bloodhoundbooks.com

Printed in Great Britain
by Amazon

87622430R00198